Advance Praise for
FALLING INTO THE SUN

"This honest, heart-felt novel not only chronicles a mother's journey to save her son, it reveals the remarkable ability of the human spirit to forgive, heal and love."

Wendy Walker, author of *Four Wives* and
editor of *Chicken Soup for the Soul—Power Moms*

"Poignantly rendered . . . a mind-stretching journey."

Angela Masterson Jones, author of *Broken Kisses*

"Few traumas match walking in on a suicide or dealing with the dread diagnosis of bipolar disorder, real life experiences Hazard weaves into riveting fiction. As one who intimately dealt with these issues throughout my practice, I highly recommend this helpful and insightful story of how family members can spiritually grow, change, adapt and, ultimately, prevail under such trying conditions."

Allen S. Kerr, Psy.D

"*Falling into the Sun* is that rarest and most wonderful of books: the kind you want to buy for all your friends and say, 'You've got to read this; it will change your life.'"

Terra Pressler, author of *Creative Juice*
and *Cracker Wisdom*

FALLING INTO THE SUN

A Novel

Charrie Hazard

Sept 2009

FALLING INTO THE SUN
A Novel

By Charrie Hazard

SPOONBILL COVE PRESS

SPOONBILL COVE PRESS
P.O. BOX 561
SAFETY HARBOR, FL 34695-0561

WWW.SPOONBILLCOVE.COM

Book Layout & Jacket Design by Zard Tompkins
www.ZardART.com

Printed on acid-free paper
10 9 8 7 6 5 4 3 2

Library of Congress Control Number: 2009921896
Hazard, Charrie, 1958-
Falling into the Sun: a novel / Charrie Hazard.—1st ed.
p. cm.
ISBN 987-0-9815410-1-3 / ISBN 987-0-9815410-2-0

To MM,
the Love of my Life,

to Michael Thomas Smith,
who resurrected my dreams,

& to Jane,
who never doubted.

*H*E SHALL COVER THEE WITH HIS FEATHERS,
AND UNDER HIS WINGS SHALT THOU TRUST ...

NO EVIL SHALL BEFALL THEE,
NEITHER SHALL ANY PLAGUE COME NIGH THY DWELLING.

FOR HE SHALL GIVE HIS ANGELS CHARGE OVER THEE,
TO KEEP THEE IN ALL THY WAYS.

Psalm 91

Chapter 1

He prays there is no life after death because he's sick to death of life. Wasn't always that way, but he won't go there. He finds the plywood in the back of the warehouse. It's dark here. Nothing exciting displayed: raw wood, aluminum trusses, cinder blocks, heavy rope. The bare bones of building—or destroying. He wants thin plywood cut in three-by-five sheets to allow overlap when he covers the windows. What kind of nails will secure wood to plaster? He might have asked yesterday but not today. He just wants some goddamn nails. And wood. And rope.

A teenage stock boy approaches. He tells the kid about the wood, refusing to look him in the eye. The teen's eyes will distract him. He knows from experience. Too much life there. He focuses on the boy's hair, blond and brushed back in a two-layered beach cut—like Matt's. The thought scorches. The stock boy can't be more than three years older than his son. He looks at the boy's apron, powdered with cement, smudged prints where he brushed his hands. Reminds him of baking rolls from scratch, Matt barely five, covered with flour, laughing as he clapped dust clouds, his nose still white-tipped when they surprised Cara with homemade breakfast in bed. Cara and he were new lovers then. She thought Matt adorable. Or so she said.

Plywood, nails, rope. Focus. Keep your eye on the ball, *Ma used to yell when she was angry or disappointed. Which was all the time near the end.*

"Nails are on aisle three," the stock boy says. "The wood will be ready in ten minutes. Pick it up in back after you pay."

He heads for the fastener aisle. It seems as long as a city block, with countless boxes of nails and screws packed on shelves reaching more than halfway to the twenty-foot ceiling. The choices overwhelm him. He reels, seasick. He grabs the first box he sees—1/8" x 1"—then looks for rope. It has to be strong. How much does he need? Two feet for the knot, another for stretch and at least three feet to tie off. Six feet, the same length as his body.

Odd thought: his body. He likes his wiry frame. Has kept it strong and lean. A sense of loss wells in him. He turns from the emotion as a nun might avert her face from a sexual tryst she's stumbled upon in the pews. Denial is a coping mechanism. He read that once.

He doesn't return the chirpy greeting of the old checkout lady. Her face is caked with powder, giving her an unnatural glow as far as her chin where the skin turns sallow. Always do to your neck what you do to your face. *Another bit of Mother's wisdom when she applied her weekly mudpacks. He doesn't return the clerk's cherry-red smile exposing stained teeth. Why is she working here? She should be home in front of a fire, reading her favorite mystery, a hand-crocheted afghan over her knees.*

She pushes the receipt across the counter. Her almond-shaped nails frosted in red are unseemly ends to her gnarled fingers.

"Don't forget your plywood," she says. "Thanks and come again."

He grabs his bag of rope and nails and walks toward the door, head down.

"You're welcome!" she calls after him. His heart skitters but he doesn't miss a step.

Does it please her to speak for him? Her voice held no sarcasm, but the chirp was gone. That must be a sin, to steal another's song, to dampen delight. There are worse sins, according to the church. The idea of ranking sins always fascinated him. How do they know that divorcing a mistake is worse than living a lie? He'll find out soon enough if the church really knows sin.

Did Cara enjoy speaking for him? What will she do? Will her tongue ache from disuse? Will she be sad, or just angry? He tries to step inside her head, her skin—but he can't. His chest is a deep freezer.

He finds himself in the driveway of the house they share. He doesn't remember the turns, the stoplights that got him here. For a moment, he can't recall why he's here—his mind a dull gray. His eyes are scratchy; when did he last cry? He knows this is a problem, not crying. Too late to solve.

He pulls into the garage, presses the remote to lower the door then cuts the engine. He climbs out of the cab. The garage stinks of exhaust fumes, rotted wood, sweaty towels. It needs airing. He hauls the plywood from the pickup's bed and nails a sheet over each window, systematically blocking out sunlight and palm fronds waving against blue sky. The nails go in easy. Too easy.

An alarm blares in the back of his brain. He's missing something, some essential detail he might later regret. He ignores the warning, impatient to be finished. The last window, overlooking the street, won't close completely. It's an awning window and the crank is partially stripped. He tries to catch his fingernails beneath the steel frame, but he's chewed them to the quick. Well shit. He nails the board on anyway. Stands back. The board shudders as wind seeps through the window's small opening. He shrugs. Good enough for his needs.

He secures the manual lock on the garage door then pulls the red cord hanging from the electric door's motor to disengage the chain drive. She'll be irritated when the door doesn't open, will cuss about remote batteries going bad too fast. What next, she'll think. He squeezes his eyes shut, causing his mouth to curl into a grimace, puts his hand on the truck hood to steady himself.

Chapter

"What is the nature of evil?"

The students look surprised, even though the reading assignment focused on society's fascination with horror films—not the modern blood and gore offshoots of the genre, but the classics, where innocence faces the dark supernatural or man struggles with his shadow self. Kate Nardek is undaunted. East Florida University ranks third in the state. The students are bright.

"Is evil within us?" She allows thirty seconds to tick off her watch. The windowless room is so quiet she can hear the fluorescent lights hum. "Is evil simply our dark side or is it the upshot of mental illness? Is Stephen King right when he claims we are all potential lynchers?"

She smiles at the discomfort on the undergraduates' faces. As the silence stretches, she opens her backpack and pulls out a compact. She purses her lips to check her lipstick then runs her fingers in exaggerated motions through her short waves of strawberry-blond hair. Her brown eyes twinkle back at her in the tiny mirror.

"Or is evil an external, malignant force stalking us, trying to corrupt?" She snaps her compact shut, making a girl in the front row jerk to attention. "Do we live in a dualistic world where God and Satan are duking it out, with our souls the booty?"

The students study the open notebooks on their desks with ostensible fascination. She leans against the podium. "You guys had your morning coffee?" she asks with mock severity, surveying the bleary-eyed expressions so common in early-morning classes. A few students smile sheepishly. "How many times I gotta tell you? Don't come in here without a caffeine fix. Now come on, I know you've all thought about evil."

"I don't," says Cleo, a slender black student in the second row. Kate smiles at the soft but firm conviction in the young woman's voice. "I figure it's best not to think about it. Thinking about evil invites it in. I refuse to believe it can touch me. If evil's not part of my thoughts, it's not part of my life."

Kate scans the students' faces. They reflect a budding thoughtfulness. She waits.

"Well, do y'all agree? Is Cleo right or simply naïve?"

"I think evil is in us," says Austin, another of Kate's favorites. With his intense curiosity and his willingness to risk being wrong, he often helps jumpstart class debates. "Both good and evil are part of our nature. We have to learn to nurture the good and curb the evil."

"Evil comes from Satan." Angie shoots Austin an impatient look, then turns to Kate. "He's out to get us. He's trying to turn us from God. We have to guard against him."

Again silence reigns, but the students' faces show interest and anticipation.

"Is this one of the themes of horror films?" Kate asks. "Can evil pop up unexpectedly at any moment, engulf us, transform us, mutilate our bodies—or worse, our souls—if we're not careful? Do we really believe that? Or do we go through the day, following our neatly planned schedules, mindlessly believing we're in control?"

"Well," Austin says, looking up from the notebook in

which he has either been taking copious notes or doodling madly. "Certainly *The Exorcist* is about Satan and there wasn't much control there. Satan even overpowers the priest. But what about werewolf movies? They're more about the monster within. That's different. If the wolf is part of our nature, we have some control—we can choose to cage it."

"Yeah, but nobody believes in werewolves," Angie says, rolling her eyes. "We all believe in Satan."

"I don't," Cleo pipes in.

The debate takes flight, expanding from the nature of evil to the value of horror films. Some students argue such films are enlightening and cathartic, allowing people to explore their dark side in the safety of a theater. Others maintain the movies themselves are evil because they encourage people to take pleasure in iniquity.

"I don't watch them," Angie declares. "They're too real. Like *The Exorcist.*" She eyes Austin. "Satan's out there with his legion of devils and he wants to get you. And he can."

Chapter 3

He carries the rope into the deserted house, throws it on the kitchen table. It's stuffy, the air overly warmed by the furnace. Cara always sets the thermostat too high. He walks through the house, making sure all the window locks are secure. He opens the front door, puts his key in the outside lock, snaps off its head with pliers, then closes the door and engages the deadbolt. He does the same at the back door, using the spare key, then drops the broken heads on the rug. The carpet is soiled inside the back door—mud-smeared rose. Matt never has learned to wipe his feet. And she never got around to buying a throw rug. Stupid to fight over such things. He wishes he could say sorry. Too late. Sorry is for when there's still a chance, still a future.

He takes a bottle of Jack Daniels from a kitchen cabinet and sits at the round wooden table where the rope lies waiting. The table is covered with an oilcloth, white with red hearts. She bought it last year at half price the day after Valentine's Day, too cheap or too despairing to buy it full price on the day of love. He puts his lips on the bottle's mouth and sucks long and hard. Great gulps of liquid fire burn his throat and stomach but don't faze the iceberg in his chest. He pulls the bottle from his mouth and licks its rim. Remembers how he used to lick her nipples to the rhythm of her moans until they grew hard and peaked. He used to get hard just thinking about her, their laughter during foreplay, his hand on her thigh, her hands massaging his chest, her eyes like a child's when telling a favorite joke. But she was all woman when she arched to him, her nails digging into his back as he pulsed within her. Then the love murmurings afterward, whispered with lips brushing ears, the breathy words causing shivery giggles.

He slides a hand to his crotch, wishing he could get hard now. But his dick is dead. Only good for pissing. It started dying when the bitching overtook the laughter. Most of it centered on Matt, what a slob he was, drinking milk from the carton, never showering, leaving his filthy clothes on the floor, sitting on her good furniture after a workout, dripping with sweat. He's a teenager for chrissake. But she'd never lived with a teenage boy. An only child herself and childless at thirty-seven, it was too much of a stretch. Then the police showed up over the BB gun. Matt was just target practicing out back, but Mrs. Lentil, behind them, claimed bullets were zipping through her yard. Bullets *for chrissake. And then the other neighbor—at least she didn't call the police—said Matt fired at her cat. The lady was nice about it and Matt caught hell, but Cara couldn't handle it. Said he could stay but the boy had to go.* I didn't sign on for this, *she said.* You're ruining my fucking life!

He takes another swig, lets his lips linger on the bottle, then slams it on the table with a crack that startles him. He pulls the rope over and begins working the end into a knot. When he was a Boy Scout, his leader called it a running knot. No one really calls it that. But the real name is too grim for young boys out fishing. Odd the useless things you learn, while the important lessons slip by undetected. He doubles one end of the rope into a long U, then brings it down again, toward the U's trough, passing it under the doubled cord. He makes eight loops around the cords, then pulls the end tight as he massages the loops into a knot. He tests it. The rope moves easily through the knot, allowing him to adjust the loop size.

He carries the rope to the garage and throws it on the floor next to the black oil slick left by her Malibu. He gets the ladder from the wall, sets it under the right steel beam of the garage door track, where it's mounted to the ceiling. The beam is stronger than the light fixture or the chain drive. He grabs the rope, climbs the ladder and begins to tie the free end to the track, making sure he doesn't leave too much slack. It takes longer than he expected.

He hears a faint whistle of wind. He's working in front of the window that wouldn't close completely. The plywood bows toward him when the whistle is high, then becomes slightly concave in the silence between gusts. The undulating wood seems alive, as if breathing, sucking in the cold air of the new year. He returns his attention to the rope. His first attempt at two half hitches ends in a gangly granny knot he doesn't trust. The rope is heavy. His arms ache. He wants the knot to hold. He was always good at knots, but not at holding on. A strange contradiction. Maybe if he could have tied himself down—but what does that mean?—he wouldn't have gotten so goddamned tangled.

A memory flickers across his mind like a home movie. He is seven, on the beach, pulling in the kite string, loop upon loop. Too frantic to twine the string on the spindle. Dusk is settling. Mosquitoes and no-see-ums are attacking with vengeance. No time to coil, *his brother Tom hollers,* just get the damn kite down. I'm getting eaten alive!

They take the matted tangle to the motel room where Ma and Pop are drinking martinis from the liquor kit. Ma, already drunk, shrieks at the waste. Not one more roll of string. No more kites until you untangle that mess. *Pop smiles at the tears then walks to the pile on the floor.* It's all loops, *he says.* Just pull the loops away from each other, one by one. *Past midnight he sits on the floor with Tom and his dad, unlooping the string, slowly shrinking the pile, transferring loops to coils, loops to coils until, mind-numbed, he falls asleep.*

He wakes at sunrise to find the string neatly coiled on the spindle, the kite ready to fly. Pop's last gift before the crash that killed him, a drunk driver—Pop ironically sober.

He knows there's a way back to a neat coil, but he's worn out by the loops and has lost faith in overnight miracles. His mind is numb, as when a child, hands full of tangled string, blame and punishment stinging him like whiplashes.

He yanks the knot tight and takes the noose in his hands— the last loop of his life. The thought tugs at the hard line of his lips, but only for an instant. He puts the noose around his neck. Best for everyone. The only way. Matt! Can't think of him now. Goddamn it!

He closes his eyes and steps forward.

Chapter 4

ate walks across campus to her van. The chill January breeze gives a spring to her step. Class discussion yielded plenty of fodder for her students to contemplate as they develop their papers. On the drive home, she mulls potential horror stories for the class to read. She also wants to show one film.

Students could harvest any number of papers from *Dr. Jekyll and Mr. Hyde*, the dual nature of man the most obvious. But there's also Jekyll's hubris, the hell springing from conscienceless freedom and, more intriguing, the desensitizing nature of evil. Each heinous act by Hyde makes the next easier. The same theme shows up in the more recent movie, *Fargo*. At a stoplight, Kate jots a note to make that connection in lecture.

Jekyll and Hyde is a good read, but the movie is outdated. Perhaps she'll show *Rosemary's Baby*. Her skin prickles. She hasn't seen the movie and is sure her students haven't, it's so ancient, so it will be new territory for everyone.

As she pulls her white Plymouth Voyager into her driveway, she hears the shrieks. Her heart pounds in answer to their piercing persistence. Her neck tingles. Barely audible words pepper the screams.

"Help me! Someone. Help me!"

Her hands tremble as she opens the van door. A breeze sweeps across her, intensifying the chills quaking her spine. She runs down the drive, looking toward her neighbor's house. There, collapsed on her hands and knees in the grass, crouches Cara. Her head is swinging up and down as if powered by her screams. Her sandy hair dances in the breeze. Kate runs to her van for her cell phone, dials the police as she races across the street. She casts a glance at the other houses on the block. Where is everybody?

The phone quits ringing. "911."

"My neighbor needs help! She's hysterical! Wait!" She reaches Cara, bends down and grabs her shoulder. "What's wrong? What happened?"

Cara continues to scream.

"What's the problem?" The dispatcher's voice is flat.

"What's wrong?" Kate shakes her neighbor's shoulder.

Cara erupts to her feet and flings her arms around Kate's neck. "Michael's dead!" she shrieks, hanging from Kate, her feet barely touching the ground. "In the garage!"

Kate drops the phone as she struggles to unlock Cara's death grip. She pushes her back, grabs her shoulders and shakes her. "How do you know he's dead?" She releases Cara, who falls to her knees. Kate scoops the phone from the ground.

"She says her boyfriend's dead in the garage!" Kate yells into the phone. The notice the Neighborhood Watch sent her last week flashes through Kate's mind: *Look out for burglars robbing houses by day, gaining access through open garages. Three houses robbed this month.* What if Michael walked in on a burglary? Was murdered? What if the killer is still there?

"Can you get in the garage?" The dispatcher's voice jars her into action. Her heart pounds painfully as she runs to the rear of the house. When she sees the garage door, her body sags. She gulps air, realizing she's been holding her breath. "The garage door is down."

"Can you see in?"

Kate runs to one of two side windows facing the street.

"The window's boarded."

"Are they all boarded?"

"I'm not sure." She steps to the second window where a board hangs diagonally, rattling against the frame. She peers over it. There, not three feet away, hangs Michael. He faces her, the rope biting his neck, his head unnaturally askew, his right ear folded against his shoulder. His eyes are black holes. She can see the ladder directly behind his preternaturally still body. She turns away instinctively, but already Michael's death mask has branded her brain.

"Oh my God," she sobs, "he's hang … he's hanging …"

"You can not cry," the dispatcher orders. "You cannot cry. I need you to tell me the address."

Kate covers her eyes with her free hand in a futile effort to block out the image of Michael's pale face and the eerie shadows where eyes should be. She draws a ragged breath then relays the address so help will come, even though she knows it's too late.

"Stay on the phone until the rescue squad and police get there. They're on their way."

Kate nods but doesn't answer. She turns toward Cara's sobbing. A burly man she recognizes as a neighbor holds Cara in his arms, trying to comfort her. He wears a white undershirt and jeans. No shoes.

"You on with 911?"

Kate nods. The man's eyes bore into her. He jerks his head toward the garage. "The window open?"

She sees a crack between the window and the sill, wedges her fingers and pulls. "It's open."

"Open the window," the man orders. "Get in there and

cut him down."

Kate backs away. "I can't go in there," she whispers.

"Don't go in the garage!" the dispatcher commands. Kate still holds the phone to her ear.

The man throws her a look of disgust. He eases Cara to the ground, where she crumples in convulsing sobs, then runs to the window.

"The dispatcher says don't go in."

He pulls open the window and climbs through.

"What's happening?" the dispatcher asks.

"He's going in the garage. A neighbor."

"Tell him not to."

"I can't. I tried. What if he can help?" No one can help Michael. She knew when she saw his face. She knew it from the garage's deathly stillness.

"The paramedics will be there in thirty seconds. Wait for them."

"I can't … I can't stop him." Kate hears the distant wail of sirens.

"Do you see the rescue squad?"

She peers down the street. "Yes."

"Okay. You don't need me anymore." With a click the dispatcher is gone. Kate stands alone at the end of Michael's driveway, waving her arms at the truck speeding toward her. Two police cars follow.

Within seconds, paramedics and police swarm the yard, break down the front door, invade the garage where Kate's burly neighbor struggles to un-hang Michael.

Chapter 5

He moves faster than light, disintegrating time, jumping dimensional barriers. Pure energy speeding to its source. A spark falling into the sun, ageless as a photon. He's aware of Cara's screaming. And the other's tears—a salty dampness he cannot taste, cannot touch, yet still they infuse him. The heaviness filling this stranger makes him sink even as he rises.

Sightless, he sees a pinwheel of fire, like a far-away galaxy, arms of light flying off, the center flashing like a cut diamond under glass, shooting crystal shafts glinting with transparent colors of ruby, emerald and sapphire. A prism held to the sun. He recognizes the light, knows it's always been. Before his birth, in the living room when he was eleven, in his son's first smile, in the garage. Right next to him. Within him. Why had he not seen it?—but he had. Why had he not acknowledged it? His life could have radiated with it, could have been one of its brilliant tendrils, had he chosen. Why did he not choose?

The center's splendor mesmerizes him, wrenches from him a desperate yearning, like that of a child, ridiculed and punched by bullies, face down in the dirt, longing for the soft touch of Mommy. It is warm, safe, inviting. Home. Yet as he races forward, he realizes with slow-growing horror he is off center. Like a poorly drawn arrow, he is awry. The realization ravages him. The arrow of his life missing this mark—the only mark. What he remembers as despair is an ear boxing compared to this bludgeoning—this sledge hammer shattering the stone of his heart, exposing to the sickle's edge tender, red tissue.

He sees every wobble of his life, every pain administered intentionally or un-, every overlooked chance to tender kindness: Turning from Cara after lovemaking, her thighs glistening with sweat, as she whispers, We need help; *slamming the door in his son's face, yelling,* Get out, goddamn you, *when Matt asks to throw the football; snuffing the clerk's song at the hardware store, each nudging him a speck farther off center. How many motes of missed opportunities did it take to put him a mile off course? An overwhelming desire to implode besets him. He yearns for the black hole of non-existence. Empty words pass through him. Regret. Sadness. Despair. He searches for the right word, the code, the key to freedom....*

FORGIVE *resounds from him. What does it mean? His high school Latin teacher reciting the etymology of words. Old English,* forgiefan, *to grant, allow, give up, completely. Latin,* perdonare, *to give thoroughly, to remit, let go. What does it really mean? He screams in soundless agony.* Oh God, forgive me! Have mercy. Let me go! *Energy can be neither created nor destroyed, his science teacher's mantra.* But you created! You can destroy. I beg you!

How long is eternity? The question terrifies him. He wills himself to dissipate—like gas released from a canister. He wants to spread across galaxies, across the universe. He wills apart the gluons of his soul—smaller than quarks, smaller even than those ethereal neutrinos scientists claim can speed undeterred through a chunk of lead trillions of times thicker than Earth. But even as he glimpses his disso-

lution, begins to turn toward it, the center moves, aligns itself with his distorted aim. The choice is his.

He chooses.

In a flash, a kaleidoscope of light and color embraces him whole, fills him with a balm so pure and strong and healing he hesitates to call it love, for it's like no love he's ever experienced. The word God *rises, but is pitifully inadequate, doesn't jibe with Sunday school. No judge here. He's in the center of the universe, or the universe is centered in him. He can't tell which. But he knows someone—or something—has noted every twist of his life since sperm struck seed, has documented each of his hurts, counted every unspent tear, has joined in every burst of laughter, rejoiced at the birth and mourned at the death of every dream. It's all before him in a song that sears as it soothes. He's a toddler who has stumbled, forehead to floor, about to cry when laughing hands lift him to his feet, give him a gentle nudge. The missteps and missed opportunities, devastating a nanosecond before, are lessons in biology, sociology, philosophy, theology.*

He rests in the center, engulfed in a warm sea rippled by elfin laughter. The laughter sings to him, I know, I know. *Lightning flashes, electrifying him, focusing his attention. Then darkness falls. Stillness settles. His thoughts tumble in free play as when sitting before a winter's fire watching flames lick logs. The song is softer than a sea breeze. Each note strikes an image: Sand dunes edging the southern Atlantic coast, dolphins playing in a boat's wake, pelicans gliding wide-winged through troughs of ocean waves. He remembers this song from another time. He was angry then. So angry he blotted it out, its magnificence a mockery of the life he'd known. He sang his own tune then, of bitterness, resentment, self-pity, the melody underscored by a descant of fear. He's not afraid anymore. What's left to fear once you've known hell?*

He listens, glad for the warm dark where he can concen-trate. Voices are in the music. Cara's dissonant with grief and anger, the other's off tune, like an orchestra member on the wrong page, his mother's quivering with an unwonted gentleness, Matt's—no, he can't yet listen to Matt's. There are other voices. Forgotten teachers who encouraged him, strangers who greeted him on the sidewalk, his childhood dog's joyful bark as she bounded after him in the woods. Every moment of his life, every person he touched or who touched him, is in this song. And above it all, a voice he recognizes but cannot name, mighty as a trumpet yet tender as a violin. Clear as a flute and more joyful than any bird heralding spring.

He craves this voice as the seedling craves sun. Desire like newfound love fills him. Take me. Take me. *The song crescendos, vibrates through the universe, shaking the stars, trembling his soul. Then softens to a hush.*

Uncanny knowledge comes to him unbidden, unwanted. Every moment of his life revealed in full light. A gift he can refuse, wants to refuse, but forces himself to accept. Cara's screams grow distant, though the strings of his soul forever quiver with their echoes. He hears the thoughts behind the silent weeping of the other as she sits in her living room. Each warm tear melts the stone splinters of his fractured heart while rending his soul. She is lost in the dark, sepa-rated from her inner light.

Why must he know this? Why must he know any of this? But the easier path, not knowing, willful ignorance is like the river Lethe; it leads to only one place. This time he chooses the song. This time, he chooses knowing.

Chapter 6

"Are you all right?" Mitch's arms tighten around Kate as she lies on her side under the covers. He pulls her back against his chest, spooning her.

"I'm okay."

"Put it out of your mind. Just sleep."

"I'm so tired," she admits. "But I'm afraid to sleep. I'm afraid I'll have nightmares."

"If you have a nightmare, just wake me."

"Will you keep holding me?" Usually he only cuddles with her for a few minutes and then moves back across the king-size bed to his space to sleep. Only during winter cold spells does he sleep pressed against her.

"I'll hold you all night as many nights as it takes."

She relaxes but the second she closes her eyes Michael is there. At first his face is exactly as she saw it earlier. But then it gains a haunting vibrancy. It undulates before her, wraith-like, its outer edges wavering. Slowly the expressionless yet gruesome visage transmutes into a leer. Her lids fly open to darkness.

"Dammit!" She groans.

"What is it?"

"Every time I close my eyes I see him. Not just him, but these awful visions. They're malevolent. God, why am I falling apart like this?"

"Give yourself a break," he soothes. "This is probably normal. It'll just take time."

"Mitch, I feel like I saw something in that garage. I mean, not just Michael, but something else."

"What?" He rises on an elbow and coaxes her to roll onto her back so he can look into her eyes. "What did you see?"

"It sounds dumb, so overdramatic. I thought I saw ..."

"Finish your sentence." She detects a hint of impatience in his voice.

"I don't know." She twists the bed sheet in her hands. "The truth is I think I saw evil."

Mitch grunts. "Kate, this is so typical of you. You saw the body of a man who hanged himself. Let's not make this more than it is. A suicide. That's all."

She closes her eyes, stinging with unshed tears, and turns back on her side.

"You're always trying to fit everything into some big picture, as if it all relates." His voice is gentler now, almost pleading. "Some things just are, for no reason. They have no great significance beyond their face-value."

Her intellect agrees, but the other within her whispers, *No.* During her sixteen years with Mitch her intellect has grown louder, increasingly drowning out this softer voice. But occasionally she still hears it. When she does, she envisions a young goddess, her golden hair flowing in curling waves, the white gauze of her gown rippling behind her as if caught in a perpetual breeze. Tonight she wishes she could talk to this goddess. She knows this being is somewhere inside her, but when she hears the voice, her intellect quickly slaps it down.

She pushes off the cover and sits up.

"What are you doing?" Mitch's voice rises with alarm. "I've made you mad. I'm sorry, but I hate to see you upset yourself. It's not good."

"It's okay. I'm not mad." She rubs her eyes then reaches for her flannel robe, soft from years of wear. "I can't sleep. I'm going to get a glass of wine and sit for a bit in the living room."

"Want me to come?"

"No. I'll be back in a little while."

"Wake me when you come to bed."

"Don't worry." She half chuckles. "I'm gonna make you keep your promise about holding me."

Wine in hand, moonlight guiding her steps across polished oak floors, Kate shuffles to the rattan sofa in the living room and sinks into its pillows. She runs her hand across the cushion next to her, admiring the muted pattern of roses against rich cream. Mitch chose the fabric as well as the formal Smithsonian-style sofa and rocker made by Henry Link. The accompanying chair and ottoman are upholstered in a subtle plaid of hues pulled from the floral fabric. The combination gives the room a light, airy look.

She sips her wine as she reviews her options. She needs to talk to someone and Mitch isn't the one. He loves her, but so often he's not in tune with her needs. Even today, when she telephoned him, still standing on Cara's lawn, nearly hysterical, sobs clogging her voice, he had asked, Do you want me to come home? She had clamped her lips into a quivering grimace. She desperately wanted him to simply say, I'll come right now. But instead, he made her ask him to choose her needs over his work—work he'd been married to longer than he had to Kate. Why couldn't he sense her need and respond without direction? Just come. She had hesitated, then said, No, you don't need to come home early.

Later, the police officer who had been so kind at the scene stopped by to check on her and convinced her to call Mitch home. You shouldn't be alone at a time like this, he had said. Why did he get it when Mitch didn't? The mixture of anger, disappointment and shame she felt when she called Mitch washes over her anew.

Typical man, Jean would say with a laugh if Kate told her. She wishes she could telephone the woman she calls godmother, though Jean wasn't installed by the church or chosen by Kate's parents. Kate asked Jean to be her godmother several years ago. Of course, of course, she had answered, tears glistening her eyes. We'll have our own ceremony. On the beach. And they did. A ritual at twilight, candles flickering in the sand. The brief words Jean wrote and they exchanged wove together truths of astrology, Hinduism and Taoism as well as the teachings of Jesus.

Jean rejects the notion of only one true path. How limiting, she often says. Why are we always trying to make God so small, so … unimaginative? Then she laughs and her laughter is irresistible. It pulls Kate in until she finds herself laughing too, safe in its warm, comfortable embrace. Many times Jean has helped her laugh at her own fears and foibles, her myriad misdirections, making them manageable, getting her back on target.

She needs Jean. She hears God in Jean's laughter—a God who in no way resembles the frowning, judgmental disciplinarian fed to her as a teen by the church and her father. She can tell Jean about the garage and knows she won't dismiss it, or her, as crazy. Kate will call her next week when Jean returns from visiting her daughter Jamie in France. It seems a long time away.

She drains her wine glass then heads to Mollie's room. In sleep, her four-year-old still purses her lips in suckling dreams. Kate strokes Mollie's velvet cheek, then her golden-brown ringlets. She crosses the room to straighten the covers over ten-year-old Reyna, whose red corkscrew curls clearly come from Kate's mom.

She heads farther down the hall to Joshua's room. The thirteen-year-old is sprawled on his bed, dressed in plaid boxers, his comforter tossed to the floor, his ceiling fan on high even as the chill night air seeps in through the cracked window. She touches his forehead. Cool. Yet she knows if she puts the comforter over him, he will throw it off within minutes. He constantly complains he's too hot. Even in midwinter he insists on having his fan on high and will tolerate only a sheet.

She pulls the sheet over him and strokes his auburn hair, the color of smoldering embers, reflective of his temperament. "Good night, sweetheart," she whispers, then heads to the other side of the house, to her bed, where Mitch's warm body waits to enfold her.

Chapter 7

The next day, Kate sees the dead Michael with her eyes open. When she rounds the corner of her dining room, he's hanging from the living room fan, his bloodless face accentuated by his cap of black, curly hair. When she opens the front door to get the morning paper, he's standing on the stoop. When she steps into the pool enclosure to sweep the deck, he's lurking by the back hedge, his lips twisted in a taunting smile. Stiff-armed, she turns the knob of the door to the garage then kicks it open while jumping back. She catches a flash of Michael hanging there. Driving Reyna to elementary school, she looks in the rearview mirror. The dark holes of Michael's eyes look back. As she walks to the lectern at the head of her classroom, his shadow hovers beside her, somber and grim.

Three days after Michael's suicide, Kate returns home from the university. As the garage door rises, she doesn't see Michael hanging from the ceiling; she sees Josh. The vision is brief but gruesome. Kate brakes, bouncing her chest against the steering wheel. She throws open the door just as a wave of nausea turns to a flood of vomit. By the time she stops retching, her face is soaked with a salty mix of sweat and tears. The vision tells her what she has known for a long time but has refused to accept. She needs help with Josh. Josh needs help.

Josh has a bad temperament. That's what Kate and Mitch have said for years. He was born crying and didn't stop for six weeks. Even as a baby he was easily frustrated and frantically impatient. Kate first consulted the pediatrician when Josh was a toddler. The doctor smiled indulgently. Is anyone else in your house impatient? he had asked. Mitch came to mind. Like father like son, said Dr. Foster, who had known Mitch and Kate for years.

Josh's impatience and stubborn insistence on his own way grew worse with Reyna's birth, to the point Kate feared for her newborn's safety. "Time-outs" became hitting, kicking, clawing fights as she dragged the recalcitrant three-year-old to his room. She would tug the door closed, but he would yank it open and try to beat his way past her. She'd shove him back in, draw the door and hold it, feeling Josh's pull on the other side. After a few minutes he'd release the knob and she would turn to leave only to hear a loud thud. When she'd open the door she'd find something of value—a new tape player, an engine from a train set—lying smashed on the floor and a large dent in the door.

How do I deal with his tantrums? she asked Dr. Foster. Josh was in first grade. His behavior was stoking a smoldering rage in her she could not have imagined before his birth. During one morning episode, she threw Josh in his room and closed the door. She tried to read the paper, but the high pitch of his wails and the thuds of his feet and fists against the walls increasingly grated on her nerves. After thirty minutes listening to his rage, she marched into his room, grabbed him by the arm, dragged him wriggling and resisting into the bathroom, turned the shower on cold and heaved him into the tub. The frigid flow drenched his face and clothes, shocking him into silence. Aha, she thought, I've found the answer. But the next time she tried this maneuver, Josh was ready and she was the one who fell over the tub into the cold stream, banging her legs and buttocks and further inflaming her growing resentment. But how could she admit this to the doctor?

Switch his bedroom doorknobs, Dr. Foster said, then lock him in until the tantrum stops.

For two hours? she asked. You want me to lock him in his room for two hours?

Dr. Foster stared at her blankly for what seemed an eternity then shook his head slightly, grabbed his prescription pad and began writing. Thank God, she thought, he understands. He ripped the sheet from his pad and handed it to her. She snatched it, sure it held the name of a trusted counselor. Instead, she read, *Taking Back the Reins: How to Regain Control of the Out-of-Control Child.*

It's a parenting book, Dr. Foster said as she stared at the paper as if deciphering Morse code. Could this be normal? she wondered.

She read the book, posted "behavior charts" on the refrigerator with magnets, bought sticky stars to denote good days. The charts, quickly covered with black X's, didn't last long. Small, angry hands ripped them down and shredded them.

The tantrums got worse in middle school. One afternoon, in a fit of anger, Josh punched Kate in the stomach. Without thinking, she kicked him in the calf. He raised his hand to strike back but she grabbed it. As they struggled, she ran her free hand over the top of the bookshelf next to them. She felt a plastic ruler, seized it and brought it down on the top of Josh's head. The ruler broke with a loud crack. They both froze, staring into each other's eyes, then Josh jerked loose from her grasp and ran to his bedroom, slamming the door. Slowly Kate turned to look behind her. Reyna, then eight, cowered on the couch, her eyes filled with fear and what Kate read as accusation. Kate walked zombie-like to her bedroom, fell on her knees next to the bed, dropped her face into her hands. God, what am I doing? she whispered. Am I a child abuser? Forgive me. Please forgive me. Let Josh be all right. Help me, God. Please help me.

Later, she peeked in on him. He sat propped against his headboard, staring at the wall.

I'm sorry I hit you, she murmured.

Get out, bitch, he said, the malevolent glare in his eyes demonic. I hate you. She shut the door. Guilt prevented her from reprimanding his vulgarity.

When Josh wasn't fighting with Mitch or Kate, he was threatening to kill them. The threats were detailed. I have a knife and I know how to use it, he said one morning, his chocolate eyes dark with rage because Kate had asked him to pick up his room. She confiscated his Swiss army knife and hid all the carving knives.

One day I'm going to get a gun and I'm going to kill you, he said a few weeks later. You have no idea how easy it is to get a gun at school. First I'm going to shoot Dad, then you. I'm going to make the girls watch, because it'll make them so upset. Then I'll shoot them.

Mitch blamed her. You're too soft, you don't discipline him, you let him get away with murder became his daily mantra. You're the problem, she'd shoot back, afraid he was right. You're too harsh and critical. He's a kid and you expect him to act like a man, to be the perfect gentleman, the perfect student, the perfect athlete.

The arguments were the only loose thread in the tightly woven fabric of their marriage.

Kate again consulted Dr. Foster, trying to make him understand without revealing the worst of the details. Guilt, horror, and shame kept her from expressing the thought that had begun to plague her: that Josh, her child, flesh of her womb, was evil.

We need counseling, she said. We fight constantly and Josh's tantrums are getting worse.

How's he doing in school? Dr. Foster asked.

Fine. His behavior is great, she said. His teachers love him and say he gets along with the other kids. He makes honor roll every semester. It's at home, with us, when he melts down.

Dr. Foster shook his head. Look, this counseling stuff is overdone and it stigmatizes the kid. All Josh needs is firm, consistent discipline. Here, try this. He jotted down the name of another parenting book: *The Road to Accountability: A Guide for Raising Responsible Teens.*

She read the book. It advised against arguing with a child in a tantrum. During one of Josh's fits, she took the book's advice, gathered the girls into the van and began backing out of the garage. A quarter of the way out, she heard the garage door whine and hum. Josh stood in the laundry-room doorway, smirking. Before she understood the significance of the sound and his smile, the garage door clunked the roof of her van then groaned. With a screech of twisting steel, the door ripped off its tracks and hung by its cables, bent and broken. Kate stopped and stepped onto the van's running board. A broad path of scraped paint and a large dent ran across the vehicle's roof. She lifted her eyes to meet Josh's. His smile hadn't wavered.

That night, like so many others, came his tears. I'm so sorry. So sorry, Josh choked out in a predictable, pain-filled ritual. I don't want to act this way. I love you, Mom. I do. I'm sorry. Later, after he fell asleep, Kate looked in on him, heard his breath ragged with weep, saw his fair face angelic in repose, and guilt swept over her triple force. How could she think ...?

Kate spits, trying to expel the foul taste of vomit. When she looks up from the driveway, the garage is empty. She grabs the open door of her van, drags herself to a stand, leans on the door and sobs. What's wrong with her? Why can't she get him under control? Oh God, he scares her. The thought calms her. She studies it. Is she afraid of him? She reaches in and turns off the engine, then sinks sideways onto the driver's seat. She puzzles together her feelings and fears against the backdrop of Michael's death mask. As much as Josh's rages scare her, his underlying despair scares her more. Now she understands why. When she saw Michael through the garage window, she came face to face with where that despair can lead. She shudders.

The university has a support hotline for employees struggling with emotional or psychological problems. She must dial it, even though the thought brings another wave of nausea. Why is she so weak? Why can't she get her son under control? She can't answer these questions. She must put them to someone who can.

Chapter 8

Kate's jaw clenches as she walks into the psychologist's office and sits in the wing chair in front of a cherry-wood desk. Dr. Emmett, medium height, with brown hair and browner eyes, sits on the far side of the desk, leaning back in a leather chair, hands folded across his slight paunch. The smells of leather and wood polish remind her of her father's den; only the stale smell of alcohol is missing.

"What's on your mind?" Dr. Emmett's tone softens the question.

"It's silly. Last week my neighbor committed suicide and I'm having trouble getting over it. I feel stupid being here. Not sure why I'm having all this trouble. I don't know why I'm here, really." Kate stares at the purse she grips tightly in her lap, wishing she could exert equal control over her tongue.

"Tell me about the suicide."

She braces herself then relates the story, giving the dry, external details but not the internal ones. Dr. Emmett listens without interruption. When she finishes, she peeks up at him. He's turned to the side so she sees only his profile. He is slightly reclined in his chair with his eyes closed.

Oh dear God he's fallen asleep. What should she do?

Wake him? The silence weighs on her. Her petty tale of death and fear has put this man to sleep. She recalls her father's comment: You came face to face with the Grim Reaper and it scared the shit out of you. Get over it.

But Kate has seen death before. As a college intern at the *New York Register,* she covered more than one body-mangling car crash. And once, when she was working for Senator Mimms, she arrived at the government center just as paramedics were loading onto their truck the naked, bloodied body of a workman who'd fallen from the top of the communications tower.

She clears her throat, gets no response. She decides to leave quietly and moves to stand.

"You must have felt great horror," Dr. Emmett says, jolting her back in her seat, "and great sadness." He opens his eyes and turns to her. The compassion she reads in his face is a salve. To her chagrin, she begins to cry like a child. She tries to swallow the great gulps of sorrow and hurt welling from her depths, but she can't. They erupt through her taut, quivering lips, producing a tortured keening. Why is she such a baby? Why can't she pull herself together? She buries her face in her hands. Tries to hide from Dr. Emmett, from this accusing voice within.

Dr. Emmett doesn't speak. Her sobs soften to whimpers. "I'm sorry," she croaks between hiccups.

"Why do you apologize?" His voice is honey. "You're allowed to cry. You should cry. It's healing, cleansing."

She grabs tissues from the box he offers and blows her nose as quietly as she can.

"You're very self-critical." His tone is harder now.

She wipes her eyes. "You just met me. How do you know that?"

"What was the first thing you said when you came in? That coming here was 'silly.' As if being traumatized by the violent death of a neighbor makes you weak."

Kate leans her head back and stares at the ceiling, ignoring the tears streaking down her face. "There was violence there. The garage was still. Yet in that stillness I felt a terrible violence. As if I could feel his legs kicking, his arms flailing.

"I talked to my father the next day. I tried to tell him about the violence that hung in the stillness. And the terrible sadness. He said, 'Suicide is violent and it's cruel to those left behind; that's why it's unforgivable.' I felt something wrench inside, as if my heart put its hands over its ears and shouted 'No, no, no, no.' It hurt so much, what he said."

"The judgment of it."

She nods, wipes her eyes then stares at the tissue. "I have to believe when Michael died, in that moment he crossed the threshold, God was there to wrap His loving arms around him and comfort him. I couldn't live if I didn't believe that."

She hears Dr. Emmett swivel in his chair and plunk his arms on the desk, knows he is leaning toward her, waiting. Kate raises her eyes to meet his intense gaze.

"I believe that too," he whispers.

"I feel so sad for him," she says between jagged breaths. "He must have been desperate."

"Yes."

"But I don't believe he was bad or evil."

"No." Dr. Emmett shakes his head; a slight frown pulls at his mouth. "He was depressed. He needed help and for some reason didn't get it."

"He was a computer programmer. A self-employed contractor. He didn't have health insurance."

"Too many people don't. It's a crime. But you didn't come here to discuss the injustices of American health care."

"No." Kate exhales heavily. "I'm having problems."

"Not surprising."

She attempts a smile. "I'm not sure how to take that."

"Let's just say I'd be worried if your recent experience wasn't troubling you."

"No need to worry." She gives a short laugh. "Truth is I feel afraid all the time. Every time I go into a room I see Michael there. Sometimes he's hanging. Other times he's just standing. And at night I have visions when I'm trying to sleep. I see his face ... and other things ... grotesque and monstrous. The other night I couldn't sleep. Around midnight I called my sister Lily. Woke her. I felt bad about it, but I was so upset. I told her about the suicide. When I got to the part where I looked through the garage window, I started to cry in an awful way. When I finally told her what I saw, I could hear her cry too.

"Then I told her how afraid I was, about all the visions. She said, 'I'm sure what you're experiencing is normal.' We talked awhile and at one point she quoted some lines from a psalm. 'I lift up my eyes to the hills. From whence does my help come?' The next lines were the ones I loved. I can't recite them verbatim, but they talk about how help comes from God, how He never slumbers while watching over us."

"The Lord will keep you from all evil," Dr. Emmett recites. "He will keep your life. The Lord will keep your going out and your coming in from this time forth and for evermore."

"Yes, that's it." She questions him with her eyes.

"I had that psalm read to me once when I was in a difficult place," he says. "You picked a good person to talk to."

"Yes, Lily is a good person to call when you're afraid of the dark. Funny, she's not much like a lily."

"What do you mean?"

"The word 'lily' conjures images of fragile white flowers bending gracefully in the wind. I wouldn't describe my sister quite that way. She has frizzy red hair that refuses to stay in a braid; strands wisp around her head like flames. She has green eyes that twinkle like a pixie's, unless you make her mad, which is hard to do. Her hands and limbs look delicate—lily-like—but they're not. I've seen her cling to a rearing horse a seasoned broncobuster couldn't seat."

"So she's tough."

"Yeah."

"Maybe her name better reflects her spirituality."

"Yeah, if you mean beautiful rather than weak, as in lily-livered. She's definitely not that. I remember at our uncle's funeral a few years back, we went up to the rail and knelt to receive communion. The church was Catholic and when the priest got to Lily, I guess because he didn't recognize her, he asked her right there at the rail if she was Catholic. When she said no, he snatched back the wafer he'd just laid in her hands and said only Catholics can eat at Christ's table.

"Lily rose from her knees and said in a gentle voice that managed to find its way to every ear in the church, 'Funny, I don't remember Jesus ever turning anyone away from his table.' I'll never forget the priest's face. It turned a violet red, like he was having a stroke. He skipped my brother and me and moved to the next communicant, stuttering, 'The bread of Christ, the body of salvation.'

"When we walked back to our seats, the eyes of the congregation were on Lily, and I saw in them a grudging admiration."

Dr. Emmett grins broadly. "I like your sister."

"Yeah, me too."

"And she's right, what she said to you that night. When paramedics or police walk into a suicide, they see a mental health professional within twenty-four hours to debrief. Every time. It never ceases to traumatize. The natural working through of the emotional and psychological fallout can take anywhere from two weeks to six months."

"Six months!"

"Yes, and that would not be abnormal. Nor would it indicate weakness on your part. More likely it would indicate profound empathy."

Kate wraps herself around this idea, tries to believe she is a caring soul rather than a milksop. "There's something else."

"Yes?"

"When I looked in the garage, I thought I saw something. Not saw, but felt something there. I can't describe it, but it made me feel ... It made me afraid. Not like I was going to get hurt, but afraid ..."

"Afraid of what?"

"It made me feel afraid for my soul."

"Interesting. Tell me what you mean."

"I can't. I don't understand it."

"You need to figure that out. Perhaps you'll write about it."

Kate flinches. "What made you say that?"

"I don't know. Just popped in my head." Dr. Emmett's smile looks conspiratorial, as if he's in on a secret with an invisible partner.

"I haven't written since I quit working for Senator Mimms when Reyna was born."

"Ah, so you are a writer?"

"*Was* a speech writer."

"Were you writing for Mimms when he first ran for office?"

"Wrote all his major speeches."

"Very impressive."

Kate looks away as she shrugs. "They were his ideas; I just made them sound good."

Silence fills the room. She drags her eyes back to his. He is staring at her with a puzzled expression. She senses a hint of disapproval. Her face grows hot. "I don't write anymore."

The psychologist's face relaxes into a smile. "Perhaps you'll write about it," he repeats. "Not for someone else, but for yourself."

She can't imagine this. As she tries, a sickening mixture of fear and dread rises in her.

"Anything else been bothering you lately? Maybe before the suicide?"

Kate refocuses. "Well, yes. My husband's and my relationship with our son, Josh. It's very rocky. We're always fighting with him, and the fights are getting violent. Then the other day, when I came home and the garage door went up, for a moment I saw … I mean I had a vision … "

"A vision of what?" Tears slide down Kate's cheeks. "You can tell me," Dr. Emmett says, his voice hushed.

"I saw Josh hanging there," she whispers. "It was very vivid."

"How old is Josh?"

"Thirteen." She shakes off her tears. "My son is very unhappy."

"Does your sister Lily have children? Have you talked to her about your son?"

"No. Lily desperately wants kids, but she can't have them. She and her husband have tried everything, but … I don't know. It's kind of a sore spot for her."

"Too bad." Dr. Emmett lightly hammers the eraser end of his pencil on his desk, apparently enthralled by its swift vacillation and the staccato tap, tap, tapping. The pencil stops and he looks up.

"Seeing your neighbor's suicide has brought into focus your concerns about your son," he says slowly. "That's good and I can help you there. But remember, your neighbor's suicide has nothing to do with you. It's not a warning or a portent of things to come. Do you understand?"

"Yes," Kate whispers.

"I'm not a family counselor, but I know a very good one. Dr. Lewis. Her office is not far from you. You live in Bay Haven, right?"

"Yes."

"I'll approve an initial ten visits for you, your husband and your son for family counseling. If Dr. Lewis feels you need more, she'll call me. It won't be a problem."

"Do I need to see you again? About the suicide?"

"No. The fears and anxiety you're feeling are normal. If, however, they begin to interfere with your regular routine then, yes, come see me again. Otherwise, just be gentle with yourself. You're a compassionate person, so your neighbor's death has hit you hard. Very understandable. Don't let anyone, including yourself, beat you up about it. You need to put a clamp on that critical voice inside you."

"I like that. My 'critical voice.' How do you know I have a critical voice?"

Dr. Emmett's robust laughter makes Kate smile. "Let's just say I've been doing this a long time."

Chapter 9

She believes he's a monster. A grotesque. He floats in the dark, these images a nightmare if not for the song. But he sees them through the song. It's all before him: Present, past, future—simultaneously. He can choose where to look, or not, at any given moment. Only tomorrow lacks the clarity of yesterday and today. It's like looking through frosted glass. When he glances toward tomorrow, he apprehends only telltale shapes, vague outlines suggesting countless possibilities but confirming none.

He looks back to that day. She won't come to him. The window is ajar but she backs away. He sees her face, pale and expressionless, closed, holding in her horror. Tears course her cheeks as she talks into the phone, her voice mechanical, her words hollow. I can't stop him, *she's saying as a man climbs through the window.*

She turns toward the siren. An ambulance speeds down the street. Two police cars follow close behind. She closes the phone, would melt to the ground if a cop didn't at that moment put his arm around her, support her against his starched blue chest. Michael always hated cops. Pigs, he called them, after they threatened to arrest Matt. He wishes he could kiss this man.

She heads to her house after the cops finish interviewing her. Stops in the middle of the road, stands for a moment, then turns. She runs back to the cop, pulls on his arm, interrupts his chatter with the dispatcher. She drags him to the street, frantically pointing west. She has remembered Matt—all the times she's seen him walking home from the bus stop—this boy who tried to kill her cat. She's back in her living room when the police meet the bus. Because of her, Matt doesn't see the mess his father made. The love in this small act fills Michael's heart to breaking. Yet she's already forgotten it. Doesn't remember doing it.

He listens to her pondering late at night as her husband snores beside her. Did he struggle? *she asks herself.* Did he regret? *She knows the answers but tells herself she doesn't. Will only go so far as to say there was violence in the stillness. That's what she told the doctor. But from her depths she saw it all. It was all still hanging there, vibrating in the silence. Cara didn't see it. It's not the kind of thing you see with eyes. Funny how eyes are so limiting. He remembers reading* Le Petit Prince *in high school French, not really in French, he cheated. Bought the English version. He remembers the fox telling the prince his secret—It is only with the* heart that one can see rightly. What is essential is invisible to the eye. *Saint-Exupéry must have heard this song many times to write that.*

As a teenager, the fox's secret held no meaning for him. What does the heart see as a belt flays the tender buttock? It doesn't see. It closes its eyes. Goes into hibernation.

Cara loved him, but she couldn't see him. He realizes he never really saw her. Yet this stranger who had no reason to care saw him. She saw everything. Saw the blood on his fingers. Saw his legs kicking back. He is there again, stepping off the ladder.

The pain hits like lightning. A scream rises within him, is choked off by the slicing rope. Oh my God oh my God. *He kicks his legs back as he tries to grip the rope. The motion swings his body erratically. Where is the ladder? He wants to step back. To take back this last step.*

God help me. Help me!

He claws at the rope. The toe of his boot hits the ladder, but he can't get a foothold. His body swings round. He's facing the ladder, but before he can reach out with hand or foot, he swings back toward the window. His neck is on fire. He can't catch a breath. Thunder pounds his temples, blasts his ears. His fingers are warm and sticky. Why is the rope so goddamn slippery? He can't loosen it. His arms ache. He wants to call out. He tries. A squeak. An abortive cough.

Oh God oh God oh God!

With supreme effort he jack-knifes his body and grabs the rope above his head. Holds on! His body is swinging out of control. He scissors his legs, desperately searching for the ladder. Hold on! *His hands fall to his sides.* Hold on hold on oh God oh GodohGod. *His arms are lead. His eyes burn, are too big for their sockets. The garage grows dim. His temples are exploding.*

He kicks back one last time, to where he thinks the ladder is. The garage is receding. He blinks madly. He hears a thud, plywood falling on concrete. A soft breeze kisses his face but can't cool his fever, can't douse the fire in his chest. The garage is pitch. He strains forward, eyes bulging, but discerns no light. He relaxes, hangs limp, hears only thunder now. It's softer. A drum. His mother's heartbeat. Love wells within him. That first love, while still inside, in the dark. Before he knew the outside of things. Before alcohol and belts, before threats and guns.

Unstrangled love. He knew that once. The drumbeat's fading now. It lulls him to peace. He's so tired. He'll rest a moment. Just a moment, then try again. He's calm now. The pain is gone. He feels only overwhelming fatigue. He'll rest. Just a second. Then ...

His chin falls to his collarbone. His legs and arms jerk convulsively—random, unspent electrical energy.

In one instant, in one innocent glance through the window, she saw it all. More than saw it, she felt it. Collided with it—with him. Soul to soul. He felt her strength in that collision. She hugged him in recognition and love even as her mind recoiled, the soul's empathy translating into heart-harrowing sadness and horror. His desperation, still heavy in the air, engulfed her. He'd take it back if he could. Would kiss away her tears. But he can't. All he can do is watch and wait patiently as she explores the dark in brief, isolated peeks, viewing the vision of her soul bit by bit, like watching a movie one frame at a time, because that's the only way she can take it.

Chapter

"Family Counseling Center, may I help you?" The woman's voice is briskly official.

"Yes, I'm calling to schedule an appointment with Dr. Lewis. Dr. Emmett referred me."

"What's the nature of your problem?"

"It's my son. My husband and I are having a lot of trouble with him. I don't know, maybe it's us."

"How old?"

"I'm thirty-eight."

"Your son." Kate winces at the slight sneer in the woman's tone. "How old is your son?"

"Oh, sorry. Thirteen. He's in middle school—eighth grade. We seem to fight all the time and the fights are becoming worse, they're—"

"You don't want Dr. Lewis. You need Dr. Galen."

"But Dr. Emmett specifically recommended—"

"Trust me, I know all these counselors. You're having trouble with a boy entering his teens. Dr. Galen is the best. I'm not saying the other counselors here aren't good, but he's the best for the situation you're describing."

"I've hardly said anything."

"You've said enough. Trust me on this."

"Well," Kate hesitates. "Okay, I guess I need an appointment with Dr. Galen."

"I'll have him call you. The doctors set their own appointments. Just let me get your vital statistics …"

Kate's insides sink as she hangs up the phone. Nothing's carved in stone. If this Dr. Galen isn't right, they can go back to Dr. Emmett's suggestion. But for now, she'll go with the flow. She smiles. Go with the flow. Jean's favorite saying. Our lives are like rivers, Jean says. We can either struggle against the current or swim with it. Either way, we end up at the sea.

Maybe this was meant to be. She grabs her purse and heads for the university.

Entering class, Kate begins the shift to her showman's persona. After years of teaching she became conscious of the conversion she undergoes when she enters the classroom—from what she considers her true self—meditative, awkward, insecure Kate—to the witty, fast-talking, self-confident actor, Professor Nardek. Today she's unsure she can complete the transformation. As she places her briefcase on the table next to the lectern, she notices Austin staring at her. She hears the end of the heavy sigh she is heaving and realizes it's the cause of his furrowed brow. She straightens, pulls her shoulders back, lifts her chin and smiles.

"Okay gang, listen up. I've got some changes to the syllabus."

"Again?" Cleo whines. "What's the point of having a syllabus if you're gonna change it every class?"

Kate's smile broadens. "That's the reason for the line in bold at the bottom of the first page—the one I had you recite the first day. 'The teacher reserves the right to change this syllabus at any time and as many times as she deems fit.' See how well I know myself? Hey! I see those eyes rolling." Chuckles rise from the class.

"Next week we were scheduled to have a class viewing of *Rosemary's Baby*. That's out." The students moan. "Sorry, gang." Kate pulls a sheaf of papers from her briefcase and begins to distribute them. "Instead, I've got a list of horror movies you can choose from. Watch the movie alone and then write a 2,500-word essay on how it exemplifies—or doesn't—one of the themes we've been discussing in class." She returns to the lectern. "For example, what does *Dr. Jekyll and Mr. Hyde* say about the nature of evil and man's relationship with God? Is Hell a physical place or a state of being? Those are the kinds of questions you might start with, but remember, they're not thesis statements. You have to decide what your answer is and *that* becomes your thesis."

"Why are you reneging on the movie?" Cleo asks, her eyes serious now.

The question momentarily shakes the self-confident entertainer in Kate. Should she tell them the truth? The thought leaps unbidden to her mind. She often uses snippets from her life to make a point. Once, defining "impunity," she had explained, it means without punishment. For example, my son thinks he can tell me to shut up with impunity. Kate then smiled sinisterly, rubbed her hands together and said in a stage whisper, He's wrong. The students had laughed, oblivious to the sad truth behind her example.

Kate hesitates only a moment. "I had a bad experience recently and I'm not up to watching horror movies right now."

"What happened?" Austin asks.

Kate straightens and smiles. "I walked into my neighbor's suicide." The shock she sees causes the smile to drain from her face.

"How?" Cleo whispers.

As Kate tells the story, part of her worries she'll cry. But she's in her teaching mode. She tells her students how she lived the cliché of hair standing on end when she heard Cara's shrieks. She tells them about her call to 911.

"It was like I'd stepped into a horror movie with all its conventions. The dispatcher asked me if I could get into the garage. I was the brainless yet determined hero during the obligatory search scene—the one who's alone in the house with the electricity off, hears a noise upstairs, knows something terrible lurks in the dark, and decides, against all common sense—or any kind of sense—to investigate." Her students are sitting forward, alert, some smiling at her jab at the genre. "There I was searching, searching, trying to get into the garage, knowing something awaited me but not knowing what. I wondered if someone was in there with a gun who'd killed Michael, who might kill me. All I lacked was an audience screaming, 'No, you idiot! Don't go there!'" The class erupts in laughter.

But as Kate tells how she looked through the window, describes Michael hanging a few feet from her, paints with words the gruesome image forever fixed in her mind, the class slumps into silence. The sadness and compassion she sees threatens to unleash the reservoir of tears she's kept dammed by her light, detached telling.

"Since that moment," she says, "that last grim image of Michael has walked with me." She sweeps her right hand to the side as if presenting someone to the class. "It's here now, beside me."

She surveys the class. All eyes are fixed on her. A somber silence stretches to what feels like the breaking point. Then Cleo, shaking her head vigorously, raises her hands and slaps her desk.

"Yeah, you done had enough horror." She smiles at Kate. "You don't have any complaints here."

Other students murmur their agreement.

"You guys have any other questions about my private life before we move on?" Kate asks, thankful for Cleo's rescue. She is greeted by headshakes and smiles. "Okay then, let's start by reviewing these movies and what themes they bring to mind."

As she pulls out of the university parking lot, she reaches for the CD case on the floor beside her seat. At a stoplight, she pops the CD into the player.

She hasn't listened to Cat Stevens since she was in high school. A few days after the suicide, she succumbed to Josh's persistent whining about how he *had* to buy a new CD with the money he'd earned mowing lawns. She took him to the music store. Josh went off in search of The Backstreet Boys, while Kate strolled the aisles, carelessly scanning display cases. When she spied *Teaser and the Firecat*, she stopped and plucked the CD from the shelf. The title filled her with joy, as if she'd come across an old friend.

In the first song, Cat Stevens sings about bending his inner ear to his soul's murmurings. Kate wonders if the singer/songwriter can tune into his soul whenever he wants? What does his soul whisper? Kate wishes she could hear the whisperings of her own soul on command—or at least the gentle voice she calls the goddess. She imagines this inner goddess now bracing against high winds.

The image triggers memories of Robert Smith, a man of sixty who has laid hardwood floors since he dropped out of school at seventeen. She met him when gathering bids for her living room. The other bids came from big companies or chains, all offering different grades of wood from the cheapest to the most expensive. Mr. Smith's landed in the middle.

All the bids except his specified number-one common as the wood grade.

I assume your bid is for number-one common, Kate said to him over the phone.

No ma'am, he replied in a thick southern drawl. We only use what's called quarter-sawn.

I've heard of it. But your bid is pretty much in line with the others, though you're using the best grade.

Mr. Smith chuckled. I found over the long haul it's less money and headaches, he said. You see, ma'am, quarter-sawn has less knots; I'm sure the others told ya. What they might not a said is it's stronger and more stable. It comes from the center of the tree, so it don't buckle like cheaper wood. I tried them cheaper woods a hundred years ago when I first started out. I kep' havin' to go back to old jobs to replace warped boards. That got costly. Now all I use is the good stuff and I guarantee my floors for life. You want the cheaper wood, go with someone else.

She hired Mr. Smith. Later she pondered his comments and decided the goddess is like quarter-sawn wood—strong but flexible, bending but not breaking under pressure of the elements. The thought made something deep within her spring like a gazelle.

Kate leans forward and restarts the Cat Stevens CD.

Chapter

When Kate pulls her van into the car circle, a teacher's aide opens the sliding door at the curb and Mollie clambers in, her hands full of colorful papers and her face beaming with excitement.

"I made something for you," she sings as the aide fastens her into her booster seat. The corner of her mouth is smudged with chocolate.

"Bye, Mollie." The aide waves at Kate.

"How was your day, little Joybug?" Kate asks over her shoulder as she maneuvers the van out of the lot.

"Good. I played with Amy on the slide. And Ms. Peterson pushed me on the swings real high."

"Wow!"

"And I made this. It's for you."

"Just a minute. If we come to a stoplight I'll look at it, but I can't while I'm driving."

"Can we get McDonalds?"

"Not today."

"Aw, please?"

"No. We had McDonalds yesterday. If you keep eating chicken nuggets you're going to start clucking."

Mollie giggles. "That's silly."

"Here's a light. Show me what you made."

Mollie hands her a sheet of black construction paper. Glued to the paper is a white moon cut out by her child's hand then painted with light shades of green, blue and yellow, giving it an iridescent quality. Silver glitter sparkles through the paint. Next to the moon, Mollie has drawn a lopsided star in pink chalk. Below the star is an equally lopsided heart and outlines of a butterfly and daisy—both smiling. At the bottom, in neat script, her teacher has written "God created the moon and the stars to shine at night." As a final touch, Mollie used chalk to draw a loopy circle along the edge of the paper, enclosing all the images.

"It's gorgeous." Something about the glow-in-the-dark quality of the moon and the childish scrawl, in the unhindered notion that hearts can float in space side by side with stars and butterflies, makes Kate's heart flip. She reverently strokes the picture, smells the chalk dust and feels its fine grain on her fingers. "Oh Mollie, I love it."

"Really?"

"I'm going to frame it." A horn blares. Kate looks up to see the light is green. Gently she lays the picture on the passenger seat. For a split second Michael is there, staring grimly as the picture falls into his lap. She blinks, making her forehead frown, and he's gone. The picture rests on an empty seat. The horn blares again.

"Okay," she calls. "Sor-reee." She pulls through the intersection as the light turns yellow.

"Was he mad?" Mollie asks.

"Yeah. He must be in a hurry. Oh well." Kate glances over again but sees only the picture. "Mollie," she says in a collaborative whisper, "I want to tell you something."

"What?" Her voice holds a note of awe.

"I see God in your picture. I see the joy and playfulness He must have felt when He created the world. You must have been very close to God when you made this."

Mollie doesn't answer. When Kate pulls up to a stop sign she glances in the rearview mirror, through Michael, through the black caverns where his eyes should be, to Mollie. Her daughter is looking out the window, her sparkling eyes unfocused. A wistful smile curves her lips, still full and red from babyhood. She is a cherub.

"You know what?" Kate continues. "I say we go to McDs for lunch and then to the craft store to find a frame."

"Really?"

"Really."

"Yeah! McDs!" Mollie claps. "Can I pick the frame?"

"We'll see." A warm wave washes through Kate even as her mind clicks off the chores she had planned to do this afternoon: Dust and vacuum the house, grade papers, sweep and mop the kitchen floor. These two detours will put her hopelessly behind. The goddess steps in, shoving aside guilt before it can take root. Chores can wait.

Two hours later they arrive home with a large piece of dusky pink matting and a sixteen-by-twenty-inch black frame. On the way in, Kate grabs her utility knife from the toolbox and a straightedge from the garage wall. In the family room, Mollie plops on the couch and turns on the cartoon channel.

"No TV on school days, you know that." Kate presses the off button and lays the matting on the tile floor.

"Just one cartoon. Please, Mommy?"

"Nope. Why don't you look at a book while I'm working?"

Mollie harrumphs from the couch, goes to the pine table off the kitchen and sits. She rests her chin in her hands and glares at the wall. Kate ignores her. From the corner of her eye, she sees Mollie occasionally glance her way, her frown deepening when she realizes her performance is going unnoticed. As Kate begins to measure the matting, she hears the high-pitched whine of school-bus brakes. A few minutes later, Reyna walks in.

"Hi, Rey," Kate calls from her position on the floor. "How was your day?"

"Fine. What ya doin'?"

"Mollie made a picture at school today. It's there on the table." Kate sits back on her heels and points. "We're going to frame it. There're some chips in the drawer and a juice pack in the fridge if you're hungry."

"Can I help?" Reyna asks.

"No honey, I'm in a hurry." Reyna's eyes droop. "Well," Kate relents, "I have to measure the picture and then cut a hole in this matting. You can't use the utility knife; it's too sharp, but you can help measure and draw lines with this straightedge."

Reyna grabs the artwork, skips over to Kate and kneels beside her.

"I want to help too," chimes Mollie, quick on her sister's heels, her pout forgotten.

Kate shows Reyna how to measure, then, after making guide marks on the matt, she allows Reyna to draw the first cut line. The process will take twice as long than if she did it alone, but her impatience dissipates as she watches Reyna— eyes earnest, a bit of pink tongue poking out of the corner of her mouth—slowly run her pencil along the straightedge.

"Now, Mollie's turn." Mollie, still smelling of french fries, snatches the pencil and pulls it down the straight-edge. She moves quicker than Reyna, who is a perfectionist. Halfway down, the pencil develops a mind of its own and wanders toward the center of the matting.

"Oh, I messed up!"

"Don't worry. That's the part we're cutting out. No one will see it."

Mollie again leans over the matting and finishes her line. Each girl gets another turn, then Kate uses the utility knife to cut along the lines. She lets the girls layer the matting and picture against the glass, then she seals the back of the frame.

"It's perfect." Kate holds the framed picture up for them to admire.

"Can we frame one of my pictures?" Reyna asks, looking at Mollie's art with newfound awe.

"Sure," Kate says. "But not today. We've got cleaning to do and I need to fix dinner."

The laundry room door slams.

"Mom, I'm home." Josh ambles into the family room and drops his backpack in the middle of the floor. His expression is dark. "What's that?" he asks snidely.

"A picture Mollie made." Kate rises from the floor. "We just finished framing it. I think we'll hang it over the couch."

"Really?" Mollie shrieks, jumping up and grabbing the edge of Kate's shirt.

"Really."

Josh slumps on the couch and switches on the TV.

"No TV on weekdays, Josh. You know that." Kate lays the artwork on the kitchen table then crosses to the TV and hits the power button.

"Leave me alone." He clicks the remote, turning the TV back on.

"I said turn it off." Kate punches the power button again.

"Go fuck yourself," Josh says, again pressing the remote.

"That's it. You're in your room." Kate rips the TV cord out of the socket. "You will not talk to me that way."

"Fuck you," Josh says. "What you gonna do about it? Fuck you, fuck you, fuck you!"

With two quick strides, Kate grabs him by the shoulders

and yanks him to his feet. "Get to your room, NOW!" She shoves him toward the hall.

He swings around and wags his index finger an inch from her nose. "Don't touch me. It's your fault. Turning off the TV."

She grabs Josh, who is half a head shorter than she, yanks him around and thrusts him down the hall. "Get going!" she says, then pushes him again.

"Goddamn bitch." He tries to turn but she grabs his shoulders.

"Get going!" She manhandles him to his room, shoves him in then plants a kick on his buttock. She slams the door and locks it, a maneuver recommended by their pediatrician years ago. "You can come out in half an hour, provided you're ready to apologize."

"Go to hell!"

She leans against the door, huffing, trying to calm her shaking body. Slowly she walks to the family room. The girls are gone. She walks through the kitchen and dining room. Peeks in the living room. Nothing. She heads into her bedroom. The girls are huddled on the far side of the bed. The TV is on, but neither notices it.

"I put the TV on because Mollie was scared," Reyna whispers. "I hope you're not mad."

"No, sweetheart, I'm not mad." Kate's eyes sting. She turns then leaps backward.

Josh stands in the doorway. He dangles a screwdriver in front of her.

"After you locked me in last time, I put this in my room."

"Give me that."

"What's wrong, Mom? You afraid?"

"Give me the screwdriver and get to your room." Her voice is low but strained. "Now, or I'm calling your father and telling him to come home."

"'Mitch, Mitch,'" he mimics in a high-pitched voice. "Always have to call Dad, huh Mom? Can't ever handle anything on your own. 'Mitch, Mitch, come save me.'"

"Get to your room."

"Okay, Mom," he says, his tone patronizing, "you win."

He begins to turn, then with a jerk, he swings back and throws the screwdriver at Kate. She flinches as it whizzes by her right ear. He smiles mockingly, turns and saunters to the kitchen. Kate follows. When he gets to the family room, his eyes fall on Mollie's picture. He glances at Kate then grabs the polished frame, raises it over his head, ignoring her shriek of protest, and slams it on the table. Kate turns away from the spray of splintered glass. When she turns back, she sees Josh pulling the picture from the broken frame.

"No!" she screams, leaping at him, trying to catch his hands. But already he has ripped it in two. With a satisfied smirk, he steps back from her and lets the pieces fall to the floor. She rushes forward and slaps her son full force across the face, her fingers striping his cheek red. Josh staggers back, his expression quickly shifting from disbelief to loathing. He raises his hand to his flaming cheek. Finally he turns and walks to his room, slamming the door behind him.

Kate looks at her hand still throbbing from the blow. Remembers the time her father slapped her across the mouth when she was a teen, making her lip bleed. Why? She can't recall. She only remembers the mortification, the crushing sense of injustice, the hatred that welled within her at that moment. She swore then she would never be like her father. And now, here she is, not only like him, worse than him. At least he could claim he was drunk.

Holding the back of a kitchen chair with one hand, she stoops to pick up the torn pieces and softly places them on the table. She leans her head against the table's edge and massages her forehead with her free hand. She hears the soft, hesitant footsteps of her daughters on the kitchen terrazzo behind her.

"Don't come out here; there's broken glass."

"It's okay, Mom, I have shoes on." Reyna puts her arm around Kate's shoulders.

She turns and weakly smiles at her daughter, who is at eye level with her. Behind Reyna, Mollie stands in the middle of the kitchen, tears streaming down her face.

"Come here, baby." Mollie runs into her arms and sobs against her chest. "It's okay, sweetheart," Kate croons. "Don't cry."

"Juh—osh bro—oke my pit—chure," Mollie hiccups between sobs.

Kate stands and lifts Mollie into her arms.

"Do you need time in Mommy's special rocker?"

"Mommy?" The older girl stands in the doorway holding the two pieces of Mollie's picture. "We can fix it. We can tape it."

Kate holds out her hand. Reyna walks to the rocker and lets Kate enfold her. The three cuddle until Mollie's sobs subside.

"Reyna's right," Kate says, breaking the silence. "Shall we see if we can fix it?"

"I'll get the tape," says Reyna, hurrying off to the kitchen. Kate kisses Mollie's wet cheeks before sliding her off her lap. They both follow Reyna, who has brought the tape and picture pieces to the dining room table. They fit the ragged edges together then tape the back to hold them in place.

"Look, it's as good as new," Kate says. "You'd never know it was ripped."

Mollie runs her hand across its surface, her face unusually grave.

"All we need now is a new frame," Kate adds.

"Today?" Mollie looks up and Kate sees hope in her eyes.

"Of course today! Just let me clean up the mess at the kitchen table, then we're off."

Mollie's beam returns.

"There's my Joybug come back to me." Kate rustles her baby's hair. "Reyna, why don't you read Mollie a book while I clean up. Then we'll go."

"Okay, Mom. Come on, Mollie." Reyna takes Mollie's hand and pulls her to the living room as Kate heads for the kitchen.

When they return home an hour later with a new frame and take-out Chinese, the house is quiet. Kate peeks in her son's room. He's asleep on the bed, his body curled around his black-and-white cat, Mischief. After she re-frames Mollie's picture and feeds the girls, Kate checks on Josh again. He is in the same position, with his back to her. She begins to retreat when she notices his hand stroking his cat.

"You want some dinner?"

"Mom, I'm so sorry," he chokes out in a strangled voice. Kate crosses the room and sits on the edge of the bed. She places a hand between his shoulder blades and massages the knots there. "I don't want to act this way," he says. Spasmodic gasps punctuate his words. "I don't know why I do. I'm sorry. I'm so sorry."

His face contorts. Tears squeeze through his tightly shut eyes.

"It's okay, honey. It's over now."

"I'm so sorry, Mom," he sobs. "I ruined the picture. I ruin everything."

"We're gonna get help, Josh. We'll see a counselor who can sort this out. Help us treat each other better, improve our relationships—yours, your dad's and mine. Okay?"

"Okay." He releases a shuddering sigh. "I don't want to do this anymore."

"I know."

Kate sits in the living room with the lights off, her feet up, sipping wine. She's just put the girls down and Mitch is reading in the bedroom. She senses Josh before she sees him—a shadow unerringly making his way in the dark to the piano. He settles onto the bench and silently strokes the keys as if caressing the face of a lover. Then he plays, his hands light and tender.

The music brings images to mind. The rugged bloom and blight of Appalachia. The renting pain of a final goodbye. A deserted, windswept winter beach.

Josh calls it fooling around when he plays like this. She once told him he should write down the music he composes on the spot—as he is now—when notes flow from some mystical corner of his being. He just shook his head and kept playing. He was drawn to the piano as a toddler. Even then, his childish slaps and pecks on the keys had a lyrical timbre that made Kate stop in her chores—the half-peeled potato or partially rinsed dish in her hand forgotten as she listened. He began formal lessons in first grade. Soon after, she had to tell his teacher not to play pieces Josh was working on or he wouldn't learn to read music. Once he heard a piece, he could play it by ear. By the time he reached sixth grade, he had stopped practicing his assignments altogether. Changing teachers had no effect. But he didn't stop playing. Even now he spends hours on the piano, creating music levels above the songs his current teacher assigns him.

More than one piano instructor has told her he's a genius. One even offered to give him free lessons if only he promised to practice. She used to nag him about practicing but gave it up. Everything is a battle with Josh. She tries to choose carefully, to engage only in the essential ones, but often fails.

She sets down her glass, leans back her head and closes her eyes. Her son's music tells a story of sadness and longing, of a harrowed heart begging for healing. The melancholy sonata engulfs her, compelling her to live its story as if it were her own. She prays God hears it and answers its lament.

Chapter 12

Kate jumps at the ringing that sounds like a fire alarm in the quiet bedroom.

"Who's calling at this hour?" Mitch complains next to her in bed. Like Kate, he's propped against the headboard, reading. She lowers her book and looks at the clock on her bedside stand. Nine-thirty. She reaches for the phone beyond the clock.

"Hello?"

"Katherine Nardek?"

"I go by Kate."

"Kate. Dr. Galen here. Sorry to call so late, but I've been busy and am trying to get caught up. I understand you and your family want to see me."

"Just my husband and I."

"I have an opening at six o'clock on March third."

"That's nearly two months from now. Can't we come sooner?"

"Nope. That's my first opening."

"Can't you work us in? We're pretty desperate. Just today—"

"You and everyone else. Seems like everyone wants a piece of me. I only have so much to go around."

Kate recoils at his tone. "Well," she says after a pause, "six is pretty early."

"I'm talking evening."

"Oh, that's no good. My husband's office is in Jacksonville. He's usually not home before seven-thirty or eight. Could we meet early, say seven a.m., before he goes to work?"

"No. My first morning appointment is at nine."

"There's no way you could see us earlier, just—"

"No. I've got people waiting in line to see me and they'll come any time I offer. If you can't work with my schedule, then I can refer you to another counselor."

Kate's mouth tightens. She wants to tell him where he can stuff his schedule, but he's supposed to be good. One of the best.

"What's your pleasure? I don't have all night."

"When's your first nine o'clock opening?" The quiver in her voice disgusts her.

"March thirty-first."

"Good grief, that's practically another month."

"Do you want a referral?"

"I don't know … No. Okay, six o'clock March third. It will just be my husband and me. I don't want my son to meet with you."

"I'll meet with the two of you alone on the third. Then I'm going to need to meet with your son. No way around it."

"I don't want my son to have the stigma of going to a psychologist. He's so young."

"Maybe you should think this through and call me when you're sure you want my help. It makes no difference to me."

Kate is caught in an undertow. She wants to tell him to go to hell. But a clarion call from deep within stops her.

"You can try Dr. Leonard, he's—"

"No. No, we'll be there."

"Okay. If you're sure. In the meantime, I'm going to send

you some paperwork to fill out to get me up to speed on the situation. I'd like you to mail it back as soon as possible, so I can review it before our first meeting."

"All right."

"Goodnight."

The abrupt click is as cold as the voice it disconnects. Kate hangs up.

"That the psychologist?"

She bites her lip as tears begin to stream down her face.

"Kate, what is it?" She turns away when Mitch leans into her. "You're crying? What's wrong?" He puts his arm on her shoulders. "I hate it when you cry."

"That was Dr. Galen." She lets Mitch pull her into him, rests her head on his chest and shakes with sobs. "God, I hate myself," she groans. "I can't make a decision. And he was such a jerk. So arrogant. 'Everyone wants a piece of me.' That's what he said. Like he's God."

She grabs a tissue from the bedside stand, blows her nose then grabs another and wipes her eyes. She throws the wadded tissues on the floor.

"And he can't even see us until March. And you'll have to leave work early." Mitch pulls her back against him. She relaxes into the taut muscles of his chest and closes her eyes.

"Look, there're plenty of good psychologists out there. We don't have to go to this guy. Call him up tomorrow and say we've changed our minds."

"He was recommended," she says between sniffs. "I don't know how to find someone good. I feel like I can't cope. I hate that. God, I hate it."

"Kate, Kate," he whispers, stroking her hair. "You've been under a lot of stress. That makes everything harder. Maybe you should see Dr. Emmett again."

"I don't want to go back to him. Like a baby running to Daddy. I want to get a grip. I've made this appointment.

Let's go and see what happens. It's just, he was so rude. So full of himself. It makes me mad."

"Then forget this guy. Let's find someone else."

Kate deliberates then shakes her head. "As much as I hate it," she says, "the thought of blowing him off scares me. Like I'd be making a mistake. I don't know why or even where this feeling comes from, but it's strong. I'm afraid to ignore it."

"The old woman's intuition." Mitch kisses the top of her head. "Okay, then we'll go see this guy, even though we already think he's a jerk, and after a few visits, if it turns out we're right, we'll find someone else. Agreed?"

She shrugs.

"Agreed?" He slips his left hand under her arm and tickles her.

"Stop!" she shrieks, but he clamps his right arm around her, binding her to him as his fingers continue to skip across her ribs.

"Okay, okay," she chokes out through laughter. "Agreed."

"That's better," he says, smiling down at her. "Just so we know who's in charge." He leans down and brushes his lips across hers.

"Mmmm, that was nice," she murmurs.

"Want more?" He wipes away a straggling tear with his thumb.

"Yes. Lots more."

He slides down into the bed, pulling her with him.

Chapter 13

Kate looks out the broad window above the kitchen sink. Reyna and Mollie splash in the heated waters of the bird-caged pool, only partially shaded from the sun by the green canopy of a mammoth oak that grows in the side yard. Their laughter comes to her in muffled bursts through the closed window as she washes breakfast dishes. She arranged swimming lessons—or what Mitch calls "survival lessons"—for each child before age one. Living in northeast Florida, surrounded by pools, retention ponds, lakes, rivers, bays and coastal waters, she wanted to give her children a chance of survival should they find themselves in water.

She watches Mollie launch face down off the pool steps, kick about two yards, then turn onto her back to float. After a rest, she flips back onto her stomach and kicks to the swimout on the far side of the pool. She pulls herself up to standing, lets out a squeal of prideful joy and shoves off again, back toward the steps. The sight of her little-girl legs, still holding a hint of babyhood, motoring her across the pool usually brings a smile to Kate's lips. But not today. Ever since the suicide, Kate has felt her vision shrouded by a gray veil, as if her life has become a black-and-white movie.

I can tell you've got your panties in a wad over this suicide, her father grumbled yesterday on the phone.

Kate hadn't known how to respond. She didn't want to discuss Michael's suicide with her dad. She had tried weeks ago, admitting she was having a hard time.

What in hell's the problem, he had snapped. You didn't know him.

I'll get over it, Kate had said hastily, then moved onto safer ground.

Yesterday he had pushed her after she denied being depressed.

Why are you belaboring this? The guy was in league with the devil and he'll rot in Hell for it. For chrissake, Kate, you're such a weakling.

Thank God for Jean. Oh Kate, she said early on, this isn't just about death or a neighbor's suicide. There's more to it. Give it time. Talk to God. Answers will come.

Kate slides the last of the breakfast plates into the dishwasher, pours coffee from the carafe into her mug and heads for the dining room. She sits at the table, breathes in the mild scent of hazelnut from her steaming mug and watches the girls through the sliders. Their L-shaped house wraps around the pool so the major rooms look onto it through doors of glass, making it easy for her to keep watch. Mollie continues her excursions between the steps and the swimout, while Reyna, head thrown back, twirls through the water in a blue plastic ring.

Kate wishes she had Jean's calm assurance, her absolute faith in the goodness underscoring everything. She wants to talk to God, but He seems far away. She thought she was close to God, but since the suicide her prayers sound stilted and harbor an undercurrent of hopelessness.

She recalls astronomers she read about, searching for extraterrestrial intelligence, listening on their radio telescopes for messages from advanced civilizations in other parts of the universe. There's a precise area on the radio dial to which they tune their gigantic telescopes—the microwave frequency band—because of its inherent emission line produced by interstellar hydrogen. Exobiologists figure any civilization advanced enough to have radio astronomy would be aware of this band—what they call a universal hailing frequency— and be tuned to it. Kate marvels that the universe has a built-in broadcast band ready to provide communication between beings light-years apart.

She smiles at her own efforts to communicate to a being beyond her ken. Maybe she's not on God's hailing frequency, for like the scientists, she hears nothing. She imagines her prayers as radio waves broadcast into space, traveling forever toward the end of the universe, never finding their mark. Where is God? Beyond the universe? She remembers a scientist explaining why they don't broadcast messages, only listen. With today's technology, a reply from an advanced civilization one hundred light-years from Earth would take two hundred years. Two hundred years. By then the author of the message, as well as his child and his child's child would be dead. But what's two hundred years to God?

She shakes herself back to the present. The girls are winding down in the pool. She drinks the last of her coffee and flirts again with an idea that has been pestering her for more than two weeks: calling Nick.

Nick is the new priest at church. She has gotten to know him through her position on the finance committee. He is young and impish with a rich voice underscored by a hint of laughter. But there's nothing childish about his sermons. While his delivery is filled with humor, his messages are adamant: We too easily become complacent in spirituality; we worship rituals, forgetting they're merely man-made tools designed to help us worship God; our well-to-do congregation is too focused on serving itself instead of the needy.

Kate has watched more than one church elder squirm during Nick's brief, pointed remarks punctuated with smiles.

But there were other sermons that kept Kate's eyes riveted on Nick, as when he explained why Jesus likened himself to a shepherd. In those days, the shepherd walked ahead of his flock, so the sheep wouldn't come upon a situation he hadn't already experienced. The sheep never walked a path untrod by the shepherd.

One of Jesus' points, Nick said, is no matter what we experience, no matter how dark or painful or lonely, God understands and enfolds us with perfect compassion. There is nothing in human experience God isn't familiar with, nothing God hasn't experienced first-hand.

Imagining God feeling the same sadness, the same horror she experienced looking into Michael's still face suggests a solidarity she never attributed to her relationship with God. She wants to experience that kinship, not just theorize about it. But she doesn't know how.

"Mom, we're getting out." A dripping Reyna hops up and down in front of the wooden side door to the bathroom, rubbing her arms against the cold.

Kate opens the slider. "Okay. Wait for your sister, then take a bath together."

"Aw, I hate taking baths with her. She hogs the whole tub. Can't I go first?"

"No. Go together. And stop whining." She shuts the slider and watches as Mollie pulls herself out of the pool and trots into the bathroom after Reyna.

"Shut the door!" Kate yells. Reyna appears momentarily before yanking the door shut with a bang. Kate heads out to cover the pool with the solar blanket, then changes her mind. The pool can wait. She walks into the kitchen and reaches for the phone.

Chapter

The minute she enters the diner, she sees Nick sitting in a booth along the windows fronting Main Street. She waves as she approaches him.

"Good to see you, Kate." He rises and gives her hand a squeeze. A broad smile crinkles his face. "Please, sit."

She slides across from him. Resting his arms on the table, Nick leans forward and grins at her, his ocean blue eyes twinkling, his wavy black hair slightly unkempt, giving him a roguish air. "How are you?"

"I want to say everything's fine," she says, "but then, we wouldn't be having lunch."

"I figured as much, but I'm betting between the two of us and God, we can get you back on the road to fine."

She harrumphs.

"Hey, I heard that. And just who is it you don't have faith in? Me or God?"

His tone and grimace make her laugh. "Well, we know the answer isn't God," she shoots back.

"Good. Shall we order before we start with the serious stuff?"

She nods and they study their menus in silence. When the waitress comes, Kate orders an iced tea and BLT on wheat; Nick, a Gyro and a bottle of Guinness.

"Hey, it's Monday," he says in reply to her exaggerated look of surprise.

"Oh my God, I forgot this is your day off. I'm so sorry."

He screws his face into a portrait of consternation. "Were you really trying to speak to God there? Because, as far as I know, the top dog never takes a day off."

"Cut it out," she says blushing even as she chuckles.

"Okay. 'Oh my gosh.' There, satisfied?"

"Absolutely."

"You know it's hard to be serious with you. You're so damn happy."

"It's easy to be happy when all is going well. It's the rough spots where we forget to listen for God's laughter. But it's always there."

She looks down at the napkin across her lap. "Well, I sure don't hear it. I've never thought of God as laughing."

"Perhaps you need to broaden your vision of Him. I believe He has an incredibly good sense of humor and is a virtual fount of joy. When we laugh we're hugging God, and He us."

Kate studies her napkin, turning over in her mind the idea of hugging God in laughter. She can't quite reconcile it with her childhood image of the ancient man with the flowing white beard and hair, seated behind the judgment bench, gavel in one hand, a list of sins in the other.

"Kate," Nick whispers. "Tell me. What is it?"

She meets his eyes. "It's just ... well ... I feel weird. This is harder than I thought. I've never talked to a priest about, you know, spiritual stuff."

The volume of his laughter startles her, even as its warmth encircles her. Still convulsing, Nick dabs the corners of his eyes with his napkin.

"I have to say, that's not a very resounding endorsement of my profession."

She feels her face growing hot.

"I'm sorry, it's just—"

"Kate, it's me, Nick. Your friend, I hope. Forget the priest bit. Talk to me."

"Okay. I want to tell you something that happened a few weeks ago. It might take awhile."

"I have all the time in the world." He settles into his seat.

"What I want is … um … I want to tell you about my neighbor's suicide."

He reaches across the table and enfolds her hand in his. "I'm listening."

"I'm so sorry, Kate, so very, very sorry," he says when she finishes. "How sad for Michael. And for you."

"Do you want anything else?" the waitress interrupts, clearing the empty plates off the table.

"I'd like coffee with cream. How 'bout you, Kate?"

She nods.

"Two cups then."

"Only be a moment." The waitress scurries off.

"I am terribly sad for Michael," she resumes. "But I'm also having trouble with him."

"What do you mean?"

"When I looked into the garage and saw his face, I immediately turned away."

"Yes. Of course."

"But as fast as I turned away, the image of his face as he hung there … I can't get that image out of my mind. It's as if in—"

"Two coffees with cream on the side." The waitress plunks steaming mugs in front of them and slides a bowl of individual creamers onto the center of the table. "Should I leave the check?"

"That's mine," Nick says, snatching it.

"I'll take it up front for you when you're ready."

"Here." Nick pulls his wallet from his back pocket and hands the waitress a credit card.

"Thanks for lunch," Kate says as the waitress darts off. "I wasn't expecting you to pay."

"My pleasure."

The coffee smells acidic, probably from sitting on the burner too long. Kate pours a creamer into her cup and takes a sip. The bitter brew scalds her tongue. She pours in a second creamer.

"That bad?" Nick reaches for the creamers.

"A bit strong is all," she says, then shakes her head. "I've lost my train of thought."

"Here's your card and your receipt. Come again."

Nick signs the receipt and pushes it aside.

"You were saying you couldn't get the image of Michael out of your head."

"In the second or two before I turned away, that image imprinted itself on my brain, my eyes. Ever since, I've been looking through it—like a veil between me and the world."

"Yes, I can understand that."

"I see his face everywhere. And I don't understand the way I feel. I don't believe Michael was evil, yet the image scares me. It's as if I've taken all the unnamed fears and dreads residing in my subconscious and given them Michael's face. And by doing that, they've become real."

"Yes." Nick runs his hand through his hair. "Hmmm. Michael has become the personification of evil for you. Your own personal boogeyman."

"That's it! And I feel so stupid, like I'm a child again afraid of the dark."

"Kate," he leans forward, his eyes piercing, "all of us are afraid of the dark; it's just most of us don't admit it."

She reaches for the creamers, dumps another into her

coffee and stirs. "What I want," she says, "is for God to take this image away from me."

"I understand." She waits for him to continue. Silence stretches. "Kate," he says, almost as a sigh. "You're asking for the wrong thing." His eyes are uncharacteristically solemn. "This image is part of your life. It's part of you now. Forever. Instead of asking God to take it away, you need to ask Him to help you turn it into a source of good in your life."

"How can Michael's suicide be turned to good?"

"That I can't tell you. My imagination's too limited. But then, my imagination compared to God's is like a grain of sand to the universe. Pray, Kate. Talk to God."

"I'm no good at praying."

"None of us is."

"I don't know what to pray for."

"Well, start by praying for Michael, that God take Michael into His loving embrace and heal his wounded heart. That He lift Michael's torment from him."

"Yes, I've prayed for that."

"Good."

"I mean, I believe Michael is with God. That God was right there with love and healing as he stepped from this life to the next."

"I do too."

"I thought the Christian line was suicide is a sin and leads to Hell." Kate frowns at the small bitterness in her voice.

Nick's rich laughter chases away her frown. "I guess it depends on how you define Christian and how you define Hell."

"Well," she says sheepishly, "if you believe as I do, then Michael doesn't need our prayers. He's already with God."

"Your prayers for Michael are part of God's love, Kate. They'll help in his healing and in yours."

She stirs her coffee, making a small vortex in the light brown fluid. "I would like to be a part of Michael's healing."

"So would I. Let's both pray for him."

"The problem is, I don't feel close to God. Since the suicide, I've felt separated from Him. As if He were far away, on the dark side of the moon. I don't feel His presence in my life. I don't know, maybe I never did."

When Nick doesn't answer, she looks up from her coffee. He is staring at her, his elbow propped on the table, his chin resting in his hand. She waits but he just stares.

"What?"

"So you feel separated from God."

"Yes."

"And that feeling is real. I mean it's true you feel this separation."

"Y-e-s ..." she says as if talking to a child.

He smiles. "What I'm saying, Kate, is while it's true you feel this way, your feeling doesn't represent the truth."

In her mind she sees God fly at light speed from the edge of the universe to the seat beside her. But it's not the God of her youth; it's a young sprite exuding light, bubbling with laughter, outstretched arms inviting an embrace. She feels the goddess within leap into the arms of this exquisite vision. Warmth emanates from Kate's chest. Her heart afire, the warmth spreads down her arms and legs to the tips of her toes and fingers. A flush melts the tension from her face. Her insides are liquid from the heat, as if a spring thaw is taking place.

"Kate?"

"God is right here, right now, isn't She?"

"She?"

"It feels like She."

Nick chuckles. "Yes. *She* is right here, all around us, within us. She's always here, Kate. Always."

"Something's happened."

"What?"

"I don't know. I have to mull it over. I feel full when

only a few minutes ago I was telling you I felt empty. It's a strange feeling, but good. Yet I feel like crying. Oh God, I'm not making any sense."

"Depends on what kind of sense you mean. I often think our minds grasp at truths the soul is born knowing."

"Thanks for meeting with me."

"It was a pleasure."

She grabs her purse and shifts in her seat. "Shall we pray before you take off?" he interrupts.

"Sure." She's never prayed one-on-one with anyone, much less a priest. She fidgets with her purse.

"Let me guess, you're nervous about praying in public." She shrugs a response. "It won't hurt, I promise."

He collects her hands across the table, closes his eyes, and sits in silence. She waits. When he doesn't speak, she sneaks a peek. His head is tilted back, but his eyes are closed. His muscles are relaxed, peaceful. She's relieved he's praying to himself.

"Beloved," Nick says in a husky voice, startling her. "Thanks for bringing Kate and me together, for allowing us to share and, by sharing, come to know you better." Kate exhales softly. When Nick said 'Beloved' she thought he was speaking to her. But before she can laugh at herself, she savors the intimacy of the word, turning it over in her mind as one rolls fine wine across the tongue to appreciate its flavor. She has never thought to address God in such a way. She closes her eyes, drinking in the rich texture of Nick's words.

"Thank you," he continues gently, "for walking with us, for surrounding us with your steadfast love, even when fears and doubts prevent us from feeling your presence. Touch our souls with your healing love. We especially ask this for Michael, who comes to you in great despair, and for Kate, whose heart is pierced by his pain and whose soul weeps at his violent death. We know you can light the darkest hell. We know you are a master artisan who can mend that which, to our limited vision, seems fractured beyond repair.

"Heal us, Beloved, and in healing bring us the confidence and peace that come from faith in your active presence in our lives. You do not comprehend 'impossible'; with you, possibilities abound. You are a God of bounty, of comets and rainbows, a God of joy, of hallelujahs and handsprings. Help us to see the world through your playful eyes and to tune our souls to the song of your laughter."

Nick falls silent. Kate hears his steady breathing, like that of a napping child. His eyes are still closed, but his head is now tilted forward. She watches the gentle rise and fall of his chest and wonders if she should move or cough—break into his reverie. She rejects the idea and waits. After what seems an eternity, he inhales deeply. "Amen," he says, then opens his eyes and smiles. He squeezes her hands then slides out of the booth, pulling her with him.

When they stand his arms encircle her. Kate returns the hug and starts to withdraw but his arms remain tight around her. The embrace feels good, as if she is enveloped in a field of positive energy. Finally, he releases her and tousles her hair.

"God bless you, Katherine Anne Nardek. May Her angels walk with you."

"Thank you, Nick. And thanks for lunch and the talk. You've given me lots to contemplate."

"And you me, which is why I'm heading to the pier with my fishing rod." He escorts her to the parking lot. "Carol will be thrilled if I bring a fresh catch for dinner for her and young Nicholas. You're welcome to join me. Fishing is a wonderfully contemplative exercise."

"No. I better be off. Got to pick up Mollie and get home to meet Reyna's bus. Maybe another time."

"I'll hold you to that." He heads toward his pickup then swings around to face her, walking backward. "Hey, try

reading the first few lines of Isaiah, chapter forty-three."
He gives a quick wave and turns again to his truck.

She watches him drive off, still electrified by his hug.
Some people have good energy, Jean said to her once. You
can feel it when they touch you.

Kate had laughingly replied, I know, I feel it every time
I hug you.

When you find a person with good energy, Jean said, you
should hug him often.

Maybe that's why all those people stand in line each
Sunday after service, for a moment in Nick's arms, to feel the
uplift of his energy. As Kate slides into the van, she decides
rather than darting out the church's side door next Sunday, as
is her habit, she'll join the line.

Chapter 15

ate flops on her back and kicks across the pool.
It's been five days since her talk with Nick. She looked up
the Isaiah verse when she got home and decided to memorize it, even though the idea grated her with images of Bible
thumping. She recites it in her mind as she kicks: *Fear not,*
for I have redeemed you; I have called you by name, you
are mine. When you pass through the waters I will be with
you; and through the rivers, they shall not overwhelm you;
when you walk through fire you shall not be burned, and the
flame shall not consume you. She especially likes the image
of waters failing to overwhelm.

As she kicks she gazes through the pool-cage screen. The
sky is clear and a touch of chill deepens its color. The spring
leaves of the oak whisper in the breeze as if sharing a secret.
She can see each leaf, crisp and new-green against azure.
Abruptly she stops kicking and stands. Her chest aches, as if
from running too hard too long. She can't catch her breath.
She looks at Reyna and Mollie playing in the shallow end of
the pool. Their skin glistens like wet sand at sunset, fine hair
fans down their backs. They are mermaids, their laughter as
inviting as any siren's song. Kate lifts her chin, letting the
wind lick her face.

It's true. She sees beauty again. The gray veil she told Nick about is gone. When did it lift? She doesn't know. She only knows it's gone. She scans the backyard. It's the same as yesterday, as five minutes ago, yet different. There's a brilliance, a newness, to everything. She sees each individual blade of grass and feels its joyful reaching toward the sun. She sees "Mr. Cardinal," as her girls call him, swoop to his nest in the viburnum hedge, a flash of scarlet against emerald. She hears their resident mockingbird trill through his repertoire with a resonance no flute can match.

"Mom, can we go in now? We're freezing. MA-UM!"

The girls have moved to the steps, where they sit shivering.

"Yes, okay," she says. "Fine."

With arms wrapped tightly across their chests, the girls scamper into the house. Kate is dazzled by their purity, by the splendor of the sky, the oak, the grass, even the shimmering pool water. Everything radiates. She measures the sun. It's not directly overhead and yet she sees no shadows. How can that be? She's afraid to move, afraid whatever spell she's caught in will break. A chill runs through her, leaving goose bumps. Or were the goose bumps already there? She pulls herself out of the heated water and dries off, shivering in the cool air, smiling at the thought of a warm shower. She scans the yard a last time and feels she is looking at an impressionist painting. She is aware of each dot of color that up close is distinct but from a distance unifies with the others to create a masterpiece.

"Thank you," she whispers. "Thank you."

Chapter 16

"Jean, it was so amazing. I felt touched by a miracle."

"Oh Kate, you were!" Jean's voice is filled with a child's awe. She settles back on the couch, folds a leg under her and sips coffee. She has the body of a fertility goddess, full and fleshy with broad round curves. The short, black curls framing her face combine with her large mocha eyes to give her youth that belies her sixty-three years. "It's as if ..." She pauses, cocks her head and gazes out the window onto her garden. "No, it was. You were seeing the world through God's eyes."

Kate freezes, her mug halfway to her lips.

"Remember ..." Jean turns back to her goddaughter, her luminous eyes and half-smile conveying a mixture of puzzlement and amazement. "Remember the creation story in Genesis? Every time God created something, He said, 'And it was good.' It's all good, Kate. You, me, meditative Reyna, your little Joybug Mollie, Josh with all his anger and challenging."

"How can Josh's anger be good? He knocked Reyna down yesterday. She hit her head on the table. Gave her a goose egg."

"Well that's not good," Jean grumps, her brow furrowing

momentarily. "Of course you can't tolerate such behavior. But …" her face relaxes, melting away the lines, "what's wrong there is not his anger, it's the expression of his anger. Josh was born angry and there must be a reason. His poor little soul has to learn something, and this anger is part of the path he must walk to learn it."

"Learn what?"

"That's for Josh to discover. You can't walk his path for him. But he's with you for a reason. He chose you. I'm sure of it. His soul looked down when it was his turn, and he chose you and Mitch."

"I can't imagine why," Kate says. "I don't know what I'm supposed to give him or teach him. Oh God, Jean, we're making a mess of it."

"No, you're not."

"We've decided to see a psychologist."

"That's a grand idea." She leans forward, cradling her mug in her hands. "Do you have a counselor picked out?"

"Yeah. It's odd." Kate swirls the remaining coffee in her own mug then takes a sip. It's lukewarm. "I fear I won't like him—yet something inside me rebelled at the idea of hanging up on him and finding someone else."

"You don't have to like him. You just need to accept whatever wisdom or insight he's meant to impart. I'm betting he's the right person, based on your intuition, which I trust implicitly even if you don't."

"We're seeing him next week for the first time. Just Mitch and me." She places her mug on the coffee table and looks up. "He wants Josh to come to the second visit. Said he won't counsel us if he can't see Josh in person. He's so damn cocky and insists everything be done his way. It makes me want to do the opposite—just to put him in his place."

Jean throws back her head and lets out a throaty, bois-terous laugh, infecting Kate, who laughs in spite of herself. "Oh Darlin'," Jean says breathlessly, laughter still ringing in her voice. "You are such a Leo. Leos love to be in charge. You know, king of the jungle." She shakes her head, chuckling. "This is going to be hard for you. Leos aren't good at being submissive. You're going to have to let go, lovely lion. Go with life's flow; trust in it. You've taken a step toward healing. Now trust in the steps the universe takes in response."

"The universe gave me Dr. Galen?"

"Perhaps. You'll have to see where this path leads. You'll know very quickly if he's a false turn." She rises from the couch and heads for the kitchen. "Ready for lunch?"

"Yep." Carrying her mug, Kate follows her godmother. She sits on the stool by the counter and watches Jean rinse the dishes, knowing she'll be shooed away if she tries to help. She looks around the L-shaped living room. She knows every piece of furniture, picture and knickknack by heart. The African painting of dark, featureless children holding hands to form a circle. The Chinese portrait of a hummingbird in stationary flight, sipping cherry blossoms. The terra cotta statue of a baby caught trying to pull himself into a cross-legged, meditative pose, his legs too short and thick with fat to make the bend. Jean bought her baby Buddha, as Kate calls it, when she divorced Kurt, the father of her children, after she caught him in his third affair. Baby Buddha was the first purchase she made as an adult solely for herself.

Jean's shelves are filled with a variety of books—astrology, numerology, Christianity, Buddhism, Taoism, Sartre, Jung, Freud, Gibran. On one side of the *Bhagavad Gita* are tarot cards, on the other, Native American sacred path cards. They all hold fragments of truth she extracts to form her own vision of God and Truth. Life fascinates and delights her. She sees each development as a new thread in the divine loom on which God weaves Life's tapestry. The unfolding picture is yet unclear and unordained even as the threads hint at an awesome interlacing of grace and purpose.

This is home to Kate, where she shrugs off worries and burdens. She feels it the minute she walks in—a sense of safety and refreshment, an acceptance that makes her completely comfortable being herself. There are no pretenses here, no struggles to find the right word, no concerns about being misunderstood. Kate cherishes her "Jean days," though often the two do little else than lounge and gab, taking breaks to eat. They talk of everything, from the mundane to the mystical, from current events to the exploits of epic heroes. But always at the center are God and life, wonder and mystery.

"Let's eat in the garden, shall we?" Jean asks. "I can lend you a sweater. But really the weather is fine despite the cold. Makes me want to sing, 'It's May, it's May, the lovely month of May,' even though it's only February. Tra la la."

Kate grins at her chirping. "It's 'the lusty month of May.' I'm sure you're partial to that song because everyone goes 'blissfully astray.'"

"It's good to break a rule now and then." Jean's brown eyes glint mischievously. "What's it called, to push the edge of the envelope? Josh is pushing your envelope." She pauses in the middle of washing a muffin tin, ignoring the running water wasting down the drain. "I just had a thought." She turns to Kate. "Maybe you're asking the wrong question. You said, 'I don't know what I'm supposed to teach Josh.' Maybe the question is, what is Josh supposed to teach you?"

An inner shift rocks Kate. She visualizes herself standing in an art museum examining a painting, trying with all her intellect to understand it, to no avail, when suddenly the proprietor appears and with a disgusted grunt lifts the painting from the wall, flips it and re-hangs it.

"I've made my special artichoke salad," Jean says, turning from the empty sink, "or would you rather have ham and cheese?"

"Salad's good."

Jean arranges dishes and the salad bowl on a glass tray and heads to the sliders leading to the garden. "Bring some napkins and water," she calls over her shoulder, "and two sweaters from my closet."

They sit at a black wrought-iron table situated on a small brick terrace under the shade of a towering maple. The soft yellows and oranges of early daffodils surround them. Each fall Jean digs up the bulbs and stores them in her freezer then replants them New Year's day—a system she worked out when the guy at the nursery told her flowers from bulbs can't grow in Florida because winters don't get cold enough. Kate was visiting her at the time and couldn't help smiling as they drove away, Jean in a rare temper, muttering, Ridiculous. Who ever heard of spring without daffodils?

The clean smell of newly laid mulch floats on the air. The garden takes up most of the small yard. Jean doesn't fancy linear, organized planting. No neat rows of petunias backed by calla lilies, no uniform squares of phlox or impatiens. Each year she plants daffodil and tulip bulbs haphazardly throughout the newly tilled garden then randomly scatters seeds of various annuals—marigolds, zinnias, cosmos—among well-established patches of blue plumbago and beach sunflowers. The result is a spring riot of color without pattern, an untamed paradise disciplined only by constant weeding and renewed each year with fresh plantings and seed scatterings. Above them, hanging from one of the high branches of the maple, chimes softly harmonize in wind.

"I love this spot," Kate mummers. "Beauty born of chaos."

"I think of it as yours," Jean says as she serves the salad. "I remember when I planted this tree. Close to twenty years ago now. Can you believe it? You had called from New York to say you'd gotten a job in Jacksonville and were moving back. Remember?"

Kate nods. She's heard this story before but warms to its retelling.

"I was so overjoyed, I went straight to the nursery. I wanted to plant something. And there was this tree—poor little thing, shunted off to the side, scrawny, neglected, close to death. Just how I had been feeling since Nathan's death. I knew right then I wanted that tree, that we could rejuvenate together, remember again that life is good. I talked the man into taking half off the price. We haggled quite a bit, but he knew all along I would have paid full price, even double, if he'd been adamant.

"The hours I spent tending this poor thing. I figured it wouldn't survive a year. Now look at it." She pats the rough bark. "My old friend." She glances at Kate and chortles. "I've become a tree hugger, is that what you're thinking?"

Kate can only smile.

"I do love this tree. It whispers to me the wind's gossip. It's home to the mockingbird whose song wakes me each morning. Its new-green buds herald spring. Its verdant leaves cool me in the heat of summer and then delight me with their autumn blaze."

"You're a poet."

"Hardly. But enough of the tree. Are we going to talk about your depression?"

Kate glances to the far corner of the yard, where azaleas ring the base of a young oak. Their purple blooms are so vibrant she can almost feel their heat. "I'm having trouble sorting out the suicide," she says, knowing there's no use equivocating. "Truth is, I felt I saw evil when I looked into the garage. I don't mean devils dancing on the windowsill. I'm not even talking about something I actually saw—" She looks down at her half-eaten salad. "I don't know what I'm talking about."

Jean lays down her fork and leans forward on her elbows,

resting her chin on her folded hands. "Your soul saw something," she says in a half-statement, half-question.

"I guess ..."

"Something that scared you?"

"Yes. When I looked into the garage, I felt overwhelming horror shake me to the core. I'm still trembling inside—at my center. Is my soul afraid?"

Jean lays her hand on her goddaughter's forearm. "Kate, I don't think souls know fear. Perhaps your soul glimpsed something, recognized something fearful to you, the ego."

"I've seen death before."

"Not death."

"Evil?" Kate asks.

"I don't believe in evil."

"It felt like evil. That's how it translated to me."

"Excuse me a minute." Jean heads into the house and returns a moment later with a pack of cigarettes and a lighter. "Do you mind?"

"Only that you're killing yourself."

"Oh Kate." Jean's laughter slips through the stretched lines of her lips clamping the cigarette she lights between cupped hands. "It helps me think."

Together they sit in silence, their salads forgotten. Kate closes her eyes and listens to the chimes above, to the woodpecker drilling a neighbor's tree. She hears Jean take long pulls on her cigarette and then slowly exhale. She knows her godmother is gazing out in the garden with unfocused eyes as she looks inward. Kate sits comfortably in the silence that with anyone else would make her squirm. She waits, relieved someone who knows her thoroughly is sitting with her now exploring why she thought she saw evil.

Jean stubs out her cigarette and pulls another from the pack.

"I thought one a day was your limit."

"I thouh of som-ing," Jean mumbles as she lights the cigarette. She pulls deeply then turns away from Kate to exhale a smoke cloud. She holds the cigarette elegantly between her first two fingers. "Maybe you didn't see evil," she says slowly, as if still testing the idea in her mind. "Maybe what you saw was the triumph of evil."

"Oh Jean! That sounds right to me, but I don't know what you mean."

"I don't mean evil as in Satan—some force that stalks you. But if God is life-creating then evil is another word for life-destroying. And what makes us vulnerable to life-destroying impulses? Despair. Despair makes us vulnerable. Bitterness. Self-doubt. Worse, self-hate. And Fear. Fear is the worst."

"I told you, didn't I, about the man who wanted me to climb through the window, go into the garage?"

"He was wrong."

"I couldn't go in."

"Because you knew there was nothing left to do."

"Yeah, I knew there was nothing left to do for Michael. But that's not why I refused to go in. I was afraid." Jean leans her head back and surveys the budding arms of the maple as she takes another pull on her cigarette. "I feel guilty about that," Kate adds.

"Why?" Jean's eyes linger in the middle-distance.

"I don't know. It sounds so naïve when I put it into words. I tell myself if it had been Jesus, he would have climbed through the window, taken Michael down and held him. He wouldn't have been afraid, no matter what he saw or thought he saw."

"If Jesus had been there, he would have gone to Cara, who was out of her mind with grief, taken her into his arms and comforted her."

The image causes Kate a pang of guilt. "We're both right. What upsets me is I didn't do either. Michael horrified me. But in a way Cara's screaming horrified me just as much."

"Kate," Jean looks at her with mock distain. "You're not Jesus. Surely you can live with that. You answered that woman's cry. You brought help even as you shook with fear. That's love. Jesus asks us to love as best we can and not get all muddled with the unachievable."

"The unachievable?"

"Perfection. We are all imperfect. But in all your flawed humanity, you reached out to help Cara and you did help her."

"They had to take her to the hospital."

"Oh God, that poor woman," Jean groans. "She'll be haunted forever. What was he thinking?"

Kate shakes her head. "There's something else."

"What, babe?"

"I've been seeing shadows."

"Shadows?" Jean mashes the end of her cigarette in the ashtray. "What do you mean?"

"I'm not sure when I started seeing them, but it was after that day in the pool, after the gray veil lifted. When I glance at something, when my eyes are moving fast, I see them. The other day I took a sweeping glance across the backyard and I saw one behind the kids' hobby horse under the oak—a dark presence behind the horse. I can't really describe it. It was like a hovering charcoal cloud, hiding, spying. It scared me to death, but I forced my eyes back over the horse, forced myself to look hard and slow, and it was gone. That's always the way. When my eyes move quickly, I see them behind things—the family-room rocker, the small magnolia in the front yard, the bed—peeking out as if in hide-and-seek. Seems everything has a shadow—everything at home, that is. I only see them at home, which scares me. I feel like I'm haunted."

"Hmm." Jean cocks her head as if to say, "How interesting," then sits in silence, her eyes studying a patch of garden. Kate can almost hear the questions Jean is throwing out to herself—What could it mean? How does it fit into this unfolding picture, this odd puzzle still missing so many pieces?

"Do they run across the floor like rats?" she asks, scampering her fingers across the glass tabletop.

"No."

"That's how I saw them," Jean says.

"You've seen them? What are they?"

Jean shakes her head and shrugs. "We all have a shadow self. Everyone and everything."

"But why am I seeing them now?"

"I don't know." Jean studies her fingers lightly tapping the table, then reaches for another cigarette. "My last one," she says before Kate can object. She inhales as if pulling on a joint. "Maybe you're seeing them now because Michael's death has given you an increased awareness, a fuller view of life, the light and splendor as well as the dark."

"They scare me."

"No need to be scared, Kate. The dark can't touch you if you're full of the light. And you are, my Darlin'. Light shines from you."

"You mean God?"

"If you want to call it that." Jean takes another leisurely pull on her cigarette. "I had a dream once, a long time ago, when I was seeing shadow rats. I dreamed I was standing by a large body of water, so big I couldn't see the far shore, like Lake Michigan or the Gulf of Mexico. A bottle had washed onto the beach—a large, old-fashioned soda bottle made of heavy glass. It held a paper inside. I pulled out the cork and shook loose the paper. It had one word written on it: LOVE. Oh, I thought in the dream, this is the wrong bottle for this message. I walked along the beach searching for the right bottle. Finally I found an old, plastic milk jug. I put the paper in it, capped it and threw it into the water where it twirled in the waves. Then I walked in up to my chest, spread my arms and floated on my back. The water buoyed me as if I, too, were a plastic jug filled with love.

"As I bobbed on the water, it came to me. It's meant to be light, Kate. Not only light as in sunlight, but light as in weightless. It's light.

"After that dream, I didn't see the shadows again."

"What happened to them?"

"They're still there, I'm sure. I just don't see them anymore. Some part of me has chosen to see only light. It wasn't a conscious decision, so I can't tell you how. It's like the day you saw the world in all its crisp glory, newly made. We're not seeing through the intellect at those times, but from some deeper place of seeing and knowing. Some truer place." She chuckles. "Makes you wonder about the intellect. Maybe it's best to be a bit crazy." She laughs harder. "Oh Kate," she says, short-winded, "you look so worried. Dear one, we're all crazy one way or another. It's just some of us are a bit more than others, or perhaps we don't hide it as well."

Kate can't help but join Jean's laughter, even though she isn't sure she agrees. She only knows if Jean is crazy, she wishes more people were.

Chapter

Kate turns the radio on low as she begins the ninety-minute drive home. She winds through city streets to the interstate. Traffic is heavy downtown, roads crowded with snowbirds. When she reaches I-95, she switches on the cruise control and lets her mind wander. "At Seventeen" plays on the oldies station, unfolding the mournful tale of high school love reserved only for the physically beautiful "in" crowd. Janis Ian could have written this song about Kate's own high school years, when "if only" was her mantra. If only she was prettier, sexier, smarter, wittier, more serious, less serious, more athletic, more academic … If only she was something, something different, then she would be popular, have friends, fall in love, be loved, know bliss, sleep at night with a dry pillow.

But she wasn't and she didn't.

Ironically, the very qualities that made Kate an outcast in high school, her independence and non-conformity, drew respect and friends in college and, finally, even dates. Boys actually claimed she was beautiful, statements she chalked up to robust sex drives. She's not beautiful. Not that she's ugly. But beautiful? Her father made it clear to her more than once that beautiful would be an exaggeration. Jean disagrees, but then Jean loves her and love blinds. Or maybe it enriches sight. Today no one would guess Jean, now seventy pounds overweight, was a beauty queen in her youth. Yet she is beautiful to Kate—every inch of her, every full, round curve. Much more beautiful than the sterile perfection of skinny cover girls on women's magazines.

Jean was Kate's antithesis in high school—an insider loved by all the cliques, asked to every prom, crowned home-coming queen, voted most popular. Was she a good actress back then, or was she always able to discern good in every-thing? Even Linda, Jean's friend since elementary school, doesn't know of the dark moments that plagued Jean's child-hood. The time when she was five and her older sister thrust Jean's hand through a window, the jagged glass shredding the tender white skin of her wrist, ripping open veins. She'd done it right in front of their mother, who dutifully cleaned up the blood and bandaged Jean, while never saying a word of comfort to her or reproof to her sister.

The story had shocked Kate. She'd never suspected her godmother had known an ugly moment before Kurt. Jean admitted she hadn't told anyone about that incident. She told it to Kate when they were talking about dark spots on the heart. Jean said her relationship with her mother is one of her few dark spots. There were other incidents, both before and after, but this is the one where Jean remembered feeling a door within her slam shut. She didn't reject her mother outright, but she never again let her see into her heart, not even when her mother was old and wheelchair-bound. Jean invited her down from Virginia several times a year, until her death, would push her along the boardwalk so she could see the ocean, hear the seagulls and feel the salt breeze. She would chat with her mother about the weather, local and national politics, the newest TV drama, but that's as deep as it got.

Must childhood have such dark moments? And why do some people, like Jean, come through them seemingly unscathed, while others carry them always, like storm clouds hanging over the soul? Kate scans the barren sand hills lining 95, as if the answer lies hidden there. Her college psychology professor once said even the worst childhood has enough good in it for a kid to get a toehold on love, should he or she be open to it. And even the best childhood can produce a child of despair if the heart is closed. Why are some hearts open from the beginning while others aren't? Josh—born crying—claims he's an abused child, yet no one has ever sawed his wrists against serrated glass. Jean, on the other hand, would snort in derision should someone be so silly as to suggest she was abused.

Kate hopes the psychologist will help Josh find a toehold. One of Jean's was her father. He must have been a lot like Jean, based on her stories about him. Sometimes he'd sneak in her room in the early-morning hours, long before the horizon glowed with sun. He'd shake her awake, order her to get dressed in her grubbiest clothes and bundle her in the car with a bag of donuts, two thermoses and a cooler of fish bait. They'd drive to a secluded spot on the James River, where they'd sit in companionable silence on the bank, their poles hanging over the water, sipping hot chocolate and coffee while waiting for a pull on one of their lines.

Once, he insisted on driving her to school, ignoring his wife's assertion the two-mile walk was therapeutic. When they got to the main road, her father headed south to the interstate. An hour later they arrived at Williamsburg. They spent the day strolling mile-long Duke of Gloucester Street, browsing the shops, eating peanut soup at King's Arm Tavern. Late in the day they stepped into the smithy, where a blacksmith dressed in colonial garb was bent before a forge heating a stick of silver and fashioning it into a delicate crescent bracelet. Jean still has the bracelet, bought hot from the fire. Later her father had it engraved, "To my life's joy." Jean wore it for years, until her wrists outgrew it. Now it sits on her dresser next to a photo of her father carrying her on his shoulders.

Jean's father flew to Florida the day she called about Kurt. Stood by her as Kurt packed his things. Her mother refused to come. If you'd kept yourself attractive, maybe Kurt wouldn't have gone looking at other women, she said. As for Nathan, the man who filled Jean's life with love, Jean's mother refused to speak to him. The adulterer. That's what she called him, though he met Jean in the divorce support group she joined after kicking Kurt out.

Nathan married Jean within months of their first meeting. He put all her children through college and treated Kate as if she were Jean's fourth daughter. He'd get on the phone every time Jean called her or she called Jean, asking about her latest boyfriend, insisting she tell him her true weight, fussing she was too darn skinny, asking if she needed cash. She lied and said no. He sent it anyway. Kate shakes her head. Seems like a hundred years ago. Yet the phone call from Jean about Nathan's death is as fresh in her memory as yesterday.

He was rarely sick, ran three miles five days a week, didn't smoke, so the heart attack was a shock. He died before he reached the hospital. Kate was living in New York then, a year out of college. Senator Mimms, who wasn't a senator at the time but a visiting professor at NYU, had just telephoned to ask her—his favorite government student—if he might talk her into coming back to Florida the following year, when his stint at NYU ended, to try her hand at speech writing. She'd said no. Then Jean called. After Kate hung up with Jean, she called Mimms back, told him she'd reconsidered. When could they meet? When she moved back to Florida to write for Mimms, she met Mitch, an investigative reporter with an attitude. He was interviewing Jean about the grass roots organization she and Nathan started to protect mangroves when Kate walked in unannounced, as was her custom. She gave Jean the maple; Jean gave her Mitch. She got the better deal.

Chapter 18

Kate walks into the kitchen, having just returned from dropping Mollie at preschool. She doesn't have class today or any errands. She used to enjoy these mornings of quiet, the house empty except for sunshine. Time to browse the newspaper or sit with the latest novel. But since the suicide, she tries to avoid being here, makes up all sorts of errands to keep her out of the house. She remembers how Jean said fear opens people to life-destroying forces. Today she refuses to give into her fears. She can't go on like this, afraid to be alone in her own home.

She pours herself a glass of fresh-squeezed grapefruit juice and carries it and the newspaper to the family room. The floor glimmers with sunlight pouring through the sliders. She curls up on the recliner, pulling her legs under her, ready for a good read. Then she hears it, sending pinpricks down her spine, making her neck tingle at the hairline. It's coming from the study, the muted click, click, click of computer keys. Someone is typing. She holds her breath, leans forward, all her concentration in her ears. There's no mistaking that familiar sound. Her heart sputters. Her hands shake, slopping juice on the newspaper. She puts down her glass, considers running from the room, out of the house. Instead, she rises, stands on the brink of action, what action she isn't sure.

The sound continues industriously. Someone is in the study typing on her computer. She can see him in her mind. Skin the color of dried blood. Long fingers with even longer, jagged nails. Eyes red as fire and more intense than those of a mad dog. Horned temple, cleft hooves, a spear-tipped tail touching the ground, his body giving off the smell of death. She imagines entering the study, seeing him busily typing. He senses her presence, stops, turns, gives her a leering smile. She takes one halting step then another toward the study door, her mind screaming, Run! Her soul wanting proof. She reaches the edge of the threshold, pauses, and with a growl of determination—or is it fear?—swings through the doorway and faces the computer.

The desk chair is empty, the room quiet. She looks under the desk. Nothing. She walks to the closet door, puts her hand on the knob, pauses, then yanks it open. Nothing but rarely worn winter clothes: plaid wool skirts, thick knit sweaters and down jackets. No one is in the closet. No thing.

The computer is on, the stars of the screen saver zip across its face. She touches a key; the screen jumps to her desktop. Odd, she hasn't been in the study today. Who turned on the computer? Not Mitch. He doesn't enter her work area unless asked. None of the kids came in before school. But one of them must have. She turns off the computer, watches it power down, then takes another look around the room. It's still empty. Leaving the study, she explores the entire house, opening closet doors, looking under beds. No one is here. By the time she returns to the recliner, her juice is warm and her brow damp with sweat.

She carries her glass to the kitchen and plunks ice in it, then splashes her face with cold water and pats it dry with a clean dishtowel. Juice in hand, she heads back to the easy chair and sits with her legs folded beneath her, the stained newspaper across her lap. All is as it should be, yet her hands shake as she lifts her glass to her lips, making the ice cubes clink. She begins to read. Halfway through a story on the growing number of virulent, antibiotic-resistant strands of bacteria, she hears it again. The soft click of computer keys.

Her chest is hollow. Her mind numb. She puts her juice down and tiptoes to the study doorway. Click, click, click comes rapid fire. He's a good typist. She charges into the room. It's empty. The keyboard is silent. She walks to the computer. It's on, stars flying across the screen. Her hand trembles as she reaches out a finger to touch a key. The screen jumps to her desktop.

She surveys the room, a new fear rises, more chilling than the other. Dear God, is she going crazy? She turns off the computer then reaches behind and unplugs it. She walks to the family room and sinks into the recliner, but before she picks up the newspaper she hears it again. Click, click, click. She knows he—it—is in there. Knows she'll never see it. She jumps up, grabs her purse and charges for the garage.

When she climbs in the van, she glances in the rearview mirror, catches a glimpse of Michael. At least that hasn't changed. She'll go to the grocery store. Buy something for dinner. Buy lots of things, until it's time to pick up Mollie. Then she'll go home. It never comes when someone else is in the house.

At the grocery store, she strolls the aisles aimlessly. Mitch usually does the shopping, but he always forgets to buy sponges for the kitchen. She throws a pack into her cart. And he refuses to buy her "feminine products," as he calls them. She throws in some tampons and pads. As she rounds the front of the cereal aisle, her eyes fall on the floral section at the far end of the store. She pushes her cart there. Perhaps she'll buy herself some roses. Mitch rarely gives her flowers, though he knows she loves them. Years ago she gave up hinting and began to buy them for herself. It's easier. In the floral section, a potted cactus catches her eye. It's not like any cactus she's ever seen. It has dozens of thin arms branching off its main trunk, each one tipped with a rose-colored bloom.

"It's called a Christmas cactus, though I don't know why." Kate looks up to see a clerk standing next to her. "Pretty, isn't it? We get a lot of them in May, around Mother's Day. This one came early.

"Do you have any others?"

"Nope. This is the only one. Just came in this morning with a load of rhododendron. Thought it was kind of weird. Probably a mistake. Too much hassle sending it back. Decided to just put it out, treat it as a gift from God."

Kate casts a sharp glance at the clerk, but she is smiling placidly at the plant.

"How much?" She picks up the cactus and examines it for broken arms. It's intact.

The clerk takes the pot from her, turns it sideways to look at the bottom. "No price. Typical. Tell you what, they usually go for fifteen dollars, but since there's no price I'll sell it to you for the same price as the rhododendrons. They're on sale today for seven-fifty."

"I'll take it."

Kate barely feels the ground beneath her feet as she walks—almost skips—through the parking lot. When she reaches her van, she carefully places the cactus on the floor, surrounding it with her groceries so it won't tip over on the drive home. What is the worst evil can do? She examines this thought as she drives. If God is with her, then the worst evil can do is kill her, kill her body. She exhales. She can live with that. There are things worse than death. She's not sure how she knows this, but she knows it with absolute certainty.

She slams the door open, calling out as she enters the house, "I'm back. And I'm bringing with me a gift from God. Do you hear me? I have a gift from God here. You don't scare me. God's here, so bug off." She walks the entire house holding her cactus and yelling her claims and threats, telling this presence she is no longer afraid. Part of her wonders if this is true, but she shoves the doubt away. Instead she focuses on a line from the Isaiah verse Nick had her read. *When you pass through the waters, I will be with you, and through the rivers, they shall not overwhelm you.*

Kate places the cactus on the coffee table in the living room. Its resplendence radiates in a shaft of sunlight coming through the bay window. She heads back into the family room, sits on the recliner, picks up the newspaper and begins to read, part of her tense and alert, anticipating. But it doesn't come. The house is silent. She forces herself to move her eyes across the print, though her brain doesn't comprehend the words. Her mind is wary, waiting. The house remains silent.

She throws the paper on the floor, leans her head back and closes her eyes, still waiting. The house is silent. She focuses all her attention in her ears, hears the ticking of the kitchen clock, the rasping call of a blue jay, the gentle clanking of the ceramic beach chimes on the porch, the rustling of oak leaves in the breeze. But no click, click, clicking. No typing from the keyboard in the next room. She looks at the clock. Time to pick up Mollie. She stands, walks to the study and surveys the empty room. She's not sure the war is over, but she's won this battle.

Chapter

ate slides into the driver's seat and shuts the van door. She glances at the rearview mirror and catches a glimpse of cavernous eyes, then they're gone.

"Hello, Michael," she murmurs, as if afraid someone might hear. "How are you today?" She keeps her eyes fixed on the mirror another second but sees only the back seat and rear window. "I know you're here," she says as she turns the key in the ignition. "I'm not afraid of you." She smiles at the lie.

The drive to Dr. Galen's office is only five minutes. Mitch is already there, having come straight from work. He rises to kiss her and they sit together. They wait for half an hour. Mitch flips rapidly through one magazine then another, stopping to look at his watch every two minutes and rolling his eyes. Finally a man about Kate's height, with broad shoulders tapering to his waist, comes through the door marked "private," leans against it and scans the room. He's dressed in a shirt and tie, camel trousers and a tweed jacket. His eyes fall on Kate.

"Mrs. Nardek?" She nods. "Will you and your husband please follow me?"

Kate can feel the irritation vibrating from Mitch as he

waits for her to go before him. They follow the nattily dressed man into a small office where he motions to a loveseat and then sits in a rolling chair, his back to them, opening a file on a desk crowded with a computer, piles of case files and various knickknacks. Mitch slides into a wing chair to the left of the loveseat. Kate sits on the loveseat and envisions a second indentation as if Michael's grim specter sits. What would this doctor think if she told him she imagines a dead man next to her? She remains silent.

The office is scattered with stuffed animals and puppets. A bookshelf running from floor to ceiling holds various games—checkers, chess, building blocks. The upper shelves hold thick books, their titles a foreign language—*OCD, ADHA, ODD*—sitting side by side with *The Complete Works of Shakespeare.* Clocks stand sentinel on his desk and the end tables flanking the loveseat. Their silent hands move across their faces indiscernibly.

The psychologist turns to face them. Kate surmises he's about her age. His thick blond hair accents his green eyes.

"Hello," he says, looking at Mitch. "You must be Michael Nardek."

"I go by Mitch. By the way, my last name is Cerveau. Nardek is Kate's maiden name. She didn't change it when we married." The counselor nods as he jots on the clipboard balanced on his knees.

"And you must be Kate," he says looking up.

"Yes."

"As I'm sure you realize, I'm Dr. Michael Galen …"

Kate jerks as if struck by one of Zeus's lightning bolts. Dear God, she's surrounded by Michaels! She immediately rejects the observation as childish whimsy. But within her, the goddess, lover of eccentric thoughts, grabs hold and begins pondering. An image rises of the first to bear the name Michael, the militant archangel, God's warrior and dragonslayer, his sword ever unsheathed, relishing the battle as much as the victory. Michael, the conqueror of rebellious Lucifer. Michael, whose name means "Who is as God."

"Mrs. Nardek!"

Kate's eyes snap to Dr. Galen.

"Are you with us?" He's frowning.

"I'm sorry," she stammers. "I was, um, lost in thought."

"As I was saying," he draws out his words, "I've read your answers to the questionnaire I sent you. I'm very goal-oriented. I'd like us to start by setting measurable goals and then track our progress."

"Yes, of course."

"Now—"

"Before we get started," Mitch interrupts, "could you tell us a little about yourself?" His voice is light but holds a skosh of challenge. "I assume those degrees on the wall above Kate detail your qualifications. Maybe you can start there."

"I'm good at what I do," Dr. Galen snaps, ignoring the diplomas. He's a pug ready to take on a Great Dane. "I have close to a hundred percent success rate with my clients. Anything else before we get started?"

"It must be hard spending every day listening to everyone else's problems." Kate can tell by her husband's tone he's dissatisfied with the counselor's answer. Mitch is in his investigative-reporter mode, asking seemingly innocuous questions, all the while searching out the vulnerability, the soft underbelly of his prey. In spite of herself, Kate feels a pang of pity for Dr. Galen. He doesn't know what he's up against.

"I love my job, probably because I'm successful at helping clients address their problems constructively." Dr. Galen looks at his watch. "Now let's move on, shall we?" With raised eyebrows Mitch rolls his eyes to meet Kate's. "As I've said," the counselor continues, "I've read your information. Seems like you've been having trouble for quite awhile. What finally prompted you to seek professional help?"

With resignation, Mitch continues to look at Kate. She stares back, her face hardening. It's none of his business. Mitch is trying to read her eyes. It's none of Dr. Galen's business. Mitch shrugs in exasperation then turns to the psychologist. "My wife walked in on our neighbor's suicide."

Other than a slight widening of his eyes, Dr. Galen doesn't move. He looks at Kate then back at Mitch. "Was it successful?" he asks, his voice slightly deflated.

"Yes," Mitch says.

Dr. Galen waits for Kate to elaborate. How does one walk into a suicide? She stares back at the counselor, her face and tongue as frozen as her heart. Turbid silence fills the room. She feels like a guitar string tightened to the snapping point. Dr. Galen glances down, seesaws his pen between his fingers, making its ends hit his clipboard in rapid fire. Tap tap tap. Tap tap tap. Tap tap tap. The pen's motion is mesmerizing. Tap tap tap. Tap tap tap. Tap tap tap.

"Okay," he says, arresting his pen in midair, "let's talk about your son."

"You've read what we wrote," Mitch says. "He's out of control."

"Tell me what you mean by 'out of control.'"

"Just yesterday he had a total meltdown because Kate asked him to empty the dishwasher. That's the one chore he has in the morning, ever since fourth grade, yet every morning it's a battle. He'd been behaving badly all morning, being rude to Kate, taunting the girls, making Mollie cry."

"Mollie is … ?" Dr. Galen begins searching through the papers on his clipboard.

"She's our four-year-old. Anyway, when Kate asked him to empty the dishwasher, he took a carving knife out of the block and pointed it at her. I had to tell him twice before he put it down. Then he took a plate from the dishwasher and dropped it on the terrazzo. Oops, he said. Then he took another out and did the same thing. I grabbed him and threw him out the front door and locked it. Then, while we were cleaning up, he broke through the pool screen and began pounding on the sliders so hard we were afraid they'd break. I went out there and I admit by then I was in a rage. I shoved him and he shoved me back, hard, right into the glass doors. He kept poking my chest, saying, 'Come on, Dad, whatcha gonna do?' Taunting me ... I don't know, almost gleefully. I swear, for the first time yesterday I thought, This kid's crazy. If you could have seen him ..."

"He's not crazy," Kate snaps.

Mitch throws her a sideways glance. "It's hell living in our house right now. I'm sure Kate's right. A lot of it's our fault, but it's hell."

"How so?"

"How is it hell?"

"How is it your fault?"

"We've made a lot of mistakes," Kate says. "We've been over-demanding, expecting him to be perfect in everything, a little gentleman." The words gush from her. She's talking too fast but can't find the brakes. "Our expectations have always been out of line with his age and development. We have much higher expectations and put much more pressure on Josh than we do the girls. And we're more critical of him. Overly critical. We—"

"I have to admit I'm the biggest offender there," Mitch interrupts.

"A good example is the first two-wheeler we bought him," she continues. "It was too big for him by two years. It's symbolic of our entire relationship. We're living the stereotype of parents of a first child: unrealistic expectations. We know we pressure him; we've talked about it numerous times, but we can't seem to stop. We can't step out of the stereotype."

"You seem to think you're bad parents."

"Obviously. We wouldn't be here if we didn't have problems. We're inconsistent. We don't follow through. Our pediatrician has told us repeatedly that if we'd just do a better job paren—"

"Who's your pediatrician?"

"Dr. Timothy Foster."

"I know him. When did you first consult him about Josh's behavioral problems?"

"Oh gosh, back when he was a toddler. Before Reyna was born." Kate relates the tantrums and disobedience that pushed her to seek advice from Dr. Foster first once, then again and again during Josh's childhood and early adolescence. The fights that increasingly grew physical. The threats that increasingly became dark and detailed. The property damage that could be as small as a broken plate or as large as a garage door ripped from its tracks. Dr. Galen listens without interrupting, his expression tolerant.

"Dr. Foster recommended one book, then another," she says after recapping a decade of parenting problems. "We read them and tried to follow their advice, and each time things seemed to improve for a while, but then everything would fall apart again. It seems the more we try to follow Dr. Foster's advice to discipline Josh, to exert control—no matter how we couch it—the worse it gets."

Dr. Galen shakes his head. "That's because you aren't the problem."

"What do you mean?"

"The problem here is Josh." Dr. Galen speaks as a teacher to a child. "Contrary to what you apparently believe, Josh is not an abused child. More likely you're the abused ones."

His words slap Kate. She has braced herself for outrage, indignation, recriminations, but not for this. She doesn't believe him. He doesn't know what he's talking about. Hasn't he been listening?

"Based on what you've written here," Dr. Galen taps the clipboard with his pen, "and what you've described today, I'd say Josh has the typical qualities of what we call oppositional defiance disorder. What I'd like you to do is take this book ..." He stands and scans his bookcase, finally plucking a dark blue paperback from the second shelf. "It explains ODD in layman's terms and suggests a very effective mindset along with strategies for parents dealing with defiant children."

Kate rolls her eyes. "Not another parenting book."

"This isn't a parenting book," Dr. Galen says, clipping his words. "This is a book about your son's disorder and how you can best cope with it. I'd also like you to keep a daily log of your interactions with Josh and bring it to the next meeting, with your son."

"So you've met with us for thirty minutes and you know, categorically, without doubt this is the problem?"

"I've been doing this a long time." He hands Kate the book. "This is a common problem. We'll have it under control within three months. Trust me."

Chapter 20

She's talking to him jauntily. She does it when she's alone. When she's driving or cleaning up the kitchen after her husband and kids have left. She greets him by name, as if he is an old friend, as if she's not afraid. He likes how the more frightened she is the more confident she acts. She's a fighter. He also likes her voice moving through him. An accompaniment to the melody now sustaining him. He only wishes she wasn't afraid. That she could see him in light. He wants from her what he was never able to give others. Why do humans see so darkly? Do they all? Certainly her vision is not as obscured as his was. She sees rays as well as shadows most times, and all the variations of gray in between. That must be why she refuses to judge him, though she abhors his choice. If only she would give herself the same benefit.

Her thoughts and prayers float past him during her nights, become lyrics in the song. She asks for forgiveness most, then patience and a loving heart. She doesn't believe she loves her son, or loves him enough, as if love can be measured. She prays for Michael, for his healing. Those prayers lift him, like a runner who has finished his first marathon. Other times she pleads: Don't let me lose my compassion. What would his life have been like if he had once contemplated such a prayer, much less prayed it?

Immediately, unbeckoned, his mother's voice intrudes. He quakes, certain the harsh cacophony of her song will destroy him even as a part of him realizes, with a horror begging disbelief, that the fierce vibration is emanating from him. He is howling out a movement of hatred he feeds by looking back to his own youth, to the day in the living room when he was eleven.

He is there. You ruined my life, *she's screaming.* I could have had a life if it weren't for you and your brother. Could have been a dancer. I had the body. *Her face is red and blotchy, her eyes dry, her nose dripping. She's pushing the barrel of the handgun against her temple—again. Cold steel against pulsing life.* Want me to do it? *Even though he's played this drama countless times, it still turns him to ice.* You don't believe me, do you? *she's saying.* But I'll do it. And when I'm gone I want you to remember it's your fault. Your fucking fault! Whoever asked you to be born?

He begs her through choking sobs. Afraid to step toward or away from her because sometimes she turns the gun on him when he moves.

You fucking baby, *she cries.* You worthless piece of shit. God, I hate you!

That last time, that last dance where, instead of flinging the gun at him, she pulls the trigger, a smile of disdain dashing across her face before her head explodes. A detached part of him stands back and watches himself fall to his knees, snot stringing from his nose mixing with tears and vomit, the gunshot still resounding. He wonders how moldy cottage cheese came to be scattered across the now blood-soaked carpet.

That was the final reality between him and his mother. Until her voice rose up. He understands why coyotes howl at the moon. His violent howling has emptied him, made room for the softer notes of his mother's song to move through, to unfold a graceful yet mournful ballad.

He sees her as a child, silent, her face averted as her hulking lumberjack father forces himself into her, saying, It's okay, sweetie pie, you're doin' good for your pa. *Blood on her lip where she's bit it to hold in the pain. That's what her father does on the nights he drinks only a little. On the nights he drinks a lot, his eyes get hard and narrow when they find her. She is Eve to his angry Adam. He blames her for his transgressions. If she isn't quick, he catches hold and then the beatings begin. He smacks her hard across the face, shoves her to the floor. Kicks. He unbuckles his belt and flails her bare bottom.*

Most of the time she gets away before he inflicts too much damage. She has scars where the belt broke skin. His words inflict more. Slut. Fucking cunt. Get out here and take what you deserve. *She shrinks into a dark corner hoping his haphazard, stumbling search will overlook.*

This is why her mother left, secretly, in the middle of the night, when her father was passed out snoring. Her mother kissed her at bedtime, as usual, but was gone the next morning. No note. No clothes missing. Her father took it out on her, especially after finding their bank account drained. She never heard from her mother again—at least not on earth. When she realized her mother was gone—really gone—she ran into the woods and cried. Why hadn't Mother taken her? Why had Mother left her with him? That was the worst scar of all.

Michael cannot hate his mother after hearing this song. Her voice is free from pain now, free from guilt, fear and accusations, regret and shame—free to tap into a love buried so deep in her center, she could not access it on Earth. She calls with a mother's love no longer shriveled by misandry or self-hatred. He knows at another time, the same time as now, he chose to ignore a similar song, held onto his hate-filled howl, even as the notes wavered in front of him, beckoning, chanting his name.

He thought the choices ended when he chose the center. But the choices never end. He remembers his high school teacher trying to explain Jean-Paul Sartre's philosophy. How Sartre maintains that every situation holds choice, even a bound prisoner has a choice to struggle or passively die. Seemingly innocuous choices we make daily, hourly, minute-by-minute ultimately define us. He remembers the example his teacher gave. An obese man decides in the morning he is going to diet. But such a choice is only good at the moment it's made. At lunch, when the man goes through the cafeteria line and sees his favorite piece of chocolate cake, he must recommit to dieting. He must re-decide. Re-choose.

He's glad this time he chose to listen. When he lets his mother's song ring through him fully and unresistingly, he feels lighter, as if a stone has fallen from his heart. How many other stones still dwell there? How many times has he howled in resistance?

What is this master opus? There are so many strands to it—this symphony of souls—each a living presence separate from him, yet a vibrating energy that both surrounds and fills his very essence. It's a mystery why some parts of the song speak to him and others don't. What stories do the strands he can't interpret tell and to whom do they sing?

He can tell from his mother's song she's been here. She's always been here. They've all always been here—even when they haven't. How can that be? He also knows the center moved for her, as it moved for him. That it moves for everyone.

Missing the mark is not the final reality.

Could a soul see the center and choose to turn away? Part of him knows this is possible. He could have at the very moment the center moved. But he can't imagine it. To see the beauty of the center, to see how far you've drifted from this sublime mark, to feel the despair of it, then notice in a blink the center move, see it align itself with your crooked path, joyously promising an all-encompassing embrace, and still say no? It must be possible, but he can't conceive it. He also knows such a choice must be hell.

Chapter 21

Kate sees it again. This is the fifth night. She's not crazy. Something on the other side of the door wants to come in, pushes the door forward. A part of her, awake to danger even in sleep, sends off a jarring alarm. The presence seems to sense her and backs out of the room, quickly pulling back the door, but not quick enough. She sees the door, half open, jerk to the spot Mitch positions it when they turn in—about two inches from the frame. She lies motionless next to Mitch, afraid the hammering of her heart will wake him. She doesn't want to be scolded again about her need to "get a grip." Stiff with fear, Kate doesn't move, doesn't breathe. She's afraid to wake Mitch. Afraid to take her eyes off the door.

It's not a burglar. She'd almost welcome a burglar, a human being. But she knows the haunting presence outside her bedroom—the same presence that types on her computer—is not flesh and blood. She hasn't seen it, just the door swing back in place when she opens her eyes. The thought of investigating terrifies her. She's sure evil lurks on the other side of the door. Feels it in her gut.

Her mind flies to the cactus sitting on the coffee table. A gift from God. Oh God, protect me, she prays. She gets out of bed. Her feet curl at the cold touch of the hardwood floor.

She hesitates, then gingerly walks to the bedroom door. God is with me, God is with me, her mind chants with each step. Her hand shakes as she reaches for the knob. She clasps it firmly, clenches her teeth and yanks open the door.

Nothing. No thing is there. Just the dining room table glowing warmly in the soft beam of the nightlight. She looks into the living room, sees the cactus' silhouette in the moonlight.

"Kate, is that you?" Mitch's voice is thick with sleep.

"Yes."

"What are you doing?"

"I'm having trouble sleeping. I thought I'd read. Sorry I woke you."

"Come back to bed."

"I will in a bit."

She hears him sigh and rustle under the covers. She steps through the door, pulling it closed behind her. Maybe Mitch is right. She thinks too much. Overdramatizes. Damn! She's such a child. Why can't she grow up? She turns on the lamp over the stereo cabinet, then searches the CD titles, finally spying the gift from Lily, a collection of meditative chants from Taizé, an ecumenical community in France. She places the disc in the player and sits down next to one of the large speakers, lowers the volume and closes her eyes as her favorite chant, "In the Lord," encircles her.

The music washes over her, the melody gentle, the voices sure, commanding her to forsake her fear and trust in God, assuring her that God is close by. Singers repeat the chant, each time adding a new element—a flute descant reminding her of the melodic trill of the warbler living in the pine off the driveway, or an oboe, bringing to mind a cat stretching from its nap. She pulls her knees up to her chin and wraps her arms around her legs, rocking to the music's sway.

She believes. She believes, doesn't she? Yes. She believes. Then why is she so scared?

Chapter 22

"Hurry and eat up," Kate says, looking over her shoulder from the stove. "We're going to take advantage of the warm front and picnic at the beach."

"Yippy!" Mollie bounces on her knees at the kitchen table. She refuses to use a booster seat but can't quite reach the table without one, so she sits on her knees during meals. Kate doesn't mind, though it bugs Mitch. Can't anyone sit at the table properly? he asks at every meal.

"I hate the beach! I'm not going." Josh's face is a tight scowl. Kate hesitates only a moment as she flips the next batch of pancakes. "No problem," she says, forcing a lightness into her voice she doesn't feel. "You can stay home."

Josh's scowl deepens. "Thanks, Mom." His sarcastic tone cuts like a razor. Kate hurries the girls through breakfast and then shoos them into the bathroom where she slathers them with sunscreen. She can hear Mitch and Josh.

"Why do you do this? You ruin everything. Your mom wanted this to be a family day. She's been having a tough time. Can't you once put someone else's needs before your own?"

"She chose the beach because she knows I hate it."

"Since when do you hate the beach?"

"Since now."

"Yeah, right." Mitch's voice drips with disgust.

"It's okay," Kate calls from the bathroom. "Let's just go with the girls and have a good time. Josh can stay home if he wants. I don't want him to come if he doesn't want to."

She packs lunch and drinks in a cooler while Mitch loads the car with Reyna's boogie board, Mollie's ring, plastic buckets and shovels, the beach blanket and chairs. As the girls clamber in the back of the van, Josh saunters into the garage, pushes roughly past Kate and climbs in.

"Thought you didn't want to go," Kate says, trying to empty her voice of the irritation she feels at his rough bumping.

"Shut up, Mom."

"Don't talk to your mother that way," Mitch says. His face is red with rage. Josh looks out the window, ignoring his father. Mitch looks at Kate. Please, she pleads with her eyes, even as her face sags. He slides behind the wheel as she climbs into the passenger seat beside him. He pulls the car out of the garage and steers to Route 1.

"Can we go for a walk on the beach and hunt for shells?" Reyna asks fifteen minutes later, just as they reach the highway.

"Of course," Kate answers.

"Of course," Josh mimics in a high-pitched tone. "Anything for your little angel." Kate hears the slap of a hand.

"Ow!" Reyna shrieks. Kate turns to see Reyna rubbing the side of her face, flaming red from Josh's strike. Tears stream down her cheeks.

"Josh, did you hit her?" Why is she asking? She knows the answer.

"No."

"Josh!"

"I just tapped her. It was a joke. She's faking, like always. She's such a fucking baby."

"That's it! No ice cream for you at the beach, and no computer for the rest of the weekend."

"Fuck you, bitch."

The van swerves violently. Kate looks over at Mitch as she grabs the dash. She can tell from his expression an explosion is coming.

"Mitch," she whispers as he stops the van on the shoulder. He throws open his door, jumps out and circles around the front. He shoves the passenger side door wide with such violence it rebounds off the end of the track. He pushes it in place, then leans into the van.

"Get out here," he says to Josh, his voice a low growl.

"Make me."

Mitch reaches past Reyna and grabs Josh by the arm; Josh struggles as Mitch jerks him from the van. Gravel crunches under Josh's body as he falls. Kate leaps from the van and joins them.

"You are not to talk to your mother that way. And you are never to hit your sisters. You got that?"

"Fuck you," Josh says, but his tears rob his voice of its bluster.

Mitch leans over, grabs him by the shirt and pulls him up, nose to nose. "Say it again."

"Mitch!" Kate pushes her way between the two, breaking her husband's hold on her son, urging him back. "Please. This isn't the way."

"What am I supposed to do, just let it go? Let him beat up a little girl half his size?" He leans around her. "You're nothing but a bully. A coward. You want to take on someone, you take on someone your own size."

Josh steadies himself against the van. He's no longer crying. "I'll take you on. Come on, Dad, want to fight?"

Kate turns and puts her hands on her son's chest. "Stop this now, Josh." He glares past her.

"Get out of my way." He swings his arm to shove her

away, hitting her in the head. The blow knocks Kate to her knees. For a moment she sees only a black curtain with spots of light fading in and out.

"Kate?" Mitch is next to her.

"I'm okay."

"I didn't mean it," Josh says. "I didn't. It was an accident."

Kate feels Mitch spring to his feet. Hears him slam Josh against the van. "An accident?" His voice is a lion's roar.

"Stop!" she screams. "Stop, both of you." She leans over her knees and cradles her head with her arms as she rests on the ground.

Mitch steps away from Josh. "Satisfied? Happy now? Making your mother cry?"

"I'm not crying." She lifts her head. "I'm just a little dizzy." She slowly pushes herself to her feet. Mitch takes her arm, then brushes off the gravel embedded in her knees.

"I'm so sorry, Mom," Josh whispers from where he leans against the van.

What is the right response? Should she be angry, forgiving, understanding, accusing? She doesn't know, so she says nothing. Mitch takes her elbow and helps her into the van. Josh is already in when Mitch gets behind the wheel.

"Let's go home," she says, locking her seatbelt in place. "I don't feel well."

Mollie begins to whimper.

"It's not fair to the girls," Mitch whispers. "Why should Josh's bad behavior punish them?"

Kate doesn't answer. She doesn't know the answer.

"Why don't we take Josh home and then go to the beach?" Mitch offers.

"No!" Josh's voice is a whine now. "I said I was sorry. Please. I want to go with you. I didn't mean to hit Mom."

"Let's just go," Kate says. She feels as if she hasn't slept in weeks. "Come on. Let's just go to the beach."

Mitch huffs in disgust but starts the engine and merges back into traffic. "I don't see why we put up with this," he says under his breath.

"Did Josh break the day?" Mollie asks, her voice uncharacteristically sad.

"Yes," Mitch growls. "He breaks everything."

Kate looks out the window, losing herself in the green haze of trees whizzing by.

Leaning back in her low-sitting beach chair, Kate watches the girls build crooked sandcastles to the music of the surf, their faces full of concentration as they dig and pile and pat their creations into shape, oblivious to everything else, fully in the moment. They plan, build, negotiate, renegotiate the lines of the structure, the width of the moat, the height of the tallest pinnacle, leaving their child worries in the van, or at home, or somewhere beyond.

Mollie runs to the surf with a bucket and brings back water to fill the moat, which drinks itself dry before she can get the next bucketful there. Reyna pats the sand, smoothing, sculpting.

Mitch is far down the beach, trying to walk off his anger, slogging through the surf like a battleship. Josh lies on the blanket before her, sullen. She wants to rescue him, but keeps getting caught in the currents. She recalls their last visit to Dr. Galen, when the counselor told Josh he was drowning. *I'm not drowning*, Josh said irritably, but Dr. Galen persisted.

When you're trying to rescue a drowning person, you never approach him head-on, he said as he leaned forward, elbows on knees, gazing intently; a slight smile playing on his lips. *When you approach a drowning person head-on,* you risk getting caught in his struggle, and you both drown.

Kate was a lifeguard in her teens. She knew he was right. She knew what he was going to say next.

That's the mistake your parents keep making, Dr. Galen continued. They try to help you by approaching you head-on and you all end up going under in the struggle. What you need is an anchor. Who could you use as an anchor?

Josh had refused to look up, refused to answer.

Think, Dr. Galen pressed. Who could be your anchor when these emotional storms threaten to sweep you out to sea, threaten to overwhelm you?

I dunno, Josh said, shrugging. You maybe?

No. I'm not at your home when things fall apart. You can't call me every time problems arise. You need someone who can be there for you. Can you think of someone?

Josh stared stonily at the rug as another prickly silence filled the room.

How about your mom? The counselor posed. Could your mom be your anchor?

Josh didn't answer.

She's very strong, Dr. Galen almost whispered.

I know she is, Josh replied quietly, but with surprising conviction.

Kate remembers the sharp pain in her chest and the sudden realization she had stopped breathing. She pulled in a shaky breath and refused to meet Dr. Galen's eyes. She shakes her head at the memory. She reviews the morning as she runs her fingers through the sand next to her beach chair, feeling its cool grit. She cannot imagine herself an anchor for anyone, least of all her stormy son. She feels adrift, capsized on the turbulent, squall-ridden sea that is Josh's and her relationship. She's bruised by the pounding waves of verbal and physical violence and angry at the squalls; angry that she is so easily overwhelmed; angry that, for the first time in her life, she's afraid of the water.

How can flotsam be an anchor?

She wishes she could ask her mother this question. A strong swimmer, a master sailor, her mother was at ease on the sea. She loved the water, which is why Kate grew up on the shores of the St. Anne River. Her mom bequeathed this love as she taught Kate and Kate's brother Greg how to navigate the river's mile-wide waters in her eighteen-foot sloop. She taught them to find peace in the murmurings of the river's placid, patinous waves lapping the shore and wonder in the wind-whipped fury of her steel gray whitecaps. Most important, she taught them to respect her.

At the tip of the isolated peninsula where Kate grew up, the river's current collided with a backwash from the channel, creating a deadly vortex hidden beneath her deceptively calm surface. At age fourteen, Kate woke one night to the distant wail of a siren. She pulled herself up on her knees to peer out her bedroom window. The doleful siren grew louder, reaching its pitch as the rescue squad raced past her house, motorboat in tow, the trailer spitting gravel as it careened behind the speeding truck. As the trailer disappeared down the road, she felt an arm tenderly drape her shoulders. She turned to see her mother standing by her bed, staring out the window. Their eyes met. Her mother's furrowed brow mirrored her own misgivings. The siren died away. After a long silence, her mother said, Come.

They walked to the kitchen. Without speaking, her mom got out two wine glasses, poured Burgundy in one, apple juice in the other. She handed Kate the latter then they wandered into the living room and stood before the picture window overlooking the dark water. They both knew the river had swallowed someone that night.

Look, her mom said, pointing to the dancing path of silver the full moon cast across the rippling water. Beautiful, isn't it?

Kate didn't answer.

The river is beautiful, her mom continued softly. But we mustn't forget how powerful she is, how treacherous she can be. She took a sip of wine, then pulled Kate close. That doesn't mean we should fear her, she said as if she had felt her daughter's trembling heart. Respect her. Hold her in awe. But don't be afraid of her. Fear is a poor counselor. It compromises us; it compromises our judgment.

The next day, her mother, Greg and Kate went sailing. The wind was high and they sailed close-hauled, cutting through the chop at a fast clip, so fast the centerboard trembled in its casing, creating a slight hum.

She's singing! Hear her? her mom called out. Her russet curls flamed with the sun's rays.

Kate nodded back at her from her perch on the bow, where she clung to the pulpit. Laughter spilled from her as the wind tore at her hair, the cold spray stung her face and the boat's song reached her ears. She looked at Greg manning the tiller with a light touch, feeling her play, gently searching for the boat's limit. His brown eyes reflected her laughter. She felt safe with these two sailors, even as the boat heeled so the leeward gunwale threatened to kiss the water.

They heard the news when they returned home. Teenagers. Not local. A late-night party at the point. Beer. Skinny-dipping. Panicked splashing. Two disappeared. Their bodies had yet to be recovered. They had committed the cardinal sin for any sailor or swimmer, according to her mom. They had entered a water strange to them without first familiarizing themselves with her idiosyncrasies. Then, when the river wrapped her long, unrelenting fingers around them, rather than giving themselves partially over to her pull, resisting only obliquely, they struggled in direct opposition, ensuring their doom.

Now here Kate is, years later, in the strange waters of Josh's anger and ugliness, swimming hard against the current, trying to fight her way back to shore. She wishes she could talk to her mom about Josh, confess her fears for him, the doubts and guilt that plague her. Wishes she could hear her mother's encouraging laughter, could seek her wise counsel on flotsam anchors. But not long after that last sail, an artery exploded in her mother's head, killing her within minutes. An aneurysm due to an inherent weakness in the vessel, the doctors said. She should have died the day she was born. Miracle she lived to forty-one.

"I'm going for a walk," Josh mumbles, interrupting Kate's musings. He pushes himself up from the beach blanket. Kate pulls the *Godspell* CD from her bag and inserts it in the boom box. She presses the forward key until she gets to "We Beseech Thee," then lets the song's plea for healing and mercy sweep over her. She sings quietly along with the chorus, where the players beg God to "come sing about love." When she closes her eyes, she hears the waves and the raucous cries of a gull join in the song.

The sound of Mollie rummaging through the large beach bag wakes her.

"What you lookin' for, honey?" Kate asks, rubbing her eyes.

"The kite. Found it." Mollie sprints back to the hard sand and unrolls the nylon. She assembles its frame, lays the kite down, unspools several yards of string, then runs down the beach on firm chubby legs. The kite drags in the sand like a puppy. She turns and runs back to it, past it, but the kite stays grounded. Kate begins to rise when Josh jogs up.

"Mollie, that's not how you do it. Let me show you." He takes the string from her and directs her to hold up the kite. "You've got to run into the wind. Follow me." The two lope down the beach and the kite takes flight. Josh turns and runs backward, rolling out the string as the kite climbs. Mollie's gleeful giggles carry on the wind as she hugs Josh's legs. He laughs—he actually laughs—and returns the hug.

They watch the kite, Josh's face clear of the storm usually shrouding it. He hands Mollie the string. She dances along the beach, the kite bobbing after her. Josh hovers, occasionally nabbing the string and guiding the kite so it doesn't lose altitude.

Kate grabs the camera from the beach bag and snaps a photo. This is what she wants to remember.

Chapter 23

ate sits in bed, ignoring the novel lying open across her lap as she listens to the music flowing from the piano. She didn't eat dinner with the family, excusing herself with a headache. Normally she would call for quiet, but tonight Josh's music soothes her irritability. It sings of the beach. She hears the gentle roll of the waves, Mollie's laughter, sees the kite skipping across the wind, sandcastles gleaming in the sun. Barely audible, a mesto bass harmony underscores the giocoso melody. How he integrates the two tempos and moods is a mystery to Kate, but the result is achingly poignant. When the music stops, she returns to her book. She doesn't look up when Josh saunters in.

"I liked your playing," she says.

He flops across the bed, ignoring her comment. His head lands softly on her legs, making her flinch. She despises herself for cringing at her son's touch. She keeps her eyes on her book, but the words have lost their meaning.

"Mom, I'm sorry about the beach."

She hesitates. She wants to say, Okay. Wants to let it go. But she knows, as sorry as Josh is now, his regret won't change his behavior tomorrow.

"Part of being sorry is committing to change so you don't

do the same thing over and over." She tries to keep her tone light. She doesn't want to lecture.

"I know," he says, frustration in his voice. "Mollie's the only one not mad at me. Dad's right; I ruin everything. I don't mean to. I just do. I don't know why."

"You don't ruin everything. You were very good with Mollie and the kite. Wait here." She walks to the living room and returns with two large photo albums. "Come sit beside me." She leans against the headboard and opens one of the books. "Look, there you are with Dad. You must have been about five, flying your new kite. That was at Nags Head. Look how happy you are, how happy Dad is."

Josh touches the picture. "I don't remember."

"The memory is in you, in some file your brain's tucked away. You've just got to search it out. It's important to remember the good things, Josh, much more important than remembering the bad." She flips a page. "Look, you and Reyna are in the huge hot tub at the condo we rented. We filled it with bubbles every night and turned on the jets." They stare at the photograph of a young Josh and an eighteen-month-old Reyna in a sea of bubbles. Both are laughing. Reyna has a white patch of foam on her head, like a hat, and Josh has a bubble-beard.

"I remember that." He smiles. She flips to the middle of the book, to a photo of an older Josh and Kate on horses. Behind them, Reyna sits in front of the trail guide on yet another horse.

"Here we are in the mountains. What was your horse's name?"

"Jasmine."

"Right. You fell in love with her on that trail ride."

"Yeah, that was fun." He grins. "I remember Dad didn't get to ride because he had to stay behind with Mollie. He led her around on a pony for more than an hour. I remember him jumpin' away when you first handed him the lead. Afraid of a little pony."

"Your dad didn't grow up around animals and he didn't mind staying behind. He hates riding. We rode horses on our honeymoon. A three-hour trail ride across moors in Scotland. Incredible. But he couldn't walk right for three days after. It kind of put the rest of the honeymoon on hold, if you know what I mean."

Josh looks at his mom, who smiles suggestively. A slow grin of understanding slides across his face. "Poor Dad."

"He hasn't ridden a horse since." She puts her arm around Josh and pulls him close. "It's easy to remember the bad stuff, honey. But there's a lot of good in our lives too. A lot of love. That's what we've got to remember, what we need to focus on. So often we forget in the heat of the moment how much we love each other. We've got to constantly re-remember. You know what I mean?" He nods.

"Your dad and I love you very much. Even when we're angry with you. Honey, you've got to understand most times anger is a mask for something deeper, like fear. That's true for your dad and me. We want the best for you, and part of that means teaching you what is and isn't acceptable. My mom used to say she disciplined me because she loved me. Otherwise, why would she endure the hard work and hassle of it, all the headaches and conflict? Now that I have children, I know she was right."

"Bet your mom never threw you up against a car."

"No, she didn't. But Grandpa Kyle could be pretty harsh. When he got mad, he'd take off his belt and give us kids a lick or two across the backs of our thighs. It hurt."

"What'd you get whipped for?"

"You know? I can't remember. I just remember the sting and the look of anger on my dad's face. The truth is, I probably didn't deserve most of the lickings I got. I was basically a good kid."

"Yeah, right."

"Once. Oh my gosh, I'd completely forgotten this."

"What?"

"You know your Grandma Ellie was a poet."

"Yeah."

"Well, one summer, when I was about twelve, Grandpa Kyle and Grandma Ellie took Uncle Greg, Aunt Lily and me to Cape Hatteras, in North Carolina, for a week. Your grandma was in one of her poetry periods, and Uncle Greg and I took up pens and began to write our own poetry. It was awful stuff, but Grandma Ellie very lovingly and patiently went over it, making suggestions, encouraging us to play with it. That was a wonderful time, sharing our 'art' together. Grandma's really was art. Mine was dah, dah, dah, dah, dah, time, dah, dah, dah, dah, dah, mine."

Josh snorts.

"Hey, it's not funny. I loved the poems I wrote. One was about a girl who dreamed she was riding a stallion through the stars. I called it 'Night Ride.' I kept my poetry in a three-ring binder and continued to write even after the beach trip. Mom was always interested, gave me gentle critiques and encouragement. After she died, I kept writing. I wrote a lot of poems about her. How much I missed her. Then one day I got in a terrible fight with Grandpa Kyle. I don't remember what it was about; I just remember him yelling at me, telling me I was an ungrateful, selfish kid, that kind of thing. A few days later, I came into my bedroom and found someone had taken my poetry from my notebook and ripped it up. It was lying in shreds on the bed. I sat on the bed, stunned."

"Who did it?"

"My dad, Grandpa Kyle."

"Wow, that musta made you mad."

"Oddly enough, I don't remember feeling angry. I felt, I don't know … almost embarrassed for Grandpa Kyle. I remember thinking, 'Gosh, I made Dad so mad he's acted like a child.' While I was sitting there, your grandpa opened the door and poked his head in the room. On his face was this ugly expression, a mixture of anger and satisfaction. He looked at me for a moment, almost in hatred, then pulled back out of the room and shut the door without saying a word."

Josh examines the picture of him on Jasmine, then looks into his mom's eyes.

"But you always talk about how much you love your dad. How can you love him if he did stuff like that?"

"Grandpa isn't perfect. And he had a very hard life before he met Grandma. His father was an alcoholic and treated him terribly. He ridiculed and embarrassed Grandpa in front of his friends. And he never gave your grandpa a birthday present—not once in his life. Instead, on the morning of your grandpa's birthday, his father would say to him when he came down to breakfast, 'Happy birthday. This is the day you killed your mother.'"

"Grandpa's mother died when he was born?"

Kate nods. "If it wasn't for your Great Aunt Rose, Grandpa would have had a very dark childhood. But his Aunt Rose took him on outings every weekend, went to all his games—he played baseball through college—took him to the zoo or ice skating on the lake in winter. Aunt Rose didn't have children of her own and kind of adopted your grandpa."

Josh stares at the photo album. "Wow, that stinks about Grandpa's dad."

"Yeah. The times your grandpa did mean things to me growing up, his dad was coming out in him. But more often Aunt Rose came through—at least while your grandma was alive. Grandpa's never really recovered from her death. But I didn't understand any of that as a kid."

"Is that when he started to drink?"

"How do you know about that?"

"I hear you and Dad talk, when you think no one's around."

"Yeah, that's when it started."

Josh flips through the photo album as Kate stares at the far wall. Pain wells in her, so fresh and sharp it steals her breath. It gushes from the wound she refused to acknowledge all those years ago when, as a teenager, she tried in vain to fit together the pieces of her shredded poetry.

"Mom!" Josh nudges her shoulder.

"What?" She faces him in surprise. "What is it, honey?"

"I said, did Grandpa ever apologize for ripping up your poetry?"

"No. Never mentioned it. He believes apologizing is a sign of weakness. Kind of like you."

"I didn't say that."

"You told Dr. Galen your dad and I are the ones at fault, that's why we're always apologizing."

"I didn't mean it like that."

"I know, honey. But we're all human. We all make mistakes, but worse than making a mistake is failing to acknowledge it and trying to right it. Otherwise, how do you move forward?"

"Were you sad growing up?"

"No, not really. I was a lot like Mollie. I woke every morning happy. It drove your Uncle Greg crazy. Once, during a family argument—I was in elementary school—Uncle Greg turned to me and said, 'You're the one who causes all the trouble around here. You get up every morning and sing.' My mother, who had been so angry a moment before, burst into laughter. She thought your uncle's statement so funny, she went straight to the study, typed it up and made him sign it. Then she dated it and put it in the family scrapbook."

Kate flips through the album. "Look, here we are at the top of the St. Augustine lighthouse."

"Mom, why does Dad hate me so much?"

"He doesn't hate you."

A tear slides down Josh's cheek. "Yeah he does. He says life is great when I'm not around."

"He says that when he's angry. That's not an excuse, but we all say things we shouldn't when we're angry. I do and so do you, when you say you're going to kill us."

"I don't mean it."

"I know. And neither does your father. But words have power and they can hurt. We all have to be more careful how we speak to one another."

He leans his head on her shoulder. "I love you, Mom."

"I love you too, honey."

"Will you do me a favor?"

"What?"

"When you're disciplining me, will you remind me it's because you love me?"

A needle pricks Kate's heart. "Yes," she says softly. "And I'll remind myself too."

Chapter 24

She wakes with a chill. Her eyes fly to the bedroom door. It's where it should be. It doesn't move. Still her heart beats like a savage war drum. She tries to close her eyes, to relax, but she can't. It's as if her eyelids are stretched open by invisible springs. She stares at the door. Waiting. The door begins to open. It moves slowly but steadily forward in silence. It stops just before touching the bedroom wall. Kate can't breathe. Something is gliding into the room. No, it must be someone. But it is not someone. It's not human. It's form-less, like a cloud, a gray cloud superimposed on the dark.

She's sure it's evil, but she tells herself it's Josh. He's had a bad dream. He seeks comfort. She's lying to herself, but she holds fast to the lie. It's the only thing preventing her racing heart from exploding. The form glides straight into the room, up along Mitch's side of the bed. She sits up and turns to the presence. It's not Josh. It has to be Josh. It's evil. I want it to be Josh. Her lungs ache, begging for air. She draws in a shaky breath.

"Josh," she whispers, her voice wavering, "are you all right?"

"Kate?" Mitch moans and turns to her. "What are you doing?" Kate looks around the room. It's empty. Mitch props himself up on one hand and rubs his eyes with the other. She looks at the door. It's still open.

"I thought Josh came in," she says, hoping Mitch doesn't hear the trembling emanating from her core.

He scans the room, then her. "Kate, you've got to stop this. You can't keep waking us. I need my sleep."

"I thought I saw something."

"Jesus Christ, Kate, get a grip. We can't go on like this."

He lies down with his back to her. She settles onto her back, her eyes staring at the ceiling, her body stiff. She wants to touch Mitch, wants him to hold her. But he's angry. He'll get angrier if she tells him she's afraid. If she tells him she thinks she saw ...

Her heart pounds. It wasn't Josh. What if it wasn't anything? What if she's hallucinating? What if she's losing her mind? She looks at her bedside clock. Two a.m. She looks at the door. Nothing.

Dear God, help me. Come sit with me. I'm so afraid. I'm so afraid. Tears squeeze from the corners of her eyes. She wipes them away, along with sweat icing her forehead. She tries to force her eyes shut, to will her body to relax. She recalls the cactus standing sentinel in the living room. She says the Lord's Prayer. She asks God to grant her peace, to let her lose herself in sleep. She studies the shadows on the ceiling, trying to make familiar shapes from them, the way she used to do with clouds when she was a child. She checks her clock again. Three a.m.

Dear God, fill my house with your presence. Fill my house with your angels. She envisions Elisha on the hilltop in Dothan, surrounded by the Syrian army. Sees his young servant quaking by his master's side, knowing all is lost. What could two men do against such an army? She searches her mind for Elisha's exact words, which her Sunday school teacher forced her to memorize decades ago. *Fear not, for they that be with us are more than they that be with them.*

Kate closes her eyes, imagining the servant's confusion. He is the only one with Elisha. Surely his master has lost his mind under all the pressure of the chase, and now the pack is advancing for the kill. Elisha must have read his servant's face. Did the expression he saw bring a smile to his lips? Was he smiling, still, as the Syrians advanced and he calmly asked God to open his servant's eyes so the young man might see what Elisha saw: the mountain ablaze with an army of angels in fiery chariots poised between the enemy and them?

Dear God, she prays, fill my house with your angels. Fill every inch of my house with angels, so evil has no room to set its foot. She imagines her room filled with blazing chariots manned by fearless archangels. The image loosens the tight knot at her core. Her body relaxes as a wave of warmth flows through her, thawing her lungs and heart. She looks at her clock. Three-thirty. She looks at the door. It hasn't moved. She closes her eyes and hugs the image of her bedroom filled with chariots of fire.

The phone rings repeatedly on the other end of the line. Finally, Kate hears a click and then Jean's warm "Hello?"

"Jean?" she manages to croak before fear swells into wet sobs, choking her.

"Kate, is that you?"

She gurgles out a wet affirmation, not a real word, but enough.

"Kate, I'm going to talk while you cry," Jean says, her

voice matter-of-fact, as if she receives this kind of call routinely. "Have you had rain? We're dry as bone here. I've had to water the garden daily, by hand because of water restrictions. The azaleas are complete water hogs. I don't know why I ever planted them."

Kate covers her eyes with her free hand. Tears wet her fingers, but the sobs have quieted to breathy hiccups.

"How is Reyna doing? Is she still playing the piano? She was so proud the last time you brought her, playing "Go Tell Aunt Rhody" with two hands. What I don't understand is why piano teachers don't start students off playing softly, what's it called? Pianissimo? Not all that banging, every-thing the same volume—forte! Has she gotten the Indian songs out of her system? I could see that driving you crazy, her left hand pounding a drumbeat of cords."

Kate smiles through her tears.

"Oh, and what about little Mollie, the little Joybug. Is she causing trouble in school? I hope so. Reyna is such an angel; you need a little spitfire to liven things up. A little hell raising never hurt anyone."

"Trust me," Kate croaks between sobs and laughter, "that's not a problem. We have plenty of hell around here."

"Oh Kate," Jean says, her voice soft with tenderness, "tell me. What is it, Darlin'?"

"Jean," she says, her voice shaking, "I'm going to tell you something and I'm absolutely serious and I'm speaking literally. I think I'm going crazy."

"Oh Kate!" Jean's voice is gentle but dismissive. "You're not crazy. You're not going crazy. What makes you think so?"

Kate tells her about the specter haunting her nights, making her heart jackhammer, engendering fear that tears into her chest like wild dogs ripping prey. She tells about it coming into her room, she thinking it was Josh and Mitch's resulting anger.

"Don't worry about Mitch right now. He doesn't understand where you are. Forgive him that. Hang on—"

Kate hears Jean fumbling, hears a crinkling noise. "Ohay, I'um ack."

"What are you doing?"

"I'm sucking on a mint. Sorry. Now tell me, why do you believe this presence is evil?"

"I don't know. I feel it in my gut."

"You're not confusing this with your neighbor Michael?"

"No, it's not Michael. That's the one thing I'm sure of. I know Michael's with God. I don't know how I know, I just know."

"Good. Now, about this presence, which did you feel first, fear or that it was evil?"

The question surprises Kate. She searches for the answer, going over in slow motion the first encounter she had with the apparition. She hears the mint clicking against Jean's teeth as her godmother patiently awaits her response.

"I guess, truthfully, first I felt fear."

"Just what I thought. That makes anything you thought after, any analysis of the situation, suspect. Fear clouds our judgment. It screws up our vision."

"You're saying I didn't see anything."

"No. You definitely saw something. But I don't believe it's evil."

"What is it then?"

"I don't know. I do know one thing, though, you're not crazy." Jean pauses. "Whatever this is, it's in some way connected to Josh."

"But I knew it wasn't Josh."

"Yes, but when you wanted to believe it was a child coming into the room, why didn't you say to yourself, 'It's Mollie'? She'd more likely come to you in the night at this stage."

"True. Josh doesn't come to our room anymore. He hasn't for years."

"But you called it Josh." Silence stretches through the line connecting them. Kate waits. "Your soul is trying to figure something out," Jean says slowly, as if she's thinking aloud, "or maybe help you figure something out."

"What?"

"I don't know." Kate hears the beginnings of laughter in her godmother's voice. "But I'm thinking we should ask God to help you figure it out quickly." Jean's full-throated laughter flows through the line, embracing Kate, priming her own laughter. Their mirth eases Kate's stomach, fends off the wild dogs, reassures her of her sanity, fills her with an inexplicable certainty: Answers will come.

"How's counseling going?" Jean asks when their laughter subsides.

"The first few visits seemed to do some good, but Josh has become increasingly angry at Dr. Galen."

"Probably because Dr. Galen is telling him things he doesn't want to hear."

"Yeah. The last few sessions Josh has talked as if Dr. Galen were his third parent. I kind of feel bad for him, as if it's three against one. But no matter how mad Josh gets, Dr. Galen keeps his temper. He's very light and humorous, which Josh hates. Josh never has learned to laugh at himself, and that gets in his way."

"Absolutely. But that may come in time. I don't know how people get through life without a sense of humor. Seems like it should be required equipment." Jean chuckles. "Now Darlin'," she continues, her voice lowering to a serious note, "I've got something to tell you. I was planning to call you today but you beat me to the punch. I've got some bad news, baby."

"What?"

"I hate to do this to you, Kate. Right when your life's rug has been whipped out from under you."

"What is it?"

"I have cancer."

Kate squeezes the phone as if it alone supports her. "How bad?"

"It's bad, honey. It's big, a tumor in my lungs, right next to my heart, making it inoperable."

Kate can't breathe, feels as if a sledgehammer has crushed her chest. "What are you going to do?" she whispers.

"I start chemo next week. The doctor warned me it's going to be bad because they want to be aggressive. She also says she's going to cure me. But you know, precious goddaughter, I'll be fine no matter what happens."

"Nothing's going to happen except you're going to spend a bunch of months throwing up and losing your hair. Then you're going to be fine."

"Yes, Darlin', I'm going to be fine. And, you know, I do feel there are little cells in me already trying to fight this dark mass."

"They must be your laughter cells," Kate says, then joins in when Jean chortles.

"What a heavenly thought. Kate, I want you to come see me. Soon. I need one of our days together."

"I'll come tomorrow."

"Will you? Really? Oh, that would be wonderful."

"I'll leave at eight so we can have breakfast together."

"I'll run out today and get your precious half-and-half. Oh Kate, you've made my day. I love you, Darlin' Heart."

"Love you, too. I'll see you tomorrow."

"Without doubt."

When the connection clicks, Kate lowers her head to her hands and weeps.

"I'm through taking off work early every other week to meet with that pompous couch pilot. You seem to think my work isn't important. It does pay the bills, or have you forgotten?" Mitch stands at the kitchen counter, his back to Kate, unfolding the newspaper.

"Mitch, this isn't going to work unless we both do it and show Josh we're committed." She looks toward the family room for signs of the kids. "Could you keep it down? I don't want Josh to hear."

"It's not going to work, period. You think this guy is really helping us? Look at the way Josh reacts to him. He tunes him out within five minutes."

She stirs boiling water into their oatmeal. "Dr. Galen did come on sort of strong at first. But Josh has got to know he's not an equal in this family, I mean, not equal to us in authority. We're the parents and he's the kid. There's a hierarchy. That's what Dr. Galen was trying to get across. Josh sees himself as the parent, wants the same authority as we have."

"Josh is a punk. A spoiled brat."

"Spoiled kids misbehave, but they don't threaten to kill their parents."

"Look, I agreed to try this because you were so upset after the suicide. But it's not working for me." He opens the refrigerator, pulls out the orange juice, then slams the door shut. "I don't like this Galen guy. He's full of himself. And he sure as hell hasn't connected with Josh. I don't see how we're going to get anywhere if Josh won't even talk with the man."

"We've only been going two months, and you've missed half the meetings."

"They're a waste of time." He lifts the cutting board off the hook on the wall and places it on the counter. "Give me a knife, will ya?" She pushes up on her toes to fetch the paring knife from its place over the stove fan. A while ago she hid the carving knives behind the faux cabinet covering the exhaust vent and a narrow cubby between the vent and the wall. "It's not worth me asking Alex for time off every other Thursday night," Mitch says as he takes the knife from her.

"What could be more important than our son? God, sometimes I feel like you love the paper more than us."

"This is so typical. You've never understood the demands of my job and you've never understood or supported the importance I place on being there, being reliable, being the go-to guy they can count on in a pinch."

"What's more important, this family or the *Daily Leader*?"

"Shit, Kate, that's not fair and you know it. My job pays for this house, the food this family eats, the vacations we take."

"I'm not asking you to quit your job; I'm asking you to take off an hour early once every two weeks for your son and this family. It's not like Alex is going to fire you because we need to see a family counselor. He's one of the most compassionate guys I know. If you just tell him—"

"I don't want to tell him. Don't you get it? Jeeesuus!"

"Don't tell him the specifics. Just tell him we're having

some problems and we're seeing a counselor. Tell him it's about the suicide and me if he asks. But he won't ask. And he won't say no. I know Alex."

Mitch doesn't answer. He's busily peeling bananas. If she didn't know better, she'd almost think he hadn't heard her.

"This isn't about Alex," she continues. "You'd rather work than try to deal with this. It's easier. The *Daily Leader* has always been your first love. I can't compete. I remember when we got married, you said on the flight to London if the president got shot or some other big news story broke, you'd fly home that day—ditch our honeymoon—to cover it."

"Oh God, not this again."

"It's as if the paper can't come out unless you're there. No one else can do the job." She stirs the oatmeal with a wooden spoon. It's too dry. She adds more hot water.

"It's my job and I want to do it."

"At any expense? At the expense of your son? At the expense of your marriage?"

"Are you threatening divorce now?"

"You know I'm not." She slams the spoon onto the counter. "But it hurts me, Mitch. It hurt me the day of the suicide when I had to ask you to come home."

"What's the complaint? I came, didn't I?"

"I had to *ask* you." She turns to him, talks to his back. "Don't you see? You didn't know, didn't understand how much I needed you. You wouldn't make the choice on your own. I had to ask you to leave work."

"How am I supposed to know you need me to come home if you don't tell me?"

"Mitch, I'd just seen our neighbor hanging in his garage. I was crying. Nearly incomprehensible on the phone. You said so yourself. If it'd been reversed, and you'd called me in such a state, I wouldn't have hesitated. The moment I heard your voice, I would have known. And I would have said, I'm coming. I'm coming. What I needed you to say to me."

"Maybe I'm not quite the intuitive you are." He places a banana on the cutting board and whacks it in half. "Did it ever occur to you I'm sick of all this. Sick of you?" He whacks one of the halves into quarters. "You've totally lost your sense of humor. You never laugh at anything anymore except with Jean. And you seem fixated on this notion of evil. God, how long are you going to regurgitate this in your mind? When are you going to get over it?" He whacks the other half into quarters then faces her, his knife suspended over the banana pieces. "Look, I got it you're unhappy with me. I just don't know what I'm supposed to do about it."

"Maybe you could start by not making me feel guilty about being depressed."

He snorts in derision. "I don't need to make you feel guilty. You do a good enough job on your own."

"You're right. I am unhappy. And I'm worried. I'm worried about Josh and also about you and me. I know I haven't been at my best these past months, but it angers me that not only do you not understand, you don't even try to understand. Dr. Emmett said it could take up to six months for me to work through this, and that would fall within the realm of normal."

"Well, thank God we're over halfway there," he says with a sneer. "I wish you'd go back to him. Maybe he can help you get a grip, help you get back to normal, to the way you used to be."

His statement stings like a wasp. He turns back to the counter and begins to dice the banana quarters. The rap of the knife on the cutting board reverberates between them. Kate retreats to the bedroom, softly shuts the door and locks the knob.

"Kate!" She hears Mitch cross the hardwood floor. He rattles the door. "Kate, for chrissake, let me in. Look I'm sorry." He rattles the door again. "Come on, Kate. Goddamn it! This is so typical. The minute something upsets you, you run away." She hears him return to the kitchen. "Shit, who's going to get the kids off to school? Kate!"

She sits on the bed and stares at the door. Something has occurred to her—a realization so clear and unequivocal she cannot ignore it, a realization that both enlightens and alarms her, as if she were a hiker who finally stumbles upon the long-sought-after path to the summit, only to find the tortuous route shrouded in fog.

Chapter 26

"Hi guys." Dr. Galen enters the waiting room, smiles at them, then studies Kate with raised brows. "Where's Mitch?"

"He's with his mistress," she says. He recoils, then glances at Josh, who either has not heard or is purposely ignoring them. "I'm talking about the *Daily Leader*."

Relief flickers across his face, making her feel guilty. What must he think of her? That she's a bitter, shriveled-up, old bitch?

"Could I have a few minutes with you alone?" she asks.

"Sure." He holds open the door to the hall that leads to his office.

"I want to tell you something." She she sits on the loveseat.

Dr. Galen places his mug on his desk. "Well, I better sit down," he says, then flounces into his chair.

She ignores his exaggerated response to her abruptness. She wants to get this over with.

"I don't want to tell you this." She closes her eyes painfully and rubs them with her fingers. "But I think I should. Then again, I could be wrong and this is a waste of time. Maybe you don't need to know. I'm not sure. Anyway," she shakes her head and looks hard into Dr. Galen's eyes, "right or wrong I'm just going to do it."

He leans forward.

"I'm going to tell you about my neighbor's suicide."

He nods, his face solemn. She has robbed him of his smile. After her first visit, she would have given anything to wipe that smug smile from his face. Now she'd give anything to put it back. Without it, he looks surprisingly vulnerable. He is, after all, a child psychologist specializing in discipline problems and parenting—which she only learned after their first visit. So suicides probably aren't his daily fare.

Kate plunges into her story, speaking rapidly. She tells him about Cara, about the call to 911, how she came face to face with Michael. Dr. Galen gasps, but she continues. She tells him about her father, who came after Mitch called him and fell into a diatribe about how he thought "that man" was strange, how he was living in sin with "that whore," how he and his girlfriend weren't "Bay Haven people" and now look what he's done—gone and given the neighborhood a black eye. That's when Kate left the living room, claiming she was tired, and locked herself in the bathroom. She tells Dr. Galen about the vomiting, over and over in the toilet until nothing came up except a primordial dry heaving that sounded somewhere between a bark and a strangled gag.

She tells him about the gray veil and about the visions, up to the night the gray cloud of what she calls disembodied evil pushed open her bedroom door and glided in. She tells him of Mitch's disgust, how he told her she had to get a grip.

Dr. Galen rolls his eyes when she quotes Mitch. "Don't get me wrong," she says, "I love him." The counselor nods eagerly. She can tell he doesn't want to offend or upset her, doesn't want to do anything that will make her stop telling this bizarre tale.

She tells him about calling Jean and how she confessed

she thought she was going crazy, then pauses to catch her breath.

"I'm not going crazy," she says. "After the suicide I went to see Dr. Emmett. He said it could take up to six months to work through the fallout. And typical for me, it seems I'm going to go the whole nine yards with this."

Dr. Galen mirrors the weak smile she offers.

"I'm not crazy. But I've been depressed and very stressed out at times since the suicide. And when you're depressed and stressed, everything looks bigger and darker and harder than it really is. Even the smallest bump can look like an insurmountable mountain. The reason I'm telling you all this is in counseling, I may not be the most reliable witness. Even now, when I said Mitch was with his mistress. I feel very angry and very unhappy with my life and I seem to be focusing it all on Mitch—unfairly so, but I can't seem to stop myself. I'm also not dealing with Josh well and may even exaggerate his misbehavior at times. Suffice it to say, I'm not at my best right now, and I wanted you to know that. And one other thing."

His eyes question her.

"My godmother Jean is very sick, with lung cancer. It's bad. We're very close. I've known her since I was four. She knows me better than anyone. She is exactly what her title says, my God Mother, a gift from God. The thought of losing her breaks my heart.

"That's it. That's all I wanted to say." She clamps her mouth shut and leans against the back of the loveseat. She feels foolish and relieved and unexpectedly exhausted. She pulls her purse onto her lap. Now that she's said what she came to say, she's desperate to leave. She begins to stand.

"May I speak?" Dr. Galen asks gently.

Kate slumps back against the cushion. "Of course."

"First, I want to thank you for this gift." She looks at him questioningly. "It helps me tremendously to understand the family dynamics of my patients, especially anything causing undue stress on individual family members. What I hear you saying is you're very depressed, with good reason, and you want me to help you protect your son while you work through this depression and the aftermath of the suicide."

"Yes. Exactly."

"I can do that."

"Thanks." Kate again begins to rise.

"Don't go just yet." His eyes, so solemn a moment before, are twinkling. "I can see you're in a hurry to leave."

She smiles reluctantly.

"Dr. Emmett is right; it can take months to deal with the aftermath of the shock you experienced. You're dealing with posttraumatic stress syndrome."

"Sounds dramatic."

"Not to me. You experienced a traumatic event, one that has had a profound effect on you, probably because you're a sensitive person. It might be good if you got some help, aside from family counseling."

"You saying I need counseling?"

"A good psychologist could help you figure out what's going on inside you, help you find the missing pieces of the puzzle. You could come see me or one of my colleagues. The practice has a number of good psychologists."

She stares at her purse strap clenched in her hands. She's afraid she's going to be sick. She looks up. Dr. Galen is gazing at her intently, a slight smile pulling at his lips, more boyish than smug. She likes this smile. "It's true I'm in a dark wood right now," she says. His smile broadens, confusing her. She looks back down at her purse. "I've been wandering around lost for a while. But I sense a clearing. And I have faith I'll make it to that clearing eventually. I may even stumble in and out of it a few times but I'll get there."

"Maybe if you had help you'd get there faster."

"I've muddled along this far on my own. Why not just muddle through to the end?"

He shrugs. "You could do that. But I'd hate for you to lose something in the process."

"I don't know what you mean. What could I lose?" Dr. Galen stares at her, as if waiting for her to answer her own question. She regrets she asked. What could she lose? Her mind? Or is he speaking of something subtler? What if *he* thinks she's losing her mind? Oh God, she's made a mess of this. She wishes she hadn't said anything. Wishes she could take it all back, start the day over.

"Kate, you are such a talented, sensitive woman. You have so many gifts, some you may not even be aware of. Why risk those? There's no shame in asking for help."

She imagines herself a bedraggled cat, nearly drowned, crawling belly-to-dirt to Dr. Galen's door and throwing herself with her last bit of strength onto his doormat. Gentle hands pick her up, put her in a basket near the living room fire, feed her warm milk from a bottle until she is strong enough to stand and drink on her own. The notion fills her with warmth even as she rejects it. How pathetic. She doesn't want or need help. She's not helpless. God, she's such a baby. Yet, even as she rages at herself, she hears the goddess. What can it hurt? she's saying. What can it hurt?

"The idea of talking to a counselor doesn't appeal to me." She wishes she didn't sound so tired and confused. "And I can't retell the suicide again. It's too hard."

"You could go back to Dr. Emmett."

"He's all the way in Jacksonville. Between teaching and the kids, it's just not practical."

"You could come see me."

He is smiling at her again, coaxingly. She shakes her head, not sure what to do. "Tell you what," he says, "why don't we make a deal? You come see me for five visits. After that, we'll evaluate whether the visits are helping and then take it from there. Five visits. That's not too overwhelming, is it?"

"Okay," she says, too tired to fight.

"Then we've got a deal." He grabs his appointment book and opens it across his lap. "Why don't you come back next week; that way you won't see me individually the same week you come in with Josh."

"I thought you were booked for months."

"Had a patient graduate. Is Wednesday at 10 a.m. okay?"

She nods.

"By the way, why were you worried about sharing this with me?"

"I guess I thought you might wonder why I was bothering to tell you all this, why I was wasting your time."

"It wasn't a waste of time. And I thank you for showing such trust in me."

The comment irritates her. She feels it's self-congratulatory: Look, I've earned your trust. "I'm not sure it's a matter of my trust in you but rather my desire to give you everything you need to help my son. The truth is, I'm not a big believer in psychology as a science."

"That's okay." His smile is unwavering. "I have enough faith for both of us." He stands. "I'm going to set you up with my secretary, so you can fill out the necessary paperwork, and I'll spend the rest of the session with Josh. Okay?" She nods but can't bring herself to return his smile. He opens the door for her and puts his hand lightly on her shoulder as he follows her out. "Thank you, Kate. It means a lot to me that you were willing to share, for whatever reason."

The warmth of his touch flows through Kate like an electrical current, bringing a blush to her face. She keeps her face averted, not wanting him to see. She doesn't speak, not trusting her voice. She is angry that the simplest act of kindness makes her melt into this spineless, emotional rag. Relief floods her when Dr. Galen heads off to fetch Josh. She can't take one more look from his smiling eyes.

Chapter 27

She sees her priest Nick ahead on the forest trail. She calls his name, then runs to him. She extends her hand in greeting, but he ignores it and instead cups her chin, caressing her cheek with his thumb. His eyes are the color of the sea, and before she can help herself, she's drowning in them.

She presses her thighs together, shields this heat that feels like yearning, that feels right even as her mind knows it's wrong. The more she tries to extinguish it, the hotter it grows. It's almost painful, this throbbing between her legs. She wants to release it, to smother it, to push it further. Nick's face moves toward hers, intensifying the throbbing that expands, tightens her chest, scorches her face. She is Eve salivating at the apple, all the more desirable because it's forbidden.

She closes her eyes as his lips cover hers. The warmth of his skin sends fire through her. He is pushing her lips apart with his tongue, hungrily, devouringly—painfully. It's too fast. She tries to pull away, but his grip is steel. He forces her mouth wide. His tongue, slimy and forked, darts in and out like a snake's, burning her with acid, plunging farther down her throat, gagging her. She sees his face. It's not Nick. It's … Oh my God. OH MY GOD!

She wakes with a jerk. It takes a moment for her to reorient. Thank God, just another nightmare. Instinctively she looks at the bedroom door. It isn't moving, hasn't moved. Then she looks over at Mitch. He sleeps peacefully on his back. She lightly lays a hand on his thigh, thankful for his presence. Still she shivers. She thinks of the Christmas cactus in the living room, its handsome roseate blooms. She has a gift from God in the house. She needn't be afraid. She keeps part of her mind focused on the image of the cactus as she files through the other images of the past few weeks.

The night before, she pleaded with God to give her another way to figure out whatever it is she's supposed to decipher. Take away these visions, she prayed. I can't do it this way. It's too scary. Give me an alternative. She wants to believe it's coincidence that the very next day, Dr. Galen suggested she come see him, let him help her find a path out of the black labyrinth in which she's lost. Is this the alternative she prayed for?

She doesn't want to see him alone. The thought of splitting herself open from the base of her throat to the base of her abdomen and letting everything spill out, allowing him to view the mess within, mortifies her. What would he say if she told him she'd exorcised her house with a cactus? Definitely something she should keep to herself. How could she explain the cactus as a gift from God?

The cactus isn't the gift, silly. Her mind stops when the goddess speaks. It's just a symbol, the goddess whispers. God's presence is the gift. God is in your house. In your life.

In a flash, Kate knows the goddess is right. She sees herself storming the house with her cactus, daring the Satan of her childhood to show his face. A giggle wells up before she can suppress it. Mitch stirs next to her. She turns away and covers her mouth with her hand, snorting softly. What a fool she is. What a child.

You are a fool, the critical voice chimes in, strangling her mirth. And that's exactly what Dr. Galen's going to think. Actually, he'll probably conclude you're certifiably insane.

Just go and talk, the goddess coos.

You're such a fucking baby. Can't handle anything on your own. Such a weakling. If you go to this psychologist, you'll be admitting you're crazy. That you can't cope. Is that what you believe?

Just go and talk.

Kate struggles between the two voices. The critical voice is stronger, but inherent in the goddess' voice is a playful indulgence that hugs her heart. She hates being weak. She hates appearing foolish. She told Jean that once. Her godmother threw back her head and laughed. If you want to live deeply, soulfully, then you have to be willing to appear foolish. Kate, we're all of us so very foolish. Just like Pooh Bear. But in Pooh's foolishness there's much wisdom. Kate thinks of Christopher Robin shaking his head over one of Pooh's cockeyed yet right-minded adventures, saying, "Silly old bear." There's so much love in that phrase, in the shake of his head, in the laughter underscoring his words.

Just go and talk, silly one. Kate imagines the goddess shaking her head, holding in her laughter with a loving smile.

Maybe she'll go. Maybe.

Chapter 28

hey're late, as usual. The girls are arguing in the back, a chaotic din Kate ignores.

"Mom. Mom! Stop! Stop!" She looks in the rearview mirror to see Reyna pointing out the window. "Mom, it's a dog. It's lost. Stop. We've got to help it." On the right side of the road, a miniature poodle with curly white hair prances along the ditch. Kate pulls over.

"Mom, it's lost. We've got to help it. A car will hit it for sure." Reyna's voice is a whine.

"Can we keep it?" Mollie asks eagerly, already in love.

"I'm sure it has a home near here." Kate hops out and crosses in front of the van to the spot where she saw the dog. It's gone. She walks to the back of the van. No sign of the dog. It's vanished. "Where'd it go?" she calls to the girls. She gets no answer. She shrugs and walks back to the driver's-side door, which she left open. There in the driver's seat, front paws on the steering wheel, is the tiny dog panting happily. Its stubby tail wags madly, shaking its entire body. The girls burst into giggles.

"Oh Mommy, he's so cute," says Reyna, who has already moved up between the front seats and is stroking the brash intruder. "And he doesn't have a collar." Kate puts her hand out to pet the dog, which attacks her fingers with fierce licks, its pink tongue quick and rough.

"Can we keep him?" Mollie asks, pushing past Reyna to pet the dog.

"Get away!" Reyna yells.

Kate picks up the dog. "Let's not argue, girls." The dog leans its head against her shoulder and tries to lick her chin. "You are a sweetie, aren't you?"

"What if he doesn't have a home?" Reyna asks. "Can we keep him?"

"Okay guys, calm down. The dog has an owner. He's just been clipped and is very clean, probably had a bath as well. Maybe that's why he doesn't have a collar. His owner was giving him a bath and he decided to go for a run."

"But what if he's lost? We can't just leave him here. What if a car hits him?" Reyna's voice holds tears. Kate looks at her watch.

"We're late for gymnastics, Reyna."

"I don't care. The dog is more important. We can't just abandon him." Kate looks at her daughters. Their faces glow with a mixture of delight and longing, their eyes bright with hope.

"We'll ask the people who live along this street if they know who owns him."

"What if they don't?"

"Then we'll take him to the humane society."

"Aw," the girls moan in unison. Their faces fall. Tears well in Mollie's eyes.

"Listen. If no one claims the dog, then we'll adopt him, okay?"

The girls shriek with glee. Kate dreads trying to explain this to Mitch. They had a huge fight when she allowed Josh to adopt Mischief, who showed up at the house one day starving. No pets, Mitch said, they're too much trouble and inconvenience. And just when you start getting use to them, they up and die. The cat stayed, but since then Mitch had been adamant on the issue: No more pets. Period. Now she's promised the girls this dog, if it's homeless.

"What if someone claims it?" Reyna asks, fear creeping into her voice.

"We'll see when the time comes." Kate's standard 'I'm not ready to address that' reply.

"Can we get another dog if this one has an owner?" Reyna has wanted a dog for two years.

"We'll see …"

"You can call in three days," the intake lady at the humane society says. "If no one claims her, it *is* a her by the way, then she's all yours."

The girls jump up and down on ballerina feet, clapping their hands.

"Don't get your hopes up. The dog looks well cared for," Kate reminds them, but already she's aligned with her daughters, hoping beyond hope this friendly scruff can come home with them, even though she hadn't set out to own such a small dog. She grew up with big dogs. A Collie, then a Newfoundland. She doesn't like small, yappy dogs. But this one doesn't seem yappy, just friendly.

During the drive home, the girls chatter madly about where the dog will sleep, where she'll eat. What they'll call her. Kate parks in the garage and turns to face them. "Listen guys, let's not mention this to Daddy yet. I need some time to get him used to the idea. So mum's the word."

"Okay, Mom," Reyna says. "We won't say anything. But what if Dad says no?"

"Don't worry," Kate says, hoping her tone sounds convincing.

Chapter 29

He sees his dog, a mutt, golden retriever and who knows what else. She's a big slobbery puppy when his father first brings her home. Licks Michael's face sticky wet every time he stoops to pet her. He loves her. Someone dumped her at the local gas station that winter evening, the temperature dropping to zero. The dog would've died. Gracie, they call her, because she survived by the grace of Dad. That's what his mom says in one of her rare good moods. Gracie lives longer than her savior. But not a full life.

One day she gets into the kitchen trash, eats day-old fish scraps. Barfs on the living room carpet. Smells worse than shit. His mother throws her glass of scotch across the room, shattering it against the wall, then chases the dog out of the house, rifle in hand. He and Tom follow screaming no, pleading no. She aims for Gracie's head but hits her back. Gracie falls on her paralyzed haunches and paws the ground with her front legs, twirling herself in circles, howling. His mother throws down the gun. Finish it, she says to Tom.

Tom's hands shake as he picks up the rifle, making it rattle. He wipes his nose on his sleeve. He inches to Gracie, opens his mouth, moves his lips, but nothing comes out. What was he going to say? I'm sorry? I love you? He cocks the rifle then tries to aim for her head, for the center of her twirling agony. Michael turns before his brother pulls the trigger, hears the shot and yelp. He turns back to see Tom by Gracie's side, his face a waterfall, Gracie lying on her side, bleeding from the chest, still alive.

I'm sorry, girl, *Tom croaks. Gracie stares at him, her soft eyes gentle, full of love. Tom aims at the dog's unblinking eye.* I love you, *he says as his finger tightens on the trigger.*

Michael can't watch. He turns, coming face to face with his mother, her mouth distorted with disgust and another, inward-looking emotion he cannot fully read. It looks like hatred. A shot rings out. Michael spins toward the sound. Gracie is still, half her head gone.

Better work on your aim boy, *Ma says to Tom. Tom turns to face her, cocks the gun then raises it, leveling it at her head.* What do you think you're doing? *she yells.* Put the gun down, now! *Michael jumps from between them. Watches as they stare each other down. Sees Tom squint his right eye over the barrel, now fixed on her forehead.* Put the fucking gun down! *she shrieks. The trees stop rustling; birds stop twittering. In silence, nature watches as the two stand locked in an eternal struggle.*

Fresh tears stream down Tom's face as he lowers the gun. She leaps forward and wrenches it from him, turns it on him, aims at his chest and pulls the trigger—so fast Michael and his brother are too shocked to move.

Click.

They all stare at the gun, expressions of horror frozen on their faces. She looks at Tom. Oh baby, I'm so sorry. What am I doing? Dear Mary, Joseph and Jesus, forgive me. *Tom's face is granite.* Oh baby, please forgive me, *she begs. Her tears amaze Michael. She falls to the ground, half crawls, half knee-walks to Tom.* Baby, forgive me. Please. I love you. I do.

Tom turns and runs into the woods. Tommie! My Tommie, *she cries through sobs. She pivots and stares at Michael as if she's never seen him before, as if she's trying to comprehend him. Then she covers her face with her hands and folds to the ground. She begins muttering. At first Michael can't discern the words. Then they come to him.*

Hail Mary, full of grace, the Lord is with thee. *His mother sits back on her calves, letting her hands fall from her face.* Blessed art thou amongst women. *She begins crawling to Gracie's body.* And blessed is the fruit of thy womb, Jesus. *She pulls Gracie's body onto her lap, strokes the dog's blood-stained neck, her gory chest.* Holy Mary, Mother of God, pray for us sinners …

She says more but sobs smother the words. She buries her face in Gracie's fur and cries. Part of Michael wants to go to her, hug her, tell her he loves her, rest his own head on Gracie's fur one last time. Instead, he backs away. The spectacle of his mother praying through choking sobs scares him more than when she held the gun. He doesn't understand his feelings, only that they're too much to bear.

He runs to the house, where he slides into the dark cave under his bed. He cries for Gracie. Cries that he left his mother alone in her agony. Cries because he hates his life and he hates God and Mary and Joseph and Jesus. He cries himself to sleep.

He sees it all, this time from a distance, wrapped in a protective, melodic detachment. His heart mourns the two boys, the demon-driven woman, the dog. Why do we hurt each other so? Why do we hurt ourselves? It's one and the same.

He holds Gracie close to him. I love you girl. *He holds close his mother.* I love you, Ma, and I forgive you. *He holds close Tom, still living.* I love you, brother. *He holds the child he was, is and always will be.* I love you, Michael. I forgive you. *He knows what it means.* Forgeifan, perdonare—*the conscious, wholehearted release of resentment and anger, the conscious, wholehearted release of all desire or will or power to punish.*

He rests in this place of forgiveness and love. It's peaceful here, the song now a pastoral. Each time he rests, he notices changes in the song, new lines woven into the melody, the song itself evolving, mirroring his journey, or leading it, he's not sure which. He hears a playful bark in the new strands. A sigh of freedom. Tom talking to Michael's son: I love you Matt, like I loved your dad.

Another stone falls from his heart.

Chapter 30

"I'm so sorry," the humane society intake lady says over the phone. "The owner claimed the dog yesterday. She was so happy, too. She asked me to thank you."

"Oh." Kate imagines the little white poodle jumping into its owner's arms, licking her face, her tiny, trembling body wagging in joy. The image should make her smile. It doesn't.

"We have other dogs here in need of a home. What were you interested in specifically?"

"A small dog. Friendly. Good with children. Maybe we'll stop by and take a look."

"We don't have any miniature poodles right now."

"Well, really we didn't need such a small dog. It's just because we found her and the girls … you know … love at first sight."

"Come by anytime then. We have lots of dogs."

Kate thanks the woman and hangs up. She's decided she's going to get a dog for the kids, despite Mitch's objections. She had dogs growing up and wants her children to have the same experiences of responsibility and unconditional love. She's already decided no pit bulls, no German shepherds, no Doberman pinschers. She doesn't want a dog from breeds routinely trained as watch or attack dogs. She had some bad experiences as a child, growing up in the boondocks, where dogs ran free.

Once, three German shepherds surrounded her as she was making the mile walk down the gravel road to Jean's house. The dogs snarled and bared their teeth as they inched ever closer to her. She screamed even as a sense of doom filled her. No one was in sight. The nearest house was a quarter-mile away. Suddenly the dogs froze. They lifted their snouts, sniffing the air, then turned their heads toward the woods. Kate followed their eyes. She couldn't see anything, but she heard a low, menacing growl, stiffening the hair on the necks of the shepherds.

The underbrush quivered, then a collie stepped from the woods. Its emaciated frame and matted fur looked nothing like Lassie from the movies. Hunched, his upper lip pulled back in an ugly grin, his growl soft but chilling, the dog moved in slow motion, momentarily suspending his paws in the air as he stalked. The shepherds returned the collie's growl, but Kate sensed a lack of enthusiasm. Instinctively, she realized that although the shepherds outnumbered this new arrival, they were afraid.

Without warning, the collie leapt at the closest shepherd, his teeth landing on the animal's neck. The shepherd yelped in pain. His pack mates shrunk into themselves and took a half-step back even as they growled. The collie and the first shepherd slammed to the ground and became a rolling ball of fur, snarls, and yelps. Then as fast as it started, it stopped. The two dogs stood menacing each other, blood dripping from the shepherd's mouth and neck, a red stream trickling from the collie's ear. The other two dogs turned and ran. The bleeding shepherd jerked his head to watch them, turned back to give the collie a final growl that held a note of whimper and then bounded after his pack.

Kate had stood frozen during the contest. The collie turned to her and looked her in the eyes. She didn't move, unsure if this dog was friend or yet another foe. The dog relaxed, gave a feeble wag of its tail, then sat. Hello, Kate said gently, still unsure. The dog gave a small bark then raised its right front paw as if introducing itself. She named him Sandy because the color of his coat reminded her of the beach. Her father grumbled as they drove him to the vet, even put an advertisement in the newspaper—lost dog, collie, purebred. But within a week, Kate's mother had fallen in love with the dog. For the next month they dreaded answering the phone, so many people claiming to have lost a collie. But Kate's mom made them describe the dog in detail. They all failed to note he had only three white socks.

Sandy was Kate's best friend growing up. Her confidante when she was sad or angry, her partner in hide-and-seek or tag, her furry blanket at the foot of the bed on winter nights. She wants her kids, especially Josh, to have such a friend.

They walk past large cat cages and down most of the rows of dog runs, stopping here and there to look. The girls hold their noses at the smell of animal waste and wet fur mixed with strong disinfectant, but they are soon oohing and aahing over a greyhound lying on a comforter. Kate shakes her head. Too sedate. They ask to pet a playful Jack Russell mix. Kate again signals a no. The card on the front of its cage says it's part pit bull. They stroll down the last aisle of dogs.

Kate worries she'll have to start checking newspaper ads when a medium-size dog catches her attention. He's sitting at the gate of his small run, his nose touching the chain link, watching her. When she looks in his eyes, his tail thumps the concrete twice. He doesn't bark or whine like the other dogs, but his brown eyes exude longing. He's a handsome dog. His head and body are black with a hint of cinnamon. He has a white ruff, four white socks and a white-tipped tail, as if someone dipped it in a bucket of paint. She walks to him and he stands. He's sleek and his tail arches over his back, reminding her of a greyhound, though he's clearly not. He wags his tail, actually his whole hindquarters, in excitement. She reads the card on his cage: "Name: Sonny. Breed: Border Collie/Lab Mix. Age 1. Family moved, could not take. Friendly. Restrictions: No children under ten."

"Can we take this dog into the play yard?" Kate asks the volunteer, a tall youth of seventeen or eighteen who's been trailing them through the maze of cages.

"Sure." He leashes Sonny, guides him to a fenced, grassy area about twenty by ten yards, then lets him loose. The dog sprints around the play yard twice then runs to Kate and sits at her feet. The girls and Josh crowd around him, petting him and cooing his name.

"He seems like a nice dog," Kate says to the volunteer.

"He's great. Not a mean bone in his body. He's been here four months. I can't understand it. A dog this handsome and friendly usually doesn't last here for more than a week."

"Is there something wrong with him?"

"Naw. Lately we've had a run of folks looking for more aggressive dogs, pit-bull mixes and such. You know, watch dogs."

Kate pulls on Sonny's ears. He grins up at her. She pulls him to a standing position and tugs his tail. He grins as if she's grooming him. He lets her open his mouth, as if it's an everyday event. The volunteer watches her with a smile.

"You can do anything to this dog," he says, "and he won't get angry or upset. He's gentle as a kitten."

Sonny is nearly as tall as Mollie. When he turns, his wagging tail pummels her. She lifts her arms to protect her face, giggling gleefully. "He's patting me with his tail, Mommy. Look."

Josh takes off running across the yard, calling out. The dog gambols after him.

"Here, try this." The volunteer gives Josh a footlong piece of rope knotted at both ends. Josh throws it. Sonny leaps after it, snaps it up and runs to the far end of the yard. Josh chases him, but the dog springs just out of reach, playing keep away. Josh manages to catch one end of the rope and the game turns to tug-of-war.

"Why is there an age restriction on the dog?" Kate asks the volunteer as they watch Josh and Sonny play.

"We write that restriction on every card. It's for liability. But you can sign a waiver. I know he'd make a great pet for kids."

"What do you think, Reyna?"

"Please, Mommy!"

"Please," Mollie chimes.

"Josh, how do you like the dog? Should we take him home?"

Josh runs to Kate. "He's awesome," he says between huffs.

Kate looks at the volunteer, who is grinning broadly. "Looks like it's unanimous."

On the drive home, the kids debate the dog's name. "I don't like Sonny," Reyna says.

"But he's been called that his whole life," Josh argues. "If we change his name, he'll get confused."

"Maybe we could change his name without confusing him," Kate offers.

"How?" Mollie asks.

"What if we name him after the sun, Sunny—with a 'u'—because he has such a sunny disposition?"

Silence fills the car as the kids reflect. "I like it," Mollie exclaims, clapping her hands.

"It's stupid," Josh says, but the hesitancy of his words tells Kate he's considering.

"Sunny. That's nice," Reyna says softly.

"So what's the vote?" She glances at the kids in the rearview mirror.

"Sunny!" Mollie squeals.

"I vote Sunny," Reyna says.

"Yeah, okay. But we've got to spell it right," Josh says. "I hate Sonny. Reminds me of an old Florida cracker."

"Okay Josh, no stereotyping," Kate says, unable to keep laughter out of her voice.

"Wait 'til Dad sees Sunny," Mollie says. Kate rolls her eyes. She can hear Mitch now. You call this a small dog?

"You call this a small dog?"

"Well he's small compared to the dogs I grew up with."

"And what were those, Great Danes?" Mitch is watching Sunny as he explores the family room, trailed by the children.

"My first dog was a purebred collie. Later we got a Newfoundland."

"You had two dogs?" Mollie skips up to Kate. "Can we have two so Sunny has a playmate?" Mitch rolls his eyes.

"You and Reyna and Josh are Sunny's playmates," she says.

"Look, Kate, by small dog I meant something a quarter of this dog's size."

"Come sit on the floor and introduce yourself," Kate says.

She sits down and leans against the wall. Reyna and Mollie run to sit on either side of her. "Come here, Sunny." Tail waving, he walks up to the trio, licks Mollie's face, eliciting giggles, then stretches out across their legs, turning onto his back, begging for a tummy rub.

The lines of irritation on Mitch's face relax as he looks at Mollie. He stoops down. "Hey, boy." Sunny sits up and slathers Mitch's face with his tongue. "Ugh! Gross." He stands abruptly, wiping his face. "Dog slobber." The girls laugh with delight.

"They were kisses, Daddy," Reyna says. She puts her arms around Sunny's neck. "I love him, Mommy. Thank you."

Kate raises a brow as she looks at Mitch. "You need to thank your dad."

"Thank you, Daddy."

"So this is what you call a small dog," Mitch says, but he can't hold down the corners of his mouth. When Kate smiles, he resigns. "Okay, but he better not poop or pee in the house."

"Oh thank you, Daddy, thank you, thank you." Mollie jumps up and dances at Mitch's feet.

"He won't, Daddy," Reyna says. "Josh and I are going to walk him four times a day, every day."

"Even when it rains?"

"Yes. Promise."

"That right, Josh?"

Josh nods. He's been watching the girls and Kate with the dog. "I want him to be my dog," he says.

"Josh already has a cat. Why can't he be my dog?" Reyna whines.

"He's the family dog," Kate says. "But you can take turns feeding and brushing him. Animals are most loyal to the people who take care of them, especially the people who feed them."

"Can I feed him too?" Mollie asks.

"Of course. We'll make a schedule."

"Can he sleep in my room?"

"No, mine!"

"He'll sleep in the family room for now," Kate interrupts, "until he gets used to the house and us and knows for sure this is his home. Then he can choose where he sleeps— on the floor. No beds. Let's feed him now. I want to do an experiment."

The kids follow Kate into the laundry room, where they've already laid out the food bowls they bought from the humane society. Kate pours two cups of kibble into the dry bowl. Sunny lunges at the food and makes loud crunching noises as he eats. When his food is half gone, Kate bends down and lifts the bowl away from him. Sunny sits and looks at the bowl longingly but makes no protest.

"Why'd you do that?" Josh asks.

Kate waits another minute before replacing the bowl. Sunny hesitates, gives Kate a questioning look, then resumes eating. "I want to make sure this dog knows it's not okay to growl at family members, even if they take his food. Some animals are very possessive of their food and will growl if you come near them while they eat. That's not permissible in this house. No dog that growls at a family member stays in this house. Period." The children look at Kate, their faces serious. "He behaved very well tonight. I'm going to do this every night for a week. If he behaves, then, Josh, I want you to try it, then you, Reyna, then Mollie. Sunny needs to know his love for you is more important than anything else, even his food." The children nod.

"Mommy, we'll never give Sunny away, will we? I mean, as long as he doesn't growl at us?" Mollie's smile has turned upside down and she looks on the verge of tears.

"No. And he's not going to growl at anyone over his food. I can already tell."

"But those other people gave him away because they moved. What if we move?"

"We're not moving, but even if we do, Sunny's part of the family. He'll come with us."

"I'm taking Sunny for a walk," Josh announces. "Look, he's already done eating."

"I'm coming," Reyna cheers.

"Me too," says Mollie, who has recaptured her smile.

"Josh, you keep a close eye on Mollie," Mitch says from the doorway. "Don't let her walk in the road."

"Okay, okay. I got it." Within a minute the leash is on, and Sunny and the kids are out the door.

Mitch looks at Kate and shakes his head. "I hope you know what you're doing."

"So do I."

Chapter 31

She pulls the chain to the living room ceiling fan. As it begins to circle, a huge horsefly zips off a blade. It buzzes around Kate's head. She bats it away, then turns to the dining room. The fly zooms back at her. She waves her hands in front of her face, irritated. The fly persists, darting at her first from the front, then the back, then the side. Coming from every direction. She flails her arms, spins around, trying to escape the pest. The fly's persistence fills her with cold fear.

"Get away," she screams. "Goddamn you!" The fly dive-bombs her. She tries to block it, but it's too fast. It makes a beeline for her neck, striking with a bite at the base of her throat. She wakes with a jolt. Even as her eyes open, she feels heat emanating from her neck, spreading down through her shoulders like an injection of fast-killing poison.

Just a dream, she tells herself, trying to calm her quaking limbs. She still feels the heat moving through her arms, her chest. She sits up and rubs the feeling away.

"What is it now?" Mitch groans next to her.

"I had a bad dream." Kate's voice shakes.

He doesn't answer. He's already fallen back asleep. She lies against her pillow, eyes wide open, heart pounding.

She looks at the door. It's where it should be. It was just a dream. But it's more than a dream. It's another version of the presence haunting her nights. The presence hasn't been back since the night she asked God for another way. The very next day Dr. Galen had pushed her, frightened her into agreeing to meet with him alone. Ever since, a war's been raging in her. Tomorrow she has her first meeting with him. Before going to bed she decided, once and for all, to cancel. She doesn't need help. She's not a weakling. She isn't going crazy. And she can't stand that arrogant pug. She can handle this on her own.

She wonders if the dream's a message. Maybe she's making the wrong choice. "Lord of the Flies" is one of Satan's aliases. She discards the idea as ridiculous, even as the goddess whispers yet again: Just go talk to him. The thought of meeting with Dr. Galen nauseates her. The thought of being stalked by evil turns her blood to ice.

She'll keep the appointment then, but he'll have to allow her to interview him before she commits herself any further. What if he's not a Christian? What if he is? What if he's one of those fundamentalists, spewing hell and damnation? She can't talk to someone like that about Michael. What if he doesn't believe in God at all? She has to know his spiritual beliefs. Even as she's working out the questions she'll ask, she knows he won't let her interview him.

How can he expect her to trust him if she doesn't know him, doesn't know the foundation of his being? Maybe he's cheating on his wife while he's sagely doling out advice to struggling married couples. What if he hurts her, leads her away from the answer, leads her astray, down the wrong path, an even darker path?

Just trust, the goddess whispers. God can work with broken tools.

She closes her eyes, breathes in, filling her lungs to

capacity, holds the air a moment before exhaling, feels her heart slow, wills herself to relax. Walk with me, Lord, she prays. Let me figure it out quickly. Bless this man. Help him help me.

Chapter 32

r. Galen walks behind her from the waiting room
to his office. She feels his eyes on her back, making her gait
stiff and unnatural. She eases into the loveseat and stares out
the narrow window overlooking an alley. He sits at his desk,
shuffles some papers, and swings around to face her, pulling
a clipboard onto his lap, pen in hand—nothing between them
but empty space. She read once "empty space" is an oxymo-
ron. Space is never empty. The air is filled with electromag-
netic fields made up of various wavelengths—light waves,
acoustic waves, hydraulic waves, radio waves—sending
signals. Animals sense many of these better than humans.
She wishes she had the innate neural property detectors of
a cat or a dog, allowing her to know by his smell or body
movements what's in his mind.

His expression is tentative, like a horse trainer approaching an unbroken, skittish filly. She wonders if the shadow-
smile playing on his lips is confidence or uncertainty. He's
got her cornered, but he's standing back. Good horse trainers
don't break the animal's spirit, her sister says. They gentle it
into submission. She's never thought of Dr. Galen as gentle.
Yet he has the same look Lily wears as she reaches out to
touch a wild horse capable of killing with one kick a man

twice her size—the same promise in her eyes: Steady. I won't hurt you, girl. Steady.

"So, what do you want to talk about?" His tone is cheerful. She's the filly now, pulling away, shrinking into the corner of the couch, wanting to trust but not trusting. She lifts her chin to meet his eyes.

"I don't want to talk about anything. This was your idea. You're the psychologist. Don't you have a plan?"

He glances at his blank clipboard, then looks up, his expression mischievous. "This is your time, Kate. You're in charge here. Tell me what's on your mind."

She shrugs. He's patronizing her. Empowering her. Psychology 101. She knows she has to play the game, although she's already impatient with it. She expected him to at least start off with some leading questions, suggesting direction, a rough road map for this internal journey he's forcing her to begin.

"I don't want to be here."

"I know," he whispers. She examines her hands, hoping he'll speak again. He twists in his seat, hitching one leg over the arm of his chair, looking like a college student hanging out with friends, casual despite his camel pants, herringbone blazer and tie.

"I suppose we could talk about Josh."

"Why don't we talk about you?"

Josh is easier. Just this morning he went into a rage when she asked him to make his bed. Pulled off the spread and sheets and threw them at her. That would be too easy. But starting out with evil—that's too hard. She doesn't want to be committed before the end of the first session. She chooses Josh. Spills out the long history of conflict that seemed to begin at his birth. All the visits to the pediatrician. All the fights. She watches the psychologist's eyes glaze over as the minutes steal by.

"Anyway," she says, finally pausing to catch her breath, "I think I'm overinvested in Josh."

Dr. Galen's sigh tells her he's disappointed. "What makes you say that?" His voice is flat.

"You know Josh plays the piano."

"Yes."

"He took up the cello for a while as well. He was good from the start. Not as good as on the piano. There he clearly has some innate ability. But his cello teacher kept telling me he was a natural. He really liked the cello, but he quit and it's my fault."

"How?"

"About a year ago, he was practicing one night. He'd only had a few months of lessons. I'd sat through the lessons, listening to the teacher, watching Josh. I've never played a cello. But that night I stood over him, correcting his every move, commenting on each note as he played it, as if I were an expert. Finally I grabbed the cello, saying 'Oh for heaven's sake give it to me.' And I actually sat down and tried to play his lesson. Of course I was terrible, but I did manage to get out a few notes, the whole time telling him how he should hold the neck, guide the bow.

"When I handed him back the bow he threw it down so hard it snapped in two. He said he hated me and he hated the cello and he was never playing again. Then he stormed off to his room. Thank God I didn't follow him. I thought about it. Instead, I went to my room, closed the door and sat on the bed. I was horrified. I thought, What the hell am I doing? I'd become the overbearing parent I swore I'd never be. I kept repeating over and over, 'What am I doing? Why am I doing this?'"

Dr. Galen leans forward. While Kate was talking he slowly inched his chair near her. Now he is a yard away, his eyes bright with interest.

"The second question is the important one. Why were you doing it?"

Her eyes falter under his stare. She looks at the bookcase beside his desk. "I don't know," she says, her mind riffling through the possibilities she's already pondered. "I don't under—" Her mind stops, hit by a new idea that's sprung up like a jack-in-the-box, causing her to jump, then slump internally as she examines its ugly face. Her heart cracks. "I see," she says, her voice unanimated. From the corner of her eye, she glimpses Dr. Galen jerk his head, beckoning. He wants her to look at him, but she stares at the wall. They sit in stony silence.

"What?" he whispers. "What do you see?"

She drags her eyes over him then returns to glaring at the wall. "Isn't it enough I see it?" she moans, unable to keep the contempt—or is it bitterness?—out of her voice. "Why do I have to tell you?"

"So I can decide if I'm on the right track." The gentleness in his voice pulls her gaze back. He smiles the way Lily does when she's just eased the halter over the horse's nose and ears and is stroking its long cheekbone. "What do you see, Kate?"

She cringes at the thought of revealing the new truth she's stumbled on. But the impulse to confess is strong.

"Suppose I was at one of Josh's piano recitals," she begins. "No, that isn't right. I was at one of his recitals." Dr. Galen's smile broadens. "Last year. Josh was going to play an advanced version of Beethoven's "Fleur de Lis." I remember when he walked on stage, I began to shake. My stomach was doing handsprings. Heart pounding. It was as if I was the one performing." She shakes her head, losing herself in the past. "I remember looking at my hands trembling in my lap and thinking, There's something wrong with this picture. But I couldn't see it."

"See what?"

"You know what." She frowns, then shrugs sheepishly under his twinkling eyes. "It was as if I was living life through him. I defined myself through his accomplishments and failures. God how awful for him, transferring my adult perfectionism on him."

Dr. Galen looks like a boy whose best buddy just walked in. Kate folds her arms tight across her chest, steeling herself.

"It's a lot to put on a kid," he says. She shies then realizes his words don't hurt. The light, matter-of-fact tone of his voice kisses rather than accuses. She rubs her upper arms and drops her hands loosely into her lap.

"Kate."

She watches her hands massage each another.

"Kate, look at me." She drags her eyes up. "You didn't cause Josh's problems. Yes, you may have become overly invested in his life for a time. Can't tell you how common that is. Most parents don't figure it out. Most kids live through it. You made a typical parenting mistake. It may have exacerbated Josh's problems, but it didn't cause them. You've got to understand that. It's not your fault."

She looks away, speechless. She doesn't believe him. She's messed Josh up. The most important job she'll ever have, the most sacred job, shepherding a child to adulthood, and she's messed it up, creating a child so full of anger and hate that at times it freezes her heart to look into his eyes. It terrifies her, the mess she's made, the mistakes, her own anger, born of impatience and frustration, her inability to love Josh as she feels she should. She imagines standing before God as He shakes His head in disappointment. I gave you this soul, He is saying. I entrusted you with this life.

"Kate?" Dr. Galen's voice jolts her back to his office. "What's the answer?"

"I guess I've got to start living my own life."

"Exactly."

"But I'm stuck."

"How so?"

"I've been stuck since the suicide. That day, I was running, running, with everything important held tight in one hand—like a set of keys—and a cell phone in the other. When I looked through the window and saw Michael, it was as if someone swung a two-by-four full force, hitting me in the chest. The impact made me drop everything.

"But when I dropped everything, it wasn't like a set of keys you could stoop down and scoop out of the dirt; it was more like helium balloons. Everything I was holding onto floated away."

"Maybe you were holding onto the wrong things."

She ponders this idea, then nods. "A major reconstruction project is going on inside me, but I don't know what's being built."

"I understand."

"Mitch and I had a fight recently, and he said in an ugly way that he wished I'd go back to Dr. Emmett, that maybe he could help me get back to where I was before the suicide."

Dr. Galen rolls his eyes with a grimace.

"It's okay. I know what he meant. I haven't been myself, and I've taken a lot of it out on him. But when he said that, I realized something."

"What?"

"I realized I'm never going to be where I used to be. I'm never going to get 'back to normal' as Mitch put it. This reconstruction project is building toward something completely different. But I don't know what. It's pushing me in a new direction, down a new path. But I can't see where it leads. I only know ..." Kate wants to be honest but is afraid Dr. Galen will misunderstand.

"What do you know, Kate?" He is staring at her in consternation.

"I know God is very close to me right now. That he is part of this reconstruction project."

"Is that why God put Michael in the garage?"

The statement shocks her. "God didn't put Michael in the garage," she says hotly. "Michael put himself in the garage."

"Good for you."

Her indignation sweeps his comment aside. "God doesn't have anything to do with death or destruction. He's not a master puppeteer pulling our strings or dictating the events in our lives. He doesn't look down on us like an oversized chess master and say, 'Oh, pawn Suzie needs a lesson in loss, guess I'll kill her baby in a car accident.' I hate it when there's a tragedy and people say, 'It was God's will.' God wills only good."

"I was just checking."

"This is the problem," she says, trying to steady her voice. "The minute you say the word 'God,' there's misunderstanding, because we each have our own unique vision of the being that word represents."

"Very true."

"What I mean by God is the compassionate, creative force within me, and within you, and in this room right now, all around us." Dr. Galen straightens in his chair, as if surprised. "God gave us the gift of life, but He also gave us free will. He doesn't manage events or us. Life simply is. I do believe, however, if we walk with God, we can find good even in the worst situations or events."

"And you want to find the good lurking in Michael's death?"

"I'm not saying Michael's suicide was good. Obviously, it was tragic. And he was in great despair. I know that. I can't change the course of his life. But his death has become a part of my life and it can have either a positive or negative impact depending on how I view it. With God's help, I can use it to good, perhaps to change the course of my life for the better. And if I do that, not only will Michael have given me a gift, but I will give him a gift as well."

Dr. Galen gazes at his clipboard. She watches his thumb as it flicks the bottom corners of the papers. She wonders what he's thinking, what he must think of her. He looks up.

"So, Michael's suicide is making you take stock." She nods. "You've already figured out you need to lighten up with Josh and start living your own life, the life you're called to live."

"I don't know if I'm called to live a specific life."

"We're all born with certain callings. Maybe you call them gifts. And it's our duty to discover and pursue them. Often we get lost on the way, living other people's lives instead of our own, following other people's dreams. All the while, the life we are meant to live is calling us. A person can't find fulfillment until he or she acknowledges that call and follows it."

"I can't imagine what life is calling me to."

"Can't you?"

She shakes her head.

"Well," his eyes crinkle merrily, "of course you must know you're an artist."

She jerks back in her seat as if stung by a horsewhip. "I've never thought of myself as an artist." Why is she angry? "No one has ever applied that word to me. Certainly I haven't."

"Well, you are."

"What makes you say that?" she snaps.

"A lot of things. The way you express yourself, the way you interpret life. But also plain old intuition. I'm a very good judge of people. It's one of my gifts." Dr. Galen shrugs boyishly.

"Really," she draws the word out to emphasize her skepticism even as she fights her urge to return his smile.

"So," he continues, his voice again jovial, "what's your fantasy?"

The question slams Kate like a Mack truck. Images of Nick leap to mind. Intimate images, his lips brushing hers, his hand on her thigh. Heat rises with the images, as does a spine-tingling alarm—longing mixed with shame. She glares at the wall.

"I don't care to share my fantasies with you," she says. But even as she speaks, a softer voice chants within her: I want to write, it whispers. I want to write, I want to write, I want to write.

The mantra shocks her. She examines this unexpected yet persistent declaration escaping from a locked trunk in the sea of her being—this childhood dream, dismissed long ago as impossible, impractical, hopeless. The mantra fights through her fear, like a woman who's fallen through the frozen crust of a winter lake, flailing toward the light, toward life-giving air. Her mantra is overwhelmingly desperate, like the search for an opening, hands pounding the underbelly of thick ice, eyes blinded by frigid water that flows into screams.

She has no idea why she's so afraid.

"Why won't you tell me your fantasy?" Dr. Galen sounds far away, as if he's talking through a bad telephone connection.

Tell him, the goddess says. It's so easy. Just say it. Say, "I want to write." Kate feels the words rise in her, feels them breaking through her fear.

"Are you afraid you'll sound silly?" he asks as she opens her mouth.

Yes! It *is* silly. It's stupid. You a writer? The next Tolstoy? Yeah, right. She snaps her mouth shut.

"Are you afraid it's too late?"

It is too late. Your life's half over. Your youth gone. That's when you should have done it. You're too old now.

Dr. Galen leans into her, but Kate continues to glare at the wall, focusing on the battle within her.

"Are you afraid your dream is dead?"

It is dead. Dead, dead, dead!

Tell him, Kate.

Don't make a fool of yourself.

It's easy. Just say it.

He'll laugh. Not now, but later, when he's writing up his notes. He already thinks you're an idiot. Of course he's not going to tell you that, just like he won't tell you how stupid this writing idea is. It's his job to make you feel good. Humor you. Encourage you. I wonder how many sorry-assed wannabe artists he's listened to over the years.

Say it. Just say it.

Silence fills the office. She hears her teeth grind. Her jaw hurts.

"It's too soon, that's all," Dr. Galen says with a note of self-assurance that grates on her. "You'll tell me. When it's time."

She turns to him. He's staring at her, brows furrowed, as if he's trying to decode hieroglyphics. Hatred wells within her. She'll die before she tells him. She looks at the clock on his desk.

"I've got to pick up Mollie."

He doesn't move. Just stares. She feels like a child waiting to be dismissed, disgusted with herself for waiting.

He leans back in his chair and smiles smugly. "I'll see you, then, in two weeks?" He writes the date on an appointment card, stands and holds it out to her. She rises and reaches for the card. He doesn't let go. She hesitates, looking at the card, her fingertips on one end, his on the other. She could let go, give up the whole thing. It's a mistake. Then she hears the goddess again. Take the card, silly.

Kate looks up. Sees the challenge in Dr. Galen's eyes.

"Two weeks," she says, yanking the card from his fingers and brushing past him. She doesn't intend to come back.

Chapter

If you look at the sand, you'll miss the shimmer of sea meeting sunrise, the ripple of a dolphin fin, the flight of a pelican. Kate raises her eyes to scan the ocean, dark as night sky, its whitecaps like stars. On the horizon, banks of clouds, fluffed like pulled cotton, herald the sun's approach with their burnt orange coronas. Wind from the cold front whips through her sweater. There is no right way to walk the beach, she tells herself as she doubles her pace, hoping for warmth. If you look at the waves, you'll miss the unspoiled shell or, perhaps, a sand dollar fully intact, surviving the surf.

Why does this voice constantly pester her? She hugs herself, bracing against the biting wind and resumes studying the wet sand in front of her feet.

She hates the pressure of this voice. Whatever she does, it questions, corrects, doubts. The critical parent, Jean calls it. The other voice, the one Kate calls the goddess, Jean says isn't a goddess at all, though she loves the image. It's from you, she says, from the unspoilt child. By unspoilt she means unsullied, pure—pure joy, pure innocence, pure awe. Irrepressible exuberance, giggling over mistakes. A child doesn't worry about looking at the beach for shells, fearing she'll miss a dolphin. She's too fully in the moment for such concerns. If a shout rings out and fingers point, she'll raise her gaze and find the ripples marking the dolphin's submergence into the sea, and she'll wait, skipping her eyes forward of the spot, never doubting she'll see the magical creature, and then—she does! The glistening gray skin, the characteristic arc of its play. She will be as lost in that moment as she was in the moment before, hunting for the ideal shell.

Kate spots a glimmer of brown ending in a point. An offering, but is it for her? She won't touch it until she's sure. She stops and squats, examines it closely, brushes wet sand away from its edges, her fingers aching with cold. It's a baby lightning whelk, tan with copper lines edging its spirals. The colors are vivid. She can see its lip, smooth from the life it held. She recognizes it—the gift she asked for at the beginning of the walk. She picks it up, runs her thumb over the tiny teeth at the end of its spirals, slides her forefinger in its mother-of-pearl mouth. She slips the shell in her pocket and continues, her eyes on the sand at the edge of the surf.

A few feet ahead runs a sandpiper, his head, back and wings gray, his chest and belly white. He's a tiny fellow no more than six inches in height, flittering on short legs, stopping abruptly to peck the sand, then back to a flickering run. He follows the surf, running after its ebb, then, with a sixth sense, turning at the last second and scampering ahead of its flow. If she gets too close, the bird flutter-hops a few feet down the beach and resumes his game of wave tag and pick and peck. He's been with her since she started the walk a mile back, an entertaining companion.

She hears it rising within her as she studies the sand, the goddess' mantra: I want to write. She knows she must heed this, which means looking first at the fear wrapped around it. The fear is thick and rank, like a putrid onion. She pulls off one translucent layer at a time, holds it up to the light to examine it like a scientist analyzing a specimen. You're no good. That's the first layer. You're not good enough to be a writer. When did she come to believe this?

From her first memories she had two fervent desires: have children and write. She remembers when her sister Lily first came home from the hospital as a newborn. Kate was six and she fell instantly in love with this tiny, helpless being, whose large eyes were filled with calm questioning. Lily had been a sweet baby. She rarely cried but rather gurgled and smiled and laughed from the beginning. Kate knows this can't be true, yet that's how she remembers it. And she remembers Lily, at a very young age, reaching to her for comfort. She remembers the first time her mother allowed her to feed Lily a bottle, how Lily sucked it down with voracious passion, her eyes on Kate's face.

Her second love flamed every time she took pencil in hand. She wrote before she knew letters. Scribbling across the page, she spoke out her story while her mother washed dishes. See my story? she'd say when her mother turned from the sink. Her mom would beam at the paper and say, It's a great beginning to your novel, lovey. Keep working on it. I can't wait to hear the next installment. Her mom's words thrilled her, even though she had no idea what an installment was. Then her father would glare over her mother's shoulder at the paper in her hand. What the hell you talking about? That's nothing but scribble scrabble.

Writing a novel became her dream. She remembers as a teenager sprawling in front of the living room fire, writing a short story fast and confidently, not sure yet of its path or purpose, imagining herself the next Mark Twain or Jane Austen. When did fear consume the dream?

The roar of a large breaker startles the sandpiper into flight. He glides up the beach, landing a good distance away. Beyond him a woman walks. Another soul braving the cold. She stops, bends, excavates something, stands and examines it, then tosses it down and walks on. Kate freezes her eyes on the spot the discarded item hit as she moves up the beach. She finds the treasure. A pumpkin-and-white Florida cone. The waves have worn a window in its side, revealing the creamy inner spiral. She puts it in her pocket where it clinks against the lightning whelk.

She remembers her first crush, Mr. Clark, her twelfth-grade English teacher. She was his pet until she gave up editorship of the newspaper he oversaw in favor of writing for the school's literary journal sponsored by his nemesis, Ms. Cray, who taught advanced placement English. You'll never be a writer, he said when she quit, his face contorted with disappointment. You don't have what it takes. At the time she thought only her heart broke. Now she wonders if something else broke with it.

She walks on more swiftly now, still scanning the sand even though she knows the sea's already given her a trove. The wind is raw and salty, stinging the back of her throat and tearing her eyes.

Did the dream die with Mr. Clark? Or in college, when her dad said he'd stop helping with tuition if Kate majored in creative writing and English literature. What are you going to do to make a living? he had said. You need to be practical. You're not Hemingway and I'm sure as hell not supporting you while you play at being him. Kate majored in government and, instead of creative writing, studied journalism.

She shakes her head. She can't blame her father. And she can't blame her teachers. These were her choices. She could have shrugged off Mr. Clark. She could have doubled her student loans. Instead, she bought into doubt. Caved into fear. She retreated—and she's been retreating ever since. Writing speeches for Mimms. Writing the minutes for the PTA. Writing newsletters for church. Clear, forceful, at times lyrical writing. Writing that got a good man elected to office. Writing that inspired a half-million-dollar gift to the church. Writing that was always someone else's voice.

Her sandpiper is back, following the sweeping foam S's edging the waves' wash. She looks at her watch and starts to turn back when her eyes catch a bit of something, white and cylindrical. When she squats to examine it, she sees the pockmarks. It's a finger of coral, a rare find. She grins as she picks it up, imagining its home reef and the abundant life it once supported.

"Kate!" someone yells from a distance.

She stands and scans the beach in surprise. Up ahead a man is surf fishing. He's seated between two rods resting in tubes planted in the sand. The rods vibrate in the wind as they bend into the surf. She can't see the lines she knows are there, straining against restraint, running out over the water and eventually disappearing into the sea. Behind the rods, a red pickup is parked on packed sand.

"It that you?"

She recognizes Nick's voice, though his face is a blur through her wind-whipped tears. As she rushes forward, he rises from his small canvas camp chair.

"Kate, I thought it was you." He walks to her and pulls her into a hug, briefly shielding her from the wind, then holds her from him at arm's length, his hands still resting on her shoulders. "What are you doing out so early? Thought only crazy fishermen got up before six on a Saturday."

"I come here every once in a while. When I want to be alone and think, or not think."

"I've intruded?"

"No, don't be silly."

"Good, because I don't plan to let you go before sharing a bit of coffee with you." He unfolds a second camp chair and pushes it into the sand next to his. A plastic cup with steam rising from it sits on a small foldout table in front of the chairs. "Please sit." He gestures to the chairs and fetches a tall thermos leaning against a small red cooler. He fishes through his knapsack, eventually producing a second plastic cup.

"Looks as if you were expecting me." She bites her tongue as heat sweeps across her face.

"I always bring extra. Can't tell when I might meet another fisherman," he pauses to pour the coffee, "or an attractive woman sorting through sand."

Her face is hot now, despite the wind. "I love the beach this time of day." She speaks too fast, pointing her face away from him, toward the sea. "The water's dazzling, and there aren't many people out."

"Yes." He hands her a steaming cup and sits across from her. "My best sermons come here, when I'm baiting a hook or waiting for a bite while watching the best fishers in the world practice their craft."

She looks at him, puzzled.

"The shorebirds," he says. "Gulls, terns, sandpipers. They use different techniques but they're all extremely proficient. When I arrived this morning a tern had just caught a small fish, the kind I use for bait. The fish was still alive, wriggling in the bird's beak, its scales glinting in the predawn light. I stopped and watched, wondering how this bird would eat this fish twice the size of its head. She flipped the fish this way and that and in an instant sliced it neatly down the center, laid it out before her like a picnic blanket and started pecking away at the soft flesh."

"How sad."

"Actually, it was extraordinary. I envied the quick precision with which she filleted that fish. And the minute she did, it was no longer a fish, but ... well, a square meal." His laughter is infectious, pulling Kate in.

"You make it sound as if no one died in all this."

"Perhaps no one ..." he leans forward with a teasing grin, "or no thing, did."

Kate pulls away from his intense eyes. She could get lost in those brilliant blues. The thought sends a shiver through her. She scans the waves as she sips her coffee. The liquid scalds her throat and lands like a fireball in her empty stomach.

"Hey!" She coughs. "What's in this?"

"This is true Irish coffee." He gives her two playful thumps on the back as she coughs to clear her throat. "Not that sweet liqueur and whipped cream stuff you get at a bar, but the coffee my dad used to drink to keep a fire in him all those mornings his fingers were so stiff from cold and arthritis he could barely bait a hook. Good Irish whiskey."

"How much of this do you drink in a morning?"

"One healthy mug is all I allow myself, unless it's unusually cold." His eyes sparkle with mischief. "So I was watching the sandpipers poking around for breakfast and they brought me to you. What were you poking around for?"

"Treasures."

She empties her pocket, gently dropping its contents on the camp table. She nudges the shells and the lone piece of coral away from each other. Nick picks up the whelk and examines it.

"It's dumb, really," she says, "calling these treasures."

"Why dumb?" He gazes at her intently as his fingers trace along the curves of the whelk.

"Naw. You don't want to know how weird I am."

"I'm a priest. Hearing confessions is my business. The weird ones are my favorite. They reassure me. Make me realize how much we all have in common."

She can't help smiling. "Well," she says, resignation in her voice, "whenever I go for a walk on the beach, I say to the sea, 'What gift will you give me today?' And then I look. Usually it's a shell. But sometimes it's a glimpse of a dolphin or the play of a sandpiper in the surf. Once I saw stingrays mating in the shallows this side of a sandbar. But usually it's shells. I have a glass jar I put them in, actually more than one. Mitch says I'm obsessed. It was a game I used to play with my mom when I was a kid. When I do it now, I feel like she's with me.

"This one," Kate picks up the cone, "a lady walking ahead of me picked up and threw back down, I guess because it's broken. I have a kind of strange superstition. Taking up an offering from the sea and then throwing it back is a sin. An affront to the sea's generosity. I've believed that since I was a child. That's why I have a bottle or vase of shells in practically every room. Probably Mitch is right. I'm obsessive-compulsive." She gives a tight laugh that dies under Nick's unsmiling gaze.

He takes the broken cone from her and examines it closely. He puts his finger through the window and strokes the pearl spiral she knows is there. "And that's why you have this one. Because the other lady threw it down."

"Yeah."

"Because it was broken." Kate nods. "Interesting, isn't it?" he continues. "Its very brokenness is what allows us to see the brilliance inside."

Kate's mind slows down. "I like that," she says, wanting to ponder this notion. "It sounds like something my mother would have said."

"And what gifts do you give the sea?"

The question surprises her. "God—umm gosh," she fumbles, as her brain switches gears. "I never thought about that. What can I give the sea? I mean, I pick up trash when I see it."

"I'm not talking save the Earth."

"I don't know. I'm not sure I know what you mean. Does the sea have desires?"

"You tell me. You believe the sea has a soul, how else could you talk to her? How could she give to you?"

"I love the ocean."

"No greater gift than that."

"But really, asking for treasures, it's just a game, a silly ritual, that's all." She regrets she's confided in Nick. He must think she's nuts.

"No it's not," he says gently but firmly. "The sea's your friend. You have kindred spirits. Wild. Free. Dictated to by no one. Not hemmed in by man's little ideas, his partial views, his petty dogmas."

He gazes out at the water. "The sea is strong, even violent at times. But also vital, life-giving and sustaining, like a woman. Like you."

She looks down at her hands nested in her lap. A heat is spreading through her center, making the deepest part of her tingle annoyingly with anticipation—or is it fear? Nick gently touches her knee with his hand.

"I'm sorry," he says. "I've embarrassed you."

"No," she croaks. She's afraid to look up. Afraid what he'll see in her face.

"I'm sorry I've made you uncomfortable. But so often we fail to say the truth to others—the good truth, the kind that builds, that brings a glow, or," he hesitates, "maybe even a blush." Kate fights the happiness rising within her. She pulls her mouth into a tense line ending halfway between a frown and a smirk. "But it's important we do," he continues softly. "Important we risk it. As my father would say, you're a bonny lass, Kate, and I don't just mean physically, though certainly that's true. You have a gentle yet strong spirit, a wise, loving soul under all that doubting intellect."

She continues to stare at her hands, speechless. Afraid to move.

"Come on, drink your coffee." He jostles her knee play-fully. "You're the ugliest, orneriest person I've every met. Does that make you feel better?"

She laughs in spite of herself.

"That's better."

"You wouldn't think I was so great—so gentle, did you say?—if you saw me during a fight with my son."

"Ah, the teen years. I'm sure you're the only one who's had words with a wayward boy."

Not just words, she longs to say. But what would he think if he knew the truth?

"Or is it more than words, Kate?" She feels as if cold water's been thrown in her face. He seems to read her mind. She turns to the sea. Her hands shake as she brings her mug to her lips.

"You're cold." He rises and walks to his truck. "Unusual to have a cold front this late in spring," he calls over his shoulder. She hears him open a door and slam it shut. Then he's back, draping a wool blanket over the back of her head and shoulders. He circles in front of her and tucks the blanket around her arms and over her lap. "There, how's that?"

"Grand." Her eyes meet his, then flicker away. She's the sandpiper, his eyes the waves. She's afraid of their touch. Afraid of herself. He settles back into his chair, sips his coffee.

"Josh is very angry, Kate. I've felt it when we've talked at church. Nothing overt," he adds quickly in answer to her concerned expression, "but an energy he exudes. He's angry and filled with … I don't know exactly, a sense of hopelessness? You didn't put that there. I know that. I also know a teen doesn't often know how to deal with such intense emotions and can at times explode in violence."

She fingers the treasures on the table, not sure what to say, wanting to wrap herself in his warm, reassuring voice. Wanting to believe she isn't to blame.

"It's not your fault, Kate."

She jerks her head up to meet his eyes. "Why did you say that?" He shrugs. "It's as if you can read my mind. It makes me feel … strange, uncomfortable. I mean, it kind of scares me. As if you can see inside me."

"Sometimes I feel I can." He looks across the water.

A silence stretches between them, filled by the wind

and the surf. "Now I'll make a confession to you," he says, turning to face her again. "I meditate daily."

She nods, unsure why he labels this trivial habit a confession.

"I've been meditating for years. When I do, I silence my mind and wait. Sometimes, when I'm still enough, when I've managed to really silence all those voices within me, I enter into this empty white space. Things and people cross through this space. Sometimes I interact with them; sometimes something just comes to me about them, not a voice from heaven per se—though I do think God has a hand in it—but a knowing. I can't explain it and it's a lot weirder than believing the sea gives you gifts.

"I rarely share with anyone these meditations or the process or what comes to me through them—not even with Carol. Like you with your gifts from the sea, I guess I'm afraid people will call me daft. But I try to act on them if they seem to suggest some action. Though often when I have such encounters, I'm at a complete loss, can't for the life of me discern the meaning. When that happens, I call up to God, somewhat irritated I must admit, saying, 'Okay, thanks. Another divine vision undevined.'" The word play elicits a wan smile from Kate. He turns his gaze back to the water. Again, they sit in silence. She hears a gull's cry over the surf, turns her head to find it diving into the waves.

"The truth is, Kate, you've been coming up in my meditations quite often the past few months. Actually, even longer. Before the suicide. And there's been a lot of negative energy associated with you. Not coming from you, but surrounding you, dragging on you." He's looking at her now, his eyes wary, unsure, giving him the air of a schoolboy.

"I've been having a hard time with Josh," she mumbles.

"Yeah, I know. Don't ask," he says in answer to her questioning expression. "Truth is, earlier I, how should I say it? I prevaricated a bit when I said I felt Josh's anger through our meetings at church."

"You mean you lied?" she says, trying to lighten the air between them.

"I'd prefer not to put it so bluntly." He grins. "But if you insist, yes, I lied. Truth is," his smile vanishes as his brow furrows, "Josh has been showing up in my meditations as well. I've even talked with him a number of times there, in that white space. He's full of fear, Kate. That's why he closes all the blinds in the house each day when he comes home from school."

"How could you possibly know—"

He holds up his hand and shakes his head. "I can't explain it. I do know sometimes this fear is so strong, it's like adrenaline flowing full force through a faucet, and he can't turn it off. It comes out as anger. Violent anger. He's a good kid, Kate. Really smart and very deep. But this fear, it takes over. Consumes him."

"He's hurt Reyna ... and me." She kicks sand with her foot, again and again, the toe of her sneaker digging a small hole. She watches the sand spray out before her, forming a miniature bulwark.

"I know."

"We're seeing a counselor."

"Good. Josh needs professional help." She feels the warm touch of Nick's hand on her chin. "Look at me Kate." She doesn't resist as he tilts her head back, but she refuses to raise her eyes. "Kate, look at me."

She feels ravished, as if he has broken through the door guarding her inner self, the one holding all the fears, doubts, superstitions and accusations. She fears he has glimpsed her soul as well as Josh's, must know of the hatred she has felt at times, of her own anger that has boiled out of control into violence. She wants to run from his visions of her. She hates herself, hates what he must see.

"Kate, please."

Her heart heavy with dread, she raises her eyes.

"Something else has come to me during my meditations."

She presses her lips together but can't stop their trembling.

"God wants you to know something."

"What?"

"God wants you to know you're perfect, just the way you are."

"Right," her voice cracks with bitterness. She turns, faces the beach, her back to Nick. "I'm perfect."

"Do you think God judges the sea when it's whipped into a fury by a hurricane and its waves crash upon the coast, sucking away sand dunes and beach cottages, even the town pier?"

"No, of course not. The sea's not human; it doesn't reason, doesn't have a ..."

"A soul? Neither of us believes that. The sea was created by God, just as you were. It's part of God, just as you are. You don't believe God judges the sea in all its various tempers, then why do you fear He judges you?"

Kate can't answer. She's never thought to make such a comparison.

"There's majesty in a storm, Kate. A perfect grandeur."

"Nothing's perfect. Certainly I'm not."

"To God you're perfect." She feels Nick's hand on her arm, pulling her back to face him. "You're one of His—excuse me, Her pieces of art. You're like this cone shell." He picks it up and places it in her hand, his fingers feathering hers. "Maybe a bit chipped here and there, but that only reveals the miracle, the flawless spiral within."

She looks at the shell in her palm, supported by Nick's long, rugged fingers.

"There's something else," he says.

"What?"

"A message. Two actually." His fingers tighten around her hand.

"Yes?"

"Follow her call."

Her fingers clasp his as their eyes meet. "That's so weird," she whispers.

"Do you know what it means?"

"Maybe. Do you?"

"Haven't got a clue."

She stares down at their intertwined hands. "You said there were two messages."

"Yes."

"What's the other one?"

"Let go."

She looks up, surprised and confused. "Let go of what?"

"That's all I got, Kate. Just 'Let go.'"

Chapter 34

"I felt so weird," Kate says, as she digs a trench in her godmother's garden. "What am I doing walking around in this man's meditations?" She stops digging, sits back on her heels and looks at Jean.

"You feel weird because you're making it sexual," Jean says from the chaise, where she's cushioned by pillows and shaded by the maple. The white cotton kimono she's wearing highlights her tanned skin and her thinning curls. "It isn't sexual. I used to meditate, back in my younger days, and I have consulted mediums from time to time—not to be confused with fortune-tellers. You should try it. It can be very interesting if you find a good one. But back to Nick. He has a gift. He's in tune with God's energy. He doesn't choose what comes to him."

"Well, how does it work?" Kate notices the dark rings around Jean's eyes but pretends she doesn't. "Does God dictate Nick's meditations?"

Jean chuckles and takes a sip of ginger ale. "That's the God-as-string-puller construct. You've said it yourself. God isn't some anthropomorphic puppeteer. He is the creative, compassionate energy at the core of life and being, the tuning vibration of everything, living or inanimate. Nick is simply in harmony with that energy. When he meditates, he opens himself to it. How brave of him to share with you. Most people wouldn't. Too afraid of what people might say."

"He mentioned that." Kate taps the first batch of purslane out of its plastic pot, careful not to damage the stems or the multicolored blooms. "I don't get why he said I'm perfect. No one's perfect." The plant is pot-bound. She loosens the root ball, lodges it at the head of the trench, then gently kneads the soil around it.

"Perhaps you're thinking as a human."

"Well, I am a human." She pauses in her planting. "I'm pretty sure I don't know how to think like God."

"None of us do. But it's a worthy goal." Jean grabs a candy from the bowl on the table. "Want a peppermint?"

"No thanks. Do you miss smoking?"

"Actually, I don't. The second I saw my lung x-ray, my love affair with cigarettes died." She sucks on the mint with her head resting against her pillows. "Back to what we were talking about. What if God believes this about all creation? What if each of us, with our flaws and foibles, is perfect in God's sight?"

The idea brings a lightness to Kate, as if, like a snake, she's sloughed off the old, dead skin and is splendidly new. "I like that," she says. "It makes me able to embrace what Nick said without worrying about, I don't know, being prideful."

"Oh Kate," Jean snorts. "You don't have a proud bone in you—if you're talking of arrogance or conceit."

Kate gives Jean a noncommittal smile then picks up the next pot of purslane. She's never gardened, and when Jean asked her to do this small chore, she worried about the outcome. To her surprise, the repetitive motions of planting are soothing.

"That brings us to the 'follow her call' and 'let go' statements," Jean says.

"Well, obviously I need to let go of Josh. Of all my fears

for him. Also back off and let him walk his own path. That's
what Dr. Galen says. He says if Mitch and I keep rescuing
Josh from his mistakes and misperceptions, he won't learn to
rescue himself."

"Absolutely. I like this man. He's saying good things to
you. But this isn't about Josh. I mean it is—but it's not only
about Josh. What about this 'follow her call' statement?"

"It's odd. Nick said that to me right after my first meeting
alone with Dr. Galen."

"Yes?"

"At one point during that meeting, Dr. Galen said, 'So,
what's your fantasy?' Immediately I thought, well … you
know … about sex."

Jean lifts her head in laughter then reclines again.

"Well, 'fantasy' has a lot of sexual connotations." Kate
can't help grinning, despite her chagrin.

"True enough." Jean wipes her eyes.

"Actually, I thought about Nick and I felt so guilty."

"Oh Kate," Jean's voice sings with mirth, "do you think
you're a wanton woman?" Kate feels heat spread across her
face. "Did you think you'd never be attracted to other men
once you married Mitch?"

"No. But I've never felt this way about another man.
He's good-looking."

"So is Mitch; you just don't see it anymore."

Kate rubs the back of her gloved hand across her forehead before picking up the last of the purslane. "I know, but
I feel Nick and I are in tune. I can talk to him in a way I can't
with Mitch. It makes me dissatisfied with my marriage."

"He fills a need Mitch can't."

"Yeah."

"But you also have needs Mitch fills that Nick can't."

"Can't think of any." Kate hates the bitterness in her own
voice.

"Honey, Mitch loves you profoundly, and you love him.

I'm not talking about infatuation, but about committed love patiently built over years. You have an incredibly strong marriage. One built on mutual respect for each other's individuality and independence. I've watched you through the years treating each other as fully vested members of your partnership. The bond between you might get frayed by this period of searching and growth you're going through, but it won't break. Mitch isn't only your lover, Kate. He's your best friend. Who first comes to mind when something good happens or disaster strikes?"

The answer flashes. "Mitch."

"Exactly. You're attracted to Nick. That will pass. You also love him and that's okay. All love comes from God. But no one man or one person can fulfill all your needs. That's a fairy-tale idea. It's not fair to Mitch to expect him to be everything for you in every moment, just as it wouldn't be fair of him to expect that of you."

"I know." Kate gloomily tucks the last of the purslane into the earth.

"You've been married to Mitch sixteen years, long enough to see all the dents in his armor. Nick's the new knight on the horizon, and from a distance his armor shines. But if you traded Mitch in for him, you'd quickly find he has dents, too, just in different places. Any knight worth his salt does. You'd just be trading one set of dents for another. I'm not telling you it's always wrong to get divorced—obviously. But I know you and Mitch; I know how strong your love is. In the day-to-day rush and riot of your lives, it's easy to forget." Kate nods.

"I can tell by your face I'm lecturing." Jean chortles. "You look like a child caught stealing a cookie. Darlin', those fantasies you're having about Nick are normal, what society calls 'falling in love.' But it's not the mature, committed love Mitch and you share; it's infatuation. It will pass, and eventually you'll come to love Nick without any sexual tension."

"I hope it comes sooner than later."

"It will. Don't worry."

Kate sits back and examines the freshly planted flowers. "Should I water these?"

"Come sit for a minute."

Kate stands, perches on the end of the chaise and takes a sip from her water bottle. "You didn't finish about Dr. Galen," Jean says.

"Oh yeah. Where was I?"

"He asked you about your fantasies and Nick came to mind."

"Right. But even as I was visualizing Nick, this voice rose within me, the voice I call the goddess. And she was saying 'I want to write.'"

Jean draws a quick breath. "Oh," she whispers, "I've got goose bumps."

"It was so strong. So unequivocal. And it kept repeating over and over, 'I want to write.'"

"Tell me you're going to."

"I want to write fiction. I always have. But somehow a long time ago, I got sidetracked. Eventually, I discarded the idea as hopeless and silly. 'I'm not good enough.' 'Who am I kidding?' 'Get real.'"

"You caved to your critical voice."

"Thanks for putting it so tactfully. Anyway, this mantra was permeated with an overpowering fear. I've been looking at this fear, trying to figure out how to get past it."

"Any ideas?"

"Well, I told you when I was talking to Josh recently, I remembered the incident where Dad ripped up my poetry."

"Oh Kate, that was terrible of him."

"It's odd. I had forgotten about it until Josh asked how my parents disciplined me."

"That wasn't discipline."

"I know. But later, after Josh went to bed, I realized, in one of those awakening moments, that I never wrote another poem after Dad did that. I realized every time I thought of either writing or reading poetry over the years, something in my mind clamped shut like a trap and something in my heart froze."

"Oh Darlin' Heart."

"It's okay. Once I looked at it, the incident lost its power. Does that make sense?"

"Absolutely."

"I started reading poetry again. Then one day, on my way home from the store, a poem bubbled up in me. I pulled off the road and wrote bits of this and that on scrap paper. Jean, the poem is about you."

"Really!"

"I wrote it, played with it, then took it to a woman at the library who writes poetry—a real poet. She was so encouraging and graciously helped me shape and polish it into its current form. I brought the final version."

"Oh read it. Read it!"

"Just a minute." Kate stands, pulls off her gardening gloves and reaches into her jeans pocket. "It's titled 'Ancient Child.'" She resumes her seat. "It's my first poem, so be gentle."

"Read it!"

She scans the paper and hands it to Jean. "I don't trust myself. I'm afraid my voice will shake."

She watches Jean's face as her godmother reads.

"Oh Kate." Jean beams as she hugs the poem to her bosom.

"Do you like it?"

"Like it? I love it! I'm honored by it, by the grace it expresses. I love this line." She holds the poem in front of her. "'Delights in the puzzle, fitting a jig of mundane to a saw of eternity.' How did you come up with that?"

"It's one of the bits that came to me in the car."

"And this: 'I am converted to her soul's sparkling vision of me. Of God. One.' Kate, your mother would be so proud."

Kate shrugs sheepishly. "I know it's amateurish, but it's a beginning. To where, I don't know. But it feels right. One thing I've realized is I've told myself for years if I can't be perfect, if I can't be Emily Dickinson or the American Tolstoy right out of the gate, then what's the use? I have to get rid of this perfectionism."

"You're on the right track, Darlin'. I can feel it." She nudges Kate's leg with her foot, then reaches for another mint. "Have you read the *Bhagavad Gita*?" Kate shakes her head as her godmother pops the candy into her mouth. Jean savors the flavor as she tilts her head back and stares unseeing at the maple's green canopy.

"The *Gita* is India's most sacred scripture." The cheek where she's stowed the mint is plump as a chipmunk's. "It's a dialogue between a young warrior-prince named Arjuna and his mentor Shri Krishna, who's God incarnate. The Hindus believe God has come to us in human form many times. Krishna was one of these God-men, as was Christ. Actually, the Hindus would say Krishna and Christ are one and the same."

"Don't go saying that in the Catholic church down the street. You'll be burned as a heretic."

"Not just the Catholics. I'm sure all the Christian denominations would bar their doors for a number of reasons, should I ever try to enter."

"Isn't that how St. Thomas died? Wasn't he thrown in a pit and speared to death in India for claiming Jesus was the exclusive Son of God, the only—what did you call it?— 'God-man?' The Brahmins would have accepted his testimony if he'd been willing to concede Jesus wasn't the only incarnation of God."

"Interesting. At one point in the *Gita*, Krishna says whenever man gets lost, when spirituality molders and materialism runs riot, 'Oh Arjuna, I reincarnate myself.'"

"Cool."

"Let's not get lost in Christian and Hindu heresy. What I was getting at earlier is Krishna tells Arjuna each person has a duty. It sounds heavier than it is. By duty, Krishna means our God-given call. We all have certain God-given gifts or talents. It's our duty, or responsibility, to uncover these gifts and use them. So God calls us to action, but He also calls us to surrender those actions to Him."

"Meaning?"

"This is what Nick was telling you," she continues as if Kate hadn't spoken. "Follow her call—if we capitalize the 'h' in 'her'—becomes follow *Her* call—God's call. And 'let go,' might mean 'surrender.' According to the *Gita,* surrendering means devoting your actions to God, following His—or Her—call, but then leaving the outcome to God."

"So I need to write without worrying about whether it's perfect or whether I get published, become famous, make a million dollars and am still being read a hundred years from now?"

"Exactly."

"Do I have to let go of it all, even the million-dollar part?"

"Kate! Stop." She shoots Kate a mock frown. "Surrendering means letting go of all your concerns about the results of your actions, as long as you're following God's call. Let God play with the outcome. You just write. Just think. If you did that, what would happen to your fear?"

"There'd be nothing to fear."

"Precisely."

Kate pulls her gloves on and dusts dirt from her knees as

the significance of Jean's words unfolds. For the first time since her initial meeting with Dr. Galen, she feels the beginnings of joy rather than dread flutter her stomach when she thinks about writing.

"I'll be back in a minute. I want to read you something." Jean slowly slides from the chaise to a standing position, then pauses.

"You okay? Can I help?" Kate is instantly on her feet.

"No, I'm fine. Just a bit queasy. I need to get up once in a while and move around. Otherwise I'll go stir crazy." She walks gingerly to the house, massaging her abdomen with one hand as if each touch of sole to ground is a punch to her stomach. Kate fetches the hose and mists the purslane. The maple leaves chat in the soft breeze, which plays a tune on the chimes. She imagines writing without fear, without expectations.

"Here it is." Jean slides back onto the chaise with a small book in her hand. "And I brought this for you." She holds out a hand towel.

"What's that for?"

"The dirt. Every time you wiped sweat from your face you left a smear."

Kate drops the hose, takes off her gloves and grabs the towel. "You could have told me," she fusses as she wipes her face.

"I was having too much fun watching."

Kate playfully tosses the towel at Jean's head, pulls her gloves back on and takes up the hose. Jean snorts as she drops the towel on the ground next to the chaise. She settles against the pillows and flips through the book.

"This is my copy of the *Gita*. Now, let's see." She scans the pages. "Here. Listen to this: 'He who dedicates his actions to the Spirit, without any personal attachment to them, he is no more tainted by sin than the water lily is wetted by water ... Having abandoned the fruit of action, he wins eternal peace. Others unacquainted with spirituality, led by desire and clinging to the benefit which they think will follow their actions, become entangled by them.'

"You see?" She closes the book. "Follow the call, but let go of the results. Don't become entangled in questions like 'Will I get published?' or 'Is this any good?' Just write."

Kate considers the words as she waves the spray nozzle back and forth above the purslane.

"The *Gita* says something else I love." Jean flips through her book. "I can't find it just now, but Krishna says it's better to do your duty imperfectly than to do another's duty perfectly, that God can make imperfect action perfect. It's amazing how it all ties together, your meeting with Dr. Galen, then immediately stumbling upon Nick and his messages, so relevant to that meeting. You know Kate, I've got an idea Dr. Galen came into your life for you rather than Josh."

Kate stops watering.

"What does Dr. Galen say about your desire to write?"

"I haven't told him."

"What! Why?"

"I don't know. I feel like I'm in a battle of wills with him and I don't want him to win. I didn't tell him at the first meeting because I had to look at the fear. And I felt angry with him. And then he said in his smug little way I'd tell him when the time was right. I decided then I'm never going to tell him."

Jean throws back her head and guffaws. Even though Kate knows Jean's laughing at her, she can't help joining in. "Oh Darlin'," Jean puffs, holding her abdomen, "you can't keep making me laugh so or I *will* end up losing breakfast." She leans back and rests, her hearty laugh calmed to a chortle. "Come sit." She motions to the end of the chaise and Kate complies. "You are such a Leo. Babe, this isn't about a battle of wills, even if Dr. Galen thinks it is or makes you think it is. You've got to tell him what you're uncovering, so he can help you start down your path."

"How's he gonna help?"

"He already has. He's made you hear your calling. You need to share with him, so he can help you get rid of the fear, guilt and self-criticism that keep you from following your path. So he can de-commission this yucky critical voice and embolden the voice you call the goddess, the voice of the child. You need to write from your child, Kate. The child is the creative, playful force within you. The laughter. The risk-taker. The child is very close to God. But your child's been beaten into the background. You need Dr. Galen to show you how to bring her back to the fore."

"Can he?"

"He's not worth the paper his degree's written on if he can't. And it won't take long. You're almost there. In just a few visits you'll have it. But you've got to be honest with him," she says in her mother-to-child voice, wagging her finger. "You've got to talk about what's important. No more focusing on Josh. This is your time."

"Okay, okay. I'm going to see him on Thursday and I'll tell him everything."

"Promise?"

"I promise."

Jean reaches out her hand. Kate catches her fingers. "I love you so, my proud, strong, silly lion," Jean says.

"I love you too, even if you are pushy." She tightens her fingers around Jean's.

"Lions can be stubborn," Jean says with studied haughtiness as she relaxes back.

"Yeah, I know. Proud and stubborn and wanting oh so much to be in charge."

"Let go, Kate." Jean is serious again. "Maybe it means entrusting the reins to someone else."

"Dr. Galen?"

"Actually, I had God in mind," she flashes Kate a frown, "but Dr. Galen could be a start. Perhaps he's a tool of God, one of God's angels. I've often thought we all are potential angels, God's messengers, vessels for His power to flow and work through. You know different sects of the early Christian church believed angels could take human form. *The Magus* lists certain people, like saints or martyrs, as angels."

"Never heard of it."

"Francis Barrett? The early 1800s? Oh, never mind. The point is, some people believe the folks who are the worst thorns pricking our sides are actually angels pushing us to confront things like fear, self-doubt or false beliefs spewed by the critical voice—things standing in the way of faith and growth in God."

"Dr. Galen doesn't strike me as divinely inspired."

"Why? Because he's not perfect?" Jean's smile holds a gentle challenge. A blush blazes across Kate's face. "It's like the *Gita* says, God works through imperfection. Maybe 'let go' is another way of saying 'trust me.'"

"It's hard to do."

"Very."

"I need to work on it."

"Yes."

"What I don't get is why did God make me a Leo if my path involves submission?"

"Maybe that's exactly why He made you a Leo." Kate can't help grinning under her godmother's teasing twinkle. "The lion is king—or queen—of the jungle. A ruler. Try to take that power and control away, and a lion can get cranky, is apt to show her claws."

"I guess it's fair to say I've taken a few paw swipes at Dr. Galen."

"How could you not? But Kate, you need to see the whole, complex, beautiful picture that is you. You tend to see only the flaws. Leos also have a great generosity of spirit. They're noble, responsible and incredibly loyal. What is the line written about them? 'Magnanimous in victory and unflinching in defeat.' They also live from the heart. They love the idea of love and tend to be hopeless romantics, not unlike a particular lion I know." Kate rolls her eyes. "But it also makes them very in tune with their souls. I see all of this in you."

"You make me want to purr," Kate says, even as her mind discounts Jean's words.

"Leos also love to be stroked with praise. But I can tell you don't believe me."

Kate doesn't answer. She can't lie.

"You're an old soul, Darlin'."

"I've never thought of myself as an old soul."

"Really? Well, you are. But you've got to get rid of all this self-doubt rubbish. It gets in your way. Holds you back from, I don't know, taking risks, following the inner voice of love and belief. Believe that voice. Act always as if you believe it, even when your brain says you don't. There's such power in belief, Kate. What we choose to believe either disfigures or crystallizes reality."

"Maybe I should start calling the goddess my Jean voice. I love your voice in me. I love your belief in me."

"What you need is to believe in yourself. You need a Kate voice saying all these things. Let Dr. Galen help you find it." Jean drinks the last of her ginger ale. "That was good. We should have a big lunch."

"Just tell me what you want and I'll go get it."

"Umm. The idea of eating and not immediately throwing up has me giddy."

"Sounds like it's been worse than bad."

"I'd be dead now if it wasn't for Linda. She's been such a good friend. She comes on the bad days and holds me as I'm making love to the toilet. Then she cleans up and insists on doing the laundry and keeping the bed fresh. I tell her again and again I can hire someone to do the dirty work, and we can just enjoy visiting, but she insists."

"I'm glad."

"And your weekly visits, they're like a breath of spring air. The house changes when you enter, Kate. The light, the air, everything lightens. I can't tell you how wonderful it is for me."

Kate beams with delight. "I'm glad you let me come. There are so many people clambering to see you."

"I keep my Fridays open, no visitors, so I have you to myself."

"I always worry I get more out of our relationship than you. I come here filled with all my anxieties and my seemingly insurmountable problems, and your laughter and wisdom shrink them down to a manageable size—from the Alps to anthills. Talk about reincarnation. That's what I feel when I leave here. Reborn. Refreshed. Ready for battle. Then I worry the whole drive home I've done all the talking, it's all always about me. That I'm not giving to you."

"How silly you are." Jean shakes her head. "Come sit here." She pats the edge of the chaise next to her. Kate slides up.

"You have no idea what you give me. The honor you show me in seeking my advice, in labeling my words wisdom. You make me feel needed and loved. And our laughter refreshes me as much as you."

Even as Jean's words make Kate glow, she feels a stab of fear. "I also worry," she says, then looks down.

"What?"

Kate feels like a four-year-old as she stares at her hands. "I worry someday you'll see the real me, all the mess inside, and you won't … I don't know. You'll be disappointed."

"Look at me, Darlin'." Kate looks into Jean's coffee eyes, now chocolate with emotion. "I love you, blessed goddaughter. I love you wholly and fiercely, yesterday, tomorrow and today. Nothing you could ever say or do—not even should you commit murder—nothing will ever change that."

Kate circles her arms around Jean's neck and leans into Jean's maternal hug, feels Jean's hand stroking her back. After a moment, Jean pushes her to arm's length. "Kate." She sniffs, then chuckles. "We both need a Kleenex." She pans her brimming eyes over Kate's face as if memorizing every feature. "Dear one, aren't we lucky? We must have been very good in our previous lives." Her laughter bubbles up again, as from a wellspring, inviting Kate to join in. Kate hugs Jean as a silent prayer rises in her. Please God, don't take this woman from me.

*L*aughter is a strand of the song. It vibrates through her and her godmother almost continuously when they're together. He sees her as a child, waking each morning singing. Her song is stifled now by all her worry about her son. If only she knew there's no need to worry. He never knew that, so why should she? Yet she knows more than he does, even as he sits here. If she will let go of her worries and fears, follow her heart, the song will rise again. Easier said than done when it's your child. He couldn't do it.

He knows he must look at this. He knows the one person he has always loved without reservation is his son, born of an intended one-night stand that turned into a loveless sexual partnership. When Amy got pregnant, she made plans for an abortion. The horror he felt still astounds him. She agreed to have the baby after he promised her one thousand dollars and that she'd never see him or the child again once they left the hospital. Why did he save the baby? He's avoided looking at Matt, refused out of fear and guilt and shame. But the music implores. He wants to move forward. He turns to Matt.

He sees Matt in his brother's house, sitting on the sofa with Tom's wife, Julie. She's telling Matt about his father, *how Michael had a hard life early on that left holes in his heart. She says it gently, her voice filled with compassion. Her being resonates with the song.*

He sees Matt outside with the golden retriever Tom and Julie bought him. Matt throws a Frisbee. The dog catches it and brings it to him, but when Matt grabs it, the dog pulls back, playing tug-of-war. The dog breaks free and runs around the lush yard, Matt in laughing pursuit. When did he last hear Matt laugh?

Julie is calling Matt to supper. When alive, Michael never realized what a gift Julie is—both to Matt and to him. From the beginning, she helped him without being asked. It irritated him then. Her showing up one morning for an unplanned shopping trip to get what she called "baby paraphernalia." They went to the drugstore, department store, toy store, buying things she said he'd need, things beyond his knowledge: rectal thermometer—ugh!—baby nailclippers, diapers so tiny he couldn't believe they'd fit anything bigger than a rat, bottles, nipples, formula, cloth diapers for burping. And things he'd never heard of, like receiving blankets and nightgowns—for a boy! Trust me, *she said. And* Onesies.

Later she spent a weekend with him, cleaning his apartment as she directed him in "childproofing" it. Best do it now, *she had said. Then there was the day they scoured nearly every consignment shop in town until they found a crib and highchair that met her approval. And a baby swing.* You've got to have that, *she said. The baby swing, more than anything else, had saved him on nights when baby Matt went on crying jags for no apparent reason.*

Her love came without expectations. Without demands. He remembers her laughing at his ignorance and confusion, at his obvious fear the first time he bathed the new baby. He won't break, she said. He never appreciated it. Later, when darkness descended, he pushed her and his brother away. It hurt too much to be around her. Her joy felt like a reprimand. What if that last time she came to see him, when he was living with Cara and life had become a Bataan march, what if he'd laid his head on her shoulder and cried? She gave him the opportunity. He remembers her hand on his arm, her eyes filled with compassion. Michael, we love you. Come stay with us for a while, you and Matt. Let us help. *Part of him wanted to put his hand on hers. Instead, he chose to turn away.*

He prays Tom realizes how lucky he is to have found this angel so willing to merge her wholeness with their brokenness. And now she holds Matt in her arms and heart, and refuses to allow him to utter one word against his father.

He loved you from the day you were conceived, *she says to him.* Because of his love you're here today.

Why do you keep talking about his love? *Matt asks.* You think I owe him? Screw that. He deserted me.

You owe him big time, *her voice firm but gentle.* You owe him your life. And the place in you where the good memories reside, before your father became ill.

I don't remember any good.

Then I'll help you.

Matt is belligerent. Even if I could, *he says,* even if I loved him, even if I believed I owed him something, it's too late.

No it's not, *she replies, taking his hand.* Here's what you do. Go out into the world and love someone with the same depth and commitment he gave you before the darkness descended. That's how you repay him.

Michael wishes he had honored Julie's love. He begs God to give him the chance. Give me a loving heart, he prays. He hears his answer in the symphony's vibrato.

Chapter

"Last time, you said you had deep-seated anger at Josh and yourself. Should we start there?" Dr. Galen says in a monotone.

"No, I don't want to talk about that," Kate says. Dr. Galen looks up in surprise. "My godmother says I have to tell you what's been going through my mind these past few weeks. About me. And I always do what she advises."

"I like your godmother." Interest replaces ennui on his face. "I'm listening."

"Last month, when you asked me about my fantasy, something happened. Lightning struck."

"Yes."

"I need to back up. Since the suicide I've been going through phases. They're so distinct I've given them names. First there was what I call the gray phase, where I felt I was looking at the world through a gray veil of horror and sadness. That came right after the suicide and lasted about six weeks. Then came the evil phase. That was awful."

Kate shivers as she buries her face in her hands. A fear still lingers in her that the presence, the disembodied evil as she's come to think of it, will return. She knows she hasn't fully dealt with it, that it lurks at the periphery of her life, watching, waiting to see what she does or doesn't do. She hasn't found the key to eradicating it.

"You were in that phase when you first told me about the suicide."

"Yes." She rubs her eyes and looks up. "Then came what I call the critical phase—meaning criticizing. To be honest, I was a total witch. I was ripping apart everything in my life. Critical of everything. Myself. My parenting. The choices I've made. But especially Mitch. Most of the critical phase focused on him—wondering if I'd married the wrong man. Was I really happy with him? There are a lot of things I can't talk to him about. I haven't been able to talk to him about the suicide. He gets irritated. Says I'm making too much of it. So you can see why Mitch might be a bit touchy."

"Yes." Dr. Galen returns Kate's weak smile.

"Jean, my godmother, was wonderful then. She loves Mitch and she manages to make me remember I love him too."

"Your godmother a psychologist?"

"No. But I think she's a shaman."

He grins. "To be any good as a psychologist you have to be a bit of a shaman. Psychology isn't so much a science as it is an art. I like to think of myself as a shaman."

Kate almost dismisses his statement as more evidence he's full of himself, but his expression stops her. He looks like a little boy revealing a secret. His unveiled eyes transmit a mixture of trust and vulnerability. Warmth surges through her, surprising her with its power. She smiles softly, the same smile she recently gave Mollie when her youngest said she wanted to be a philosopher, then asked what a philosopher was. Kate shifts her eyes away from Dr. Galen's intense gaze, afraid of what he might see.

"Anyway, during all these phases I was also into what I call the music phase, and I'm still in that. After the suicide, I started listening to music I hadn't played since college.

John Denver's old stuff. That drove Mitch nuts. One day I played 'Eagle and the Hawk.' Mitch said Denver sounded like someone was stepping on his toes." Dr. Galen chuckles. "I also went back to Jim Croce. Old songs by James Taylor, Bob Dylan. Even Godspell. Some new music, too, mostly spiritual. Chants from Taizé. I was looking for songs that captured where I was."

"Did you find any?"

"Yeah. An old Denver song. "Sweet Surrender." Here are the lyrics."

She pulls a sheet from her purse and hands it to him. He nods as he reads.

"I identify with having no idea where I've been or where I'm going. Since the suicide I've felt disconnected from myself, or the self I thought I was. I keep reviewing my life, what I've accomplished, what I haven't, asking, What does it amount to? What's worth noting and what isn't? One thing I've realized is there's only one question at the end of life. Only one. And it's not, 'Was Mary a virgin?'" Dr. Galen leans forward, his elbows resting on his knees. "It's, 'Did you love?' That's the only question. Since the suicide, I've been looking back at my life, trying to see what the answer is thus far, and I've been looking ahead, trying to figure out how I can make it better. Then you came along asking about my fantasy, and I realized there's another question—perhaps not as important as the first, but still important."

"And that is?" He is now writing rapidly on his clipboard.

"'Did you live fully and deeply?' Or, stated inversely, 'Did you compromise?'" Dr. Galen looks up, his expression a mixture of surprise, interest and something else she can't quite read. It almost looks like introspection. She shoves the idea aside as absurd. She's not telling him anything he hasn't heard a hundred times. People must come here every day with their "profound epiphanies."

"When you asked me about my fantasy," she continues, wanting to get this over, "I realized why I was ripping my life apart. I was looking for the compromise—the place I had failed to live fully. When you asked that question, it was suddenly there, right in front of me. Powerful, unequivocal, shrouded in fear. And it wasn't Mitch. I couldn't tell you then what I saw. I was angry with you. But also I had to look at it—especially at the fear."

Dr. Galen regards her intently, his pencil frozen over the clipboard.

"Now I suppose I have to tell you what the compromise is."

"No, you don't."

"Yeah I do. We both know that." She pauses, gathering strength. "When I left Senator Mimms, I stopped writing. No, that isn't even it." Dr. Galen relaxes into a smile. "The truth is, I've never done the kind of writing I wanted to do. I was a good speechwriter. I got an honest man elected to office, changed laws, got bad laws abolished. I was well known. On a first-name basis with the governor. My pen had power and I used it for good. But it wasn't enough. That's what I kept feeling. I'd go to the grocery store and look at the checkout clerk or the man stocking shelves, or I'd go to the park and see mothers pushing their kids on swings, and I'd wonder, 'Is that enough for them?'"

"You were unfulfilled."

"I guess. And it made me feel guilty. I can't tell you the number of times I've said to my sister I wanted something to show for life. She always says I have my children. But it isn't enough."

"Raising children is a worthy calling, Kate, but it's not enough for you."

"But it's enough for some people?"

"Yes."

"I've felt guilty it wasn't enough for me."

He shakes his head. "No need for guilt. You're an artist, Kate. It's your destiny."

"My destiny? That's an awful big word to apply to me. I've never thought of myself as having a destiny." Dr. Galen cocks a brow. "Well, actually," she says sheepishly, then looks at the rug. "Jean read me something from the *Bhagavad Gita* recently ..."

"Kate?"

His gentle prod brings her back to his office. "Mitch has been pressing me to do something to get out of this funk. He wants me to get my doctorate. I've been teaching as an adjunct at the university and I'm good. If I get my doctorate, I could get tenure. He swears Harvard will accept me. He's been pushing hard lately because I've been so depressed, and—you know—critical."

His face falls. "You'd just be exchanging one voice for another, neither one yours."

She ignores the interruption. "The other night he asked me again if I'd made a decision about pursuing my doctorate. I told him, 'Yes. I've decided I'm not going back to school and I'm not going to teach next year. Instead, I'm going to write—write for myself. Essays. Maybe fiction. But *my* writing."

"Excellent!" Dr. Galen lights up, his eyes intense with joy and something else. Approbation? Admiration? ... Love? His expression both pleases and confuses Kate. She looks at her hands, hating the wildfire flaming across her face. She peeks up. He's still grinning at her with unabashed glee. She looks again at her hands as a sea of pleasure flows through her. She loves his smile. Wishes she could hug him.

"What did Mitch say?"

"He was surprised. I'd never shared my dream with him. He's worried about the money. Losing my salary will crimp our finances. And frankly, I'm thinking I won't be going back to the university for several years. I want to give this dream a bona fide chance. I told Mitch I want to commit to it for five years. We have some savings we can draw on, but it's going to be tight."

"So he agreed?"

"We talked about it a long time, then out of the blue he said, 'You're going to need a laptop to do this right.' And off he went to Office Depot."

"Good for him."

"Yeah, he really loves me." She hears the awe in her voice. How long has it been since she's marveled at her husband's love?

"So, where do we go from here?"

Her attention snaps back to Dr. Galen. "Actually, I need your help with something."

"Anything."

"I have what Dr. Emmett calls a critical voice."

"Really? I hadn't noticed."

She dimples at his soft sarcasm. "It's very persuasive and I've listened to it for years. It's told me this dream of writing, which I've had since childhood, is stupid, impossible. I've always given into that voice. Now I want to choke it and ..."

"And?"

"This is going to sound dumb—or crazy. You're going to conclude I'm a multiple personality."

"Because you have other voices in you?"

"Yeah."

"We all do. We all have many voices or selves that make up the self."

"Well, one of the voices in me I call the goddess. She doesn't talk much, though she's been talking more lately."

"And what does she say?"

"Well, mostly ..." Kate grimaces and wrings her hands. "She says, 'I love you.'"

"Yes!"

"And when I was deciding whether I'd actually continue to see you after that first session—and my critical voice was saying all sorts of ugly things. 'You're a weakling, a fucking baby'—excuse me, I'm quoting—this other voice kept saying, 'Just go and talk. Just go and talk.'"

"Yes." The word is like a caress.

"And when you asked about my fantasy, that was the voice I heard saying, 'I want to write, I want to write.' She kept saying it over and over, urging me to say it out loud. I almost did, in that first session. But then you spoke. You said, 'Do you think you'll sound foolish?' And my critical voice jumped right in, saying, 'Exactly, it's foolish. You're a fool.' Then you said something like, 'Do you think your dream is dead, and it said, 'It is dead!' It got the upper hand and I couldn't say it. I couldn't say, 'I want to write.'"

"But you've said it now."

"Yes." Kate looks down. She can't keep looking into Dr. Galen's eyes. "I guess what I want is to make the critical voice softer and the goddess louder."

"Yes."

"Can you help me?"

"Absolutely." He stands and examines his bookcase, then plucks a book from a shelf. "I'd like you to read this." Kate looks at the title, *Art as Yogic Path*. "In Hinduism, the yogas are paths to God. This book will help you retune yourself, help you make the small voice of love and creativity—your goddess voice—the refrain of your life."

"I like that metaphor. I believe the goddess is very close to God."

"So do I." Dr. Galen settles back in his chair. "There's something else I want you to do. I want you to keep a journal. Write in it every day—preferably in the morning, before the mad rush to school and work. But it can be at other times. When you have a quiet half-hour. I want you to write two pages of stream-of-consciousness—whatever comes. Don't reflect, don't edit, just write. Then flip a page and write a page of art—a scene, a part of an essay, a character sketch, a memory. Doesn't matter. Whatever comes. And something will come. If in the beginning you get writer's block, then describe a recent incident, Mollie eating her breakfast, the homecoming of the new dog. You got what I'm saying?"

"Yes."

"Two pages stream-of-consciousness, one page of art. I want you to do this for one month, while you begin reading this book. Read a chapter a week. Each chapter has some exercises and meditations. You don't have to do all of them, but I'd like you to do at least two from each chapter. I especially like the Apache warrior one where you walk around blindfolded." Kate's eyes widen. "Don't worry. That doesn't come until chapter eight. And don't worry if you feel weird. It's just between you, the book and God.

"I want you to come see me again in a month and we'll see where you are. After that, I'm not sure you'll need to see me alone too many more times."

"You make it sound easy."

"Nope, it's not easy. But you've already done the hardest part. You've committed to a path, to your path."

She gathers her purse and starts to rise.

"You're not leaving yet." Dr. Galen motions her back into the chair. "We're not done." She sits, resigned. "Look at you." He chuckles. "You were all ready to rush out of here. You said you were taking stock of how well you've loved in your life. What were your conclusions?"

She looks at the carpet and fiddles with her purse strap. "At times I've found the answer disappointing." She shrugs. "At other times, obscure. I haven't loved my dad as well as I could have. Or Josh. But I also know the answer is tricky." She catches Dr. Galen's eye, feeling on surer ground.

"Love doesn't always mean saying 'Yes.' Sometimes it means saying 'No.' It can mean staying, but sometimes it means leaving. There's no guidebook. Every situation is unique and asks, 'What does love call for here?' Often with Josh, I can't discern the answer. I so wanted to be the 'Jean voice' to my children, but I've made a mess of it with Josh."

He shakes his head. "To make mistakes is not to fail, it's to grow. You think Josh struggles because you're a bad mother? That's not it. He struggles in those places where his emotions are most engaged. Emotions, with all their power and complexities, are difficult for him. It's easy for him to behave at church or a friend's house, where his attachments are superficial. But with you, his love is strong. If he didn't love you and Mitch so deeply, there'd be little conflict between you. One thing I'm certain of, Josh chose you, Kate. Before he was born, he chose you and Mitch."

The assertion startles her. These were Jean's words.

"He needs you. But you also need him. What is Josh supposed to teach you?"

Kate jerks. She's heard this question before as well. Dr. Galen's echo of Jean gives the idea a holy weight. She remembers Nick's belief that God speaks through people. "It's an important question," she says, shaking her head. "I don't know the answer. Patience probably. What it means to love the unlovable."

"I think it's something else as well, and Denver's song points to it."

"What?"

"Trust."

"As in trust you?"

"Yes. But not just me. All the people you've reached out to for help. And trust yourself, trust that voice within you saying, 'I love you.' Trust the good things you say about yourself. Trust yourself, Kate. Trust God."

"Trust involves letting go of control. It's not one of my strong points. Jean says it's because I'm a Leo."

"Perhaps your need for control arises from your perceived—or I should say misperceived—sense of inadequacy." She straightens at the suggestion. "We are all inadequate, Kate, yet in all our inadequacies we are all perfectly adequate. Let go of yourself. Drop the reins."

"I'm not sure I can."

"Are you a fossil?"

Kate laughs. "Where'd that come from?"

"Are you?"

"Of course not."

"Then you can change."

Kate grins sheepishly and nods. "I've also been reviewing my relationship with God."

"Yes."

"I want to walk with God."

"You do walk with God."

"Well, yeah, in that God walks with everyone. But some people are completely unaware of Her presence. They're in their own invisible, insular bubble, like people walking on a crowded New York City sidewalk with eyes straight ahead and glassy, failing to acknowledge the folks jostling by, brushing their shoulders. Others acknowledge Her presence, but only with stiff formality—walking with Her in polite yet awkward silence.

"Then there are those who take Her hand and walk with Her in friendship, talking with Her, confiding in Her, laughing with Her along the way. And finally, there are those special few who link arms and walk with Her in close unity, like lovers, whose faces glow when they gaze into each other's eyes. That's how I want to walk with God.

"I've been listening a lot to another Denver piece, 'Annie's Song.' He wrote it as a love song to his wife, but I sing it as a love song to God. The sensations and desires he expresses—'Come let me love you, let me give my life to you, let me drown in your laugher, let me die in your arms'—articulate my yearnings for God."

Dr. Galen shakes his head grinning, as if he's heard a good joke.

"What?" she asks.

"You honestly don't see it, do you?"

"See what?"

"Kate, you're already there."

"I don't think so."

"I know so. Just like Denver writes here," he waves the sheet Kate gave him, "there's a spirit, a light guiding you, shining through you. Apparently you're the only one who doesn't realize it. You're like a fish swimming in the heart of the ocean, scanning this way and that, saying, 'Where's the water? Where's the water?'"

"And you know this how?"

"Sorry, can't give away trade secrets. Just trust me. I know." His mischievous twinkle makes Kate chuckle.

"Is it permissible for me to love you?" she asks.

"Actually, I think it's required."

Kate can't help but join his laughter.

Chapter

Sunny is barking and pawing the door when Kate answers the knock. Her father brushes past her into the foyer. "Dad, what are you doing here?" Sunny nuzzles in, sniffing.

"Hello, yourself," he shoots back. "Hey boy, come here." He cradles the dog's head and strokes his sleek body. "Good boy." He stands, cups his mouth with his hands and yells. "Any monsters home?"

"Grandpa!" Mollie cheers from the family room where the TV blares. She jumps into his arms, making him tip backward. Kate steadies him then snatches Mollie and deposits her safely on the floor.

"I got somethin' for you, little monster." He pulls a Tootsie Pop from his pocket and holds it just out of her reach.

"Thank you, thank you," she chants, bouncing on her toes, grabbing for the prize. He drops it into her hands.

"Got another one for Reyna." He raises his eyes to the older girl, who stands in the doorway, watching. "If you want it, you'll have to come get it."

Reyna shuffles across the tile, accepts the candy and gives her grandpa's legs a listless hug. "Thanks," she mumbles and heads for the family room.

"Mollie, go with your sister. And take Sunny," Kate says. When they're gone, she faces her father. The smell of alcohol permeates him. "Why are you here, Dad?"

"I read your story." He ambles to the living room. "The one with flowers in the title."

Kate's stomach tightens. "How did you get that?"

"Found it when I was here last week." He plops on the couch. "I came when you were gone on one of your 'Jean days' so I'd get invited in. Saw Mitch and the kids. Josh is turning into a shit if you ask me. Where is the little turd?"

"Sailing camp." She follows him and stands next to the wing chair. "Please don't talk like that in my house."

"I'll talk any goddamn way I please."

"You had no right."

"No right to what?"

"To go through my papers, to take my story."

"I'm your father; don't tell me about parental rights. By the way, it's garbage." He stands and takes a swig from his pocket flask. She looks at her watch. It's eight forty-five in the morning. "Woulda thought the rugrats would be back in school by now." He sits down and puts the flask on the coffee table, knocking over an empty juice box left by one of the girls. He picks it up and chucks it at her. "Still no good at keeping house."

"How much have you had to drink?"

"My first sip of the day." He takes another swallow. "You know, Mitch tells me time and again his greatest disappointment in life is he's a better cook than you. Pretty bad to be your husband's greatest disappointment."

"It's a joke, Dad."

"Believe what you want."

"You should come back when you're sober."

"Who says I'm not sober?"

"Dad …"

"I came here to talk about your so-called story. You can't publish it."

The knot in Kate's stomach twists a notch tighter. She knows he's going to rip this fragile first attempt to bits. "I really can't talk now." She remembers all the times her brother Greg told her to kick him out. "We were just leaving for the zoo."

"Yeah, right. Mollie's in her nightgown."

Kate yells over her shoulder, "Mollie, I told you to get dressed so we can enjoy the zoo while it's still cool."

"We're going to the zoo?" Mollie and Reyna squeal in unison.

"Hurry up!" Kate turns back to her father. "The animals retreat to their dens by midday."

"Sounds like last-minute planning."

"After the zoo, we're stopping at Jean's. She hasn't seen the kids all summer."

"Fuck!" The word explodes. "I should have known. Always runnin' to Jean. Never could handle life on your own." Her father takes another pull on his flask and stands to prowl the room.

"That's not true and you know it."

"I don't know any goddamn thing." He seizes her mother's miniature crystal sailboat from the piano and tosses it in the air as he skulks. "Every time I talk to you, you're trottin' off to Jean's or you've just been there."

"She's sick." Kate bites her lower lip. Why is she explaining? Why is she even talking to him? She hates herself.

"If you ask me, she got what she deserves, smoking like a chimney her whole life."

"Good God, Dad, how can you say that?"

He stops mid-stride. "You've got gall asking me that. You say you love Jean, then you write this shit about her. I'm telling you, publish this story and you can fuckin' kiss Jean good-bye." The words are a sucker punch to the chest.

"What do you mean?"

"She'll never speak to you again. Telling all her sordid secrets, making Jamie into a slut."

Kate grabs the top of the wing chair. Her body shakes as if she's just come from a dip in the arctic sea. Sharp icicles pierce her lungs.

"Did you hear me?"

She wonders if he's still on his first bottle. He isn't the stereotypical drunk. Never slurs his words. Never stumbles. He's never sloppy. Just mean. Meaner and meaner with every sip. Whiskey is a whetstone to his tongue, making it razor sharp.

He circles the room, kicking away Sunny's chew bone. "Don't you ever pick up around here? Thank God your mother's not here to see. You quit the university, so you should have plenty of time for housekeeping. Yet this place is a pigsty. What the hell you doing, wasting all your time writing crap?"

"Dad," she says, her voice trembling, "how much have you had to drink?"

"Don't try to change the subject. Your story sickened me." The crystal ship sails higher with each toss. "Jean was your mother's best friend, ever since you and Jamie became playmates. Your mother was Jamie's godmother for chrissake, or have you forgotten?"

"Of course I haven't forgotten. Would you please put that down? It's one of the few keepsakes I have of Mom's."

"How the hell you get this?" He snatches it from the air and shakes it at her. "I gave it to your mother. You stole it, didn't you?"

Kate's eyes narrow and her face hardens. "Mom gave it to me."

"So you say, lying bitch."

Kate glances over her shoulder. "Dad, I want you to leave."

"I want you to leave," he mocks in a falsetto. He resumes pacing. "Back to your so-called story. It ain't fiction. Anyone who grew up with you is going to recognize everyone in it. It's a bad idea when authors start writing about their own people. They end up being downright hated. Remember that Georgia author, Jack Cantbury? Canterry? Somethin' like that. His neighbors recognized themselves in his book and ran him out of town on a rail." He swipes the flask from the table, takes a gulp and gasps.

"Plannin' to show this shit to Jean?" he continues. Kate sinks into the wing chair. "I take that as no. Because you know I'm right." He stops in front of her, wags his finger in her face. "I'm telling you this 'cause you're my daughter, and if your own father won't tell you the truth, who will? You need to choose between this trash you call writing and the people you love."

"Dad—"

"Go back to speechwriting. Now that's something you could be proud of."

"I'm sorry, you've gotta go," Kate chokes out. "I promised the kids."

"Of course." He tosses the glass ship high, almost to the ceiling and steps back. It shatters across the wood floor. "Oops." He takes a long pull from his flask, then startles. She follows his gaze to see Reyna in the doorway. Kate turns back to her father. His face crumples briefly before he slips his flask back in his pocket. "Don't worry, sweetie," he says, "I'll let myself out."

The front door slams. Kate stares at the floor glittering with crystal shards.

"Mom, why'd he do that?"

"It was an accident, honey."

"No it wasn't. I saw him. He did it on purpose."

"Grandpa was angry; that's all. Sometimes when people get angry, they do mean things."

"I hate him."

"No, Reyna, you shouldn't hate."

"He's always angry and he's always mean to you."

Kate pulls her daughter onto her lap and hugs her. "Grandpa's sick. He has a disease that makes him act this way."

"Can't a doctor fix him?"

"Nobody can fix him until he wants to be fixed." She looks into Reyna's eyes. "Do you know what I mean?"

"I guess." Reyna snuggles against her mom. "Why doesn't he want to get better?"

"I don't know. It's complicated." They sit in silence. Kate wonders what to do. She'd been so excited about her plan to send "Flowers" out this week to *Le Chance*, an obscure literary magazine open to "emerging writers." Jean would never see it. But what if she did? What if by some odd twist of fate, Jean read it and then, as her father predicted, turned from her? Kate tries to envision Jean's face in that moment—a portrait of disapproval chiseled in marble—but her mind can't quite capture the image. It's like trying to paint on water. With every brush stroke, the picture ripples into distortion.

Maybe she should throw the story in the dumpster. The thought hurts like hoarfrost, tipping the balance in the war raging within her. She gives Reyna a squeeze. "You ready for the zoo?"

"Yep. So is Mollie."

"Okay. Let me clean up this mess, then I've got to make a phone call and we're off."

"I can sweep it up."

"No, honey, I'll do it."

"I want to." Reyna's eyes plead.

"Okay, get the broom." Reyna trots off to the kitchen while Kate heads to the bedroom. She dials Jean's number.

"Hello?"

"Jean?"

"Kate! How good to hear your voice. How are you?"

"I'm great. We're going to the zoo this morning and I was wondering if we could stop by after, maybe bring dinner from the Chinese restaurant on the circle."

"Oh, how lovely. I could do with a little egg drop soup and some of that vegetable egg fu young. I was having a gray day." The warmth of Jean's words loosens the hard knot in Kate's stomach. "But do you think I'll scare the girls? I'll have to put on my wig."

Kate laughs. "You could never scare the girls, with or without a wig. How are you feeling?"

"I've been dizzy a lot lately. Don't know where that's coming from. Actually fell down day before yesterday and couldn't get back up. I was out getting the mail. The men at the fire station down the block saw me wallowing on the curb and came to my aid. They're such darlings."

"Good lord, Jean, what does your doctor say?"

"Going to see him next week. But don't worry. Today's going to be a good one; I can tell. I was up early and Linda took me for my Procrit shot. It gives me a lift. Just wish it would last."

"I'm glad. I've been worried about you."

"Bless you, babe. I'm holding my own."

"I also called because I need to tell you something." She feels like a tightly drawn quiver.

"What is it, Darlin'?"

"I wrote a short story."

"Oh, how exciting!"

"Dad read it."

"Really?"

"He took it from my study without asking."

"Oh Kate, that was wrong of him."

"He hated it."

"W-e-l-l, that's not really a surprise, is it? The question is, do you like it?"

"Yeah. I like it a lot."

"Wonderful! Are you going to get it published?"

"Well, that's kind of why I called. The story's fiction, but it's based on my childhood and—"

"Of course, that makes sense. All your writing will ultimately come from your life, don't you think?"

"Yeah. The thing is, you're in it."

"Am I? I'm honored." Kate can't help smiling at Jean's childlike joy.

"Dad says it dishonors you."

"Oh Kate," Jean snorts, "you couldn't possibly dishonor me."

"One of the main characters is based on Jamie and, of course, her mother's based on you. I wrote about you and Kurt and his affairs and some about Jamie when we were kids—how she idolized her dad and ended up dating guys like him, giving herself away on the first or second date, devaluing herself, delving into physical intimacy before establishing the foundation that makes it meaningful."

"All the things we've talked about."

"It is fiction. I've changed a lot of things and added or exaggerated some things to make a point. The characters aren't really you and Kurt and Jamie and me, but they're based on us."

"Yes." Jean draws out the word. Kate can't decipher the meaning behind the lowered tone in her voice.

"Remember when Jamie discovered Mac was having an affair, but she hadn't decided if she was going to divorce him? You said she really had decided deep down, that all her actions pointed to divorce, she just wasn't ready to say it. You compared it to the death of a dream. She knew the dream was dying; she just wasn't ready to let go."

"Yes, I remember."

Kate hesitates. How can she tell her the rest?

"Honey, I'm still not understanding the problem."

Kate plunges forward. "Dad said if I publish this story, I'll put our friendship at risk, that you'll hate me for revealing your secrets. And he says I've made Jamie into a slut."

Jean's laughter bubbles across the line like a clear mountain brook. "Oh, how silly. Nothing you could write about me or Kurt could make me angry, even if you made him Satan incarnate and me the fool who thought he was God, which frankly wouldn't be too far from the truth. And the times we've talked about Jamie, I've always been impressed with your insight and empathy. You understand her so well, and you've never judged her, only loved her."

Kate relaxes against the headboard as she listens. She closes her eyes, feels so light she could fly. She's sprung from a trap.

"Darlin', listen to me. Telling the truth can't be wrong if you do it with love." Kate nods but doesn't speak. "Kate, is your dad in one of his black holes?"

"Yeah. And he's drinking. It makes me angry. I know it shouldn't, but it does."

"He needs help."

"The new antidepressant Dr. Brown gave him awhile back hasn't done much. Actually, he's worse than ever. And when he drinks, he rips apart everyone and everything around him, as if he needs company in his hell."

"He has a lot of demons. It's hard to love others when you hate yourself."

Kate runs her hand through her hair. "I hadn't thought of Dad hating himself."

"When he spews all that ugliness, he's projecting. It's all about him. As much as it hurts you, honey, your pain is a mere pinprick compared to the knifing he's giving himself. It's essential we love ourselves, Kate. Jesus understood that. That's why he added the very important clause, 'as yourself,' onto his demand to 'love your neighbor.' I also think when he told us to love our enemy, it wasn't so much for our enemy's sake, as our own. Hatred only poisons the one who hates."

"Well, you sure put a damper on my self-righteous anger," Kate says glumly.

"Oh Kate," Jean chuckles, "I didn't say you couldn't be angry. You'd have to be a saint not to be, when someone who's supposed to love you hurts you so. Besides, anger is important. It marks our boundaries. Your dad stepped over the line. He was out of bounds. It's not only right but it's important you tell him that. Just do it with love. Don't respond to him in kind."

"No worry there. I've found when it comes to the jab, he's a much better swordsman than I. But back to 'Flowers,' can I bring it today? I'd like you to read it."

"Not if you're asking permission," Jean says in her bossy-mother tone. "Don't ever ask permission to write, Kate, no matter what. You understand me? You've gotta fly free, treasured one. Fly free."

Joy wells in Kate. "I'm going to bring the story because I *want* you to read it."

"In that case, I'd love to. I love your writing. I have a special Kate folder where I keep the letters and emails you've sent me. I re-read them when I'm down. I've thought so many times over the years what a talented writer you are."

Kate breathes deeply, luxuriating in the weightlessness Jean's words give her. She is bounding across the moon, each step a long, high spring.

"Now get those kids to the zoo," Jean says. "Wish I could fast-forward through the morning to the moment my lovely goddaughter shows up with her precious chicks in tow."

"We're leaving now. And Jean … thank you."

"Nothing to thank, dear heart. But I want to tell you something, something important. Never, Kate. Never let fear—your fear or the fear of others—stop you from living, stop you from following your dreams."

"I won't."

"Promise me."

"I promise."

"Kate, I want you to remember this promise when I'm gone."

"What do you mean? You're doing great. The doctor's last report—"

"I know, I know. I'm going to be fine. But someday I'll be moving on, and you need to remember this promise."

"I will."

"Pinky swear?"

Kate smiles. Jean got that from Mollie. "Pinky swear."

"Okay, now get on the road. I'll be counting the minutes until you arrive."

"How was the zoo and your visit with Jean?" Mitch looks up from the pizza he's cutting for himself.

"Daddy!" Mollie flings herself into his arms.

"Wonderful," Kate says, giving Mitch a peck on the cheek. "I left her my short story. Mind if I check my e-mail? I want to see if she's read it."

"Didn't you say you just gave it to her?"

"She was sitting down to read it when we left."

"Okay, but then can we get rid of the kids, turn off the computer and have an evening—adults only?"

Kate grins. "It's a date." She heads to the bedroom and logs onto her computer. Sure enough, there's an e-mail from Jean. She highlights it, but her finger stops just above the key to open it. What if Jean hated it? Worse, what if the e-mail is filled with tepid praise. She sits up straight, presses her back hard against her chair and taps the enter key.

Kate, RUN DO NOT WALK TO THE NEAREST PUBLISHER!!!!!!!

I couldn't put it down ... great ending ... would write more but looking for a box of Kleenex ...it was very, very touching and the messages thru out were magnificent.

WOW WOW WOW ... am I proud of you. More later.

Me.

Chapter 8

Sunny pushes his nose over the edge of the bed and nuzzles Kate's cheek. It's dark. Mitch and the girls are still sleeping. She hears Josh in the kitchen preparing a bowl of cereal. School started last week. Now he's a ninth-grader, he leaves the house at six each weekday morning to make the three-quarter-mile trek to the bus stop. He's eating at the kitchen table when she shuffles by in her robe and switches on the coffee.

When he looks up, she digs deep for a smile and the love in her eyes Jean has urged her to greet Josh with each day, no matter what has come before.

"Drive me to the bus stop?" he asks her.

"Nope."

"Aw, come on. Please. You're just trying to irritate me."

"Not at all. I have to walk the dog. Besides, the exercise is good for you."

"Yeah, right. You could walk Sunny after. Come on, Mom. You never do anything for me."

She doesn't bite. She stirs half-and-half in her coffee then heads back to the bedroom to dress in the dark. When she returns, Sunny is on her heels, panting excitedly. Josh is in the family room, pulling on his backpack.

"Would you like Sunny and me to walk you partway?" She knows better than to offer to walk all the way. On top of everything else, he's at that roll-your-eyes-at-everything-Mom-says age. The "this isn't the '60s, Mom; things have changed" age.

Last year he'd tolerate being seen with her on those rare occasions she drove him to school, but only because he got a break from walking, and only if she didn't look at him or speak to him once they hit school property. One fall morning they drove with the windows down, enjoying the cool air and, she thought, each other. But when they pulled into the school's car circle, Josh grew apoplectic. "Turn it off, turn it off," he hissed, pointing to the radio. In a panic, he scanned the sidewalk for peers close enough to hear. God forbid anyone should know his mom listens to James Taylor. She remembers making a mental note to be more careful.

Josh shrugs at her offer to accompany him. "Yeah, sure." His voice is neither enthusiastic nor annoyed. Does he want her company or is he humoring her? Perhaps her offer warms him but he's embarrassed to show it. Not likely. Possibly it makes no difference to him; he couldn't care less. Probably she's already put five times more thought into his answer than he has.

She's in the dark when it comes to her son. He doesn't share much, and she tries to resist the temptation to pry—though she often fails.

"So how's school?" she says with a false air of carelessness as they trudge through the gloom.

"Fine."

"Have you made friends?"

"Yes."

"Who?"

"You don't know them."

"Tell me about them."

"It's none of your business."

They walk wordless the rest of the way. He's lonely, she thinks, trying to sooth herself. And he's terribly unhappy. She continues striding beside him in what she hopes is a companionable silence that offers him the opportunity to talk.

The next morning, they again leave together and leisurely stroll three blocks through the neighborhood to busy North Road. Suddenly Josh speeds ahead.

"Get back, Mom. Get back!" he yells.

Surprised, she stops, but fails to retreat.

"Go back," he orders over his shoulder.

Too late. A school bus—not his, but headed for his school—zooms by in a shadowy blur, leaving a vague impression of faces pressed against black glass.

She hurries after him.

"Leave me alone," he groans, waving his hands as if she's a pesky mosquito. "Go away."

She pulls back on the leash but Sunny resists. Only his white ruff and tail tip are clearly visible. The rest of his mocha coat blends into darkness. He wants to catch up with Josh. He strains against the growing distance, doesn't understand why they walk separately. Josh is now a small silhouette against the predawn haze. The heavy backpack strapped high on his shoulders makes him appear oddly inhuman, enigmatic.

She peels down a side street then turns at the next block to walk parallel to Josh. When they reach Harbor Avenue, she tries to veer east to Crescent Bay, but Sunny anchors his haunches and won't budge. He looks west and whines softly. She can't see to the end of the block, but she knows Josh is there, waiting alone in a crowd of peers.

She yanks Sunny up and they finally reach the bay then turn toward home. This is the part of the walk she loves. She scans the horizon for signs of dawn and lets her mind wander through a maze of worries, ponderings, memories, to-do lists, and then, a half-remembered quote. Something to the effect that we all, at some point, must face the painful, inexorable truth that we walk through life alone. There's something right about that assertion, yet also something very wrong.

"One of them chickened out," a cop said in a recent news story on what started as a double suicide. "Happens all the time."

Some things we must do alone. Maybe that's what the survivor of the failed suicide pact realized at the moment of execution—there is no "we" in dying, only "I." But how awful if that were true about living.

"Looks like we're back to walking alone," she tells Sunny.

The next morning, when he's about to leave for the bus stop, Josh calls out: "Mom, you ready?"

Kate's shocked.

"Maybe you should turn around the block before North Road," he says sheepishly after they turn the first corner.

"Did they see me?"

"Yeah."

"How do they even know I was with you? That I'm your mom?"

"They know."

"I don't understand why it's such a big deal. I'm just walking the dog."

"I don't want to put up with all the trash."

"Did they tease you?"

"Forget it. Just turn at the corner, okay?"

As requested, she takes a side street as Josh continues toward North Road. He calls to her to have a good day—a rare endearment. She wends her way south about a mile through residential streets then heads to the bay for the home stretch. Across the bay, the sun shoots angry orange arrows from below the horizon, signaling its approach. The rays reflect on mud flats exposed by an ebb tide, turning the muck into a patchwork of black and crimson resembling a river of molten lava. The colors remind her of the smoldering turmoil inside Josh.

Perhaps they have ridiculed him. Perhaps it's just a figment of fear. Either way, he doesn't understand the tough-guy swaggers of his peers are nothing but flimsy shields they wield in desperate attempts to protect their own tender vulnerabilities—not unlike the armor Josh pulls on the moment he walks into Dr. Galen's office. Inside, each of those boys is just like Josh, a paradoxical mix of uncertainty and conceit, fear and foolhardiness, high hope and endless doubt. But Josh is struggling with more than the usual teenage angst. From where does his rage come? Why does he constantly insist he is an adult and should be treated by his parents as their equal? Why does he sneer so at everything? Does he hate himself? The thought sends a shiver down her spine.

If Josh could only realize he must hold onto the boy in his metamorphosis to man. If she's learned anything from Jean, it's that true maturity comes by discarding the fear of appearing foolish and re-embracing the child within. She hears Jean's laughter, sees Dr. Galen's impish smile, then grins at herself. She's only just figuring this out, is still incredibly insecure, too often concerned that others approve of her. She's spent years trying to develop the tough skin she thinks Josh needs, only to realize, belatedly, she's a better person tender.

Perhaps Josh is right to push her away. Perhaps a part of him knows he must learn to walk alone before he can truly walk with others. She would love to save him from his loneliness and pain, but she can't. Jean is right. To do so would deprive him of the richness that comes from discovering his own path, no matter how steep. She remembers Nick's message: Let go. Why must it be so hard?

As she draws near home, the sun's forehead pushes above the horizon, spurring her. She must wake Reyna and Mollie and hustle them off to school. They are still in the open-face, singing-heart, hugs-and-kisses-in-public age. She vows to enjoy every second.

Chapter 39

"Mom, I'm home." Josh walks into the family room and tosses his backpack on the floor next to the couch.

"How was your day?" Kate asks from the kitchen.

"It sucked."

"Don't use that language."

"Come on, suck's not a bad word."

"It's not allowed in this house."

"Jesus."

"Sorry you had a bad day. What happened?"

"Never mind." Josh sits on the couch and turns on the TV.

"Josh, you know the rules."

"Give me a break. I don't have any homework."

"No TV on school days, period."

He clicks off the TV and wanders into the kitchen. "What's this?" he tears off a paper taped to the refrigerator.

"Please put that back. It's Reyna's report card. She got four A's and two B's."

"Woo-hoo," he says, rolling his eyes.

"By the way, where's yours?"

"I forgot it."

"What'd you get?"

"I forget."

Irritation prickles Kate like a porcupine. She strides to her son's backpack, opens it and starts rummaging.

"Hey, get out of my stuff!"

"If you don't want me to search your backpack, then give me your report card."

He grabs the pack from her and pulls out a wadded sheet of paper. She lays it on the table, smoothes the wrinkles and scans it. A in English. B in history. B in honors science. A in PE. D in math. "A D! You got a D in math?" She turns to her son in disbelief.

"It's just one class. How come you don't say anything about the A's and B's? You only look at what I do wrong."

Guilt burns Kate like a branding iron. "Why didn't you tell us you were having trouble?" she asks, lowering her voice.

"I didn't know until I got the report card."

"How can you not know you're failing a course?"

"A D isn't failing."

"It is in this house." She reviews the report card. "Under comments, your math teacher wrote you haven't been handing in homework. That true?"

"I don't know. Who cares?" He grabs the paper, rips it in half and tosses the pieces on the floor.

"Mom, can I have a snack?" Reyna stands in the center of the family room, holding Josh's Magic 8-Ball.

"Give me that!" He snatches the ball from her. "That's mine."

"Hey!" Reyna whines. "Mollie and I were playing with it."

"Too bad."

"Josh, give it back to her. Now!" Kate says, anger rising in her. "Then pick up your report card and tape it back together. You've got to hand it back in, signed."

"Sure, Mom. Wouldn't want to upset your little angel." He throws the ball at Reyna, hitting her in the chest.

"Ow!" Reyna staggers backward. Tears erupt. "Mommy!"

Kate sweeps her up. "You okay, baby?"

"You okay, baby?" Josh mocks.

"It hurts," Reyna says, but the tears have stopped.

Kate lowers Reyna to the floor and wipes away her tears. "Go wait in your room with Mollie, okay?" Reyna nods.

Kate grabs the 8-Ball off the floor and throws it in the trash.

"What are ya doing?" Josh demands.

"I've told you since you were a toddler, use a toy as a weapon, it goes in the trash."

"That's stupid. I didn't hurt her. She's already stopped crying."

"That's the rule."

"Well, fuck that." He pulls the 8-Ball from the trash and pushes past Reyna to his room. Kate storms after him, takes the 8-ball from the shelf where he's just placed it and heads for the laundry room door. She slams the toy in the large garbage can outside. Josh follows, pushes his mother aside and digs the 8-Ball out. He runs to his room and locks the door.

Kate follows and rattles the knob. "Josh, open up. Now!"

"Fuck you."

"Open this door now, or you'll be in worse trouble."

He opens the door. "Come in, Mom, but you won't find it. Look all you want."

She looks around the room. The 8-Ball is gone. Her eyes fall on Josh's hand-held Pac Man. She seizes it. "Fine, if you won't give me the 8-Ball, then I'll take this."

"No! That's my favorite game!"

"Give me the 8-Ball then."

He hesitates, considering. "Go fuck a sheep."

With Josh on her heels, she takes the game to the garage. She grabs a hammer from the pegboard.

"What are you doing?" Fear strains his voice. She places the game on the workbench and raises the hammer. "Stop! I'll give you the 8-Ball. Stop!"

Kate smashes the Pac Man. Bits of clear and yellow plastic fly in every direction. Electronic innards hang from what's left of the game's shell.

"There," she says, her voice trembling. "Now it's settled."

Tears stream down Josh's face. "That was my favorite," he croaks, surveying the mess. "I played it all the time. Uncle Greg and I played when he visited. He couldn't get the hang of it, and I even wrote in my journal about it, how much I liked Uncle Greg, even though he couldn't play Pac Man."

Kate lays down the hammer. Her anger dissipates as quickly as it erupted. Looking at Josh's face, she feels empty and ashamed.

"I'm sorry, Josh, but—"

"It was my favorite toy," he says belligerently, "and you knew it."

"Josh—"

"Two can play at this game." He grabs the hammer and runs to Kate's room. Before she can stop him, he grabs the Belleek vase Mitch bought her on their honeymoon, puts it on the floor and hammers it to pieces.

He stands and faces her. "How's that make you feel."

"Pretty awful," she says slowly. "But not as awful as when I smashed your Pac Man. How about you? How did it make you feel?"

The anger drains from his face. "It didn't feel as good as I thought it would," he mumbles.

She pulls him to her. "I'm sorry, honey. I was wrong. I let anger get the better of me." His arms encircle her; his chest heaves as a new round of tears wrenches him. "I guess this is one we'd better put in our log for Dr. Galen." Josh nods against her. She pulls him closer and gently rocks him. "I'm so sorry, honey. I'm so sorry."

"How you guys doing?" Dr. Galen looks at Josh, who is examining his nails, ignoring the question and the counselor. Silence weights the room.

"Do you have a log for the past two weeks?" Dr. Galen looks at Kate.

"Yes." She hands him three typed pages. "I wrote up a typical meltdown, so you could get an idea of how quickly things go bad. On the good side, Sunny and I are still walking Josh partway to the bus stop most mornings. It's given us some peaceful time together."

Dr. Galen looks up. "Great! Josh, you enjoying your early morning walks with your mom?"

He shrugs. Dr. Galen stares at him briefly, then continues reading.

"Have you read this?" he asks. Josh shrugs. "Josh, I'm talking to you." The counselor's voice is soft.

Kate looks at her son. He's already retreated into his battle armor. She saw him putting it on as they sat in the waiting room. They'd just come from a pleasant dinner together, but the moment they entered this building his expression changed to a surly resolve, and his speech became clipped and rude. Sitting across from him in the waiting room, she knew he was preparing for battle. She read it in his face, in the way he pulled his body into himself, hunched in the chair as if ready for an attack.

"I don't need to read it," Josh says. "It's all lies. You always side with my mom. She lies all the time, but you believe her."

"Says here you threw a fork at your dad while he was

eating dinner last week. Almost hit him in the head. Says you threw it so hard, and I quote, 'it stuck in the wall and vibrated.'"

"That's an exaggeration. I barely tossed it."

"Did it stick in the wall?"

He shrugs again.

"You might have killed your father had it hit him in the temple."

"Yeah, right."

"Why'd you throw the fork?"

"I don't know. I don't remember."

"Josh wanted us to order some magazines for a school fundraiser," Kate interjects. "We agreed to order three, but he wanted us to order four more, so he could win a Game Boy. We said no, so he ripped up the entire order and started yelling and cursing. He was in the kitchen. Mitch and I decided to sit down to dinner in the dining room and ignore him. Then Mitch saw Josh from the corner of his eye making a winding motion. He ducked just as the fork whizzed by."

"Josh?" Dr. Galen waits. Josh stares at his feet. "Josh what was going through your mind when you threw the fork?"

"I don't remember."

"You don't remember what you were thinking?"

"No! I told you already. I remember being mad they wouldn't help me win a Game Boy. But I don't remember what I was thinking when I threw the fork. Why don't you ask Mom what she was thinking when she took a hammer and smashed my Pac Man? That's in there too."

Dr. Galen skims the rest of the log and looks at Kate with raised brows.

"It wasn't my finest moment," she says sheepishly. Dr. Galen chuckles.

"It wasn't funny," Josh growls.

"How did you feel when you smashed the Pac Man?" Dr. Galen asks, ignoring Josh.

"I felt horrible. I've apologized to him more than once. I tried to buy him a new one, but they don't make that model anymore. I did buy him a Pac Man game he can play on the computer, but it's not the same. I still feel bad about it."

"What about you?" Dr. Galen turns to Josh. "Was revenge sweet?"

Josh looks around the room, then down at his feet. "It didn't feel that great."

Dr. Galen nods, writes another note on his clipboard and looks back over the papers Kate gave him. "Josh, could you excuse us? I'd like to talk to your mom alone."

"Be my guest." He leers at the counselor and drags himself up. "Why don't you get Mom to give you a blow job while you're at it." He saunters from the room, slamming the door behind him.

Kate shrivels with embarrassment. She stares at the carpet. "He says that kind of thing a lot."

"Really?" Kate hears Dr. Galen scribbling.

"Yeah. Especially about our neighbor Jack and me. Jack's a bachelor. It's mortifying."

"Why?"

"Isn't it obvious?"

"Do you think Josh's statements reflect on you?" She lifts her shoulders. "They don't. They reflect on Josh."

"Yeah, but I'm his parent. Oh God, why does he say such awful stuff?"

"That's what I want to talk to you about."

"You going to reprimand me about the Pac Man?" She continues to stare at the rug, like a child caught shoplifting.

"No." She can tell by his tone he's smiling, but she doesn't dare look up. She has come to both love and hate this third Michael in her life. At times, he's much too cheerful. His green eyes twinkle as Mitch, Josh and she pour out their souls. He is undaunted by the violence they describe, the pent-up anger they harbor toward one another, the hopelessness they embrace. She often doesn't understand his cheer. She used to wonder if he found their problems amusing. Was he laughing with them or at them? Now she believes his smile comes from the ever-enthusiastic, ever-optimistic elf within him.

"If that's the worst story I hear this week," Dr. Galen continues, "it will be a good week. Kate, you've got to learn to not engage with Josh in the heat of the moment. When he misbehaves, tell him once, then ignore it. When he comes home the next day, have the consequence in place. That will prevent this kind of fight and the inherent escalation."

"Every parenting book I've read says consequences should be immediate, or they lose impact."

"True for most kids. But Josh isn't most kids."

"I'm not sure I want to ignore Josh when he's just hit Reyna with an 8-Ball. What message does that send to the girls?"

"Absolutely, you cannot ignore violent behavior that puts a family member at risk. But I'm talking about what happened after. Once Josh got the 8-Ball out of the trash the first time, you could have said, 'I'm not going to fight over this, but tomorrow, when you get home from school, there will be consequences.' If he asks what, don't explain, just repeat, 'There will be consequences for your behavior.' Then, when he's at school, dispose of the 8-Ball, or institute whatever consequence you deem fit. Take the power cord from the computer. Hide the cookies. Whatever.

"I'm not telling you to give up on parenting, but you want to avoid direct confrontations with Josh whenever possible. You have to develop strategies ahead of time that allow you to enforce your parental authority without having an all-out battle." She nods.

"What I really want to talk about is your log," he continues.

"What about it?"

"Says here Josh comes home from school most days and goes directly to bed."

"Yeah. He started that a few weeks ago."

"Kate, I think he's suffering from acute anxiety or depression, or perhaps both."

"Because he's going to bed?"

"That's one clue. But his behavior here and at home, his constant surliness and negativity also suggest anxiety and depression."

"You mean clinical depression?"

"Yes. Or possibly anxiety disorder. They're closely related."

"You're talking about a chemical imbalance?"

"Yes. There are medications, called selective serotonin reuptake inhibitors, or SSRIs that—"

"He's not taking an antidepressant."

"Kate, there are—"

"No! This is so typical." She leans back against the couch, her arms folded tightly across her chest. "Last spring, you said Josh was a defiant child, what did you call it, oppositional something?"

"Oppositional defiant disorder."

"Right. You said you were one hundred percent certain. That you'd have us straightened out in a few months. Now, after five months, you're pushing drugs. I knew this would happen. Typical American approach. Got a problem, pop a pill."

"Look, Kate, I'm a psychologist. I don't like to admit I can't solve a problem on my own. But Josh isn't just oppositional defiant. He's got something else going on. I'm certain—"

"Just like you were certain before?"

Dr. Galen rolls his eyes. "Look, you need to trust me—"

"That's what you said at the end of our first visit, when

you gave us that book. Now I suppose you're going to give me a book on depression and anxiety disorder."

He slowly surveys Kate's face, making her fidget. "What I'm wondering," he says, "is why you're so frightened of a drug that could cure your son."

"Who said I'm frightened?"

He holds her eyes with a hard stare. He's playing with her. A battle of wills. Who's going to blink first? She vows she won't blink, won't drop her eyes before he does. But even as the thought forms she recalls Jean's words—it's not a battle of wills. Her resolve crumbles; her eyes shift to the window, making her angrier.

"You ever use antidepressants?"

"No."

"Anyone you know use them?" She doesn't answer. "Kate?"

"Isn't our time up?" She looks at her watch.

"Kate! Anyone you know ever use antidepressants?"

"Look, I happen to know there are side effects."

"Yes, but if they're bad—"

"Like suicidal impulses for one. That's what happened to my dad."

Dr. Galen sits up as if called to attention. "Now that I didn't know." Kate twists her hands. "What happened?"

"When he started taking them, he was just depressed. Well, not just depressed. He was drinking, too, and full of anger. But then he started saying how easy it would be to end it all. How much better it would be. One day he told Lily, my sister, he was going to shoot himself. She took him straight to the doctor, ending that experiment. He's on something else now. I don't know what, but it's not working. If anything, he seems worse than ever."

"Well, that helps explain your reaction. So depression runs in your family?"

"Just my Dad."

"Another clue. You never mentioned your dad suffers from depression."

"You never asked, and you never suggested depression might be a problem until today."

"And when you say he was drinking, you mean ..."

"He drinks a lot. All the time."

"An alcoholic."

"Yeah, I guess."

Dr. Galen jots another note. "I understand it's scary to consider treating a child with drugs," he says. "Reactions like your dad's are rare, but I'm not going to lie—even if I wanted to it's pointless, since you already know they can occur. But we'll keep a close eye on it. Kate, if Josh is depressed, would you deprive him of medicine that can improve his life? I've had clients tell me after they began taking antidepressants they felt as if they'd walked out of a cave into sunlight. They never knew what it was like to feel good; by 'good' they meant what you and I call normal."

"My reaction isn't just about Dad. I've read a lot of articles about how doctors are prescribing drugs for kids right and left these days, especially for boys. How we've pathologized boyhood. I've read how boys who misbehave in kindergarten or first grade are immediately put on Ritalin or some other drug, and they turn into zombies. It's the new way of handling discipline problems or kids who don't fit the increasingly narrow mold held by our schools and society."

"I agree drugs are generally overused for adults as well as children. But in this case they're warranted. I wish you'd trust my judgment. That's what you're paying me for, isn't it?"

"I don't want to drug Josh, mess around with his chemistry when he's still developing. And, frankly, I worry about his essence. He has a loving and compassionate soul buried under all his anger. I don't want that essential part of him numbed or put in perpetual sleep."

"We won't let that happen. There are dozens of antidepressants out there. We'll find the right one for Josh. One that makes him feel good without deadening him."

She clamps her jaw shut and glares at the wall.

"Listen, I know a good psychiatrist. He's Native American, practices holistic medicine. Why don't we let him evaluate Josh? If there's any way to treat Josh without drugs, he'll find it."

"No."

Dr. Galen rips a sheet of paper from his clipboard and writes on it. "Here's his name and number." She stands as he holds out the paper. "Call him, Kate.

Chapter 40

"Look! We've got the whole beach to ourselves," Jean says.

Kate parks the van next to a cabana. "October in Florida. My favorite time. Perfect weather and still off season."

"I'm so glad you brought the kids."

"Yeah. Good old teacher planning days."

Josh, Mollie and Reyna burst from the van with the dog in tow. "Can we take Sunny for a run?" Josh asks.

"Absolutely, but don't let Mollie get behind." Sunny and the kids jog to the surf. "Jean, wait for me." Kate circles the van and supports her godmother as she climbs out and shuffles the short distance to the cabana.

"Oh, how wonderful," Jeans says, puffing from the small exertion as she sinks into one of the two chaises nestled in the cabana's shade. "I've always loved Arrowhead Point and have missed coming here. Feels like I've been cooped up forever."

"Just let me unload, then we can relax." As Kate pulls the cooler, beach blanket and sand toys from the van, a man approaches Jean.

"You folks want to rent for the day, half-day or by the hour?"

"Half-day. We won't be longer than that, will we Kate?"

"Half-day's good, but let me pay."

"No. You drove, I pay. How much?"

"Twenty dollars." The man peers under the umbrella. "But for someone good-looking as you, I'll take ten."

"Oh, you're too sweet," Jeans says, handing him a bill. "Thank you."

"You ladies have a good one."

"Wasn't he nice?" Jean asks after the man strolls down the beach. "I think it was my bald head under this Dolphins cap."

Kate hands her a ginger ale and sits in the second chaise. "Nope," she says, popping open her own drink. "It was your eyes. I think when he looked into them, he saw your inner light."

"Oh Kate!"

"It's true, Jean. You don't see it. It's others looking at you, listening to your words, feeling your compassion, who see it—the light of God burning in you. I hope you don't mind me saying so."

"How could I mind? I'm touched."

"Mom!" Josh yells as he and the girls run to the cabana. "Can we set Sunny free? We want to throw sticks in the water for him to fetch."

Kate surveys the beach. She sees dots of people at the point, at least a quarter-mile from them, but no one close.

"Okay, as long as no one's around. Just don't let him play in the ocean too long. He'll end up drinking the saltwater and then have the runs the rest of the day."

"Mommy, look at this!" Mollie lies in the sand, swishes her arms and legs, then jumps up to admire her creation. "An angel!"

"Beautiful."

"Come on, Mollie," Josh says impatiently.

"Mommy," Mollie plops on Kate's legs, "do you believe in angels?"

"I believe you're an angel."

Mollie beams then frowns. "But I mean real angels, like in the Bible."

Kate shakes her head. "No, honey."

"Oh Kate," Jean snorts.

"Mollie, let's go!"

"Just a minute, Josh," Jeans says, then turns to Mollie. "Come here, little Joybug." She holds out her arms and Mollie slides onto her lap. "Of course your mother believes in angels."

"Do you?" Mollie asks Jean.

"Absolutely. I think there's an angel here right now, watching over your little soul. Don't you?"

Mollie nods vigorously, then plucks at a button on Jean's shirt. "But how come I never see him? How come he never talks to me?" She looks up into Jean's eyes. "The angels in the Bible talked to Mary about baby Jesus."

Jean hugs her. "We live in a skeptical age, babe."

"What's that mean?"

"We don't believe in things we can't see, that can't be proven by science. Back when Jesus was a baby, people accepted miracles and angels as part of everyday life. I believe angels are just as real and active today as they were then, but our disbelief and fear get in the way of their work."

"Mollie, we're leaving." Josh turns and starts walking toward the water. Reyna and Sunny follow. Mollie slides from Jean's lap and trots off. After a few yards, she hesitates, then dashes back to Jean and grabs her hand.

"Do you think if I tell my angel every night I believe in him and I'm not afraid of him, he'll talk to me someday?" she asks, her eyes earnest.

"Maybe." Jean says, stroking Mollie's hair. "Anything's possible with God and His messengers." Mollie kisses Jean's cheek then runs after Josh and Reyna.

"Remember, not too much saltwater!" Kate yells.

"Okay!" The kids sprint off, an unleashed Sunny at their heels.

Kate turns to her godmother. "I like what you said about angels."

Jean catches Kate's hand and squeezes, then turns her gaze to the children. "Josh is good today."

"He's always better around other people. I told you Dr. Galen says he's depressed. Wants to put him on an antidepressant."

"It makes sense." Jean sounds like a child who's just discovered buried treasure. "Josh is full of rage, just like your dad."

"Josh isn't an alcoholic. We've kept an eye on that. He isn't drinking."

"But what if alcoholism is only part of your dad's problem? Tell you the truth, I've thought from the day I met your dad his drinking was self-medication for some deeper problem he's never addressed, never knew to. But Josh has a chance to address it."

"Yeah, maybe." Kate takes a sip of ginger ale and tilts her head back, letting the sea breeze cool her face. She's glad it's overcast. Jean couldn't bear the heat of a sunny day.

"It's more than depression with your dad. That would explain his lack of joy—that's what depression does to you, it robs you of joy. But it doesn't explain your dad's rages."

"Maybe that's the alcohol."

"Perhaps, but that's for your dad to figure out. You've got to stay focused on Josh. Dr. Galen's right, a psychiatrist can help you sort this out.

"How amazing, Kate. We have all these chemicals and neurotransmitters and whatnot in our brains, and in most people they're balanced just right—a miracle in itself. But if they get out of whack, they can create such a sense of deep despair or anxiety or rage. That's all this is, Kate, some kind of chemical imbalance. Nothing Mitch or you did caused this. And the good news is, modern medicine can probably correct it, if you'd just get over your phobia about drugs."

Kate laughs in spite of herself. "I do hate drugs," she admits. "Except your Procrit," she adds as an afterthought.

"I love that one. In fact, I'm addicted to it," Jean says with a giggle. "And you know what? I don't care."

"How are you feeling? Really?" Kate faces Jean. The weight and hair loss make her godmother's dark eyes look huge, like an owl's.

"The chemo's not as bad as it was in the beginning. But I have to be honest with you. If they haven't gotten rid of the tumor by the end, I'm not doing chemo again. This is barely living."

"Oh Jean …"

"Darlin' it'll be okay. If worse comes to worse, I'll get hospice in, and I'll have a Cosmo every night. When you come, I'll get one of those guys from the firehouse to wheel me along the boardwalk, and we can drink while we watch the sunset. The men over there are so kind. They've been checking on me several times a week."

"Remind me to go over and kiss each one of them when we take you home."

"I'm sure they'll love that."

"And we won't need hospice. You're going to be fine."

"I'll be fine whatever happens. I need you to know that."

"I do," she whispers.

"Now, back to Josh. Why are you so afraid of the drugs?"

"It's more than just my usual aversion. These drugs haven't been tested on kids. Josh's brain is still developing, and now we're going to give him drugs that will change the balance. The doctors admit they don't know if there are any long-term side effects. I want to do what's right, but I'm afraid. Afraid if I do, afraid if I don't."

"You want to know without doubt you're doing the right thing?"

"Exactly."

Jean chuckles. "Darlin', life rarely provides such luxuries. You've got to go with the best course based on what you know now. And you know Josh needs help. This is more than spoiled child syndrome or teen angst."

"I know, I know. I've already made an appointment with the psychiatrist."

"Wonderful!"

Kate can't help smiling at Jean's enthusiasm. So often her godmother reminds her of Mollie, all joy and awe. "I wanted to talk to you about something else."

"First I need some chips. I'm having a salt craving."

Kate fetches a bag of potato chips and some napkins from a basket. "Want anything else? I've got sandwiches and deviled eggs in the cooler."

"Later. This is fine for now. Sit down and talk to me." Jean opens the bag, pops some chips in her mouth and offers the bag to Kate.

"No thanks, I'll have some with lunch."

"I want to go first," Jeans says. "I've been meaning to ask if you've had any more visitations at night."

Kate grimaces. "No, thank God. They stopped after I began seeing Dr. Galen. But I worry every night, afraid that presence will return. When I wake in the dark, I instinctively look at the door to see if it's moved."

"It can't hurt you, Kate."

"I know. But it scares me."

"We've missed something. Something important. It's interesting the visitations stopped with Dr. Galen. There's a connection there, I'm sure."

"I wish I knew. I'd love to feel free of that thing."

"You'll figure it out; I know it." Jean munches more

chips. "Mmm! These are wonderful." She offers the bag to Kate, who takes a handful. "Now, your turn."

Kate smiles at Jean's show-and-tell tone. "I've been considering what Nick said, you know, about what he heard in his meditation."

"That you're perfect?"

"No."

"You should think about that more than you do. But anyway, what?"

"About letting go."

"Oh, yes."

"Once, back when I was still working for Senator Mimms, he took his staff on a weekend retreat. The emphasis was teamwork. One exercise we all had to do was called a trust fall. One of us stood on a high platform and the rest of us formed two lines facing each other beneath the platform. Each person on the ground clasped hands with the person across from him, forming this long net of hands and arms for the person on the platform to fall into."

"Got it."

"When you fell, you had to do it with your back to the people on the ground. You had to stand with your heels at the very edge and then just fall backward, trusting the folks on the ground to catch you."

"And did they?"

"Every time."

"How fun."

"When it was my turn, Jean, I was terrified. The first time the instructor told me to fall back, I refused, said I wouldn't do it. He was a young man, probably a college student, and he said in this fetching southern accent, 'Now, ma'am, if those folks down there can catch me, they surely can catch a little thing like you.' I told him I'd only do it if he'd put his hand on my shoulder until the last second.

"Jean, it scared the hell out of me."

"But you did it?"

"Yep."

"And they caught you?"

"With ease. But I trembled the rest of the afternoon. It amazed me how afraid I was. I'd just seen these same people catch a two-hundred-fifty-pound executive. Yet I was still scared. Now it occurs to me God is calling me to trust fall into Her arms."

Jean's hand freezes in the chip bag. "Oh Kate, yes."

"But I don't know how to do it."

Jean's rich laughter rings out as a descant to the lapping surf, the children's shrieks and Sunny's bark borne on the breeze. "That's because you're approaching this as an intellectual exercise. It isn't. It's a spiritual leap. The knowledge is instinctive. Just like the baby bird knows when it inches to the edge of the nest, even though it's never flown before, even though it has no proof, that something will rise up and catch it. It *believes* without proof. That's called faith."

"How do you know what a baby bird thinks or believes?"

"I'm sure I was one in an earlier life." Jean chuckles. "The point is, Kate, don't think about it, just do it. Trust, babe."

"Funny, Dr. Galen said he thought Josh was supposed to teach me trust. He meant trusting him and the psychiatrist, that kind of thing. But it's bigger than that. I'm supposed to learn to trust life, trust in its inherent goodness. Trust God no matter the circumstances."

"Yes, oh yes. That's what it's all about. Oh, Kate, it's so good to fall into God. Free-falling is so good."

Chapter
41

Reyna is quiet. She didn't fuss as a baby. Kate remembers insisting to the pediatrician something was wrong: She never cries. The pediatrician just laughed, said Kate was too used to Josh.

She remembers walking by three-month-old Reyna, who was in a curved baby seat that sat on the floor and rocked when the baby moved. Reyna was holding her hand out in front of her, arm straight, examining her fingers as she turned her hand palm in, palm out, palm in, palm out. She was completely absorbed in this new power she'd discovered. Or possibly it was the magnificence of the hand itself that captured her. What does a hand look like to a baby? A star? A truncated octopus? An angel?

The scene defines Reyna. She's an observer. She quietly takes in her surroundings, rarely commenting. What goes on behind her earnest eyes is often a mystery. As she grew older, Reyna's intelligence became clear. In first grade she was tested for the school's program for exceptional children. She scored so high on the IQ test the school psychologist telephoned Kate.

I picked her up from class, he had said. Imagine what I was expecting. Here is a child who still talks baby talk, still counts on her fingers. I was wondering, "Why am I doing this? What idiot recommended her?" Then we started the testing and I thought it'd be over in ten minutes. Ninety minutes later I didn't want to stop. To tell you the truth, I don't often enjoy my job. Testing three to four kids a day. Most of them unequal to the task, pushed by parents who think their child is a prodigy. But your daughter, she scored in the top half of one percent in both math and verbal. Do you realize how rare that is?

Kate didn't. Hadn't really thought much when Reyna's teacher had asked if she could be tested. Didn't know what to say to the psychologist.

I had to call you, he continued. She's truly gifted. The range of knowledge she displayed. The minute details she notices. Her IQ is much higher than ninety-nine percent of the kids who qualify for the gifted program, and they're all in the top two percent. So you can see …

Kate wasn't sure what the psychologist wanted her to see. Reyna is smart. Kate already knew that. Reyna takes in everything. She knew that, too. What does Reyna do with it all? What does she make of the world she examines in "minute detail"? as the psychologist said. What's going through her head now, as the orthopedic doctor wraps her forearm and hand in a cast so the fracture at the base of her thumb will heal, so her hand—the one she examined with such awe years ago—will work properly?

"How did it happen?" the doctor asks, smiling at Reyna, who is intently watching his hands. She doesn't answer.

"Her brother kicked her," Kate says reluctantly.

The doctor's hands stop wrapping. He stares at the half-formed cast, then looks at Kate. He wants more. She sits in silence, wondering if he's considering reporting her for child abuse. A year ago the thought would have scared her.

"Is this a typical display of sibling rivalry in your house?"

he asks lightly.

"My son has problems. He's seeing a counselor—a psychologist—and a psychiatrist. He's on an antidepressant."

The doctor examines Kate's face, as if trying to read the unspoken story behind the hint of her words. He turns back to Reyna and finishes the cast in silence. "Are you mad at your brother?" he asks when he's done.

Reyna looks at the cast. She has chosen light blue. She rubs the damp gauze that will tighten around her arm as it dries. "He gets mad a lot," she says softly. "But I love him."

"You're not angry he kicked you? That he broke your thumb?"

She shrugs. "I forgive him." She keeps rubbing her cast.

"Very generous of you," he says jovially, his hand falling on her shoulder. He calls the nurse in. "Helen, please take this young lady and get her a treat and a sticker. We have lollypops. You like those?" Reyna nods. "Good. Your mom will be out in a minute."

As the nurse ushers her out, Reyna throws a forlorn look at Kate. She doesn't want to go with this strange woman. Kate smiles encouragingly, tries to soothe her with her eyes before the nurse breaks their connection by closing the door.

The doctor has his hand in his pants pocket, is jingling change there as he stares at the floor. "How long has your son been in counseling?"

"About eight months."

"What's the diagnosis?"

Kate rolls her eyes. "The first diagnosis was oppositional defiant disorder. But then the psychologist said my son's depressed, or suffering from anxiety disorder. He's been on an antidepressant for several months. The first one made him worse. The one he's on now seems to be helping, but he still has violent meltdowns. His counselor wants me to talk to the psychiatrist about changing the dosage."

"And your daughter?"

"What about my daughter?"

"Is she getting counseling?"

"No. Just my son, my husband and me. Why do you ask? She seems to be dealing with it. She's not angry."

"So I see. The problem is, she should be." Kate feels as if a rock has been dropped in her already overloaded backpack. "You don't want her to develop the mentality that it's okay for someone to abuse her. That love means accepting all. She can forgive her brother, but she can't tolerate his abuse."

Kate nods, even as her face falls under the weight of his words. "I suppose you're right. I've been so focused on Josh. I'll look into it—counseling for Reyna and I guess Mollie, too."

"Mollie?"

"My youngest. She's just turned five."

"I know someone. A woman. She specializes in children and play therapy. She holds group sessions."

"I don't want Reyna in with a bunch of delinquent kids. She's an innocent."

"No, no. I agree. These are kids like Reyna, from homes where there are problems and violence not of their making but that affect them." The doctor grabs his notepad from the counter and begins to write. "Talk to this woman. Here's her name and number. If you don't like her, then find someone you do. But don't let this go."

Kate takes the paper and looks into his face. His expression is serious but his eyes have a light, a warmth she recognizes. For a moment she feels she's looking into Nick's eyes, or Dr. Galen's.

"Nice to meet you, Mrs. Nardek. I'll need to see your daughter in three weeks for a checkup and then, if all goes well, in six weeks to remove the cast."

"Okay." She turns to the door. The doctor reaches around her and opens it. She feels his other hand lightly touch her shoulder.

"Hang in there," he says softly. "It will all work out." She turns to give him the best smile she can muster, which she's sure is feeble.

"Thank you," she says. "Thanks for everything."

He waves her down the hall. "See you in a few weeks."

Chapter 42

"Why do I have to leave?" Josh is belligerent.

"I need to talk to the doctor alone for a minute." Kate fears Josh is going to stay glued to his seat and make a scene. She can see in his eyes he's considering it. Finally he shrugs up from the couch and saunters out.

"Hurry up," he orders before leaving. Dr. Niyol stands and shuts the door, then settles again into his high-backed leather chair. He's tall and broad-shouldered, with skin the color of milk chocolate. His coarse black hair sports a few streaks of gray. He's in his late fifties, Kate knows from reading his brochure, but he exudes the youthful strength of a warrior as well as the wise calm of an elder.

Dr. Galen said Dr. Niyol was as apt to recommend St. John's Wart as Paxil to his patients. She read an article he wrote in *Psychology Today* decrying the amount of drugs Americans take to treat emotional problems easily managed through diet and exercise. The need for antidepressants would decrease by seventy-five percent or more, he claimed, if people simply exercised aerobically thirty to forty minutes a day—the natural cure for anxiety, mild depression and stress.

"I forgot to tell you I read your article on the overuse

of drugs," she says. Dr. Niyol nods. His eyes, the color of coffee beans, are hard to read, as is his brief smile. "Obviously you believe Josh is one of the twenty-five percent who really need medication."

"Absolutely."

She examines the intricate leather lacing of the dreamcatcher behind him. It spans the wall above the desk. She can tell it's handmade. She shifts her eyes to the opposite side of the office where above a couch hangs a hand-woven wool blanket, its brilliant colors depicting large geometric designs characteristic of the Navajo. She longs to lose herself in the pattern, follow the threads on their journey from one side of the blanket to the other, marveling at how they interweave. But she knows she can't. She promised Dr. Galen she'd talk to Dr. Niyol about either increasing or changing Josh's antidepressant. She'd rather study the blanket.

"The Paxil seemed to help for a while," she says, bringing her eyes back to the psychiatrist. "After he'd been taking it about three weeks, he told me one day he felt different, he felt a way he never had before. I asked him what he meant. He said he woke up and Mischief, his cat, was sleeping beside him, and he thought, 'How wonderful, here's Mischief.' Then he remembered he had a party at school and felt excited about it. Then he remembered a friend of mine was coming over after school with her kids, and the thought made him happy.

"I said I didn't understand what was different about any of those feelings, and he said, 'I woke up and felt good and excited and happy about the day.' He said he usually wakes with dread."

"In other words, he experienced what it's like for a well person to wake in the morning."

"I guess. But he seems moodier than ever. Unpredictable. Then, last week he flew into that rage. I didn't tell you when he was here, but Reyna was sitting on the floor putting on her shoes when he began to kick her. She rolled into a fetal position and held her hands up to protect her head. He was kicking at her head when he broke her thumb. He still claims he didn't hurt her."

"Yes. He refuses to take responsibility for his actions. He was very angry when you told me about your daughter. What did he say, you were ratting on him?"

Kate lifts her shoulders. She hasn't completely recovered from the mortification of Josh yelling at her to "shut up" in front of Dr. Niyol.

"Dr. Galen wanted me to ask you about Josh's medication," she says. "Does he need a higher dose or maybe a different antidepressant? I don't understand why between the counseling and the Paxil he's not getting any better. Is it us? Have we just totally messed him up?"

"It's not you, though you'd like to think so, wouldn't you?"

"Why do you say that?"

"Because if it were your fault, you could fix it." Dr. Niyol stares at Kate, letting his statement penetrate. "But it's not your fault, and you can't fix it by fixing yourself. You're not broken, Mrs. Nardek. From everything I've seen, Josh is lucky to have you and your husband as parents."

"Then why isn't he getting better?"

The psychiatrist folds his hands in his lap and clears his throat. "Mrs. Nardek, you have to consider Josh is bipolar."

"Bipolar?"

"What used to be called manic-depressive. You have to consider—"

"No, I don't!" Her heart has leapt to her throat.

"Mrs. Nardek, if it were just depression or anxiety, he would have responded to treatment by now. And while at times the antidepressant seems to make him feel better, he's now having episodes of mania. You've said it yourself. You go for a short time where he seems calmer. You feel you're moving forward. Then boom. He's volatile, angry, in a violent rage. You're back at square one—or worse. I know Dr. Galen has wondered aloud to you about this 'backsliding,' why you can't seem to maintain forward progress. It's not you. It's what we call cycling."

"Cycling?"

"Moving from manic to depressive states and back again. Bipolar adults might stay in one state or another for months, but children tend to cycle more frequently. Josh is likely a rapid cycler, meaning he goes back and forth from depressive to manic states within a period of days or even several times in one day."

"I don't want to hear this. I don't believe it." She is trembling. She grabs the arms of the chair, ready to lift off.

"Mrs. Nardek—"

"I can't tell you how upset you're making me."

"It doesn't hurt to consider the possibility. That's all I ask."

"It doesn't hurt you. He's not your child."

"It makes sense, given your family history of alcoholism and depression. Actually, from what you've told me of your father, I strongly suspect he's bipolar as well. Please, take this book and read it." He slides a book off his desk and holds it out to her. "Then let's meet again in two weeks, when you've had time to consider."

"I don't understand." She ignores the proffered book. "If Josh is bipolar, where are the manic states? Isn't he supposed to have these incredibly high-energy, creative states? Almost euphoric?"

The psychiatrist drops the book in his lap. "That's what I'm trying to tell you. What this book will explain. Bipolar disorder manifests differently in children. The manic state often displays as what we call raging or emotional storms. This is true in some adults as well. When Josh is calm but surly and somewhat unhappy, he's in the depressive state. When he's volatile and violent, he's manic."

"Great. You're telling me my son is bipolar, but we don't even get the upswing? This is the third diagnosis. First he was oppositional defiant disorder. Then he was depressed. Now you say he's bipolar. What next?" She massages her forehead with her hand. She wants to cry but feels dry, as if she's already spent all her tears.

"I know this is difficult." Dr. Niyol leans forward. Kate can feel his eyes on her, silently pleading. "All these disorders are closely related. They're like cousins. And they share many of the same symptoms. But Josh isn't getting better. And someone is going to get hurt—badly hurt—if we don't treat him.

"Are you going to wait until he puts you or your girls in the hospital? Last week it was a broken thumb; what if next week it's a crushed skull? And it's not only you and the girls at risk, Josh is as well. I'm fairly certain he enters into what we call mixed states, where he stalls in transition and experiences both the raging and increased energy of mania as well as the despair and feelings of worthlessness brought on by depression. This puts him at a high risk of suicide."

"Suicide?" She doesn't mean to whisper.

"Yes, suicide." Dr. Niyol's voice is gentler now, less urgent. "I want Dr. Galen to give Josh a few tests to get a better idea of your son's perceptions, his interpersonal style, his concerns, his sense of self-worth, things of this nature."

"Will the tests confirm your diagnosis?"

"No. They may provide additional information to help us in treating Josh, both medically and in counseling, but there are no definitive tests for this disorder, only a best guess based on the evidence. You will have to trust my experience and my instincts."

"Just trust."

"Please, take this book. It's the best one I've found on adolescent bipolar disorder. It's written specifically for the layman—for parents like you." He holds it out.

She takes the book without looking up, stares at the cover. "If you're right, then what?"

"He shouldn't be on an antidepressant alone, that can make his condition worse."

"Great." Kate doesn't try to swallow her sarcasm.

"We'll add a mood stabilizer. There are a number of different ones. Some work well on one patient but not others. Some can even make the raging worse."

Kate looks skyward. She feels beat.

"It's not a science, but trial and error will find the right combination."

She looks at the table fountain in the corner of Dr. Niyol's office. She wishes the gentle babbling of water could ease the ache in her throat.

"Mrs. Nardek, you should be happy—"

"Happy!"

"Happy that today we have medications to treat your son, to enable him to live a normal life. This is treatable. A hundred years ago, even fifty years ago, your son most likely would have ended up in an institution."

"Yeah, I feel real lucky." She hears the irritation behind Dr. Niyol's sigh. She doesn't care. She hates this man. Won't come back. Won't read his stupid book burdening her lap.

"Read the book, then we'll talk."

"What about counseling?"

"He needs to continue. Medication will only get him halfway home. Counseling must get him the rest of the way."

Josh is waiting for her outside.

"What'd he say?"

"Nothing."

"What's wrong?"

"Nothing. I want to go home. Get in the van."

Josh walks to the passenger side. "Why'd you have to tell him about Reyna? You made it sound like I really hurt her."

"You did!"

"No, I didn't," Josh sneers. "I barely touched her."

"Josh, you broke her thumb. You broke it."

"She's a cry baby. Besides, it wasn't broken; it was just fractured."

Kate freezes, her hand on the keys, about to turn the ignition. She stares at Josh, trying to read his dark expression, trying to fathom whether he really believes what he's saying.

"Josh, when you fracture something, you break it."

"She didn't really even need a cast. The doctor said the cast was just to make sure she didn't hurt it while it was healing."

"The doctor said if she fell on it again, it would shatter and then she'd need surgery."

"You exaggerate everything, Mom. And you lie. You lied to Dr. Niyol, and you lie to Dr. Galen, just to make me look bad."

"I don't have to make you look bad," she snaps. "You do a good enough job on your own." Regret instantly washes over her.

"I hate you." His voice is low and menacing.

"I'm sorry. I didn't mean that."

"Someday, Mom." Josh glares at her, his eyes steel slits. "Someday."

She doesn't bother to tell him not to threaten her, that it's not acceptable. The reprimand will only lead to another rant. She can hear him: I didn't threaten you; I just meant you'll realize the truth someday, said so indignantly he might even convince her—until the next time.

When they arrive home, Josh heads for the living room. Kate pays the babysitter and rummages through the refrigerator gathering leftovers for dinner. Cacophony reverberates from the piano—lightning and thunder, steel-gray whitecaps pitted with cutting rain, howling winds.

She pauses, one hand on the refrigerator door, the other on a container of day-old meatloaf. She hears it in Josh's music, what Dr. Niyol called an emotional storm. She closes the pocket door between the kitchen and dining room and leans against it, trying to shut out Dr. Niyol's words, trying to shut out her son's song.

ate watches Josh run for the ball. He kicks it just before it travels out of bounds, keeping it in play. The game is almost over, and his team is in a frantic rush to score the winning goal. Josh is a mediocre soccer player, but he loves the game and has done well in the city's recreational league, where the emphasis is on fun and sportsmanship. His coach this year is wonderful, makes sure everyone, whether star or stumbler, gets the same amount of playing time.

She watches Josh boot the ball to the center of the field where a teammate takes a shot. The ball flies over the net, missing the goal by inches. A collective moan rises from the parents sitting along the sideline, then applause and shouts of, "Good try," "Hang in there."

A few minutes later the referee, a boy perhaps a year older than Josh, blows three long blasts on his whistle to signal the end of the game. Kate waits as the team meets with the coach for a short critique of the plays and to collect drinks and snacks. After a bit, Josh rambles across the field to her, ball in hand.

"We coulda won."

"A tie is good."

"Yeah, but we need at least one more win to make the playoffs."

"Well, you've got two more chances. I'm sure you'll get there." They stroll along the edge of the long expanse of soccer fields, passing ongoing games.

"I thought you played really well tonight. The best I've ever seen."

"Really?" His face glows with pride for a moment, then falls. "I'm not very good, even when I play my best."

"Hey, you had an assist."

"You saw that?"

"What do you think I'm doing on the sideline, knitting?" She bumps him with her shoulder and actually elicits a chuckle. They're passing a field where a peewee game has just ended. An ugly babble of young voices stops them. On the field, the young members of one of the teams—apparently the losing team—has surrounded their goalie.

"You suck!" yells one of the players. "If it wasn't for you, we'd a won."

"Why don't you do us a favor and get injured before the next game!" yells another. The boy in the center looks close to tears.

"Aw, you gonna cry now? You big baby. Go play on your sister's team."

Josh dashes toward the group. Kate follows him a few steps, then stops, wondering what he's going to do, not sure if she should interfere. He runs up to the boys, towering over them.

"Hey, what's going on here?" he demands, his voice deep with authority.

The boys look up at him. He's sweaty and his uniform is dirty from the game. Kate senses this gives him added power in the eyes of these kids. Nobody answers his question.

"Are you razing your goalie?" He catches the eye of each boy. One by one, the boys look to the ground. "Maybe your coach forgot to tell you, but this is a team sport. You win together and you lose together. Either way, it's never one person's fault."

"Yeah, but he missed every shot they took," one boy says, his voice now more whiny than accusing.

"Well how'd the other team get the ball down to your goal to take a shot in the first place? What were the forwards doing? Who are the forwards?" Several boys reluctantly put their hands up. "Who plays midfield?" More hands go up. "And, where are the fullbacks, who should have been protecting the goal and the goalie?" More hands.

"You guys—all of you—lost the game. And instead of yelling at the goalie here, you should be saying sorry for all the shots on goal."

Some of the boys peek at the goalie. The sense of shame rising in the group is almost palpable.

"Hey, what's going on?" An athletic man in khaki shorts and red T-shirt runs up to them. He stands a head taller than Josh. "Who are you?"

"You their coach?" Josh asks, undaunted.

"Yes."

"Well, you've got a bunch of sore losers."

"I beg your pardon?" The coach's tone is stern.

"Yeah, losers. And I'm not saying that because they lost their game. They were all ganging up on the goalie, blaming him for losing."

The coach surveys the faces of his young players. "Is that true?" No one answers.

"It's easy to be a team when you win," Josh says. "But what really counts is how well you lose."

No one speaks for a moment, then the coach holds out his hand to Josh. "My name is Brian Catwell."

"Joshua Cerveau." Josh shakes the man's hand.

"I want to thank you for intervening. I had no idea this was going on. You're absolutely right. What demonstrates a team's quality and character is grace in both victory and defeat. I'll be giving my guys a stern talking to at our next practice and some extra laps around the field to give them time to meditate on it." Josh grins. He starts to head back to Kate.

"Excuse me, Josh?" He turns back to the coach. "I've been in need of an assistant. We practice once a week, on Tuesday evenings. You interested?" Josh looks at Kate. She sees the eagerness in his eyes and nods.

"Yeah, sure."

"That your mom, there?"

"Yes sir."

Coach Catwell strides over and introduces himself to Kate. "Can I borrow your boy for a minute, so we can exchange information?"

"No problem," Kate says. "You don't mind if I check you out with the league, do you?"

He laughs. "I'd worry if you didn't. We'll be right back."

She watches Josh jog beside the coach to the far side of the field. When he returns, she puts her arm across his shoulders as they head to the car.

"I can't tell you how proud I am of you."

"It just made me so mad, all of them picking on that one kid like a bunch of bullies."

"I know."

"Mom, can I tell you something?"

"Of course, honey."

"The whole time I was talking to them, I was scared."

"You sure didn't show it. No one would have ever guessed."

"And I wanted to cry. I felt so sad for that little boy."

"Oh Josh, that's a good thing. It's called empathy. Being able to identify with another person's pain. It's a good, good thing."

He stops and turns to her. She realizes his face is wet with tears. "Mom, why can't I be good all the time?"

She looks within herself. With effort, she pushes away her anger at Dr. Niyol and the fear feeding it. "Well babe, Dr. Niyol has a theory he wants us to consider."

"What?"

"He believes you have a kind of mood disorder."

"Is that why you were so upset after the meeting?"

"How did you know I was upset?"

"I can tell." He shrugs. "What's a mood disorder?"

"Come on, let's talk in the car." She unlocks the van and slides in. Josh clambers into the passenger seat, throwing his ball in back. She turns to him.

"You know how Derrick has diabetes?"

"Yeah."

"Well, the problem is his body doesn't produce enough of a certain chemical to keep everything in balance."

"Insulin."

"Exactly. Well, our brains also produce a lot of chemicals and sometimes those chemicals get out of balance, just like with diabetes. And just like with diabetes, you can take medicine to restore the balance."

"It's not Derrick's fault he has diabetes."

"Exactly, honey. And if Dr. Niyol is right, it's not your fault you have a mood disorder."

"Do you think he's right?"

"I don't know, but we have to be willing to consider it. If he is right, it's going to take a lot of work to get you to a better, healthier place. Dr. Niyol says medication can help a lot with your anger and general unhappiness. But he says medication is only half the cure."

"What's the other half?"

"Counseling."

"I hate counseling. You guys all just gang up on me. Tell me how bad I am."

"Most people, given their druthers, would rather not have to go to counseling. But in our case, we all need it. For years your dad and I thought the problems we were having with you were all about discipline and ..."

"That I was bad."

"I never thought you were bad," Kate says, closing her eyes and praying God forgives her the lie. "But I felt your behavior was bad. Do you see the difference?"

"I don't know. Kind of."

"We all need to work at counseling so we can forgive the mistakes and all the hurts of the past and try to move forward with love and understanding."

"Can mood disorders be cured?"

"Sometimes," Kate says. "But some mood disorders are always a part of you, like diabetes. You don't really cure them; you manage them with medication. Many people do that and live normal, successful lives."

"I don't want to be sick, Mom. I don't want to have a *disorder*."

"I know. But if Dr. Niyol's right and we figure out the proper treatment, you could get well and feel good, and maybe we could all get along better. Wouldn't that make you happy?" She wonders who she's trying to convince most, her son or herself.

Josh stares at the dash, his face a mask. "Come on," she says, "how 'bout we stop at Annie's Stand and get an ice cream before heading home. I want to celebrate your first foray into manhood."

"What?" Josh looks at her with surprise.

"Josh, I can't tell you how adult you sounded back there, talking to those boys, and then to their coach. It gave me goose bumps. I felt I got a glimpse of the man you're going to be, and I was so proud of you, so proud for you." A pink wave spreads across his face. "Oh my God, Josh, you're blushing!"

"Am not," he says belligerently, turning to the window.

She laughs and she starts the engine. When she hears Josh joining in, she sends a grateful thanks skyward.

Chapter

The phone is ringing when Kate walks through the door, her arms full of groceries. She slides the heavy bags onto the counter and reaches for the handset. She hopes it's Jean with the test results from her recent PET scan.

"Kate?"

"Yes. Linda?" She barely recognizes the voice of Jean's neighbor.

"Kate." Linda's voice is taut, yet Kate can tell her lips are trembling like a compromised dam, the walls slowly giving way under pressure, trickling leaks—innocuous hints of impending disaster.

"What is it?"

"Jean ..."

Icy fingers grip Kate's heart. "What about her?"

"Baby, she's dead."

Kate's mouth falls open. Her body sags like a marionette whose strings have been severed. She stares out the window over the sink, not seeing the pool shaded by oak leaves, the hunter green hedge, the red flash of cardinal wings.

"Kate, are you there? Kate!"

"I'm here." She can barely form the words.

"I tried to call you earlier but only got the machine. I couldn't tell the machine."

"Went to the grocery after getting the girls off to school," Kate says, her voice a monotone.

"Last night we had a thunderstorm." Linda is crying now. "It wasn't anything, really. It came in off the ocean. It was windy but nothing like Agnes. Jack and I were eating dinner. We had all the lights out, enjoying the lightning. Then we heard a terrible crash. At first we thought lightning had hit. We looked out the front window and didn't see anything. Then the back. That's when we saw it." Linda is weeping.

"Saw what?"

Linda sobs uncontrollably.

"What did you see?"

"Jean's maple," she chokes out. "It came down on her house, practically cut it in two." She stops to draw a shuddering breath. "It was pouring rain. We ran to Jean's, calling to her. The lights were off, the electricity cut off. Jack ran back for a flashlight.

"She didn't answer, Kate. The tree fell directly on her bedroom. We couldn't get to her. Then the firemen came. Bill called them when he went for the light. They had to cut their way to her with a chainsaw. She was under the tree. The chief said she must have died instantly. At least she didn't suffer, Kate." Linda adds, her voice cracking. "She didn't suffer."

A tremor, like an earthquake, runs through Kate. Her body shakes uncontrollably. She sinks to her knees, collapses against the cabinets, her hand holding the phone frozen at her ear. She hears Linda trying to swallow her sobs.

"Kate, are you there?"

"I can't … I can't talk right now." She reaches up and gently places the phone on the counter. She can hear Linda's voice calling her, then finally a click. A dial tone. She wonders why she's not crying. Why she doesn't feel anything. Some part of her is standing aside, watching her, giving a running commentary: What's wrong with you? Lost your ability to feel? Thought you loved her. But even this voice—usually so loud and persuasive—is the buzz of a mosquito.

She brushes it aside as she looks into the emptiness welling within her. A vacuum, a black hole. Her chest has a desperate, grasping pain, as if all air has been knocked from it. In her mind, she sees Jean. The tree. The storm. The crash. She can't make sense of the images. They are incomprehensible, like ink blots. What do you see? asks the psychologist. Nothing. I see nothing. Black ink spilled on white paper.

A single tear slides down her face. The phone is speaking again. "If you would like to make a call, please hang up ..." She'd like to call Jean.

She lies on the floor, pulls her knees to her chest, feels the cold tile against her cheek, tastes acid bile. She hears the ticking of the kitchen clock. And then another sound, not yet sound, sharp as spear points, ripping her open, eviscerating her, splintering her heart like harsh pitch shattering glass. All before it ever reaches air.

She covers her ears as a guttural, inhuman wail fills the house. Wonders what poor animal is making this god-awful noise.

The drive to Jean's house blurs by. Kate remembers getting in the van, then parking half a block from Jean's, the ninety minutes in between lost. The house Jean and Nathan called home for more than a decade, and then Jean without Nathan, is crushed.

The top of the maple sprawls across her front yard, blocking the drive, reaching into the road. Branches aflame with Florida's late fall give the disaster an incongruous beauty. Kate walks to the thick limb blocking the driveway, toys with a leaf of fiery gold, one of dozens on the long fingers shooting from the branch.

"She loved you," she whispers. "She loved you so. Why?" The tree was healthy. She knows it. Jean had it checked after Hurricane Agnes, when she was in bed most of the time from chemo. Kate was visiting when the cigar-smoking arborist knocked on the door. Go with him, Jean had ordered in a teasing tone of parental authority. Report back to me.

This tree ain't goin' nowhere, the arborist had said in a backwoods drawl after examining the ground around it, his cigar clenched in his teeth. The hurricane didn't faze it none. He laid a large, rough hand gently on the rugged bark and slid it down to where trunk met earth, his head bent so close to the tree his ear almost brushed the bark. This tree ain't shifted since it was planted. He looked up the line of the trunk reaching for the sky. Growed straight as an arrow. It's a strong un, full of vigor. It'll be here long after we's gone. Mark me. He had refused to take Jean's check.

"So ironic." Kate starts at the voice, then swings around to face Linda. "Didn't mean to sneak up on you." Her voice trembles. Her face is blotchy from crying. "Oh God," she moans, throwing her arms around Kate, her tears slicking Kate's neck.

Kate absently strokes Linda's back as she gazes over the older woman's shoulder, wondering who will clean up this mess. After a moment Linda backs away and blows her nose into a limp hanky. She grabs Kate's arm and pulls her to the curb, where she sinks. Kate sits next to her.

"The firemen asked me to identify her once they got her out," Linda says between sniffs. "A formality. They all knew her. Loved her like their own mothers. Took an hour—getting her free. I sat here in the rain listening to the chainsaw. They brought her out on a gurney, all wrapped up except her face." She pauses to blow her nose again, then wads the handkerchief in one hand and covers her eyes with the other.

"The chief said it was strange. Frankly, he looked freaked." Kate feels Linda glancing at her but can't take her eyes off the gray asphalt at their feet. "Said the tree fell at a slight angle to her bed. Fell across her, crushing her entire body except for her head. The trunk was right next to her head, practically on her pillow. The chief said it made him think of lovers. What a goddamned thing to say."

She shakes her head and wipes her streaming eyes. "He said Jean's eyes were open and her mouth was in an 'Oh.' Said she didn't look afraid, but more like she'd just opened the door and unexpectedly seen an old friend. Of course, they'd closed her eyes and mouth by the time I saw her. Oh Kate!" Linda leans her head on Kate's shoulder, her voice shuddering with sobs. "She looked like she was asleep."

Kate can't find words. The lexicon of her mind is blank. She stares at Linda's hands twisting the soaked handkerchief. She places her hand lightly on Linda's forearm. "She loved this tree," she says softly.

"Yeah, she did," Linda croaks. "She'd sit in her garden and talk to it when she thought no one was around. I'd hear her when I was working in the yard. She'd tell it about her life, her day, even her cancer. She demanded to go out there and sit alone Monday, after the doctor told her the cancer had metastasized in her brain. Turns out that's what was causing her dizzy spells."

"I didn't know."

"She didn't tell anyone. Told the damn tree, that's how I knew. I was eavesdropping. Probably shouldn't have, but she wouldn't tell me what the doctor said, didn't say a word on the drive home."

Linda places her hand on Kate's shoulder and hitches herself up, then reaches to help Kate stand. "I'd like to get hold of that damn arborist," the older woman says. "I knew he was full of shit. I knew the hurricane compromised that tree. But Jean was convinced the guy knew his stuff." She shakes her head. "Doesn't make sense. She was a good judge of people."

Kate remembers Jean in her bed, leaning forward, her eyes eager-bright. Does he know what he's talking about? she asked after the arborist left. Kate sat on the edge of the bed and thought of his hands, calloused and thick-skinned from heavy labor, yet so gentle when he stroked the tree, and his sloppy speech belying his sharp eyes.

Yes, he knows, she answered.

The county extension agent recommended him. I have to say the cigar took me aback.

He knows nature, Kate said, not from books but from some deeper place within him. When he was examining your tree, stroking it, I felt he was communicating with it, having a spiritual dialogue.

Oh Kate, I like him, Jean said. I like seeing him through your eyes.

"You all right, honey?" The corners of Linda's bloodshot eyes are crinkled with concern.

Kate looks at the pavement as she runs her hands through her hair. "Yeah, I'm just … I don't know." She walks slowly to the limb in the driveway and fingers the leaves. "I'm …" She wills her voice steady. "I'm gonna take some of these and wax them."

"Why would you want to?"

"Can I get around back?" Kate asks, ignoring the question. She likes Linda and is grateful for the loving care and loyal friendship she gave Jean. But she desperately wants to be alone. She's a time bomb ticking down to the last second.

"You can go through my yard. I won't go with you. I've had enough of this tree."

They walk in silence along the sidewalk as it curves around Jean's corner lot to Linda's house.

"When you're done, come get some coffee," Linda calls

as Kate heads around the side of her house. "I'll make it fresh."

Kate follows the stone path leading from Linda's back door to Jean's yard. Half of Jean's garden is gone, excavated when the maple fell. A large circle of roots rises at the base of the tree like a web woven by a titanic spider or, perhaps, Arachne in a frenzied effort to save herself from Athena's wrath. Jean introduced her to the strange and fantastic world of the Greek gods and heroes when Kate was a child. She read the stories aloud, laughing with Kate and Jamie over the madcap love affairs of Zeus, ever plagued by the jealous Hera, or mourning the magnificent Achilles, felled by the sop Paris. Oh what tangled webs we weave, Jean would say, then add, with eyes twinkling, that's Sir Walter Scott, not Homer.

She circles the crater left by the fallen tree, touching the webbing of roots as she passes, causing dirt to crumble to the ground. She inhales the smell of green wood and fresh earth, clean dirt as Jean called it—Gaea, who fell in love with Uranus. Earth and Sky star struck—that's what she smells, here in Jean's garden at the edge of winter.

From her pocket Kate pulls out a Swiss army knife, the one Mitch gave her when they married, because her mom had carried one. She's used it maybe a dozen times in sixteen years, mainly to cut the plastic that ties shoes together in low-end department stores so the kids could try them on. Now she walks to the base of the tree's trunk and carves out a piece of bark about two inches long and an inch deep—deep enough to get the meat of the tree. It's still green, life still courses through its veins. How long does it take an uprooted tree to die? To die instantly suddenly loses meaning. Her eyes burn at the thought.

Linda is wrong. Bless her, but she's wrong. Last night's thunderstorm didn't bring down this tree, this titan who had just months before withstood 115-mile-per-hour winds.

The tree fell of its own accord, from some inner will and spirit—the same spirit that brought the cockeyed grin to the arborist's face. It didn't fall; it flung itself on the house, on Jean, sacrificing one hundred years or more of life to save her from a few months of ungodly, drawn-out death. Love returned. Everything, even those things we think of as inanimate, has a spirit, Jean used to say. Everything has its own energy.

"Thank you," Kate whispers as she rubs the wound she's left. She shimmies onto the tree then lies forward, wrapping her arms around the trunk, resting her head against its coarse skin, breathing its scent. Slowly she opens the gates inside her, gingerly releasing the tears she's held tight within, afraid of being overwhelmed, of drowning in a salt sea. She stays an hour, unmoving save for her heaving chest, giving the maple its last watering.

Chapter 45

"Typical," Kate mutters, hearing the doorbell as she steps from the shower. "Coming!" She quickly roughs a towel over her body, then wraps it around her head, yanks on her robe and heads for the front door, tying the robe as she walks. The bell rings again just as she opens the door. Her irritation dissolves when she sees Nick.

"Kate, I came as soon as I heard." He steps over the threshold and wraps her in a bear hug. "I'm so sorry," he whispers. "So sorry."

The warmth of his body is a balm. She leans into his shoulder and closes her eyes. She didn't realize until this moment how tired she is. She rests against him as seconds tick by, then pulls away. He holds her by the shoulders and surveys her.

"Did I get you out of the shower?" he asks, apparently noticing her attire for the first time. "I can stop back later."

"No. I'm so glad you came. Can you give me a minute to pull on some proper clothes?"

"Absolutely. Mitch home yet?"

"He's on his way. Probably get here in half an hour. Would you like something to drink?" She throws the question over her shoulder as she heads to the bedroom. "There's wine, beer and ice tea in the fridge."

"Mind if I have a beer?"

"Help yourself."

A few minutes later, she returns dressed in jeans and a blue flannel shirt. Nick sits on the couch flipping through Mitch's latest *Sports Illustrated*. He tosses it aside as she settles in the chair catty-corner from him. He's holding a bottle of dark ale and offers her one from the coffee table.

"Thought you could use this," he says.

"Thanks." She takes a long sip, enjoying the bitter frost that leaves her throat warm. "How did you hear?"

"Mitch called me."

"Mitch?"

"Uh-huh. Said you needed some moral support. He's a good guy."

"Yeah," says Kate, still in shock over Mitch's thoughtfulness.

"When did it happen?"

"Night before last."

"Why didn't you call?"

"I was gone most of yesterday. I drove down. I wanted to see …" She hesitates, takes another sip. "I was going to call you today; I was going to call some other people too. My sister Lily. My brother Greg. But I couldn't. Every time I picked up the phone, something froze in me. I couldn't say it. I can't say it."

He takes her free hand in his. "Saying it the first time is the hardest."

She bites her lower lip to stop its trembling as she looks into his eyes, but the kindness there is too much. She looks away. "I don't want to cry."

"It's okay to cry. You'll probably cry a lot over the next year, at times you'd least expect. Mourning can be irritating that way."

"I'm not sure I'm even there yet. I'm in this place where I feel I simply can't endure. If anyone has been the face of

God in my life, it's Jean. I brought her my mess and she saw only beauty." Kate's voice cracks on the last words. She looks down as her eyes water. "I can't imagine never hearing her laugh again."

"Her laughter will always be with you. It rings in your heart."

"I can't hear it," she whispers.

"You will, once the screaming pain of her death recedes a bit."

She inhales deeply, sips her beer, then meets his eyes. "All her kids are coming in from out of town over the next few days. They asked if I would put together the memorial service."

"Would you like some help?"

"Could you?"

"It's actually part of my job description."

"Well, we're not holding it in a church. Jean didn't subscribe exclusively to any one denomination or, frankly, to any one religion. We're having it on the beach near her house. Her kids want something nontraditional, you know, spiritual but not religious."

"Something befitting her soul."

"Exactly."

"When is it?"

"Monday. I know it's your day off."

"I don't have any plans. How can I be of use to you?"

"Could you come and lead it? I know it's a lot to ask."

"I'm honored. Truly. Listen, why don't I write up some ideas and pull passages from various places and we can go over it on Friday."

"That'd be great."

"Is there anything special you'd like included?"

She stares out the bay window fronting the street. "My mind's a blank."

"I'll gather a bunch of stuff. Give you lots of choices. Do you want music?"

"I was hoping you'd bring your guitar."

"I'd love to."

"Oh, there is one thing, a hymn. Actually, I'm not sure if it's a hymn. I heard it at a picnic years ago."

"A song?" he asks. She nods. "What's the name of it?"

"I have no idea. I don't even know the first line. But there's a phrase in the chorus, something about trees clapping their hands."

He grins broadly. "I think I know the very one. It's based on Isaiah, chapter fifty-five, verse twelve. I'll have to look it up for the exact wording, but I can quote you Isaiah."

"Okay."

"You will go out in joy and be led forth in peace; the mountains and hills will burst into song before you, and all the trees of the field will clap their hands."

"That's it! Or very close to it."

Nick looks at her questioningly.

"It's not appropriate? I want the memorial service to be a celebration of sorts. Jean wasn't afraid of death. She saw it as simply moving from one dimension to another."

"It's very appropriate. It's also one of my favorites. But I've never had anyone request it for this kind of occasion. Actually, no one's ever requested it. I'm wondering how it came to you."

She frowns. "You're going to think I'm crazy."

"I already think you're crazy."

She can't help smiling as he beams at her. She tells him about Jean's maple. How Jean rescued it, how it grew healthy and strong, how Jean loved it, and how on that last day she told it she had reached the end of her current journey.

"They say the maple fell—knocked down by the storm's winds." Kate looks at the floor. She can no longer face Nick's eyes, afraid of what she might see in them. "I don't think it was a passive act. I don't think the maple fell, I think it ..." She can't say it. It sounds stupid even to her own ears. But she believes it. Nick doesn't speak. They sit in silence. Finally, she peeks up at his face. He's staring at her.

"You know, my wife hates that verse from Isaiah," he says. "Whenever it comes up in the lectionary, she shakes her head and says, 'How can trees clap their hands? Trees don't have hands.' It's one of the few places our visions don't meet."

He leans forward, elbows on knees. "You see, she believes Jesus was speaking metaphorically when he told the Pharisees that, should they quiet the crowds singing and cheering his entrance into Jerusalem, the rocks and stones would take up the chorus."

"Do you believe that, that the stones would sing?"

"The real question is, did Jesus believe it? If he did, I would have loved the Pharisees to silence the crowd, to hear the song of the stones released by perfect faith. That would be something."

"Then you don't think I'm crazy?"

Nick shakes his head. "Not a mite."

"God, I love you."

"The feeling's mutual," he says, playfully tousling her damp hair.

Chapter 46

itch and Josh are arguing. It's almost ten p.m. Josh should be in bed. Their voices rise, Josh's demanding, Mitch's adamant. Kate can't hear from the bedroom what Josh is insisting on. She rushes to the living room as his escalating shouts combine with Sunny's excited barking.

"What's going on?"

"He's an asshole; that's what's going on," says Josh, facing off with his father in the center of the room. "I never get anything I want. I'm sick of it."

"Josh," Kate says, incredulous, "you just got a sailboat for Christmas and the cell phone you said you couldn't live without."

"Now he wants a TV and laptop in his room. I told him no. None of my kids will have TVs in their rooms, period. I told him we'll talk about the computer when his behavior improves. Maybe for his birthday. That's not good enough for him."

"Goddamn right it's not, motherfucker."

"Josh," Kate hisses, "don't talk that way."

"I'll talk any way I want, bitch."

Mitch lunges at Josh, grabs the front of his shirt and drags him so their noses almost touch. Sunny barks high-pitched warnings as he leaps around them. "You will not talk to your mother that way! You hear me?"

Josh throws his arms up, breaking loose, then shoves his father away. "Don't touch me, fuckin' asshole." Sunny charges between them, his bark taking on a gravelly note.

As Mitch stumbles back, Josh picks up the clay pot holding the Christmas cactus and hurls it. The pot flies at Mitch's head. Kate flinches in sympathy as her husband raises his arms, trying to deflect the blow. The earthen pot hits his outstretched hands and crashes to the floor. Mitch falls back, landing on his butt. Sunny yelps as potsherds, dirt and cactus flowers spew across the polished wood planks.

They all stare at the mess in stunned silence. Kate's eyes harden at the sight of the Christmas cactus lying upside down, its arms smashed. She looks at Mitch, who is pushing himself up off the floor. "Are you all right?"

"You goddamn shit. I'm going to kill you." He rushes Josh. Kate jumps to snatch his arm.

"Mitch, stop. We can't do this," she pleads.

He glares past her at Josh. "I'm calling the police."

"Yeah, you do that, little pussy. Can't handle your big, bad son. Have to call your little friends down at the station. I'm so scared."

"Josh, stop it," Kate orders over her shoulder. "You're already in enough trouble."

"Get a broom and clean it up," Mitch growls through clenched teeth. His face is violet as he leans into Kate.

"Fuck you." Josh sits on the couch and begins sorting through the mail Kate left on the coffee table.

"Mitch, just back off," she whispers. His body relaxes against her. "I'll clean up, then we'll call Dr. Galen. We'll deal with Josh tomorrow." Raising her voice, she adds, "Josh, there will be serious consequences."

"Fuck you, bitch."

Kate fetches a broom and dustpan from the kitchen and begins to sweep. Mitch watches a moment then storms to their bedroom. He's feeling exactly what she's feeling: impotence. Despite counseling and drugs, Josh is still out of control. No, he's worse. The thought stops her mid-sweep. She needs to call Dr. Niyol before she calls Dr. Galen. She looks at her watch. Oh well, she's paying enough to have them answer a late-night call now and then.

She sees a menacing shadow from the corner of her eye and swings around just as Josh springs forward, wielding the letter opener over his head like a dagger. He plunges his arm toward her chest. She staggers back, brandishing the broom as a shield. Her scream is lost in Sunny's vicious snarl. The dog is in the air between them, then on Josh, knocking him off his feet.

Josh howls in pain as the letter opener clatters across the floor. Sunny retreats as quickly as he attacked. He stands in front of her now, facing Josh, hackles raised like a testy porcupine, his throat vibrating with a menacing warning.

"He bit me! He bit me!" Josh curls in a fetal position, holding his wrist, crying.

"What in God's name happened?" Mitch runs from the bedroom and surveys the scene. "Did the dog bite Josh?"

"Josh came at me with the letter opener." Kate's voice is emotionless, as if she's recounting the scene of a play. "He could have killed me. The dog jumped between us. He bit Josh's hand."

"I wasn't really going to stab you," Josh moans. "I was only trying to scare you. I was just kidding. Look at my wrist! I'm bleeding."

Kate looks at Sunny. "Sit, boy." The dog sits, then turns and stares at her. "What did you do?" she whispers, squatting in front of him. Sunny lifts his right paw, placing it lightly on her knee and looks into her eyes. He looks just like Sandy. She shakes her head. He doesn't look anything like Sandy. Her chest tightens as something like fear, though not fear, expands like a helium balloon within her. She could swear she glimpsed Sandy in those eyes.

"MOM! Don't you care the fucking dog bit me?" Josh's tears have turned to outrage.

"He barely broke the flesh." Mitch is leaning over Josh, examining his wrist. "God, it sounded like the dog was eating him."

"He bit me. He ought to be shot."

Kate stands and puts her hand on Sunny's head to steady herself. "No one's getting stabbed or shot in this house. Josh, go clean up your wrist, then wait in your room."

"What are you going to do?"

"I'm going to talk to your father. Then we'll decide."

Josh stands and glares at Sunny. He feigns a kick. The dog doesn't waver. "I'm gonna kill that dog. Just wait and see." Josh saunters to the hall, then stops and turns to Kate. "It was just a letter opener, Mom. It wouldn't have hurt you."

An explosion of anger decimates Kate's detached calm. She grits her teeth as she takes two long strides to the letter opener, scoops it off the floor, seizes Josh's arm and drags him to the kitchen.

"Whatcha doin'?" he whines. She grabs an apple from the refrigerator, slams it on the counter, lifts the letter opener over her head and snaps her arm down. The cleanly sliced apple halves rock on the counter. The letter opener lies between them, beaded with juice.

"Big deal. It's just an apple."

"GET TO YOUR ROOM!" She wants to strike him, but she holds her arms stiff at her sides, her hands balled.

"God, nobody can take a joke around here." He heads to the bathroom. "Assholes," he mumbles.

"You okay?" Mitch asks after Josh leaves. Kate wanders back to the living room and drops into a chair. Sunny sits next to her and rests his head on her knee.

"I can't stop shaking. Mitch, he scared me."

Mitch stands behind her and massages her shoulders.

"What do you want to do?"

"I want to call Dr. Niyol, ask him if Josh's medication could be making him worse. Then I want to call the police."

"If we call the police, they may arrest him. It will go on his record."

"I can't help it. I can't have a person in this house, whether my child or not, actively threaten to kill me. I want to call the police."

"Okay. I'll call right now." Mitch heads for the kitchen.

"Mommy?" Mollie peeks from behind the rocker at the far end of the room, tears streaking her face.

"Mollie, what are you doing up?" She holds out her arms and her youngest runs into them.

"Josh and Daddy were shouting. Then Sunny barked ..." Mollie buries her face in Kate's shoulder and sobs.

"Honey, it's okay. We just had a disagreement. It's over now."

"Muom—mee, are we—ee going to ge—get ri—id of Sun—unny?" she chokes out between sobs.

"No, baby. Why would you ask that? Sunny's going to stay right here. He's our dog. Now come on, take a deep breath, like this." Kate inhales through her nose, fully expanding her lungs. Mollie imitates her. "There. Better?" Mollie nods. Kate holds her daughter close in her lap.

"But you sai—aid, Mommy. You said if Sunny ever bi—it anyone he couldn't stay—ay."

"Well," Kate strokes Mollie's hair, "I suppose there are exceptions for everything. Besides, Sunny didn't really bite Josh. He just scared him."

"So we can keep him?"

"Yes, baby." She gives her a quick squeeze. "Now, how would you like to lie in my bed for a while?"

"Can Sunny stay with me?"

"Absolutely." Kate carries Mollie into the master bedroom and tucks her in the king-size bed. She calls Sunny, who lies next to the bed, then she bends over and kisses Mollie's forehead.

"Thanks, Mommy."

"Okay, little one. Now go to sleep."

"Can I sleep here all night?"

"Okay, but just tonight. Deal?"

"Deal."

Kate heads back to the living room where Mitch sits with the phone in his hands. "I've put a call into Dr. Niyol's answering service," he says. "They say he'll call back in a few minutes. The police are on their way."

Sirens approach in less than five minutes.

"What's that?" Josh says, running from his room. "Did you call the police?"

"Yes."

"You called the police?" His cold mask of indifference crumples into fear. Fresh tears erupt. "They're going to arrest me. They're going to take me away. Please, Mom, I'm sorry. I didn't mean it," he wails. "I didn't mean it!"

She knows the tears are real. Knows beneath all the anger and rage is a scared, confused boy. "I'm sorry, baby. But you crossed a line."

"Please, Mom, please." The doorbell rings. Josh turns and runs to his room.

A short, burly officer follows Mitch into the living room. He holds out his hand for Kate to shake, introducing himself as Officer McNeil. Kate tells him what happened, tells him about the doctors, the diagnoses, the drugs, how they're still in a trial-and-error period.

"You've got three choices," Officer McNeil says when Kate finishes. "You can ask us to Baker Act him, or—"

"Baker Act him?" Mitch interrupts. "I thought that was only for extreme cases."

"Under the Baker Act, police can take into custody any person who appears to be a danger to himself or others due to a mental disorder and admit him on an involuntary basis to a psychiatric hospital. The hospital evaluates the person and decides whether he indeed presents a danger and needs to be committed or whether he can be released and treated as an outpatient."

"The other options?"

"We can arrest him. But then he's in the criminal justice system, and, frankly, you don't want that. At least not at this point. Lots of bad stuff goes on in jail, and there're a lot of bad influences. Doesn't really sound like your son's a criminal, and it wouldn't be smart to expose him to that element."

"What's left?"

"You can let me speak to him. I understand your son's ill, but his illness shouldn't define him."

Kate shakes her head. "Last month, I took him to meet with the school resource officer—Deputy Johnston—because Josh keeps threatening to kill us. Deputy Johnston told Josh he was committing a crime when he threatened us, that he could be arrested for it, and told me in front of Josh to call him if Josh did it again. Josh was very polite during the whole thing. Listened attentively to the deputy, saying, 'Yes sir, yes sir.'

"But the minute we hit the parking lot, he called the deputy a, and I quote, 'fucking asshole,' and said mockingly, 'Was I supposed to be scared of the big, bad policey man?' He called me a bitch for ratting on him and said if I ever did it again, I'd be sorry. So, you see how much effect a talk from a deputy had.

"I'm not sure what to do." Kate looks at Mitch. "I'm not sure having another officer talk to him is going to make a difference."

"I'd like you to let me and my colleagues take a crack at the boy," Deputy McNeil says, bringing Kate's attention back to him, "give the kid a bit of a reality check. In the long run, it'd be better for him to avoid an arrest record now. If we can't shake some sense into him, then the next time something happens, we'll Baker Act him. But for now, my advice is let us talk, take it up a few notches from Deputy Johnston."

The phone rings. "Could you excuse me a minute? That's his doctor."

"Yes, ma'am."

Kate answers the kitchen phone.

"Mrs. Nardek? Dr. Niyol here."

"I'm sorry to call so late, but we've had a bad meltdown tonight. The police are here." She relates the evening's events. "Is it possible this new mood stabilizer you put him on is making him worse?" she asks.

"It's a distinct possibility. Don't let him take any more. I'll call in a new prescription tonight. Do you have an all-night pharmacy near you?"

"Yes. The CVS on A1A."

"Okay. I'm going to call in a prescription for an antipsychotic—"

"An antipsychotic?"

"This is just a temporary move. This drug also works as a mood stabilizer, and it takes effect quickly. I'd rather he not be on this long term. But for now it's warranted. Have him start it tonight, if you can, or first thing in the morning."

"The police are here. They said one option is to Baker Act him."

"Is Josh still out of control?"

"No, he's calmed down, but he's scared. The police want to talk to him."

"The Baker Act is really for patients who can't regain control. If Josh is no longer exhibiting violent behavior, then he'll be released within twenty-four hours. It will be a lot of headache and little, if any, gain. Let the police talk to him."

"Dr. Galen tells me Josh is refusing to participate in a

meaningful way in therapy, which is as important as the medication. He'll have to learn sometime what happens if he doesn't fully treat his disorder. Better now, when we have some control over the consequences, than when he's an adult with no one there to explain or protect him. If you have any more problems, any at all, call me immediately."

"Okay. And I'm sorry to have—"

"No need to apologize. That's what I'm here for."

Kate leans on the kitchen counter after hanging up, then heads back to the living room.

"That was the doctor. He's prescribed a new medication for Josh. But he also thinks you should talk to him," she tells Officer McNeil. "You won't hurt him, will you?"

"No ma'am. But we might scare him a little."

She looks at Mitch. He nods. "Okay," she says. She finds Josh in his bedroom sitting in the far corner, partially obscured by the bed. "Honey, Dr. Niyol called. He said this latest medication could be making you worse, so we're going to try something else. I'm going to send your father out for the new prescription. Meanwhile, the deputy wants to speak to you."

"Please, Mom. I'm sorry. I didn't mean it."

"If you don't come out, he'll have to come get you. That would be worse." He pushes up from the floor, drags his forearm across his nose and follows her to the living room.

The deputy is holding the letter opener, repeatedly smacking its blade against his palm. "You threaten your mother with this?" His voice is as sharp-edged as the blade.

"I didn't mean anything," Josh mumbles.

"You're going to have to come with me." Josh turns pleading eyes to Kate. "Your parents will wait here." The deputy takes Josh's arm and escorts him out the front door.

Kate peers through the curtains. Another sheriff's car has arrived. The deputies frisk Josh and put him in the backseat of the first cruiser. She pulls away from the window. She can't watch.

Thirty minutes later, Deputy McNeil knocks on the door. "Your son would like to speak to you if you're willing," he says to Kate. She nods. Officer McNeil motions Josh forward.

"Officer McNeil, sir, may I have your permission to enter the house, sir?" Josh croaks, tears streaming down his face, nose dripping.

"Yes."

Josh enters and walks to Kate. "Officer McNeil, sir, may I have permission to speak to my mother, sir?"

"Yes."

"Mom, I'm very sorry I threatened you with a letter opener," he chokes out. "I'll never do it or anything like it again."

"Okay, honey."

"Officer McNeil, sir, may I have permission to go to my room, sir?"

"Yes, you may." Josh heads to his room without looking back.

"Ma'am, here's my card." Kate turns to Officer McNeil. "We were pretty hard on him, but it's worth it if it keeps him out of jail down the line. I put my cell number on here. Call me if you have any other problems. Even if I'm not on duty."

"Thanks."

"There's one more thing, ma'am."

"Yes."

"I don't want your son's lasting impression of law enforcement to be negative. He seems to be a good kid at heart. I told him that. But he's pretty upset with me right now. I was wondering if you'd mind my stopping by in a week or so to check up on him, maybe take him to lunch down at the grill, see how he's doing?"

"Not at all. That would be wonderful."

"My pleasure. Now, I just need some information from you to file our report."

After Officer McNeil leaves, Kate tiptoes toward Josh's room. Before she gets halfway down the hall, she hears the shower. She rests her ear against the bathroom door, hears him choking out abortive sobs. She knocks. He doesn't answer. She cracks open the door.

"Josh, I'm putting your new medication next to your bed. Make sure you take it, okay?"

No answer.

"Okay?"

"Okay, Mom."

She heads back to the living room, where Mitch sits on the couch, examining his hands.

"Josh in bed?"

"He's still in the shower. He's still crying."

"Well, maybe this will make an impression."

"God, I hope this was the right thing to do."

"Kate, we can only do the best we can. There's no point second-guessing. This Officer McNeil seems to have Josh's best interest at heart."

"I hope so."

"Come here." She slides onto the couch and leans into his chest. He strokes her hair as he rests the side of his face against her head. "I love you. We'll get through this." She closes her eyes, enjoying the safety of his arms. The clock ticks off thirty minutes before she gets up to check on Josh. He's in bed, his back to the door. She hears his ragged breathing, is sure he's still awake.

"Josh?" He doesn't answer. "I love you."

"Go away." His voice is jagged from crying.

She retreats and looks in on Reyna, whose bedroom is next to Josh's. A shiver runs through her at the thought of leaving Reyna here, on the far side of the house from the master bedroom.

She walks to the garage and takes down the saws, the hammer, the screwdrivers, the hatchet, anything Josh might wield as a weapon, and locks them in the trunk of Mitch's car. She walks to the kitchen, collects the carving knives, steak knives, the long-pronged grilling fork and takes them, too, to Mitch's trunk. Then she heads back to Reyna's room, gathers the sleeping child in her arms and carries her to the master bedroom, laying her next to her sister.

"What are you doing?" Mitch whispers from the doorway.

"I can't sleep tonight unless our bedroom door is locked. And we can't lock the door if the girls are out there."

"Honey, it's over. Josh has gone to bed."

"I know I'm probably overreacting, but I'm not going to ignore my instincts. Either we lock the door, or the girls and I go to a hotel."

"Okay, okay, we'll lock the door." Mitch surveys the bed. "How are we all going to fit? You know Mollie; she'll take up half the bed."

"I'll sleep on the floor."

"Are we going to do this every night?"

"Let's just take it one night at a time." She spreads a comforter on the floor next to the bed and fetches a pillow from the closet. She kneels, arranging her nest. Sunny circles the blanket and lies in the middle of it.

"Guess you won't be sleeping alone," Mitch says, his smile sad and longing.

"It's just tonight, honey."

"Why don't we let Sunny sleep on the bed, and I'll sleep on the floor with you?"

"But you always say the dog isn't allowed—"

"It's just for tonight. Isn't that what you said?"

"Yes," she says, holding out her arms. "Just for tonight."

Chapter 47

She wakes to the sound of giggling. For a moment she's disoriented. Why is she on the floor? Then it all comes back in a flash of ugly images. Mollie is on the bed giggling and snuggling with Sunny. "Shhh," Kate hears her say, then more giggles.

Kate sits up, coming face to face with Mollie. The child's smile flips to a frown. "He didn't mean to get in the bed," Mollie says. "He's sorry."

"It's okay." Kate pats her daughter's cheek. "We thought you and Reyna could use some Sunny love last night."

"You mean it's all right?"

"Just this one time."

Mollie throws her arms around Kate's neck, squealing joyfully.

"Hey, what's all the racket? It's not even six-thirty."

Mollie scrambles out of bed and jumps under the blanket on the floor, pressing up against Mitch. "What's this?" he says in mock dismay. "Where'd this goblin come from?"

Mollie giggles. "I'm not a goblin."

"Remind me again why we had all these children." The soft light in Mitch's eyes belies his plaintive tone. He ducks down with a burst of protest punctuated by laughter as the tickling begins. Kate marvels, yet again, at the light Mollie brings them. No matter the events of the previous day, she wakes with a smile and a song.

The contrast between this little pip and Josh is stark. Kate often thinks Josh's soul missed the helping of joy when going through the serving line of attributes before birth. Later, when Mollie came through, the angels said, Hey, somehow we ended up with an extra helping of joy. Why don't you have it?

As she watches Mitch gently wrestle with Mollie, she laughs to herself at how adamantly he fought having this third child. When Kate first met him, Mitch often declared he didn't want children. He hated hearing a whiny child or wailing infant while eating out. It had the same effect on him as dragging fingernails across a chalkboard. He'd scowl painfully, his lips forming an ugly, tight frown. From the beginning, Kate made clear her uncompromising stance on children: She wanted them.

Why do you want them? Mitch asked her one evening as they snuggled on the sofa in his two-bedroom condo overlooking the Atlantic. They're so messy and so, so … inconvenient. I make my decisions and try to arrange my life based on the maximum convenience. He puffed up with that last statement, causing Kate to burst into laughter. What's so funny? he had asked, his expression ambivalent, as if he couldn't decide whether he should be hurt or join in her hysterics.

Most things worth having in life are terribly inconvenient, Kate said once she caught her breath.

Like what?

Like love. It can be very inconvenient at times to love another person, because you can't just worry about yourself anymore—what you want or what's best for you. You have to take the other person into consideration; sometimes you have to compromise. It's out of your way to drive me to work when my car is in the shop, but you do it.

Yeah, but that's different.

Kate just smiled. She had told Mitch more than once not to fall in love with her if he was adamant on his no-kids stance. He kept asking her out. When he finally proposed, he agreed to have children. After Josh was born, he said his end of the marriage bargain had been fulfilled. But Kate shook her head. I said I wanted children, not a child. Children. Plural.

Three and a half years later, they had Reyna. Mitch was enthralled with this baby girl who never cried but only stared intensely. So was Kate. Her desire to have children was as old as her first memories. It blossomed from her essence. Once Josh was born, she'd insisted they have a second child, not so much to fulfill her own desire—Josh had done that— but as a gift to her son.

Kate knew her own siblings were her greatest teachers in lessons of compromise and flexibility, bending with life's flow. As a teenager with two other kids in the house, all needing to get somewhere and only one car among them, Kate learned on-the-spot problem solving. Rearranging plans or working out new ones to accommodate everyone's needs if not fully, at least partially, was a fairly common requirement. Her brother might be ten minutes late for football practice (requiring him to run ten extra laps), or she might miss the first half hour of play rehearsal or, conversely, have to show up a half-hour early, but generally they figured out a way for everyone to get where they needed to go.

Mitch, an only child, never had to do such juggling as a kid. When he got his driver's license, his parents immediately gave him a car, so he could do what he wanted when he wanted without concern for anyone else's plans. Consequently, he tended to be far more rigid than Kate early in their relationship, easily upset by a change in plans, especially if it required a compromise from him.

When you have only one child, he grows up thinking the universe revolves around him, Kate said when Mitch first balked at having a second child. No matter how much you as a parent are aware of the problem, no matter how much you work against it, in fact, the universe does revolve around him.

You're saying only children are spoiled? Mitch asked, raising his eyebrows like Groucho Marx.

I'm saying only children tend to be self-centered.

I'm not self-centered!

Well …

Mitch lowered his chin and peered at her as if over the rim of glasses, giving her what she playfully called "the look."

After Reyna's birth, Kate agreed to Mitch's insistence that two Cerveau-Nardek babies fulfilled their obligation to keep the world properly populated. More than a year passed before Kate began to feel the yearning within her. But this time it wasn't from her, wasn't born of her essence. The first time she brought up a third child, Mitch exploded. We decided this after Reyna was born. Now you're coming back at me? The answer is no.

Kate didn't understand this persistent calling deep within her but, try as she might, she couldn't ignore it. Each time she broached the subject, the arguments got uglier. Why are you doing this to us? Mitch would ask. We had an agreement and now you're reneging. It's dishonest and it's unfair to me. You're asking me to do something that will make me unhappy for the rest of my life. Kate would leave the room crying, guilt, resentment and anger wrestling within her. She'd go a few weeks trying to ignore this ever-present call within her until her heart felt it would break from sadness and sharp-edged fear. Then she'd go to Mitch and they would fight, again.

One night Mitch was in his usual sprawl on the floor reading his latest techno-thriller. Kate came into the room and quietly sat in the rocker near his feet. I need to talk to you, she said. No more kids, he answered, his voice hard as stone, his eyes fixed on his book.

You said recently if we have another child, you'll never be happy.

That's right.

You're wrong. The minute you look into our new baby's eyes, you'll fall in love, just like you fell in love with Josh and Reyna.

I won't fall in love with another four years of diapers, being awakened in the middle of my nights by crying and worrying about yet another four years of college tuition.

I'm going to tell you something you probably won't understand, because I don't understand, so I'm not sure I can really explain it. He laid down his book, sighing heavily.

Okay, I'm listening.

There's something in me. It's like a voice—not even a voice, really. More like another life inside me beckoning to be born, calling out to me. I feel its call as clearly as I hear your voice.

I love you, Mitch. I don't want to make you unhappy. But I have a fear, similar to yours, that if I ignore this voice it will forever haunt me—like an aborted child. It angers me that you're asking me to ignore this inner calling. What scares me is I'm not getting over the anger. It's not like me. But for some reason, as hard as I've tried, I can't let this go, and I'm afraid down the road, once the other kids are grown, this anger simmering inside me will have built an impervious barrier between us, one too old and fortified by years of bitterness to break down. I've thought about this a lot. I've thought about divorcing you.

Now, wait a minute. He pushed himself up on his elbow.

Mitch, listen. I've *thought* about divorcing you, but I've decided as powerful as this thing is within me—this life begging to be born—I love you, and if I have to choose, then I choose you. But I need help getting over my anger and resentment. So I want us to go to counseling, to help me figure out how to let go. I tried. I can't do it by myself.

He stared at her open-mouthed, his eyes flashing panicked confusion.

I don't want you to be unhappy, he said finally.

And I don't want you to be, either.

Let's talk about it tomorrow, he said, his voice weary.

Okay. Guess I'll finish up the kitchen.

Later, when Kate walked from the kitchen to their bedroom, she saw Mitch lying on the floor staring at the ceiling, his book untouched where he had dropped it earlier.

The next day, Mitch snuck up behind Kate and wrapped his arms around her as she washed the breakfast dishes. So, when do we start making baby number three? he whispered, nuzzling her ear. Kate remembers later telling Jean the story.

My God, the man will do anything to avoid counseling, she said, throwing them both into a fit of laughter. Kate chuckles at the irony.

"Hey, what's so funny?" Mitch asks as he holds squealing Mollie at arm's length with one hand and tickles her with the other. "I think your mom needs some tickling," he says, turning to Mollie. "Let's get her." Before Kate can escape, the two are on her, pulling her into a wrestling match of love and laughter.

Chapter 48

ate takes Sunny for his six a.m. walk. When she returns a half-hour later, she falls back in bed, fully dressed, telling Mitch to wake her by seven-thirty so she can get the girls up and ready for school. She is so tired. So very tired. She vaguely hears Mitch hustling the girls through the morning routine, fights to wake, struggles to open her eyes, but her lids are lead.

Mitch doesn't wake her. The phone does, four hours later. Long enough for her to have a series of gut-twisting dreams that evaporate upon waking, leaving nothing behind save an insubstantial sense of anxiety.

"Hello." She hears the slow heaviness of her voice.

"Kate?"

"Yes."

"It's Lily."

"Lily."

"I woke you. I'm so sorry."

"No, it's okay. I needed to get up," she tries to say lightly, embarrassed at having been caught. "I got up early and then went back to bed."

"Wish I could do that, but the horses won't wait."

"Yeah." Kate leans her elbow on the bedside stand and rubs her forehead.

"I had to call you, now you're into writing. I just read a great book; it's a novel about a ballet dancer. I want you to read it. I'd love to discuss it with you. Gosh darn, Sis, it's so well written and powerful. Made me laugh and cry, sometimes at the same time."

Lily continues to extol the book, not realizing each sentence of praise is a knife slash. *You'll never finish your book*, Kate's internal critic laments over Lily's excited chatter. *You're kidding yourself. You can't write. Even if you could, you won't. You're lazy. Afraid of the truth. Your dream is nothing but a stupid fantasy.*

"… know you're busy with the kids and all, but I want to hear from you on this," Lily is saying. "I want your opinion."

"I'll read it. I'll check it out from the library today." The thought fills her with dread. She knows she'll read each line as a reprimand of her own lame efforts to write her novel. Within her, the dragon of jealousy sears her with its fire-breath and cuts her with whips of its barbed tail.

Lily asks about the kids. Kate hasn't told her, hasn't told anyone about the latest diagnosis and test results. Phrases from the written report of the personality tests Dr. Galen gave Josh flash before her: Self-sabotaging … overly critical of self and others … feels lost, empty, inadequate, hopeless … overwhelmed … sees himself as a perpetual failure … easily frustrated … isolates himself socially … inflames others to alleviate anguish caused by lack of self-esteem and feelings of guilt … symptoms indicative of bipolar disorder.

The worst sentence, the one that made the page shake in her hands, noted Josh's answers not only signified severe depression and anxiety but also revealed "dangerous ideation." *What does that mean, dangerous ideation?* she asked Dr. Galen. His expression told her. Thoughts of suicide.

"Things are going well," she tells Lily. She can't bring

herself to discuss Josh. She read the book on bipolar disorder, and for the first time his behavior and all his symptoms made sense. Even the fact he's hot all the time—temperature dysregulation, Dr. Niyol called it.

She can't bring herself to share with Lily the failed drug trials, the introduction of antipsychotics after the letter-opener incident. Risperdal put an end to the physical violence, but Josh is still surly, his attitude often hostile. A wave of grief is building in her and has been ever since her last visit with Dr. Galen, when he told her Josh is one of his most difficult cases. She fears, like a tsunami, this grief will crash upon and devastate her.

"Kate, you okay?"

"Yeah, fine. How are the horses?" The question sounds feeble to her own ears. "Did the one mare ever deliver?"

"Last night, actually. A chestnut colt. Was a long labor. At one point I got a little worried, but Sally pulled through. We won't breed her again, though."

"Gonna retire her?"

"Just from breeding. She's still a great teaching horse for the little ones. Oh Kate, you'd just love this new student I have, Jacob. He's thirteen. Isn't that Josh's age?"

"He's fourteen now."

"Well, his mom brought him to me after Christmas break because he's goofing off in school. Too much skateboarding with his friends, showing off for the girls. He got caught sneaking out at night a couple of times. She said he needs to be taught discipline, and she had heard from Amy Wilcox—I teach her daughter—what a great teacher and mentor I am. That was so nice of her to say.

"So now I've got this thirteen-year-old hotdog out at the barn three afternoons a week. He doesn't give two cookies for horses and would much rather be riding a trail bike."

"Sounds like a pain."

"Funny thing, he really isn't." The words pour from her in

a rush of enthusiasm. "I don't put up with any of his shenani-
gans. Can't tell you how many times he's had to clean stalls
since he's been here, and though he acts resentful, he's developing a grudging respect for me. At least, I hope that's what's
going on. Really, he's a good kid at heart, and I'm connecting
with him. By the end of the year, he just may be a bona fide
horse lover and making better grades in school to boot. I'm
enjoying working with him despite the headaches. Gives me a
taste of what it must be like to have a son."

"That's great, Lily." Kate keeps her voice cheerful with
effort. She doesn't want Lily to hear her dragon hiss at this
boy's mother. Doesn't want her sister to know she'd give
anything for Josh to goof off skateboarding with friends, for
Josh to have friends. "Listen, hon," she says, "turns out I've
slept through all my morning chores. Why don't I give you a
call later this week when I have more time to talk."

"Sounds good. Call the barn first."

"Okay. And I'll start on that book."

Kate hangs up, then lowers her head in her hands and
weeps. Her despair is like malaria, causing her heart to ache
and her soul to blister with fever. She runs through a mental
list of names. She needs to talk to someone. But who? She
can think of only one person with whom she feels safe
sharing her fear-fed grief: Jean. Her heart rips. She picks
up the phone and dials Mitch. She knows his love for her
is deep and solid, but he will, nevertheless, say the wrong
words. She yearns for his love even as she braces herself
against his awkward attempts at comfort.

When he answers the phone, she can't speak. Her throat
is clogged with sobs.

"What is it? What's wrong?"

"I'm depressed," she croaks.

He waits patiently.

Finally, she relates between wet hiccups her conversation with Lily. When she finishes, her grief again gushes out in a torrent.

"I feel so hopeless. Josh is never going to be normal, whatever that is. And Dr. Niyol's predictions don't help— that Josh will quit taking his medications several times when he gets to be an adult, that he'll probably be committed at least once before he fully accepts and addresses his illness. And I feel I never get it right with him. That if only I were a better parent, things would be better. Then I tell myself the doctors say that's not true. It's not our fault. But I feel so guilty about all the times we assumed he was bad rather than realizing he was ill."

"Kate."

"God, the whole family is in therapy. Seems like every day I'm running someone to one counselor or another. And the house is a mess, and I haven't touched the computer in weeks. Then I remember what Jean said about not trying to write the great American novel first time out of the box. Think smaller, one page at a time. She kept saying, patience, your time will come. Oh God, I miss her. But then I think, it's all just excuses."

"Excuses!" Mitch sounds incredulous.

"Excuses I use so I won't write. I haven't written a word since Jean died. I feel like I'm never going to write." She blubbers like a child whose world has ended because her big brother smashed her favorite doll. The phone is silent. Between sobs, she begins to worry they've been disconnected. "Mitch?"

"Kate." His voice is hushed by tenderness. "You're going to write. And we'll do whatever we have to with Josh. One day at a time. Why don't you take a walk? It's a nice day."

"I should clean the house," she says between sniffs.

"Take your other son for a walk. You'll feel better." Since the night the police came, Sunny rarely leaves Kate's side when she's home. He still plays with the girls, comes running when Reyna calls him to dinner, still licks Josh's face when Josh lies on the floor watching TV, but he has imprinted on Kate. He follows her everywhere. If she sits, he lies at her feet and licks her toes. If she gets up, he's on her heels. When she works in the kitchen, he lies in the doorway watching her. His devotion is alternately endearing and annoying. Mitch finds it amusing.

She sullenly follows Mitch's advice. Sunny walks ahead of her, keeping the six-foot leash taut. He bounces along, his body collected. His legs are springs barely allowing his paws to touch ground, reminding Kate of the dressage horses Lily trains.

Those horses are Lily's babies. Unexpectedly she thinks of her younger sister on that day years ago, crying softly next to Kate in the car on the drive home from the clinic, saying over and over, "The doctor said there'll be others." Neither of them could have known Lily had just destroyed the only baby she'd ever conceive.

In the years since, they've never discussed the abortion. Lily later met and married Nat. They tried for years to have a baby, their sensuous, spontaneous lovemaking slowly deteriorating to a dry, mechanical chore. Then came the repeated attempts at in vitro fertilization. Then discussions about adoption leading to arguments and angry silences that made the air in their home thick and heavy. If Nat couldn't have Lily's baby, he didn't want any.

Finally resignation set in. Lily lost herself in her horses, Nat in his engineering. They made peace with each other and with their life. Now they seem happier than most couples and argue less than Kate and Mitch. Yet, lingering between them is the ghost of the child they never had.

Sunny jerks the leash, almost yanking it from Kate's hand as he jumps for a squirrel sitting unperturbed two feet beyond the leash's range. It's as if the glorified rodent knows the dog's limitation and is baiting him. Kate resists the urge to free Sunny to teach the cocky critter a lesson. She doesn't want to spend a half-hour chasing him through the park. Within a day or two of owning Sunny, she figured out no one ever trained the dog to follow orders, and in Sunny's mind, chasing squirrels is much more fun than walking on a leash.

Instead, she takes Sunny to the small beach at the far end of the county park on Crescent Bay. She sets him free and guards his escape by sitting on the wooden steps leading from the sand to the top of the seawall. She looks across the still water to the far shore dotted with expensive waterfront homes.

She wishes she had Lily's faith. She remembers Lily's tear-choked voice the night of Michael's suicide, quoting the Bible, her gentle energy flowing through the line.

Lily's deep faith was a gift from the abortion. After the procedure, without conscious thought, Lily began killing herself. Part of her died with the baby, and that dead part became a slow-spreading gangrene no one noticed. The truth lay hidden under winter sweaters and long overcoats. She was constantly dieting, but so was every girl Kate knew. And she swam daily. Exercise is healthy, she said. She urged Kate to join her each night for a workout at the Y over Christmas break.

One evening Kate did. The lap lanes were congested, the water over-warm. She swam a half-mile, occasionally slapping hands with one of the four swimmers sharing her lane. She wanted to leave. Lily was still going strong. Kate swam another half-mile. By the end she was ready to murder the thirty-something guy in Speedo cap, goggles and tight racing trunks. He passed her at the end of the lane about every third lap, making her swim the first half of the next lap with his feet kicking in her face, chlorine singeing her mouth and nose.

Lily was still lapping, still doing flip turns. Kate hung on the edge of the pool at the end of Lily's lane and counted. Ten, fifteen, twenty.

How long are you going to swim? She asked after grabbing Lily during a flip turn.

I'm almost done, Lily sputtered, wiping her nose.

How many laps you doing?

Two miles. Then she was gone, kicking off like a dolphin. Kate didn't return to the Y. The evening was too long and irritating. She didn't think of it again until the first warm day of spring, when Lily showed up at the house in shorts and a T-shirt. There was nothing underneath but skin pulled tight over bones. Kate could see the indentions her radius and ulna made at the elbow, could see the ligaments connecting them to the humerus. She looked like a Treblinka survivor.

Should I lose a few more pounds? Lily asked as she pushed her hands against her abdomen, her ribs rippling her shirt. The question shocked Kate as much as her sister's appearance.

My God, Lily, what have you done? Jean said when Kate dragged Lily to Jean's house. Kate didn't hear the answer. Jean pulled Lily into her bedroom and shortly after drove her to Jean's gynecologist. Lily admitted to the doctor she hadn't menstruated in months. Even so, he had a hard time convincing her she was ill. When he finally did, months passed before Lily could eat what one might call a normal meal. She felt full after a few bites. That and all the aversions she'd developed. Kate remembers the many arguments at the dinner table. Bread's too fattening. We want fattening, remember?

Later, when no babies came, Lily said it was the anorexia that damaged her. She hadn't told Jean about the abortion. The doctor must have known, even if Lily didn't tell him. He insisted Lily see a counselor.

I'm not sending you to some shrink; I don't care what the doctor says, their father declared. I know what'll happen. You'll go see him for months, then come out saying you're messed up 'cause your mom died when you were young and your father punked out. It's always the parents get the blame.

Jean managed to talk their father into letting her take Lily to the priest at the new Episcopal Church in Wheatling. Father Jess' white hair belied the fire that flamed in his light blue eyes. Lily went to see the priest often. Neither she nor Father Jess talked to anyone about what transpired. It's my business, Lily said. Confidentiality, Father Jess replied.

Over the next months, Lily's body filled in, curves returned, her cheeks came alive with color. She later said Father Jess saved her life by introducing her to God. I took you to church when you were a kid, their father would grumble when Lily made such statements. But Father Jess' vision of God was far more compassionate than that of the young preacher who had served at the Baptist church of their youth.

Kate thought it ironic that the younger man was the more judgmental of the two, eager to help Jesus get a head start on separating the sheep from the goats—his favorite passage. Lily said she once asked Father Jess about that passage. He answered, There are no goats.

Kate often wondered how Father Jess reconciled this unequivocal statement to the teachings of the church. She wished she'd known him well enough to ask. Many times when she was younger, listening to Lily talk of Father Jess, she'd found herself yearning for a Father Jess of her own—a mentor on her wavelength who could bring her closer to God, who could broaden her understanding.

Jean pops to mind. She realizes with a shock that God answered those whispers from her heart so long ago. Not then, but years later, long after she'd forgotten her wish.

As this insight unfolds in all its richness, she hears it. At first, it doesn't fully register. Just a light tinkling of falling water. Then it deepens into a cascade of music growing richer as the waves lap their way down the patch of beach toward Kate.

The bay's song is a gift from God. Kate's eyes focus on the water's ripple as she listens to the goddess. God is right here, silly. You aren't alone.

It's the wake of a boat, you idiot, her mind sneers. Why do you see God in everything? You are so naïve.

Kate rolls her eyes. Here goes the critical voice, on a soapbox, urging her once again to be rational. It dawns on her how close this voice is to her son's when he's in one of his moods. Man created God so he wouldn't be afraid of dying, says Josh, who hasn't studied Marx though he sounds like a disciple. He gets angry when she refuses to agree that the father of one of Reyna's friends, a lawyer living in a two-story mansion on the bay, who drives a BMW when the Jag's in the shop, is rich.

Depends on how you define rich.

Stop trying to sound like Jesus, Mom. I'm so sick of your spirituality shit.

She scans the horizon. Sure enough, a small white tug silently glides beyond the beach that only now bears the brunt of the boat's pulsing motion. "God," she whispers, "if I'm not alone, if you're really here, why am I so depressed?"

It's not depression, says the smaller, softer of the warring voices within her. It's a crisis of faith.

It's hormones, you dope, comes the retaliatory salvo. Look at the calendar.

Instead she looks at Sunny. He is down the beach, digging madly, spewing sand in all directions, creating a crater. He stops, jumps to one side, then leaps back, his body wriggling with excitement. He barks, then digs again.

Why can't she be like him? Why can't she take joy in the moment, dig for no reason, yesterday forgotten, unworried about tomorrow? Why can't she simply let go, believing in the intrinsic goodness of life? The query leads her into a maze of thoughts that dead-ends at the same terrible question: What is the point of it all?

It's a question she can't answer alone. When she's alone, she sees no point.

You're not alone.

A boat made those waves.

She steps down to the beach, picks up a stick and whirls it across the water. Sunny bounds chest deep into the bay. The stick is beyond his depth. He dives anyway to where he thinks the stick is, then rises on his hind legs, pawing the water, his head barely above the surface. He spies it, glides open-mouthed to his quarry, snaps it up, then paddles to shore, his breath coming in huffs.

He drags himself from the water, carries the stick to within a yard of Kate, drops it, then puts his paw on it in challenge. She doesn't move. This goads him. He shakes his coat free of frigid water, spraying her. Then he bows, wiggling his rump in the air, wagging his tail like a flag, inviting her to play. She yanks off her sweatshirt, throws it on the steps and lunges for the stick, but already he has snapped it up and is halfway down the beach. She runs after him. He prances in circles around her, just out of reach. He gambols, cavorts, shakes the stick at her, teasing her into the chase.

Finally, they're both winded. She picks up a new stick and throws it far over the water. Sunny swims for it. When he returns, dripping, stick in mouth, she is back on the steps, noticing for the first time the air's crisp, cool promise. He shakes off another spritz of water then lies at her feet and gnaws his catch.

Kate pulls on her sweatshirt and savors the sun's warmth. All is quiet. But the stillness feels less empty now.

She is stunned. Mitch said the right thing. She feels better.

Then she hears it again. Trickling music, like a harp. She looks up the beach. Another wake is lapping down the shoreline. She runs her eyes across the bay. Squints to see farther. She stands and strains forward, slowly scanning the water, a strange mix of disbelief and something close to fear gripping her.

No boat.

There's a rational explanation, the critic declares. But deep within rings the elfin laughter of a child.

Chapter

osh and Kate slide the twelve-foot, sloop-rigged dinghy off the trailer and into the water. Mitch revs the van's engine and pulls the trailer up the boat ramp, then parks.

"What are you going to name her?" Kate asks as they wait.

"I've been thinking I'd like to name her after the stars."

"How 'bout *Big Dipper*?"

Josh laughs. "*Little Dipper* is more like it."

"That's not a bad name."

He shrugs. "Actually, I was thinking *North Star*. Isn't that what sailors use to navigate?"

"Yep. *North Star* is nice."

"What's this about the *North Star*?" Mitch walks onto the dock that borders the boat ramp and holds out his hands for the bowline. Josh tosses it to him, and Mitch pulls the boat alongside the dock then secures the rope to a cleat.

"That's what I'm going to name it," Josh says as he and Kate slosh out of the water. "What do you think?"

"I like it." Mitch stands and surveys the water. "I'm no sailor, but it's a bit breezy, don't you think?"

"We'll be fine," Kate says as she helps Josh with the rigging. "We've just got to watch the cat's-paws."

"What are cat's-paws?"

"God, Dad, they're little gusts of wind," Josh says scornfully. "Don't you know anything?"

Kate scans Crescent Bay, ignoring Josh's unpleasant tone. The water is coarse from wind, but no whitecaps. She wishes her mom were here. She hasn't sailed in years and never on a boat this small, with such a narrow beam and so much sail. She knows the combination means speed but also an unforgiving nature. She would have preferred a Sunfish, but this boat was practically given to her by an elderly parishioner who first offered it to Nick.

She spent nearly a month cleaning and polishing the fiberglass and reworking the rigging. She finished just before Christmas and glowed when Mitch proclaimed in surprised admiration that the boat looked new. The sight of Josh's face Christmas morning when he glanced out the living room window and saw it parked on the front lawn still makes her smile. She unfastens the bowline.

"Mitch, hold the boat like this, pointed into the wind." Kate climbs in the cockpit where Josh is waiting, his hand on the tiller. "I'll pull up the mainsail, then you push the bow out and jump in."

She quickly hauls up the crisp sail; Mitch gives the bow a shove and jumps in just as the wind catches the sail and the boat heads into the bay, already heeling slightly.

"I want to put the jib up, too," Josh says from the stern.

"Let's see how we do with just the mainsail first," Kate says. "And put your life jacket on."

"I don't need a life jacket."

"Put it on. You, too, Mitch. The bay's deep." Kate pulls on an orange life vest, as does Mitch.

"It's not like we're gonna capsize," Josh whines.

"You never know." She holds the tiller while Josh pulls

on his vest. The dock rapidly recedes as the boat glides toward the center of the bay.

Josh brushes her hand away. "Let's see what this baby can do."

Kate's muscles tighten. She looks at Mitch sitting in the bow. He is calmly surveying the water. Josh hauls in the main sheet and cleats it, then jerks the tiller toward him, pointing upwind. The boat heels dangerously.

"Fall off! Fall off for chrissake!" Kate grabs the tiller. "Ease off the main sheet!"

Josh refuses to relinquish the tiller, his chocolate eyes now ebony with rage and wounded pride. As they each struggle for command, the boat lurches wildly, almost jibing.

"Let go of the tiller, Josh!"

"Get away!"

"Jesus, Kate, what are you doing?" Mitch clutches the edge of the cockpit.

She yanks the tiller from Josh. "I'm trying to prevent us from capsizing! You don't cleat the main sheet when you're sailing close-hauled, especially with all these puffs."

"I suppose you know more about sailing than I do?" Josh's voice quivers with anger.

"One summer of lessons doesn't make you an expert."

"You're just afraid, Mom. I know what I'm doing."

"Really, Kate, everything was pleasant until you started yelling."

"Look, this is a new boat. I'd prefer we get to know her slowly, okay? Not try to find her limit on the first tack."

"Give me the tiller." Josh shoves her arm. "God, I was just having some fun."

"You can have the tiller as long as I control the main sheet."

He glares at her as she snatches the sheet from him and lets it out. "God, you're such a chicken," he sneers.

They sail in silence. Kate looks at Mitch. He shakes his

head at her, his face a portrait of reproach. When they return home two hours later, Josh stomps off. Mitch follows him, leaving Kate to hose down *North Star*'s hull and fold her sails alone.

Chapter 50

"Mommy, it's Uncle Greg!" Reyna calls, her voice a song, "It's Uncle Greg!"

Kate dashes from the bedroom toward the front door, unbelieving until she glimpses her brother's curly auburn hair and his undeniable smile. She runs into his arms. He lifts her off the floor in a hug that's warm and sweet.

"What are you doing here?" she asks, after Greg gently releases her.

"Had a two-day conference in Jacksonville. Thought I'd surprise you."

"Is the conference over? Can you stay?"

"Conference ended at three and I don't fly home until Sunday night, so I'm yours for the weekend."

"Yea!" Reyna squeals, lifting her arms. Greg sweeps her up and settles her on his hip.

"And how's my little mouse?" he asks, nuzzling her nose with his.

"Fine." Her eyes beam adoration.

"You been sailing with your brother?"

"No, Mom won't let us." Greg looks at Kate in surprise.

"Uncle Greg, wanna see our new dog?" Reyna asks. "He's in the backyard with Mollie and Josh."

"You bet."

"Don't take long," Kate calls as her brother strides to the back door, carrying sixty-pound Reyna effortlessly. "I'll have a beer waiting for you."

"Sounds good," he calls back.

Kate fetches two beers from the fridge. She feels like dancing. She hasn't seen Greg since Jean's funeral. Even then, he only flew in for the day and it was so hectic they didn't get in a real visit. Now she has him for a whole weekend. Not quite the whole weekend. She knows Mitch will insist on taking him out on a "guys only" afternoon of college football and beer at the local sports bar. But that's okay. Her husband's friendship with her brother has been one of the unexpected joys of her marriage.

Greg lets himself in through the family room slider. "Great dog."

"Yeah, he's been wonderful for the kids. Come on," Kate beckons with her head, "let's sit in the living room."

"Just a minute. I brought you something." He retrieves a binder from the duffle bag he left by the front door and sits in the center of the sofa. She perches on the end, facing him.

"What is it?"

"Mom's poetry." He hands her the binder. "When you told me you were writing, I knew you should have this—that Mom would want you to have it."

"I haven't been writing lately."

"You will."

She reverently strokes the navy blue cover. "Where'd you get it?"

"I hid it after Mom died. I was afraid Dad would destroy it."

"Like he did everything else?" Greg nods. She opens the binder and flips through the typed pages yellow with age, reading the titles. "I remember some of these, but some I've never seen."

"It's interesting reading, especially the ones about Dad."

"Oh Greg!" Kate lays the binder on the coffee table and flings her arms around her brother's neck. "Thank you, thank you. What a gift. It's a treasure. Priceless."

He glows with delight. "Just make copies for Lily and me when you get around to it."

"I will. I promise." She pulls away and again strokes the binder.

He takes a swig of beer. "Hey, what's this Josh tells me about the new boat? He says you've only been out twice. What gives?"

"Well … I don't know," she says haltingly, picking up her own beer. "I think I need sailing lessons."

"You don't need sailing lessons. You know how to sail."

"When we go out, it's no fun. Josh handles the boat the same way he handles life; he's too forceful with the tiller. He thrusts it jarringly rather than coaxing it through a series of small adjustments. He makes me so nervous. Every time we heel, I start yelling for him to fall off. We've even had fights over the tiller."

Greg's boisterous laughter fills the room. "Kate," he says, "tomorrow Josh, you and I are going to take your boat out, and we're going to capsize her."

"No, we're not."

"Yes, we are," he answers gleefully, his brown eyes twinkling. "We're going to capsize her. Then we're going to right her. And then you know what we're going to do? We're going to capsize her again."

"No!" She plunks her beer down on the coffee table.

"Now Kate," he says in the same patient, cajoling tone she's heard him take with his stubborn three-year-old daughter. "We must have courage. We must not take counsel of our fears." He laughs again, now with a note of victory, for he hears her joining in.

"Kate," he says after a pause, "have you ever capsized?"

She shakes her head. "No. Never."

"You've got to. When I taught sailing, it was the first exercise I made my students do once they could handle the boat."

"Mom never capsized." Again she is belligerent.

Greg is beside himself now, roaring with laughter rich and irresistible. "Kate," he says finally, breathlessly, "how do you think Mom became such a good sailor?"

Her surrender is implicit in their shared laughter. He reaches over and pulls her to him, circles her shoulders with his arm. She leans her head on his chest, closes her eyes and imagines sailing on the bay with her brother and her son.

In the vision, she puts Josh's hand on the tiller. They sail close to the wind, making the boat heel and the centerboard hum, waiting for a gust. When it comes, they hold firm the main sheet. A purposeful mistake. And they won't be alone. How she suddenly knows this, she can't tell, but she knows. Her mother will be with them, in Greg's laughter, in the sea spray, in Josh's smile when *North Star* sings—and begins to tip.

Chapter

The phone rings. She snatches the handset from the kitchen wall.

"Oh Kate!" Jean's voice is full of its customary awe. "I saw everything, from the moment I was born to the moment I died, and it was all wonderful."

"Jean!" Saying her name fills Kate's voice with tears. "Oh Jean, I miss you so."

"I know Darlin'. But it's your time to stand alone." A hint of laughter underscores her words, as if she is stating an obvious fact Kate has missed. "You have everything you need, babe. You always did."

Kate can't speak. She holds the phone tight as she cries.

"There's something else, dear one. I saw what we missed."

"What? What did we miss?"

"It wasn't evil; it was an angel."

The hairs on Kate's arms stand; goose bumps ripple her flesh. As her mind whirls through the events of the past eighteen months, something powerful rises in her, quivering her body.

Images fly before her. The Archangel Michael, swordless, his laughter-filled eyes beckoning as his dancing fingers type on the keyboard. Nick singing of clapping trees. Dr. Galen's leprechaun smile. Mitch's kiss. Her neighbor Michael's hollow eyes. She sees Mollie dancing next to Josh, clutching a kite string, her joyful shrieks part of a song that holds Jean's laughter, the maple's thundering crash, computer keys clicking in a seemingly empty study, Josh's dissonant chords, Sunny's excited bark when digging. The silence of Michael's garage.

Kate is a fledgling taking its first plunge from the nest, hurtling toward ground. But she isn't afraid. Knows she has wings, though she's never used them. Knows she can fly, though she's never tried. The knowledge is older than her body, deeper than her brain. She hears the whistle of wind, the rustle of feathers. *On their wings they will bear you up, so that you will not dash your foot against a stone.* She flings out her arms, ready to embrace the unfathomable, join in Her laughter, die in Her song. She sees everything, not from ground level, but from the wonder-filled eyes of a plummeting eaglet.

Oh Kate, it's so good to fall into God. Free-falling is so good.

Her own laughter wakes her. Her face is salty wet. She turns to her bedside stand. The clock flashes two a.m.

"I miss you, Jean," she whispers. "God knows how I miss you."

Everything is wonderful. Jean's cancer? Everything. Their struggles with Josh? His rage? The repeated mistakes? It's all wonderful. Michael's suicide? Everything. Even Kate? Wonderful.

She pushes back the covers, steals out of bed and heads for the study. She sits at the computer, presses the "on" button, watches it power up, then opens her word processing program. She stares at a blank page for a minute, an hour; she has no idea how long. Finally she writes, "Wonderful." She savors the word, then hits the return key and clicks out, "Full of wonder."

Her fingers tremble as she again hits return. She presses her hands to her face, rubs them together as if warming them. What did Jean once say? *What we choose to believe either disfigures or crystallizes reality.* Her fingers hover over the keyboard as if afraid the letters are acid tipped. She draws in air until her lungs are achingly full, slowly exhales, then types.

"I believe in angels."

Chapter 52

She bangs on the door a second time. "Dad, you in there?"

The lock turns, the door swings open and her father squints at her against the morning sun.

"What the hell you doing here?"

"You say I don't come to see you. Well, here I am." Kate brushes past him into the foyer. Her nose wrinkles at the rancid smell of his breath.

Her father scratches his chest and yawns, then hikes up his pajama bottoms. The elastic's shot. "What time is it?" he says.

"Eleven. You just getting up?"

"Yeah, thanks to you."

"I brought your favorite Danish. Would you like me to warm it up?"

"I'm not hungry." His glance sweeps over her. "Well, look at you. All sunshiny and full of yourself." His voice has the flat tone of a hangover.

"Actually, I am, and it feels good." She heads to the kitchen and shrugs her purse onto the counter. She sees an empty fifth of whiskey atop an empty jug of cheap chardonnay in the trash. No wonder he doesn't want to eat. "Well, I'm eating, even if you're not."

"To what do I owe this pleasure?"

"I was worried when I didn't hear from you since New Year's. I left several messages on your machine the past couple of weeks."

"Didn't feel like talking."

"I thought maybe you were feeling down about Jean."

"Fuck Jean. She got what she deserved."

Kate clamps her jaw, biting off a violent explosion. Should she leave? No. She's going to finish what she's started. She puts the pastries in the oven and turns it on. She works to keep her voice even, "That's awful harsh."

Her father saunters by, a contemptuous look on his face. "As ye sow, so shall ye reap." He drops into a chair at the wooden table in the breakfast nook adjacent to the kitchen.

"True. By the end of Jean's life, it was clear what she'd sown. When people heard about her cancer, they came from all over, from across the country to see her. Others called. Sent flowers. It was a spectacle. You should have seen it."

He shrugs. "Lot of good it did her. I need a drink."

"I'll make coffee." She measures the water and grounds, switches on the pot and leans against the counter. "Must have hurt her that you never called or visited."

His eyes narrow. "Why would I?"

"Good God, she was Mom's best friend. When Mom died, she practically raised us."

"Oh, now *she* raised you."

"You know what I mean. You were working fourteen-hour days."

"To keep food on the table, a roof over your head. Guess that doesn't count."

"That's not what I'm saying. I'm just saying Jean was

good to us." She wants to scream, Why is everything about you? Instead, she lets out a long, slow breath. They watch the coffee brew in silence, its heavy aroma filling the kitchen. When the coffee maker gives a final steamy gasp, she pulls mugs from the cabinet above the sink and fills them. She sets them on the table, then brings over the Danishes on two plates.

"I wish you'd tell me why you're here then get the hell out." He breathes in the sugary tartness of the apple pastries then automatically pulls a flask from his pajama-top pocket and doctors his coffee. Kate pretends not to notice.

"Actually, I do have something on my mind."

"Wonders never cease."

"First, I wanted to get back the copy of 'Flowers in Winter' you took."

"Too late."

"What do you mean?"

"I chucked it. I told you it was trash. Hope to God it was your only copy."

She cringes at his cruelty. "It wasn't. But that's not the point."

"Well, get to the point."

"The point is you owe me an apology."

"Like hell! For what?"

"For sneaking into my study and taking my work. For reading my story without permission. For ripping up my poetry."

"Are you kidding me? Where's this shit coming from? Your poetry? That's gotta be over fifteen years ago. Maybe you want me to apologize for fathering you, too."

"No," she replies in the exaggerated calm of a scolding parent. "Just for what I said. I'm not demanding an apology." She looks at him until he returns her stare. "But you owe me one."

"Forget it." He tears a corner off his Danish and stuffs it in his mouth. "'oo da 'ell do 'ou 'hink 'ou are?" He swallows, then empties half his mug. "I'm your father, for chrissake."

"Even so, you had no right."

"I have every right," he sneers. "You're as bad as your mother. Wasting your time on this shit. Poetry." He sprays spittle with the last word.

"You never said it was a waste when Mom wrote."

"You're not your mother!" The crash of his fist on the table rattles the plates.

"I didn't say I was."

"Where'd it get her? Struck down in the prime of life."

Shaking her head, Kate lifts her hands, palms up. "The two aren't related."

"Where did any of it ever get her? Always running off to that church with Jean, coming back with all that feel-good crap." He feigns an ethereal air. "'God is love,'" he says in a mock soprano. "Well, where the hell was God when she was dying?"

"Dad—"

"She only saw what she wanted to see and ignored the rest."

"Like?"

"Like death!"

"Maybe she didn't—"

"Like sin and damnation! Like the fact Satan's out there gathering us up and only a lucky few make it through the eye of the camel. And that's Jesus I'm quoting."

"It's *needle*. And I doubt Mom believed in Satan. I know I don't."

"Since when?"

"Since now."

"Then you're a goddamn fool and fools are Satan's own. I'm not surprised. You never had the sense God gave an ant. You had a respectable job and threw it away to write garbage. That's what your short story is and that's what all your so-called poetry was. Garbage. Too much idle time. Think you'd have your hands full raising kids. But no, just like your mother, you neglect the kids to—"

"Mom never neglected us—and I don't neglect my children."

"I suppose Josh is proof of that."

"Leave Josh out of this!" Kate's voice is a vibrato of growing rage.

"Don't you talk to me that way, ya little witch. You don't know anything about your mother. Always sneaking away to her study, typing out nonsense."

"It wasn't nonsense."

"What do you know?"

"I've read it."

"And after all these years I suppose you can quote it to me."

"Actually, I read it again recently."

"Like hell. Where'd you get it?"

"Greg."

His face deflates like a balloon. "Greg?"

"He hid Mom's poetry notebook when you were storming the house with the baseball bat, smashing the china and the crystal. Her bookcase, her typewriter."

"I couldn't stand to look at it after she was gone," he mutters.

"He gave it to me after I told him I was writing. There's a poem titled 'To Kyle.'"

He stares at the table.

She goes to her purse and pulls out a piece of paper. "It's short." He doesn't answer. She sits at the table, clears her throat and reads:

Tenuous
the balance
between you
and me,
a shift of wind
foretells
the storm at
sea.
Scudding clouds
already veil
the sun,
light shatters
with the lamp,
and love is
done.

But I will
gather up
the pieces
on the floor,
and when the storm
subsides,
mend them
once again
as I have done
before.

Kate looks up. Her father's eyes remain fixed on the table. "Dad, she loved you. She still loves you—"

He sweeps his plate and mug off the table with a crash. "She's dead!" He grabs the paper from Kate, rips it in two and waves it in her face. "Maybe if she'd focused more on us instead of this crap, she'd be alive today."

A piece of pottery rocks on the tile floor. Kate stares at her father in disbelief. Unexpectedly, Jean's words resonate within her: *When he spews all that ugliness, he's projecting. It's all about him.*

"Is that what you believe?" she whispers.

"Goddamn right."

Her words come slowly. "Oh my God, I'm so sorry."

Before she can comprehend, before she can blink, her father springs to his feet and strikes. The slap whips her face toward her shoulder.

"You think I want your pity?" he bellows. His hand hovers above her head, ready to strike again.

"You bastard!" She launches to her feet, overturning her chair with a crash, and hits away his hand. "I hate you!" She turns, kicks aside the chair and heads for her purse.

"That's it! Run away, like always. You piece of shit. You're nothin' but a cheap imitation of your mother." His words stagger her like an arrow to the heart.

"I thought you might amount to something. When you were working for the senator. Even when you went to the university. But now look at you. You're nothing but a house-wife and a mother—and a lousy one at that—playing at being Hemingway. Friends ask about you kids. I tell them about Greg's engineering degree and his work for the government. I even tell them about Lily's horse farm—at least she's a champion at something. But you? I don't mention you. You're nothing! Nothing!"

She whirls to face him. "You son of a bitch!" Her voice vibrates with her effort to contain the lion's roar rising within her. "There's nothing cheap or lousy about me. That's you talking about you! You're nothing but a pathetic, stinking dru—"

Kate! She hears Jean's voice as if she were in the room. Teasing laughter underscores her words. *It's all wonderful.*

She surveys the mess at her feet, then her father's haggard face. Even this.

She closes her eyes and draws a deep breath, willing her clenched jaw to relax, commanding the wounded lion to retreat.

"You're wrong, Dad," she whispers and opens her eyes to meet his glare. "I'm the best there is. I'm quarter-sawn wood."

"What the hell?"

"I'm beautiful and I'm strong. I'm a good mother and a good writer. I'm an artist."

"Shit."

"But even if I wasn't. Even if I were only a mother, even if I were homeless on the street, it wouldn't change a thing. The truth is I'm wonderful. And Mom is wonderful too. I'm certain, wherever she is, she knows all this and is incredibly proud of me."

"Get out." His voice is weary.

She looks at the floor where pieces of her mother's poem soak up spilled coffee. She stoops to retrieve them.

"Leave it and get out!"

She gathers the pieces, shakes off the coffee, then walks into the kitchen for her purse. She turns to her father.

"I also know you're wonderful." He stares back slack-jawed. "Mom loves you. If only you weren't so blinded by bitterness and self-hate." She shakes her head. "You didn't kill her, Dad. God didn't kill her. Do you hear me? No one's responsible for her death."

"You don't know anything."

She rubs her throbbing cheek. "I know one thing. You've got to stop drinking."

"Forget that."

"You need a doctor. Not a general practitioner like Dr. Brown, but a mental health professional. A psychiatrist who—"

"You think I'm crazy?" His eyes are wide with disbelief.

"Dr. Niyol believes Josh is bipolar. He said it can run in families, especially families with alcoholism."

"You sayin' I'm crazy!"

"I'm saying you should look into the poss—"

"Get out!" He hurls his flask. She doesn't flinch. The bottle misses her and pings off the far wall. "Goddamn you! Goddamn your soul." He slumps into his chair, leans against the table and rests his head in his hands.

Kate grips the kitchen counter to steady herself. "I love you." She's surprised by the assurance in her voice. "And if you ever need help, I'll do my best to be there. I also want you to know I forgive you. Do you hear, Dad? With my whole heart I forgive you. For today, for yesterday. For everything."

He dismisses her with a grunt.

Wobbly as a foal, she reaches the threshold to the foyer then pauses, turns back. "There's one other thing you should know. As much as I love you, I will never again let you shred me verbally the way you shredded my poetry. And if you ever strike me again, I'll charge you with battery."

Her father doesn't move.

"Goodbye, Dad." She shuts the door softly behind her.

Chapter 53

Kate's footsteps reverberate as she walks down the center aisle of the deserted church. She loves this old church, built in the eighteen hundreds in Tudor Gothic, the sides of the long nave lined with bay windows brilliant with stained glass.

She heads for the small chapel off the nave and kneels before the stand of prayer candles. Only a few are lit. She closes her eyes and looks inside herself. Michael is still there, grim but no longer frightening. She opens her eyes and lights a taper from one of the candles, then lights a candle of her own.

"God, this is for Michael," she whispers. She watches the flame flicker. "God," she says, her voice stronger, "I want to talk to Michael." She waits a moment, as if giving The Creator time to fetch him.

"Michael," her tone is gentle, tentative, "first I want to tell you how sorry I am you reached a place in your life so dark and full of despair you could see no light to lead you through it. I'm sorry for all your suffering, for the difficult path you had to walk. You must have been in a terrible place to believe self-destruction was the solution. I'm so, so sorry." A tear slides down her cheek.

FALLING INTO THE SUN

"I wish I could have helped you. I wish you hadn't killed
yourself. I used to wish I hadn't seen it, but I don't anymore.
Seeing your suicide brought great good to my life. It made
me take up my dream of writing, which I'd forsaken out of
fear years ago. I'm working on my novel again and it's good.
I don't feel lost anymore. For the first time in my life, I feel
fulfilled, I feel like I'm doing what I should be doing. I've
got a new theme song—Jim Croce's 'I've Got a Name.' Ask
him to sing it to you." Kate smiles at the idea.

"I also want you to know that seeing your death pushed
me to get help for my son, which led me so unwillingly to
Dr. Galen. Actually, God crammed him down my throat as I
kicked and screamed.

"He has helped us so much, Michael. Given us the kind
of help I wish you could have had. My son is still struggling,
but he's slowly getting better, and I thank you for that. The
drugs have helped him turn a corner, and I hope when he
matures a little, he'll start working in his counseling sessions.
I hope he makes that choice.

"Most of all, Michael, your death brought me closer to
God. I know you're with God. I've known that from the
start. I guess what I really want to say is this: I love you. I'll
always love you. You'll forever hold a place of honor in my
heart. God bless you, Michael. Now and forever."

Kate leans on the communion rail, resting her head
on her arms. She feels lighter. She inhales the sulfur still
lingering in the air from the struck match. She listens to the
candles sizzle as they eat oxygen. She listens to the hush of
the sanctuary.

"Thank you, God," she finishes. "Thank you for letting
me speak to Michael."

She rises and turns to the nave. On the far side, a man
prays in the otherwise empty pews. Odd, she didn't hear him
come in. She hopes he didn't hear her. She decides to leave
through the side door off the chapel. As she turns she notices

the person lift his head toward her. She reaches the side door in three long strides, puts her hand on the knob, then takes a last glance at the nave. The person is gone.

A chill runs through her. She lets go of the doorknob and creeps to the nave, looks up and down. It's empty. She tiptoes toward the pew where the figure sat, a knot in her gut growing harder with each step. A yard from the spot where she saw him, she stretches, looking over the back of the pew.

"Kate?" She jumps a foot off the ground before swinging around. Nick is standing in the narthex, his hands on his hips. "You don't need to sneak around the church, you know. You're welcome anytime."

"Were you just here a minute ago, praying?" she asks breathlessly.

"No. I've been in the office," he says as he walks down the aisle.

"I thought I saw someone."

"Haven't seen anyone but you." He pulls her into a quick hug. "But you're a welcome sight, though I have to say I'm surprised. What brings you here on a Friday morning?"

"I wanted to light a candle and say some prayers. On Sundays it's so crowded. I wanted privacy."

"Am I intruding?"

"No, I'm done. I'm glad you're here, really. I received the nicest letter from Jamie, Jean's daughter."

"I remember."

"She's doing pretty well though she misses her mom terribly. We all do. She wrote again about Jean's funeral, how lovely and comforting it was and how much she appreciated your help. She's coming next month to spend Easter week with us. We were wondering if you, Carol and Nicholas would join us for Easter dinner?"

"We'd be honored."

"Great!"

"But you still haven't told me what you were stalking just now."

She turns and looks at the pew. "I thought I saw someone over there."

Nick walks to where she points, looks under the pews. "No one here, but someone left this Bible out." He picks it up. "Open to one of my favorite stories."

She walks to him and reads over his shoulder. "Oh, it's Peter trying to walk on water."

"Stormy water. A gale was blowing."

"Why is it one of your favorites?"

"I love Peter. He's so enthusiastic, yet he's such a bumbler. He reminds me of me."

"I don't think of you as a bumbler."

"We're all bumblers." He grins broadly. "But how can you not love Peter. He so wants to follow Jesus, so longs to be close to God. Yet he often jumps to wrong conclusions, misunderstands, loses faith numerous times, often at crucial moments. Even so, Jesus and God never lose faith in him. God works miracles through him and even puts his mistakes and flaws to good use."

"What do you mean?"

"Well, take this story here. What's it about?"

She reads through the passage. "It's about faith."

"Yes, but not only that. It tells us what causes us to lose faith. Do you see it?"

She takes the Bible from him and re-reads the passage. "'But when he saw the wind, he was afraid and, beginning to sink, cried out, *Lord, save me!*'"

"Exactly. It's about fear. Only when he became afraid did he begin to sink. Fear is the single biggest block to living a full life. When we give into fear and worry, we abandon hope as well as trust. Peter learned this firsthand. Imagine, he could walk on water—not just water, but whitecaps—right up to the moment he allowed fear to overthrow faith."

"He could walk on water," Kate echoes, playing with the idea. She leans against the end of the pew. "You're saying we could all walk on water if we just had enough faith?"

"Don't look at me, this is Jesus' idea," he says, his eyes gleaming. "But the water is a metaphor. What the story tells us is we can do anything our hearts desire, if we simply believe."

"I believe that with all my heart."

"So do I. But the story doesn't end there."

She looks down and reads aloud: "'Immediately Jesus reached out his hand and caught him. *You of little faith,* he said, *why did you doubt?*'"

"There. Even when we doubt, God is with us, catching us as we fall."

"You've just summarized my life story."

"It's the story of all our lives. That's why I love Peter. He's everyman."

"Sounds like a good sermon." She can't stop the teasing smile pulling at her lips.

"Am I sounding preachy?"

"You never sound preachy. I'd say passionate is a better word. And profound."

Nick's laughter resounds through the church. "Coming from you, I take that as high praise. Hey, I'm just heading out for lunch. Care to join me? I've got a lot of Peter stories."

She shakes her head as she hands him the Bible. "Thanks, but I've got to run and meet Reyna and Mollie's bus." They walk toward the narthex. "School's out early today. I just came in for a quick prayer about—" Kate staggers, then grabs Nick's arm to steady herself.

"Kate, you okay? Good gosh, you're pale. Here, sit down." He pulls her into a pew and sits next to her.

"I just saw something," she says, staring ahead blindly.

"What?"

"I was about to say I'd come here to pray about Michael."

"The neighbor who hanged himself?"

"Yes. I don't know if I can explain it. It's going to sound weird. You know how I used to see Michael's image everywhere?"

"Yes."

"Well, that eventually stopped. I could get in the car and look in the rearview mirror and all I saw was the mirror and real images. But his image was still in me, I mean, when I'd take time to look around inside myself, it was still there."

"Yes, I understand."

"Remember how you once told me Michael's image would always be with me, and what I needed to do was pray for it to become a source of good in my life?"

"I do."

"I did that, even though at the time I didn't know what I was praying for. Well, recently, I've realized how coming face to face with Michael's suicide changed my life. In good ways. So today, when I was praying, I thanked Michael and told him I loved him. Bizarre, huh?"

"Not at all."

"You never think anything's bizarre." She can't help smiling as she turns to Nick.

"Been in the God business too long, I guess."

"Anyway, just now, when I was about to mention Michael, I took a peek inside myself and there he was, but he had changed."

"How?"

"He wasn't heavy and grim anymore. He was ... he is light. I'm looking at him right now, and he's all light."

Chapter 54

How long has he been here, in the Heart of Hearts? That's what he calls this place. Long enough to review his life, meditate mystery, listen to her prayers. This last must be a gift, this knowledge of her. He doesn't understand, but doesn't question. Knows there's meaning. A door he can walk through—or not.

He knows all the people she loves—the son, the husband, the daughters, the godmother, the priest, the sister and brother. Even the bulldog counselor with the child's heart. Knows them not as she does, for he sees not through her mind, but through her soul.

He loves these people because she loves them. And she loves him. Her prayers and thanks swirl around him in a joyful allegro.

How long? Time doesn't exist here. He may have been here an eternity in the lapse of just one of her days. He only knows the end approaches. He can tell by the song. It's gentling into adagio. The drums are taking over, their rhythm a heartbeat, at first faint but growing stronger with each pulse. He knows the vital beats signal his time to choose. He doesn't know how he knows.

He has two requests. Both scare him. One is impossible. But nothing is impossible. Even so, he knows another child is not her desire. It's not part of her dream, not part of the path she's following. He asks anyway.

I choose her, *he pleads.* Please, let me be with her. I CHOOSE HER! *The music wells around him, the answer indiscernible. The song softens to a whisper, inviting his second request. He's afraid. What if he's asking too much? What if the answer is no? Too frightening to contemplate.*

I want the song. *The cry comes from his core.* Don't let me forget the song. *He has known song-less existence. It's worse than any conjurings of human torture. Hellfire is nothing compared to an untuned heart.*

The song surges to crescendo, ferocious in its grandeur, gentle in its explosive power, shaking the universe, breaking him free of the center.

He's not ready. What's the answer? He must know before he goes. It's a mistake. He needs more time. But the song is unrelenting, the drumbeat like thunder. It whirls him through the stars, past shoreless suns. He sees creation vast and infinite, he at the center, or it his center. He can't tell which, is not sure of the difference. It feels like a dance. Then blinding speed.

He's a comet plunging through the universe, past countless galaxies, toward Earth. Friction disintegrates memory until only lessons remain. Cleansed by fire, he plummets into darkness, a warm, pulsing sea. He is wrapped tight, confined but safe. Only the drumbeat remains. A comfort. A metronome. A lifeline.

Chapter

The phone jangles Mitch and Kate out of their embrace.

"We're in a goddamn hotel two hours from home and we still can't get away from the phone," Mitch moans. "Don't answer it."

"What if it's the babysitter?"

"Okay," he sighs with resignation.

Kate picks up the handset. "Hello?"

"Kate? Lily."

"Lily?"

"Honey, I'm so sorry to bother you on your special weekend away. I made Josh give me the number. I had to tell you. I couldn't wait. Not even a day."

Kate props herself against the headboard. "What?"

"You're not going to believe it."

"What?"

"I don't believe it."

"*Lily.*"

"Okay, Okay. Here goes. I'M PREGNANT!"

"No! Oh my God!"

"It's true. I took three home pregnancy tests before I finally went to the doctor. You know how neurotic I am. I wanted to be sure. And they had told me it was hopeless. Especially after the last in vitro failed. Kate, it's a miracle. That's what the doctor said and I believe it."

"Oh Lily, so do I. I'm so happy for you. I'm stunned. I wish I could come across the line and hug you."

"Don't worry, I'm getting plenty of that from Nat. But Kate, I have a big favor to ask you. Oh, please say yes."

"What?"

"Say 'yes' first."

"Okay," she laughs, "yes, I'll do it. Now what is it?"

"I want you to be our baby's godmother. I mean a real godmother. I want this baby to have the kind of relationship with you that you had with Jean. I so envied you. I hope you'll forgive me for it, but I never had that with my godmother. Just a postcard once a year on my birthday.

"Kate? You there?"

"Yes."

"Are you crying?"

"No," Kate croaks, making them both laugh.

"Well, will you?"

"I already said yes. But I'll say it again. Yes! Oh, yes!"

Lily squeals like a child. "You've made Nat and me so happy."

"Lily, it's you who've honored me. I'm not as wise as Jean, but I'll do my best."

"You'll be wonderful without even trying. Look how great you're doing with Josh. How you sorted it all out and got him back on track, I'll never know. I've been reading about bipolar and mood disorders in kids ever since you told me. From what I've read, Josh is lucky. So many of these kids are misdiagnosed, or not diagnosed at all, just treated as juvenile delinquents, ending up in jail."

"Yeah, well, we had a lot of help. Some of it literally out of this world. But we're still a long way from home. Josh isn't physically attacking us anymore, thank God, but he's still refusing to cooperate in counseling. He's so angry and rude. His language at home is atrocious."

"Ugh."

"Yeah, makes Mitch furious. But underneath all the foul words and bully posturing, I think Josh is terrified. Did I tell you the psychiatrist said he has anxiety disorder, maybe even oppositional defiant disorder along with the bipolar?"

"Oh Kate."

"They're all related—or similar. I'm not sure. I don't think the professionals are really sure."

"Well, you've picked wonderful people to help sort it out. I love Dr. Galen."

"I know. It's just gonna take time. Josh is so darn smart, but he's about three years behind in maturity. He argues about taking his medication and wouldn't if we weren't on him every day. And he still blames Mitch and me for everything—even when he hits Reyna or steals money from my purse. It's our fault because we've been such abusive parents."

"Oh geez, I thought you were past all that."

"Seems like we take a step forward, then two steps back. Dr. Galen says it's easier and less painful for Josh to blame us then to look inside himself. He calls it the victimhood game, and until Josh drops it and takes responsibility for his actions, he's not going to progress. He says that may not happen until Josh hits rock bottom."

"Rock bottom?"

"You know, gets Baker Acted—committed against his will by the police or a judge."

"Kate, no!"

"Odds are that will happen at least once before he hits his mid-twenties, at least according to everything we've read and everyone we've seen. And there's little Mitch and I can do about it. We've provided him with all the tools he needs, but he has to choose to use them."

"And he will. I know it. Maybe not today or this year, but down the road. He's so smart and I think he has a very true and compassionate soul. He'll figure it out. I felt it in my gut when you visited last month. And he's playing in the jazz band at school! That's gotta be good for him, musically and socially."

"Yeah, I still don't know how the band director talked him into that—even after Josh told him he couldn't read music and wouldn't practice."

"I bet he loves it."

"Well, he's been playing a lot of jazz lately, if that's any indication."

"Baby, he's gonna be fine. Tell me you believe that."

"Yes," Kate says slowly. An image of Peter walking on water flashes before her. "Yes, I believe it. With all my heart."

"Good. Now I'll let you get back to your romantic weekend with Mitch. You guys are long overdue. Hope I didn't interrupt anything, you know, intimate."

"You didn't. I'm so glad you called. Hope I didn't dampen your joy by blathering on about Josh."

"Give me a break. You'd better talk to me. I was so mad when you finally told me everything—mad that you'd waited so long, depriving me the right and the joy of being there for you."

"You and Greg have always been here for me. More than you know."

"Okay, but no more secrets. Deal?"

"Deal."

"Now get back to your hubby. I love you, Kate."

"Love you too, little momma. I'll call you next week."

"Okay. Love to Mitch."

Kate hangs up and stares out the window. Exaggerated snoring interrupts her thoughts. Mitch lies next to her, his eyes closed, his hands peacefully folded across his chest. She smacks him on the thigh.

"Wake up, you faker. That was Lily. She's pregnant!"

"Great. At least someone's having sex."

Kate slides down in the bed. "Well, let's pick up where we left off."

"You were on the phone so long, it kind of killed the mood." He pouts dramatically. She gently strokes his chest.

"She asked me to be the baby's godmother."

"She couldn't have asked Monday?"

"She's excited. They gave up hope years ago." She tickles her hand down across Mitch's bare abdomen, eliciting a gasp.

He pulls her to him and slides his hand over her rear, her naked thigh. "Maybe you could demonstrate in detail," he kisses her ear, "how this conception came about." He kisses her neck. "Maybe with some hands-on instruction." His lips capture hers.

Chapter 56

He loves this dark, wet place. A drum pulses without and is answered by a smaller beat within. Sometimes he hears other things, lilting tones, though muffled. He vaguely recognizes them, is drawn to them, but they are not where he is. He is here. They are out there. He spends eternity here until the dark sea, always calm, begins to roil. Waves massage him—first gently, then with growing pressure, channeling him against his will, overpowering his newborn strength. He fights, tries to hold back, but the waves keep bearing down—stronger and faster, stronger and faster, pushing him forward. Forcing him, once again, toward the light.

Acknowledgments

Profound thanks to the many people who helped and encouraged me in this endeavor, especially my godmother, Jane Carrigan, my dear friends Diane Rado and Sherry Peterson, my brother, John W. Hazard Jr., and my wonderful "Write Women," Diane Masiello, Junia Ancaya, Terra Pressler and Angie Jones. Their enthusiasm, insights and critiques were invaluable. An added thanks to Angie for her poetic suggestions and thorough final editing.

I'm also indebted to the people who read early drafts of the novel: Lynn Duke, John Foster, Chuck Hawkins, Linda Barley and the members of the Old Sames Book Club: Elaine Formby, Lee Beneke, Joan Ciampini, Tootie Erwin, Martha Forbes, Jo Ellen Mendel, Lori Badders, Pat Hazel, and Fran Barnhisel. The Old Sames women were strangers to me when they agreed to be the test book club for *Falling into the Sun*. Since then, they have become treasured friends.

I thank my parents, Helen K. Hazard and John W. "Jack" Hazard Sr., who told me I could achieve anything I set my heart and mind to, and extend further gratitude to my mother who graciously allowed me to use her poem, *To My Father* (titled *To Kyle* in the novel). And I will forever treasure the love and endless encouragement I received and continue to receive from my husband, Mike Moscardini, and my children, Leo, Ellie and Emma. They never stopped believing in my writing or me.

I am grateful to the following publications in which early portions of the novel appeared—*Sunscripts: Writings from the Florida Suncoast Writers' Conference; Palm Prints; Wordsmith*—and to SkyLight Paths Publishing for permission to quote from the following published work: *Bhagavad Gita: Annotated & Explained,* Translation by Shri Purohit Swami with Annotation, copyright 2001 by Kendra Crossen Burroughs (Woodstock, VT: SkyLight Paths Publishing, www.skylightpaths.com).

Finally, many thanks to the very talented graphic artist, Zard Tompkins, for the beautiful cover design and interior layout and for touting the novel to all her friends and any stranger she happened to meet either in America or in Dominica.

Falling into the Sun

A Reader's Guide

About the Author

Ancient Child

Discussion Questions

Resources

Readers can print out this guide at

www.CharrieHazard.com

About the Author

harrie Hazard grew up on the Potomac River in Hallowing Point, Virginia, a small, isolated community at the river's end of Mason's Neck Federal Wildlife Preserve. She was one of seven children in a rather chaotic household run by highly intellectual, talented and loving parents, both of whom were children of alcoholics. Her father, John W. Hazard Sr., a journalist, author and editor, was executive editor of *Changing Times Magazine* (now *Kiplinger)* during Charrie's youth. He spent his evenings writing books, humorous columns and short stories, such as "The Flying Teakettle," which after first appearing in *The New Yorker* was made into the movie *You're in the Navy Now,* starring Gary Cooper. Although her father was somewhat aloof during Charrie's childhood, and a strict disciplinarian, he nevertheless instilled in his children a strong sense of ethics, integrity and generosity.

Charrie's mother, Helen K. Hazard, was a poet and author of children's stories as well as the director of Gunston Hall School, a private elementary school which specialized in children with learning disabilities. She taught ancient history and had her young students read classics, such as Homer's

Iliad. As reflected in her collected poems, *Footnotes Along the Way* (available at Amazon.com), Helen struggled with depression but tenaciously held to the belief in the goodness of life and its primacy over death.

As a teenager, Charrie spent much of her free time either sailing the Potomac with her parents in her father's nineteen-foot sloop or riding the family's chestnut hunter through the wildlife refuge, often bareback and accompanied by only the family dog. Otherwise, she had her nose in a book. The bookshelves of her home were filled with classics. With her mother's encouragement, Charrie became a voracious reader of literature and poetry. She quickly graduated from *The World of Pooh* to *A Little Princess* and *Little Women* to *Pride and Prejudice* and *Huckleberry Finn* to *The Brothers Karmozov* and *Les Misérables*.

Though her parents were members of and attended the historic Pohick Episcopal Church, her mother's spiritual views were quite liberal and often defied the boundaries of organized religion, including the idea that only one religion held the key to God. Instead, Helen believed God revealed Herself through not only the world's major religions but also great art and literature. Consequently, she introduced Charrie to such spiritual works as *The Prophet* by Kahlil Gibran; *Man's Search for Meaning* by Viktor E. Frankl; and *Wind, Sand and Stars* by Antoine de Saint-Exupéry.

By the time she was a high school senior, Charrie knew she wanted to be a novelist. After graduating from The College of William and Mary with a B.A. in history, she discussed this dream with her father. He encouraged her to go into journalism to develop the habit of daily writing and to learn to write on deadline. Charrie took a job as a feature writer at the *Lynchburg News & Daily Advance,* was soon promoted to the news side and, over the next two years, won numerous awards, including two first-place awards for investigative reporting from the Virginia Press Association.

One of these honored her twelve-part investigative series on the Lynchburg Training School and Hospital, at the time the nation's largest institution for the mentally handicapped. The series exposed patient neglect and abuse, low employee morale and poor working conditions, and touched off state and local investigations that led to corrective measures.

She then took a job with the *St. Petersburg Times,* where she started as a police and court reporter, graduated to special projects and ultimately became a member of the editorial board, writing editorials, by-line columns and Sunday *Perspective* pieces. Her favorite columns and editorials were those that called for justice for the disenfranchised whose voices would otherwise go unheard.

She continued to use her investigative reporting skills, leading her, at times, to break news in her editorials. She exposed, for example, negligence on the part of the Florida Department of Health and Rehabilitative Services (HRS) that contributed to the death from abuse of seven-month-old Eddie Elmore. Charrie wrote the editorial despite an HRS official's threat to press criminal charges against her, personally, should the *Times* publish information from the HRS abuse report, which state law protected from public scrutiny. (The local sheriff's office mistakenly included the report in the criminal investigation of Eddie's death, a copy of which Charrie received through a public records request.) The *Times* editors published the editorial.

While working at the *Times,* Charrie began to date Michael Moscardini, who at the time was the paper's national editor. They were of very different temperaments—Charrie was outgoing and optimistic; Michael was an introvert and a self-proclaimed pessimist—and of those who knew them both, few thought they were a good match. They married a year after they met.

After ten years as a successful journalist, Charrie nevertheless felt unfulfilled. She also had come to believe she was not a good enough writer to become a novelist. After the birth of her second child, she left the *Times* and pursued her M.A. in English at the University of South Florida. While working on her degree, she had her third child. But her attention became increasingly focused on her oldest child and only son, whose volatile temper was leading to increasingly violent confrontations.

After earning her M.A. she taught English and writing at St. Petersburg College and writing at the University of South Florida (USF). She might have made that a full-time career, but for a life-changing moment: She walked in on her neighbor's suicide. He had hanged himself in his garage. The sight caused her to envision her son in the same position. Charrie realized then that the kind of despair that drove her neighbor to suicide fueled her son's outbursts. She sought psychological help for her son, who ultimately was diagnosed with anxiety disorder.

The suicide also forced Charrie to come to grips with the legacy of alcoholism in her family and her own issues with anxiety. It also drove her to re-evaluate her life and her beliefs, a process encouraged and guided by her son's psychologist, Dr. Michael T. Smith, and her godmother and spiritual mentor, Jane Carrigan, a close friend of Charrie's mother. During this period she read and was profoundly influenced by Julia Cameron's *The Artist's Way* as well as India's sacred scripture, the *Bhagavad Gita.* She resurrected her dream and wrote several award-winning creative nonfiction essays before starting a novel titled *In Our Midst,* which chronicles the parallel journeys of two women thwarted in the pursuit of their dreams. But often, when she sat down to work, her neighbor's suicide bubbled up. Finally, she put aside the unfinished *In Our Midst* and began to write about her neighbor. The result was *Falling into the Sun.* Though loosely based on her experiences, it is a novel.

Charrie currently teaches writing at the University of

Tampa and is working on her second novel. She is a member of the National League of American Pen Women, Inc., and is a former program director of Lifelong Writers, the now defunct membership arm of The Florida Center for Writers at USF. She also is a board member of the Gunston Hall School Foundation, Washington, D.C., which provides scholarships to elementary and secondary school students with learning disabilities who cannot afford the specialized education they need. She has won six major journalism awards. Her creative nonfiction has been published in a number of literary journals and has won prizes from organizations such as The National League of American Pen Women, Tampa Writers Alliance and Mount Dora Festival of Music and Literature.

She lives with her husband of twenty-four years and their three children in Safety Harbor, Florida. The marriage, as it turned out, was a keeper.

For more information, visit Charrie's Web site:
www.CharrieHazard.com.

Ancient Child

Delights in the puzzle,
fitting a jig of mundane
to a saw of eternity.

With unvarying marvel
hunts through all traditions,
from stars, to awakened one,
to carpenter unwooden,
for jagged bits of truth,
wide-eyed at proof
when piece locks into piece.

Lips tremble as, mystery-laden,
the piecemeal picture rises:
beauty, smudged but unsullied.

Eyes weep with wonder,
seeing One in all.
Giggles gush
over murky flaws,
sanctifying me with
a wellspring of love
unclouded by censure.

I am converted
to her soul's sparkling
vision of me.

Of God. One.

—for Jane

Charrie Hazard, February 2003

DISCUSSION QUESTIONS

1) Where does the title *Falling into the Sun* appear in the novel? How does it operate as a metaphor?

2) As Michael flies toward the center of creation, or God, after his death, he realizes that, "like a poorly drawn arrow, he is awry. The realization ravages him. The arrow of his life missing this mark—the only mark." But even as his despair threatens to destroy him, he sees the center move, aligning itself with "his distorted aim" (pp. 17-18).

The word sin originates from the Greek archery term meaning "to miss the mark." Michael later realizes that the center "moves for everyone" and that "missing the mark is not the final reality" (p. 110). What does this mean? Do you agree with Michael's perception? How does this idea square with more traditional Christian concepts of judgment of and punishment for sins?

3) Chapter Two begins with Kate asking her students about the nature of evil. What different views of evil does the novel present? Does Kate's view of evil change over the course of the novel? If so, how and why?

4) In what ways is Nick a traditional Episcopal priest? In what ways is he not? What other spiritual traditions does he draw on in his approach to life and God?

5) When Kate was young, several teenagers drown in the river on which her family lived. Kate's mother, sensing her daughter's distress, told her that though the river is beautiful "we mustn't forget how powerful she is, how treacherous she can be.... That doesn't mean we should fear her.... Respect her. Hold her in awe. But don't be afraid of her. Fear

is a poor counselor. It compromises us; it compromises our judgment" (p. 121).
Jean tells Kate that fear can be life destroying (p. 86).

Analyze the many fears that plague Kate during the novel. How do they affect the different aspects of her life, from addressing her son's illness to pursing her dreams? Does she ultimately overcome them and, if so, how?
Do you agree that fear is one of the biggest blocks to living a fully realized life? Why?

6) Early in the novel, Kate realizes she hears God in Jean's laughter (p. 23). Later, Michael notes that "Laughter is a strand in the song. It vibrates through [Kate] and her godmother almost continuously when they're together" (p. 211). Why is Jean's laughter so healing?
How does Jean view God? Are Jean's beliefs borne out through Michael's experience in "the center"?

Kate says to Nick, "If anyone has been the face of God for me in my life, it's Jean." (p. 291-291). What qualities in Jean do you think account for this?

7) What are the likely physical and psychological legacies of Kyle's alcoholism on his children and grandchildren? Do you believe Kyle will ever seek professional help, as Kate advises him to do at the end of the novel?

8) Do you believe Kyle loved Kate's mother? From what little the novel reveals, how do you envision their relationship? Who does Kyle blame for the death of Kate's mother?

9) Compare Kate's first major confrontation with Josh early in the novel (pp. 53-55) and her final confrontation with her father (pp. 337-345). Are there any parallels? How has Kate

changed? Do you believe it is realistic that Kate could forgive and continue to love her father, as she claims she does, in spite of his on-going treatment of her?

10) During his time in "the center," Michael comes to a fuller understanding of the meaning of forgiveness (p. 158-159). What does it mean to truly forgive, according to Michael? What qualities make such forgiveness possible?

11) The working title of this novel was *Of Angels and Archangels*. How does that title relate to the book? Who are the "angels" in the novel? What concept of angels does the novel advance?

Resources

Children afflicted with mood disorders often are misdiagnosed at least once since many of these disorders have similar and/or overlapping symptoms. Mood disorders are treatable, but finding the right medication or combination of medications can be tricky and scary. The links below can help.

American Academy of Child and Adolescent Psychiatry
www.aacap.org

Anxiety Disorders Association of America
www.adaa.org

Attention Deficit Disorder Association
www.add.org

Child and Adolescent Bipolar Foundation
www.bpkids.org

Children and Adults with Attention Deficit Disorders
www.chadd.org

Children With Oppositional Defiant Disorder
http://www.aacap.org/cs/root/facts_for_families/children_with_oppositional_defiant_disorder

Depressive and Bipolar Support Alliance
www.dbsalliance.org

Juvenile Bipolar Research Foundation
www.bpchildresearch.org

National Alliance for the Mentally Ill
www.nami.org

National Alliance for Research on Schizophrenia and Depression
www.narsad.org

National Association of School Psychologists
www.nasponline.org

National Institute of Mental Health Publications
www.nimh.nih.gov/health/publications/

National Mental Health Association
www.nmha.org

Obsessive-Compulsive Foundation
www.ocfoundation.org

The Bipolar Child
www.bipolarchild.com

About the text fonts:

*T*he Zapfino typeface *(featured not only within the cover design as a graphic element but also for the dropcaps and chapter numerals) was designed by Hermann Zapf and originally released in 1998 by Linotype.*

Body copy is in Times New Roman, designed by Stanley Morison and Victor Lardent, and is a trademark of The Monotype Corporation.